Bound Across Time

He met her eyes and held the pouch out to her. She took it with trembling fingers and opened it. She gasped. It was her locket. She withdrew it and held it in the palm of her hand. When she looked up, he was smiling.

"I feared that you wouldn't know what it was and then I would be insane."

"You're not insane, Brenden." She closed her fist around the locket. "But we were brought together for a reason. We can't pretend the content of our dreams means nothing."

"I'm not. 'Tis the very reason I wanted you with me."

Audrey moved closer to him and placed her hand over his. "But I'm sure I'm not here to help you. I'm here to stop you from making a mistake."

He shook his head and sighed. "I have told you, lass, I can't pay heed to your words unless I know the source!" She swallowed. "I'm from another time. The future. . . ."

A Time for Dreams

JEN HOLLING

HarperPaperbacks
A Division of HarperCollinsPublishers

HarperPaperbacks
A Division of HarperCollins*Publishers*
10 East 53rd Street, New York, NY 10022–5299

This is a work of fiction. The characters, incidents, and
dialogues are products of the author's imagination and are
not to be construed as real. Any resemblance to actual
events or persons, living or dead, is entirely coincidental.

ISBN 0-06-101407-9

Cover illustration © 1999 by Judy York

First HarperPaperbacks printing: August 1999

Visit HarperPaperbacks on the World Wide Web at
http://www.harpercollins.com

❖ 10 9 8 7 6 5 4 3 2 1

For Mark

⫸ *prologue* ⫷

DROCHAID CASTLE, SCOTLAND, 1980

At first Audrey thought there was nothing special about the castle. It wasn't any different from the dozen or so others she'd seen over the past year. Her mother had a passion for castles, said it was her Scottish roots. There were all the normal castle things to see: chapels, tapestries, goblets, portraits of people with strange, lashless eyes, and always something that had belonged to some long-dead king.

Then she saw the corridor. A wide arched doorway and a hall. At the other end, she could just make out flickering lights.

She pulled on her father's hand. "Let's go there."

"Where?" He looked blankly in the direction she pointed. "That's a wall."

"Are you crazy?" She walked closer to it and pointed again. "There's a hallway right there."

He raised his eyebrows. "Whatever you say, pumpkin." He rejoined the tour. Audrey looked from him to the corridor. No one else seemed to notice it either. Intrigued, she entered.

The sound of her footsteps echoed strangely. The corridor was illuminated somehow, but she couldn't see any lights. Each step she took seemed to push the arched doorway farther away. Suddenly the end was directly in front of her. She stepped into a passageway with torches burning on the walls, then looked back down the corridor. She could see the bright electric lights and a few people standing around. That was odd. The corridor appeared much shorter than it actually was.

She hesitated for just a moment before deciding to explore. This must be part of the castle no longer in use. But if it wasn't being used, why bother lighting the torches at all? A thrill of excitement ran down her spine at the thought of castle ghosts and finding passageways long out of use. Maybe she'd find the hidden treasure or a magic sword from the times of King Arthur.

Audrey hadn't been walking long when the sound of footsteps caused her to panic. She would be in trouble if anyone caught her here. She looked around frantically for someplace to hide. Not seeing any means of escape, she started back the way she had come, intending to dart back into the mysterious passageway that would lead her to the tour in progress.

She looked over her shoulder and saw a man approaching. She started to run, then stopped. It wasn't a man after all, just a tall boy, and some of her fear left. He was bigger than she was, but his face was young. He saw her and stopped, too.

He was fifteen or sixteen years old. But there was something odd about him. His clothing was strange. He wore pants that ended just above the knee, with hose covering his knees and calves and ugly shoes that looked more like shapeless slippers. His shirt or coat or what-ever it was had a high collar with a frilly little ruffle on it. She covered her mouth and snickered.

He cocked his head to the side and stepped closer. "Pray tell, what amuses you?"

Audrey stopped laughing but kept her hand over her mouth, her eyes widening. He sounded like the other Scots, but different somehow.

"You . . . your clothes . . ." She dropped her hand. "Is there some medieval fair going on around here? They didn't say anything about it on the tour."

He frowned. His hair was reddish-brown and wavy. A curl fell across his brow. As he came closer, she could see his eyes were an unusual light-green color.

"What manner of dress is this that you wear? It isn't proper for a lass to be roaming about in—breeks?" He phrased the last word as a question, apparently not knowing what to call her jeans. "From whence do you hail? Your speech is odd."

Audrey swallowed hard. Was this one of the ghosts she was so eager to find? Surely not. He looked real, solid. She reached out and touched his arm. He didn't move, just watched her action with interest.

"What business have you here? I haven't seen you about before." He looked her over studiously.

"I . . . I'm lost," she lied. "I'm looking for my father."

"Who might he be?"

"Captain Daniel Williams." His frown deepened and she hurried on. "We're stationed at Croughton in England. We're here touring the Scottish castles."

He looked alarmed and grabbed her arm. "Your father's an English soldier?"

Audrey shrank away from him and started babbling.

"American. And he doesn't like to be called a soldier.

Airman really. See, he's in the air force. You would call someone in the army a soldier or a grunt, maybe. Or is that a marine? No, those are jarheads."

He looked at her in utter confusion, shaking his head slightly. "Come with me," he said, and started pulling her. She jerked her arm away, and he made a grab at her. She felt a pull at the chain around her neck and then she was free, running back to the corridor. She heard his footfalls behind her.

"Wait!" he yelled.

Once again the hallway seemed to extend, her running getting her nowhere but farther away; then the doorway was there in front of her. She stepped back into the bright electric lights, slightly out of breath from the exertion and fright.

The tour had moved on, so Audrey hurried after them, looking furtively around for the strangely dressed boy. She spotted her parents in the midst of the small crowd of tourists and slipped her hand into her father's. He smiled down at her.

She didn't see the boy again or anyone else dressed like him. She was beginning to wonder if it had really happened. Had she talked to a ghost? Or had she passed out and had some strange dream? Her parents were looking in one of two glass display cases, and she stood close, afraid to stray far from their side.

"Look, Audrey!" her father cried excitedly. "It looks just like your locket."

Audrey peered into the case. Sure enough, there it was. Looking old and tarnished and chainless. The hair on her neck prickled as she read the placard next to it: "Sixteenth-century locket from the Countess of Irvine Collection." Her hand slowly rose to her throat, only to find it bare.

* * *

SCOTLAND, 1980

That night, after returning from the castle, the dreams began. Sometimes Audrey saw the boy, except now he was a man. She knew it was him from the eyes—those unusual light-green eyes could belong only to him. His hair was darker and short, but his clothing was the same. Sometimes he looked at her earnestly, other times sadly. She could never hear his voice, though his lips moved and she knew he was trying to tell her something.

She also saw a woman. She was always richly clothed in velvets and silk and praying with a rosary. Then came the executioner. His face was dark and inscrutable. He held an ax, sharpened to a glistening edge. There were often variations in the chain of images, but it always ended the same way. The woman mouthed the only words Audrey understood in the whole dream.

Sweet Jesus, she would say, as blood filled her mouth and ran across her white skin.

DROCHAID CASTLE, SCOTLAND, 1570

Brenden lay in bed, staring at the back of his brother's head. He would be lying on his back, but since his father had practically beaten the skin off his arse, that wasn't possible. Thinking about the beating made the heat creep up his neck.

He couldn't sleep. The events of the day kept running through his head. Surely the lass hadn't walked through a wall. "Witch," he muttered under his breath, then froze. The blond head in front of him didn't move, and he exhaled.

He hadn't really believed there were English soldiers about, but he'd thought it a good idea to inform his father of the incident. To his surprise, his father not only had not believed him but had also accused him of stealing the locket and lying about it. A severe beating followed.

Afterward, Brenden covered every square inch of the castle looking for the lass but was unable to find her. Had it even happened? Could he have imagined it? He knew he'd seen her walk through that wall, her skin blending right into the stones as though she were made of air. He'd touched her, though, and knew she was real.

He'd thought she was sweet when he saw her. Her eyes were enormous and gray, gazing innocently at him. She looked about ten and wore such strange clothing. She'd commented on his own clothes as though they were odd to her. He frowned. He didn't know what to make of the incident but planned to get the locket back.

He sighed and began drifting to sleep. His dreams were troubled, filled with strange images. She was in them.

1

"What am I doing? What am I doing?" Audrey muttered to herself. White-knuckled, she gripped the steering wheel, peering over it for road signs. She could make out the faint outlines and muted greens and browns of the landscape through the thick, swirling fog. Not that seeing it would have helped. It had been sixteen years since she'd been here.

She breathed a sigh of relief when she saw the sign and turned to follow the road into town. What was she doing? Sure, she needed a vacation, but was this the answer? Coming back to the place that had haunted her for sixteen years? Would it matter? Or would she discover she'd imagined it all and never find an end to the dreams?

She parked in front of the inn, which sat on the outskirts of the small town. The quaint wooden sign proclaiming it MacMann's creaked in the wind. She laid her forehead on the steering wheel. This time she would visit the castle alone. No mother and father to laugh with and enjoy the sights. The husband who had promised to face this moment with her—gone. No hand to grip tightly if she became frightened. Just her. As it had been for the last three years. Even more than that; for the years spent with Alex, she might as well have been alone.

She gathered her purse and suitcase and went inside. This was the third time she had made reservations to stay here. The last two times, she had canceled at the last minute, unable to go through with such an enormous undertaking. But this time she was practically forced to come. Her commanding officer had strongly suggested she take some time off. He didn't care for the idea of someone who slept less than two hours a night walking around base with a loaded semiautomatic weapon and being in charge of an entire flight of security police. He took her to the airport himself and told her he hoped the haunted look in her eyes wouldn't return with her.

Audrey signed the register and went up to her room. It was small but pleasant. Was she really going to do this? What if there were no corridor? The memory of the day she had stepped into the strange passageway was still vivid. And yet at the same time, it often possessed a dreamlike quality, making her doubt it ever happened. Doubt she had ever owned a silver locket.

She shook her head. It had to be real; it was the only explanation. She knew the dreams were connected to the incident from her childhood, but it wasn't until the past year that she had been drawn to return. The dreams were driving her mad. They had not only become more intense, but now they were invading her waking moments with their residue. And her inability to go back to sleep afterward was affecting her work. Being in charge of the security for the American side of the Royal Air Force base was difficult when she couldn't keep her eyes open and jumped at shadows.

It was the portrait that had done it. She had been lulled away from her comfortable flat by well-meaning friends intent on yet another sight-seeing excursion. They stopped at a portrait gallery and that was when Audrey saw her. She didn't really look like the woman from the dreams who was getting her head cut off, but there was something about her, the straight nose, the high noble forehead, the proud tilt of her chin, the eyes of deep amber, that told Audrey that this was a likeness of her. She was Mary, Queen of Scotland. And she had been executed in 1587 at the block.

Audrey stepped out of the shower and vigorously towel-dried her hair. She might as well get it over with; it was almost time for the tour to begin. What would she do with the remaining two weeks of leave if this proved to be her imagination? And if it wasn't, would two weeks be enough? How would she know what to do? She combed the tangles from her hair and pulled it into a long, wet ponytail. She slipped on some jeans and a T-shirt and hurried out into the mist.

The castle hadn't changed much. It wasn't as big as some of the others she'd toured in the past and was much cruder. The main part of the keep still stood, although it was showing its wear; the stones were gray and weathered with age. The outer curtain wall was in disrepair, crumbling and completely gone in places. There were no buildings inside the castle walls, but she remembered being told that at one time it had functioned like a small village within, with brewery, woolshed, and bakehouse. The chapel was gutted and open to the elements. There was a circular drive, obviously a recent addition, with cars parked along it.

Once inside, it seemed smaller than she remembered. A few other people were wandering around the hall, looking at the paintings, tapestries, and display cases. The walls were covered with rich wooden paneling and an enormous chandelier hung from the vaulted ceiling. She walked tentatively to the cases and peered in.

There were only two, and nothing of interest to her in the first, only some miniatures of people long dead and documents yellowed with age. She looked at the miniatures closely, but none revealed the man or woman from her dreams. She went to the second case—and there it was. The silver locket. A silver watch with only an hour hand and a dagger flanked it. Her heart thumped wildly in her chest. It was such a simple locket; she was surprised they found it worthy of display.

"Doesn't look like much, does it?" Audrey looked up to find an attractive red-haired man standing next to her. Freckles dusted his fair skin.

"Uh . . . no." She felt strangely guilty, knowing it was of no historical value. But he didn't know that.

He smiled. "Ian MacKay. I'm leading the next tour."

"I'm Audrey Williams. The Countess of Irvine—the one who wore this locket—who was she?"

"She was wife of the sixth Earl of Irvine. She was quite a woman for the time she lived in. She founded a university, was sheriff of a shire, and did various things for the poor on her estates, giving alms and such. Saved some witches from the stake. It's been said she never took this locket off."

"Wow," she breathed. But how did the countess get her locket? Was she the boy's mother? And what had any of this to do with Mary, Queen of Scots?

"Aye, and a woman of great beauty. There's a painting of her hanging in Creag Liath, the seat of the Earls of

Irvine, if you find yourself over that way." He looked at her strangely, then shook his head.

"What about her husband, the earl?" Audrey asked. "Did he do anything of merit?"

"Brenden Ross, he was a fair lord. But that's not what he's remembered for." He leaned closer. "He was a Marian."

"A Marian."

"Aye, he was a follower of the Queen of Scots. She was beheaded in 1587 by Queen Elizabeth. He was loyal to her to the end. He constantly dabbled in treasonous plots to put her back on the throne. After she was executed, he became outlawed. He took to the heather and disappeared for a time."

"And he was never captured?" she asked in amazement, looking back at the locket.

"Not for want of trying! The soldiers harangued his wife for a while. It wasn't as important to King James as it was to Elizabeth."

"Why did he want to help Mary?"

"I haven't any idea what his motives were, but probably he was a closet Catholic. Or had some grand dream of setting her upon the throne of both countries. The lords of that time were a greedy, power-hungry lot. Utterly corrupt." He grinned as though the concept was delightful. "As for Queen Mary, she was executed after almost twenty years of imprisonment for plotting to kill Queen Elizabeth."

Audrey stared hard at the locket, as if it would speak to her of what all this meant. But it was silent, looking out of place among the real antiques. She had purchased a book about Mary, hoping in her reading to find the answer that made everything fall into place. That never happened. It only confused her more.

"I remember reading about them," she mumbled, trying to piece the puzzle together in her head. "One of them murdered her husband, King Henry, then raped her and forced her to marry him, right?"

Ian nodded, his smile growing warm at her apparent interest and knowledge of the period. "That would be the Earl of Bothwell. The marriage didn't last long, and the other lords forced her to abdicate in favor of her infant son."

That was when Mary had fled to England and asked her cousin, Queen Elizabeth, for aid. Elizabeth imprisoned her for almost two decades and finally executed her. It was this execution that Audrey believed she witnessed over and over again in her dreams. She could never make sense of it before. Though it was still a mystery, she was beginning to see connections. A man who plotted to rescue Queen Mary had lived in this castle. His wife wore Audrey's locket. Was this the man in her dreams?

"Are you visiting us on holiday?" Ian asked, interrupting her thoughts.

"I live in England right now. Croughton."

"Are you military, then?"

"Yes. Captain Williams, chief of security, and last in a long succession of Captain Williamses."

"Chief of security?" He looked impressed. "The last, you say? Why would such a bonny lass say she's the last?" He was still smiling at her in a way that was beginning to make her uncomfortable.

She gave a little shrug, reluctant to go into that aspect of her personal life . . . or lack of it. "Has anyone ever . . . disappeared around here before?" She shifted, feeling ridiculous asking such a question.

His expression immediately became guarded. "What do you mean? Disappeared?"

She toyed with a lock of brown hair that had fallen over her shoulder, examining it. "You know, disappeared without a trace. After coming to this castle."

"There are some stories, most my father told me. Why do you ask?"

Her throat was thick, her mouth dry. She swallowed hard. "What were the circumstances of the disappearances?"

He scratched his head. "Well, some people just disappeared, leaving everything behind. But that sort of thing happens everywhere. Is that why you're here, Captain Williams?" He gave her a suspicious look. "Investigating a disappearance?"

"No, I'm just here on vacation. Were any of these people ever found?"

"I don't know. Like I said, I've only heard tales." He was still looking at her oddly. He glanced at his watch. "It's time for the tour to begin."

She followed him to where a group of people were gathered. He began by explaining to the small crowd that the castle's name, Drochaid, meant "bridge" in Gaelic. It was assumed to be symbolic, because the castle was near the highlands, in effect a bridge to them. But no one really knew for certain what it meant. He showed them various points of interest and told a legend about a bastard son of one of the earls, purported to be a warlock, who haunted Drochaid with his familiar, huge black devil-dog. Audrey felt a chill. She was beginning to believe anything was possible. Witchcraft seemed tame in comparison to the mysterious corridor.

She saw it as they were passing through a wide hallway. It was just as she remembered. It branched off the main corridor she was in, looking like a passage connecting two parts of the castle together. She could make out a flickering of torchlight at the opposite end. The passageway was even more unusual, since there were few internal corridors in Drochaid Castle; doors or staircases connected the rooms to each other. A quick survey of the group told her what she already suspected; it was a bare wall to them.

Audrey wasn't sure what to do. Should she just walk through? She was terrified—and how would it look? Would it look like she walked through the wall? The group was moving on, but she hung back. She went to a tapestry and pretended to study it.

When she was certain no one was looking, she took several deep breaths and stepped in. It was exactly as it had been the last time, as if she were sealed off from the rest of the world in a bubble. She heard nothing of the outside world. Inside, all the noises she made echoed loudly. She looked closely at the gray stone ceiling and walls and floor, searching for the means of lighting, but found nothing. The corridor simply—glowed.

She began walking, her heart beating loudly in her ears. When the corridor lengthened with that dreamlike quality, she stopped. It continued moving for a moment before it stopped, too.

She had had a few sessions with a therapist after Alex's death and had told him about the dreams. He had recommended a book. The book stated that anyone had the power to change his or her dreams. That sounded good to Audrey, so she tried it. It said to do a dream check. If she looked at an object while dreaming and then looked away, when she looked back, it would be different. But if she was awake, it would stay the same. The knowledge that she was in a dream was supposed to empower her to change it.

It didn't. The dreams were relentless and unchangeable. But perhaps the technique could be useful. Audrey looked at her tennis shoes. She looked at the wall, then down again. Still tennis shoes. Her heart sank. It wasn't a dream. She started down the corridor. The lengthening began again, only to stop suddenly with the doorway directly in front of her. She felt slightly disoriented and braced her hand on the stones that formed the arched doorway to steady herself. A faint vibration tingled through to her fingertips. She snatched her hand away and vigorously rubbed it until the unsettling feeling was gone.

Through the doorway she could see a torch in a sconce and shadows along the walls. She had just started to step through when a woman wearing a long brown gown with a white kerchief tied around her head hurried by with a fistful of candles. When the woman had gone, Audrey stepped through.

It was quiet in the hallway, but a quiet with substance. She could hear the crackling of the torch and feel the damp cold envelop her. She stepped back into the corridor and sank down onto the stone floor.

"Oh my God!" she whispered. "This is real! This is really real!" Now what would she do? But she knew. There were preparations to make.

The inn boasted a little dining room, which was where Audrey sat picking at her dinner as she tried to determine what to do about her discovery. When she had decided to come to Drochaid, it had seemed so easy. If it were real, she would go through, find out the reason for her dreams, and end them.

But now she was here and it was real. And she was paralyzed with fear. What about Mary, Queen of Scots?

She was beheaded in England. How could she be the woman from the dreams? To what point in the queen's life was she traveling? What was the significance of dreaming about Mary's execution? The more she discovered, the more confusing it all became.

She would be going to the sixteenth century. What would she do once she got there? The answer wasn't going to jump out at her. Maybe she could get a job. Then what? What if she were working in the wrong place? What if she never saw the queen or the green-eyed man? Would she just wander around in the sixteenth century forever? Audrey shuddered at the thought.

She paid for her meal and went back to her room. She unpacked the items of clothing she had brought for this very purpose and looked at them critically. The woman who had walked by the corridor was dressed plainly. After seeing the portrait and making the decision to return to Drochaid, Audrey had poured over catalog after catalog of women's fashions, looking for something similar to what the woman in the dream was wearing. It had become an obsession. But Audrey wouldn't want to draw attention to herself by dressing in fine materials. She would want to look like a servant or commoner. This eliminated one of the dresses she had brought.

She settled on a gray wool skirt. It was plain and heavy. If worn with a shirt, it would suffice until she could get her hands on something more appropriate.

She gave it one last look before hanging it in the closet. It would have to do. If she went. The dreams weren't so bad, she reasoned. Maybe she should wait another day. She could go to that other castle and look at the painting of the countess. She could have a dress made.

Audrey felt herself relax as she slipped between the

sheets and turned out the lamp. That's what she'd do. She wouldn't make any rash decisions.

Audrey was walking behind the woman. A long white veil hung down the woman's back. There were other people around, but she couldn't see their faces. Her heart was filled with a hopeless despair. The woman in the veil turned to her. Her amber eyes were calm and beseeched Audrey to be also. The woman pressed rosary beads into Audrey's hand.

The woman walked away and climbed a scaffold. He was here somewhere—Audrey knew it. He had to help. She looked around and saw him. He was dressed like the other soldiers. A short auburn beard hugged his jaw, but she still recognized him.

"Do something!" she screamed at him.

He turned and his eyes were filled with sorrow. No one heard her scream except him. She looked down at the rosary beads clutched in her hand. She looked back at the woman, now chanting something in Latin, and down again. She held the locket. It was a dream.

Audrey looked back to the man. He still watched her with those light-green eyes, the color of jade. He was the only one who could stop what was about to happen, so she ran to him. She expected him to recede and stay just out of her grasp like he always did. She was startled when her hand closed around his forearm. White, puckered scars surrounded his wrist.

"Can't you stop this?" she begged.

He shook his head sadly.

"You can! I know you can!"

He grabbed her arms and pushed her face into his chest. "Don't look," he commanded.

She pulled away and turned. The woman's head was on the block, and the executioner's ax was high over his head. Falling now, falling down swiftly, missing its mark and hitting the back of her head. The woman mouthed, *Sweet Jesus.* Audrey dropped to her knees in agony, trying to tear her eyes from the sight.

Wake up! Audrey screamed at herself. The green-eyed man grabbed her again, pulling her up and turning her to face him. "Audrey," he said, his voice deep and smooth, with a Scottish burr, "I need you. You must come back."

Something bumped against her foot. It was the woman's head. Her glazed eyes stared up at Audrey, with her lips still moving, continuing the chant.

Audrey screamed.

Audrey sat shivering by the window, trying to steady her nerves. This was, by far, the worst dream yet. She awoke in a sweat, barely able to breathe. The strangest thing about this dream was the hearing and feeling. No matter how bad the previous dreams had been, they were completely devoid of sound. Although she had often reached for the people, she had never been able to touch them, nor had they grabbed at her, as the man had done. She could still hear the soft, deep burr of his voice caressing her ears.

He was the answer, whoever he was. He was the boy she had met sixteen years ago. He was a man now, and she had to find him. She didn't know what to do once she found him, but she was certain this was the only end to the dreams. If she kept stalling, pretty soon her leave would be over, and she would have to return to England, accomplishing nothing.

It wasn't even dawn, but Audrey knew sleep would be elusive for the rest of the night. She pulled her lone suitcase across the bed and unzipped it. What, if anything, should she take with her? She considered shampoo, a toothbrush, and toothpaste. But she would be viewed with suspicion if someone saw them. None of those things were used in the sixteenth century, and the plastic would certainly attract unwanted attention. She sat heavily on the bed. There really wasn't much to take. She had no photographs with her. Everyone she loved was dead anyway. She decided to get dressed.

She French-braided her long hair, leaving a fat braid hanging down her back. She looked in the mirror and started to apply makeup. Another useless addition that would do nothing but call notice to herself. She put the makeup away and surveyed herself critically. Her skin was good, and she never wore much makeup anyway. She decided to go without.

She read until the dining room was open and went down to breakfast. She thought about items she might need to acquire after she passed through the corridor. She remembered reading that everyone carried around their own dirk, or knife, for eating. She looked down at the dull butter knife next to her plate. That certainly would not do. She needed something sharp.

Her hands were shaking so badly she had to put the spoon down. Was she really going through with this? Was it safe for a woman alone? Somehow she doubted it was. How would she find employment? Surely you didn't fill out an application. *Maybe I should bring my résumé*, she thought a little hysterically. Her stomach began knotting up and she felt herself backing out again. She wasn't prepared enough for this. She would go to the library, do more research. Come fully equipped with a bag of sixteenth-century coin. Perhaps even bring a gun for self-defense. She would feel much better with a sidearm.

And she would dream. Every night. Forget about sleep. They were talking to her now! They were grabbing her and telling her to come back. She had no choice. She breathed deeply. She could do this. She was a military woman and had the training to survive in many unlikely and hostile situations. She had lived half of her life in Europe and Asia, first as an air force brat, then becoming an officer herself, and was accustomed to different cultures and trying to blend or at least attract as little attention as possible. She had spent the three years before she came to England in Turkey, gaining the respect of men who had no respect for women. She learned their language and proved to them she could do her job. *She could do this.*

And she had to do it now. Not only could she not afford to purchase antique coins and period implements, but she didn't have the time to have them made or search out suitable substitutes. It was almost winter and very soon Drochaid would be closing its doors to tourists until spring. She could put it off no longer. That must be why he had talked to her last night. He was telling her it was time.

Audrey planned to arrive at the castle after the tour had begun. If it was already in progress, maybe no one would see her. She fingered the lump of gold jewelry she had tied in a handkerchief. It was all she had of value that she assumed would also have value in the past. She would need some way to pay for food and clothes, especially if she could not find immediate employment.

The cavernous hall was empty, except for the volunteer stationed at the door to collect tourists' pound notes. She walked briskly through the castle to the corridor. It looked menacing. A yawning opening into the unknown. She stood before it, trying to grasp the courage she felt last night after the dream.

"Miss Williams? Audrey?"

She jerked around to see Ian MacKay.

"Back again so soon? See something interesting on the wall?" His brown eyes were dancing with amusement.

She shook her head dumbly.

He cleared his throat. "You look. . . nice." He looked her over from head to toe. "Not at all like a soldier or a bobby."

She felt conspicuous and guilty. Her cheeks and neck instantly became hot. "Well . . . yes . . . uh, thank you. I'm not exactly a bobby or a cop. . . . Military security is a more apt definition and I . . . uh . . . have to be somewhere later and I need to wear this. Since it was all I brought, well . . ." She had no idea what she was saying. A problem of hers—she got nervous and started babbling.

"A date?"

"As a matter of fact, yes, well . . . something like that. Actually, no." She was not a practiced liar either and smiled sheepishly. He laughed.

He leaned against the corridor opening. To Audrey it looked as though he was leaning against thin air, like a mime. With some difficulty, she closed her mouth. What now?

"How long are you staying here?" he asked.

"Not long. I plan on leaving very soon; today, in fact."

"After your engagement, right?"

She gave him a strained smile, not answering. He continued making small talk until she was perspiring. She could hear the rest of the tour coming back and was desperate to leave. She had stopped paying attention to what Ian was saying when she realized he was asking her a question.

"I'm sorry, what did you say?" She glanced nervously in the direction of the voices.

"I was asking you to dinner."

She searched for an excuse, until she realized this could work for her. "Sure, sounds great. I'll see you then." Maybe he'd go away now that he'd completed his objective. He straightened from the wall, pleased but confused.

"You're staying at the inn?"

"Yes."

He scratched his head. "Seven sound good?"

She nodded, still smiling.

He hesitated, then finally started walking away.

She was going to wait until he was gone, but the tour was almost in sight, so she stepped inside. She turned to see Ian staring, wide-eyed, at the wall she had just disappeared through. His mouth was hanging open.

Damn! She didn't want anyone to see this. He walked to the wall mouthing her name. He reached out with a tentative hand and touched it. He looked around. The tour streamed in behind him, and a few people glanced at him curiously. He ran a hand through his hair and stared hard at the wall. He turned abruptly and left.

Audrey wondered if he would show up at the inn for their date. The idea of him still wanting to go out with her after she had walked through a wall made her laugh. She took a deep breath—and walked into the past.

❧ 2 ❧

It took Audrey a long time to finally walk through to the other end. And once she had, she loitered in the passageway, not far from her time-traveling corridor. She hadn't seen anyone yet and was afraid to make an appearance. When she finally heard footsteps, she almost lunged back to her corridor. She forced herself to be calm. She would have to talk to whomever it was and see if that person could help her.

A young woman approached. She wore a gown made of coarse brown cloth. A cream-colored hood covered her hair, though Audrey could see her light-brown hairline.

"Is something amiss, lass? Ye're starin' like ye've seen a ghost." Her accent was thick, but Audrey understood her. The woman surveyed Audrey's attire with raised eyebrows but didn't comment.

"Um, well, actually, I was told there might be work for me here."

She looked about the passageway. "Naught here. But we might put ye to work 'n the kitchen." Her eyes brightened. "Ye must be the lass Mistress Douglas sent over! Gibson'll be grateful! We have a houseful, what with milord arrivin'. We're needful of the extra hands."

Audrey jumped on this information. "Yes, that's me. Here for my lord."

"Come on then, there's work to be done." She inclined her head for Audrey to follow.

Audrey hesitated. "I don't have suitable clothing," she began, and the woman gave Audrey's attire another once-over. "I can pay you for a gown," Audrey said. She slipped one of her two modest rings off. It was a small emerald. It was probably worth more than a servant made in year. The woman took it, examining the green stone.

The young woman considered her for a moment, her hand closing tightly around the ring. Audrey suddenly feared she might refuse and accuse her of theft. "Come wi' me," she said at last. They walked down the passageway, up several flights of stone steps, and into a tiny room at the top of the castle.

"What's yer name?" the woman asked. She opened a wooden chest and began rummaging.

"Audrey."

The room was sparsely furnished. Straw mats lay in front of a fireplace. There was a scarred wooden table with stools pushed underneath, a shelf with a pot on it, and the chest she was digging through. Scented straw covered the floor, but the underlying smell of urine made the lavender nauseating.

The woman straightened suddenly. "Guendolen." She pointed to herself and smiled, showing Audrey her missing teeth. Guendolen handed her some clothes. "Here, try this."

She busied herself at the fireplace as Audrey surveyed the pieces of clothing. One was a long bone-colored gown that was worn beneath bodice and skirt. The wrists of Guendolen's shift were dingy and graying, but the one she gave Audrey was clean.

Audrey undressed and pulled it over her head. It felt scratchy. The neck was low and square, and the full sleeves were cuffed snugly at the wrists. To her dismay, it was pulled taut across her chest.

Guendolen turned to watch her. "My shift's a wee bit tight on yer bosom, but it'll do, aye?" Guendolen looked at her own small breasts and grinned wryly.

Audrey picked up the remaining two garments. They were made of the same brown cloth as Guendolen's dress. One was a skirt, which Audrey slipped on and tightened with the strings at the waist. Guendolen was shorter, and the skirt and shift hung just below Audrey's knees. The other piece was a vestlike bodice that laced up the front. Guendolen helped her pull the strings tight. Audrey caught her breath. It was stiffened somehow and very tight. Her breasts felt squashed. She looked down, and to her horror, they were trying to escape from the dress.

She looked at Guendolen's dress, which had a more modest neckline. "I can't wear this! I'm falling out of it!"

Guendolen frowned at Audrey's chest. "Why? 'Twill be a fine day when I fill a gown out in such a manner." Seeing she hadn't assuaged Audrey at all, Guendolen tugged at the top of the shift until it covered more of Audrey's breasts. "I dinna have a partlet, but ye canna tell unless ye bend over."

After slipping the cap on her head and tying it beneath her chin, Audrey remembered the jewelry she had brought, wrapped in a handkerchief. There were no pockets in the dress, so she shoved it into her cleavage. When she looked up, Guendolen was inspecting the skirt Audrey had taken off. She dropped it on the table.

"Whence are ye from? Yer speech is queer."

Audrey swallowed hard. "England," she blurted out, almost cringing, ready for the expected shriek of "liar."

"England, aye? I never met an Englishwoman before. What brings ye to Scotland?" She craned her neck, trying to see behind Audrey.

"My mother was Scottish, and I'm on my way to see her family. I need a place to stay and earn some money for a while." Audrey looked nervously over her shoulder, but saw nothing. "What?"

"Is it true what I've heard aboot Englishmen? They have tails? Long and hairless like rats?"

"What?" Audrey asked again, and laughed at such an absurd notion. "No, Englishmen don't have tails."

Guendolen frowned in disappointment and looked at the ring Audrey had given her. Audrey hoped Guendolen would assume it was the only thing of value she owned. When Guendolen looked up, Audrey didn't see any signs of suspicion or disbelief in her eyes and exhaled the breath she was holding.

"Gibson will be expecting us," she said, leading Audrey out of the room.

The kitchen was big and warm, with vaulted ceilings and several fireplaces lining the walls. Servants were rushing around. In their hurry to get there, Audrey's breasts were squeezing out of the dress again. She noticed that most of the women in the kitchen were showing some cleavage, so she didn't feel so uncomfortable.

Pots, pans, and cooking utensils hung from iron hooks at the far end of the room. In the center of the room sat a huge table covered with various pieces of meat in different stages of preparation. Guendolen led

Audrey to a very short, round, rosy-cheeked woman who could only be Gibson. She presented Audrey to her without a word.

Gibson looked Audrey over thoroughly and raised her eyebrows—a feat that didn't seem possible, had Audrey not seen it, considering that even her forehead was fat.

"Have her bring in some flagons of ale, and when the meal is done, I want her in the scullery."

Guendolen motioned for Audrey to follow. She led her down a short flight of steps into the larder. Barrels and sacks lined the walls. Wooden shelves were stacked with cheeses wrapped in cloth, dried fruits, and meats. Guendolen filled four pewter pitchers from a barrel and handed Audrey two. The smell of the ale was very strong. Audrey didn't care for alcohol but had an urge to take a deep drink from one of her pitchers. Perhaps if she got drunk, she could handle this.

"Servers dinna speak unless spoke to, aye?" Guendolen said, on their way back through the kitchen. Audrey nodded. "Always serve the lord's table first; they must always have food and drink."

"Got it."

She heard the boisterous great hall before she saw it. They entered from behind a partition that hid the kitchen from sight. Audrey halted and watched Guendolen. She squeezed between two men, one of whom slapped her on the backside, and swapped a fresh pitcher for an empty one. She gathered some empty platters and returned to the kitchen.

"Go on!" Guendolen urged.

She took a deep breath and reassured herself. She could do this! She was a modern woman. She could handle a bunch of sixteenth-century men.

There was one very long table and several smaller rectangular tables set up around the hall. Audrey went to the nearest one. The hall was different. The polished paneling of the future was gone, replaced with stone walls and newer-looking tapestries. A chandelier hung from the ceiling, but it was made of wood and suspended by chains. Scores of candles burned in it. The huge fireplace blazed brightly. That, combined with the heat from so many sweating bodies, made the hall comfortably warm.

The men were dressed in knee-length pants. Some wore close-fitting jacketlike doublets; others had tunics over their shirts, secured at the waist by leather or rope belts. A few of the men were surprisingly well groomed, not at all what she had expected. The rest were, alas, exactly as she'd expected. Long hair and scraggly beards, filthy shirts. There were a few women, dressed in finer clothes than Audrey wore, but they were near the head of the longest table.

She headed for an open space so she wouldn't have to squeeze between anyone. A few of the men leered at her chest, and one said something to her, but his burr was so thick, she couldn't understand him. He tried to grab her hips. She moved away quickly.

She hurried back to the kitchen. Guendolen handed her a large platter with several roast chickens on it. "These go to the head table, but dinna serve the lord or lady. 'Tis his squire's duty." Guendolen was laden down with dishes and indicated for Audrey to follow her.

They headed for the long table, where a few women sat. Most of the men there looked clean. Their hair was short and neat, and they ate with some semblance of manners.

Audrey stopped short with a gasp. Sitting between

two enormous fat men was the green-eyed man from her dreams. He poked at his food with a sharp knife but didn't eat. One of the men beside him was apparently telling a joke of some sort, although she couldn't understand him with his mouth full of food. He threw his head back and laughed, bits of food tumbling from his mouth. He punched the green-eyed man in the shoulder as though saying, *Get it?* Green Eyes did not smile and made a subtle turning move with his broad shoulders, discouraging further conversation.

Her heart thundered against her ribs, and she willed herself to move forward so she wouldn't be standing there gawking at him, but she couldn't. He took a drink from his pewter mug and set it down, looking into it. He looked the same as he did in her dreams. Wavy, collar-length auburn hair, light-green eyes fringed thickly with russet lashes. A strong, square jaw covered with a few days' growth of dark whiskers. He was wearing a plain black doublet, with a high rounded collar, unadorned except for the row of small silver buttons down the front. A bit of the collar of the white shirt he wore beneath showed, but she could still glimpse the muscular column of his neck.

"He's a bonny lad, no doubt about that. But I believe he's spoken for."

Audrey turned to Guendolen. She was on her way back to the kitchen but had stopped to lean over Audrey's shoulder, admiring him.

"Who is he?" Audrey whispered hoarsely.

"Brenden Ross."

Audrey's hand fluttered to her throat. He was the one Ian MacKay had told her about. "Spoken for? He's married?" That must be the great wife Ian had gushed about, the one who had Audrey's locket.

Guendolen pulled Audrey closer to the wall. "Nay, not married, though I believe his father has a match in mind. 'Tis rumored the only woman he has time for is the whore Mary Stuart." She gave Audrey a conspiratorial look. "I hear that's why he's here. He's plotting to restore her. Perhaps he has designs on the kingship?"

Audrey looked at her in surprise. "Really?"

Guendolen shrugged sheepishly. "Nay, I dinna know for certain. Ye know how people talk." When Audrey still made no move toward the table, Guendolen said, "Get ye gone now. Ye must never keep the head table waitin', and they're ready for those birds."

If that was why Brenden Ross was at Drochaid, from the look of him, he wasn't having much luck. She started forward, glad to get a closer peek. She was drawn to him. He looked so troubled. She felt as if she knew him. Sixteen years of dreams made him seem like a friend in this sea of strangers. She could feel his unrest, and it made her nervous and edgy.

She looked at the platter in her hands. He was seated at the head table, and there was an empty space right in front of him. He was deep in thought and not taking any notice of the din around him. She leaned over, placing the platter in front of him, and the two fat men immediately attacked the chickens with gusto. She grabbed an empty pitcher to take back to the kitchen. Brenden Ross lifted his mug to his lips, then stopped in midswallow, his eyes lingering on her chest. She realized, belatedly, the way she was leaned over put her cleavage on display for him. His eyes traveled slowly up her neck to her red face and widened in horror.

He spit his ale right into her chest. "God's blood!" he exclaimed.

Audrey stared back, heart in throat. She tried to

straighten and walk away, but she was rooted to the spot by the eyes that were staring into hers with recognition. His mouth opened and closed a few times, as he tried to find his voice.

"It's you," he finally managed to say.

That broke the spell. She ran to the kitchen.

"Wait!" His voice rang out. Audrey stopped at the partition. She looked back and saw Brenden Ross struggling to extricate himself from the bench he sat on between the two stout fellows, only to bring the bench crashing backward.

She ran back down to the larder to catch her breath and collect her thoughts. Lukewarm ale trickled between her breasts; she dabbed at it with a towel. How was it possible he recognized her? It couldn't be! They had both been children, and he had to have been of the same mind as she, thinking it was really a dream or his imagination.

She didn't know what to do. He was the reason she was here. She was looking for him! So why did she run? She was no longer certain this was a good idea. What was she going to say to him? "Hi, my name is Audrey and I'd like to follow you around for a while and see if my bad dreams go away. And by the way, I'm from the twentieth century."

Audrey groaned, covering her face with her hands. "I'm so stupid!" she muttered. Her first impulse was to leave and come through better prepared later. But she was already working in the kitchen. She might not get this opportunity again, especially if she disappeared. She sighed, filling the empty pitcher.

On her way to the hall, she passed Guendolen, who gave her a strange, raised-eyebrow look. Audrey's eyes went to the empty place where Brenden Ross had been sitting. She was scanning the room for him when she felt a large hand wrap itself around her upper arm. She turned and looked up into eyes the color of jade. They were emotionless, as was his face. He pried the pitcher from her grasp and handed it to a passerby.

"Come with me," he said, and dragged her from the hall.

"You're hurting me!"

He ignored her. His hand bit into her arm, and she started to get angry. Was this the attitude of men in this time? They thought they could just haul women off anytime they felt like it? She dug in her heels and yanked hard on her arm. He wasn't expecting it, and she pulled free. He didn't grab her again.

"I said, you're hurting me," she repeated loudly. Now that he was standing, she saw what an enormous man he was. He stood at least six feet tall. His shoulders were broad, and his chest and arms huge. He hadn't looked quite so large in her dreams. Or so menacing. In the dreams he always had a sad, soft expression on his face. Now he looked cold and unfeeling. Perhaps seeking this man out was a mistake.

"Forgive me," he said suddenly, and smiled. It was a lovely smile, his teeth straight and white, but it didn't reach his cold green eyes. His burr wasn't as strong as the others she'd encountered so far; his words clipped purposefully. Audrey had an overwhelming urge to run and began backing away from him. He saw the move, and the green eyes narrowed.

"I have to get back to work." She raised her chin a notch and started walking away. She expected him to grab her again. When he didn't, she stole a furtive look over her shoulder. He followed a few paces behind.

She turned back to him, hands on hips, summoning

all the bravado in her person. "Just what is it you want from me?"

"I reckon if I follow you long enough, you'll start walking through walls."

Audrey's breath caught in her throat. "Don't be ridiculous!" she managed to sputter. "What do you think I am? A ghost?"

He laughed, a deep, rumbling, pleasant sound. "Not that it hadn't occurred to me, lass. But nay, I don't think you to be a spook."

He took a step toward her, and she, a step back. He smiled again, but this time his eyes softened. He held up his hands in a gesture of defenselessness. "I didn't mean to hurt you. You took me by surprise, is all. Please, I must talk to you."

He *was* the reason she was here. But he scared her. He held his hand out to her. She looked at the large, powerful hand extended in invitation and saw the scars surrounding his wrist. How did a man get scars like that? Was he bound at some time? Tight enough to cause such wounds? He followed her gaze. Something passed across his face and was gone. He stepped forward again, as if trying not to frighten a spooked animal. He gently grasped her hand. It looked so small and white in his large tan one.

"Come. Talk with me a bit. I won't hurt you."

He led her into a sitting room and closed the door behind them. Richly embroidered tapestries hung over the paneling. There were no rushes in this room. Instead, a large Turkish rug covered the floor. The wooden planks and rug were meticulously clean. Several low-backed wide chairs were situated about the room. He led her to one near the stone fireplace and motioned for her to sit.

She sat on the edge of the chair, wadding her skirt between her hands. He offered her wine, and she accepted the silver goblet with trembling fingers.

"Who are you?" he asked, turning to face the fireplace. He was powerfully built. Narrow hips and large muscular thighs were enclosed in leather breeches. He wore knee-height black boots, well made, but like the rest of his clothing, simple and unadorned.

"Audrey Williams."

"Are you English?"

She cringed inside. The truth was out of the question. She was certain women were not part of whatever constituted the sixteenth-century armed forces. She also didn't know much about the American colonies of the sixteenth century or sea travel. So trying to stay close to the truth wasn't plausible.

"Yes," she answered hesitantly.

He turned and raised an inquiring eyebrow. "Whence do you hail?"

"Croughton."

"That's odd, as I've never heard an Englishwoman speak so queer."

Audrey's cheeks burned, but she stared back defiantly.

He shook his head. "Nay, you're no Englishwoman." When she held his gaze silently, he advanced, circling her chair and inspecting her. "I'll wager you're no serving wench, either."

His suspicion was making her angry. She understood his curiosity, but she wasn't about to be put on trial concerning her origins. Besides, she couldn't think of a better lie.

"If you're through, I'd like to leave."

"Where's your husband?"

"Dead."

"Who takes care of you then?"

"I take care of myself."

"Are you a witch?"

"No."

"Why are you here?"

"I'm working."

He stood directly in front of her, rubbing the dark whiskers on his chin. "Explain how you walk through walls."

Audrey stifled a laugh. As if she could explain it! She looked at him innocently. "I don't know what you're talking about."

"If you're not a witch, pray impart to me how you've haunted my dreams for sixteen years?"

Her chest tightened. He dreamed of her, too. What was going on? What could this mean? The first thing that occurred to her was a ridiculously romantic notion. They dreamed about each other. She was lonely, a simple fact she wasn't afraid to admit. For the past three years, whether she knew him or believed him to be real or not, he had been the only man in her life.

Then the rest of her dreams came rushing back. The executioner. Brenden Ross was plotting to rescue Mary, Queen of Scots. A plot that would fail. Maybe that's why she was here. To help him save her.

"What happened . . . when we were children?" she asked suddenly.

He sat on the hearth across from her. "So you have no more idea of what this means than do I?"

"No."

He lowered his head, running both hands through his thick hair. When he looked up, his expression had changed. His eyes looked into hers deeply and searchingly. "I was sixteen when I saw you. I've never been sure, till now, that it happened." He smiled. "My father beat me for lying and thieving."

She gasped. "Thieving?"

"Your bauble."

"Oh." She touched her neck reflexively, wondering where her locket was now but not wanting to ask. He followed her gesture and then moved his eyes lower, his gaze lingering on her breasts, which were probably falling out of her dress. She blushed furiously.

He looked back into her eyes. "I've dreamed of you near every night since. For a while, the lass you were then. But most"—his mouth curved into a smile—"as you are now."

She was having a hard time breathing. She was transfixed by the growth of auburn stubble covering his jaw, bristling around the soft, full lips. She cleared her throat and looked away, fingering the strings that tied her cap securely under her chin. They suddenly felt like they were strangling her.

"Well, uh, yes. It's all very strange." She set the goblet down and grasped the neckline of her shift, pulling it higher over her chest. He arched an eyebrow in amusement, then stood abruptly and went to the door.

"Well, we'll sort it out, I've no doubt."

"Wait a minute. Where are you going?"

"I expect you'll find this room more comfortable than the servants' quarters. We'll talk again in the morn." He left, and she heard the door lock.

"You're locking me in?" she said in disbelief. She ran to the door and tried in vain to open it. "You bastard!"

She wandered around the room in frustration, picking up her goblet and draining it. She went into the connecting room and surveyed the bed. It was a monstrosity of a bed, made of walnut and carved with swirling designs. The coverlet was rich gold velvet, embroidered with a crest of some sort. She almost swooned toward it.

She didn't realize how exhausted she was until that moment. How long had it been since she had a good night's sleep?

She stripped down to the shift and kicked her shoes off. She slid under the coverlet and quilts with a sigh. The feather mattress and pillows were soft. In seconds she slipped into a deep dreamless sleep.

Audrey was awakened by someone shaking her. Candlelight danced off Brenden Ross's face, making her think she was within a dream. She closed her eyes and snuggled deeper into the mound of quilts.

"Rouse yourself!" He shook her harder.

She sat bolt upright. "Where am I? What time is it?" She pulled the quilt under her chin. "What are you doing here?"

"It's past midnight. You're in my bed and we're leaving. Get dressed." He tossed a gown at her.

She stared dumbly at the dress. "Where are we going?"

"We'll talk later."

Audrey's senses were beginning to return. She remembered the last time she'd spoken with him and his locking her in this room. "I'm not going anywhere with you."

"You don't have a choice. I'm leaving, and I mean to take you with me."

"But that's kidnapping!"

"Call it what you must," he said impatiently. "Get dressed."

Audrey pulled the dress closer but made no move to put it on. "Why do we have to leave now? Can't you wait until morning?" She lay back against the pillow, fatigue sweeping over her again.

"I must leave now. Get on with it!" He was dressed for travel, wearing a dark wool mantle wrapped around his shoulders and a sword at his hip.

She threw back the quilts and crawled out of her warm cocoon. "I think maybe the dreams were a warning. To stay away from you!"

"Indeed?" His face was bland.

"First you slobber all over me in the hall!" He flinched a little, which spurred her on. "Then you manhandle me in the hallway and coerce me to come to your room, 'just to talk.' Next thing I know, I'm your prisoner!" She glared at him. "Trouble! That's what you are!"

The door opened a few inches, and a young man with curly black hair poked his head in. "What's keeping you, Bren?"

"We'll meet you at the stables," Brenden said in dismissal. The young man raised his eyebrows and backed out.

When Brenden turned back, his expression had softened. "I must go, but I won't leave you behind. I haven't suffered through years of nightmares only to have you run off because you don't like my manner." He smiled apologetically. "I will attempt to conduct myself proper from this time forward, aye?"

Audrey smiled slightly at his resorting to charm. He should have tried that first. She examined the dress to see how to put it on. It was heavy black velvet with a large, and very stiff, cream-colored ruff at the neck. He took it from her and held it out like a coat. She slipped her arms into it. He touched her shoulders lightly, turning her to face him.

"'Twas the best I could do. It's a fair sight better than the rags you were wearing earlier." His hand brushed her breast as he fastened the series of ribbonlike buttons that ran upward from the base of her ribs. He glanced up at her sharp intake of breath and touched a lock of hair that had escaped from her braid. "It looks bonny on you."

Audrey backed away, frowning. She didn't have any choice but to go with him, even though her better instincts were screaming not to ride off alone with this dangerous man, but she wasn't about to make it enjoyable for him.

She looked for her shoes and her head covering. They were gone, along with the dress she had worn earlier.

"Let's go," he said, grasping her arm and dragging her impatiently from the room.

"My shoes!" She tried to pull away.

"Forget the damn shoes!"

Audrey's annoyance was mounting by the minute. He pulled her into the passageway and held a finger to his lips. He led her through room after room until they came to a door leading out of the castle and into the courtyard. The ground was not gentle on her tender feet and she cried out in pain from sharp stones. She stumbled at one point and fell against him. He hooked a huge arm under her knees and swept her up. She glowered at him.

"I haven't time for this display of feminine distress."

Audrey poked her finger into his chest. "You are a bully."

He carried her into the stable. "Aye, that may well

be. But you're a shrew. I liked you better in my dreams, when I couldn't hear your yapping."

She was about to retort when he tossed her in a haystack. Before she could fight her way out of it, kicking and sputtering, the young man who had stuck his head in the door earlier was hauling her up.

"Get your hands off me!" She raised her arm to fight back. He caught it easily and twisted it behind her back.

"Gavin! Release her!"

Her arm was dropped immediately, and she stood trembling in rage in front of a huge russet horse the same color as Brenden's hair. He was astride it with his hand extended in invitation. She turned and saw Gavin in a stance of readiness in case she should bolt.

Audrey reluctantly gave Brenden her hand and slipped her bare foot into the stirrup. He pulled her into the saddle so she sat sideways across his lap, her shoulder in his chest. He wrapped an arm around her waist and spurred the horse forward.

As they rode out of the stable and into the night, he whispered, "You didn't think I'd let you disappear from my life again, did you?"

◄ 3 ►

There was a chill in the air, but the dress Brenden had brought Audrey was warm. The stiffened ruff itched and smelled strongly of sweat and a cloying flower scent. She yanked it away from the sensitive skin of her neck.

Brenden grabbed her wrist. "Be still!"

"This thing is driving me crazy!" she said through clenched teeth.

He pushed the ruff back at her. "You're about to scrape all the hair off my face."

"What is the purpose of these stupid things anyway? They itch; they're uncomfortable; and they look hideous. Why would someone want to wear one?" She pulled it away from her neck again.

"Dammit, woman!" He grabbed the ruff with one hand and the front of her dress with the other. She gave a little cry when she realized what he was doing and slapped at his hand to stop him, but it was too late. He ripped the ruff halfway off, then yanked a few more times to complete the ruin. He held it up for her to see and, with a smile of satisfaction, tossed it into the darkness.

Her jaw hung open, and she made an incredulous, puffing sound. "What in the hell did you do that for?" She turned to glare at him. "Now the only dress I have is ripped."

He smiled and his green eyes traveled down the curve of her neck. "It's not so bad. You said you didn't like it. I did you a favor." He pursed his lips and looked sideways. "Truth be known, I didn't like it, either."

"You said I looked bonny!"

"Well, you do . . . you just look better without the ruff."

She caught Gavin looking at them with raised eyebrows. He quickly looked away when she saw him. He nudged his horse and rode ahead.

"The last time I saw you, you were acting the same. As though you'd never seen this manner of clothing before."

He seemed to be waiting for a response from her, and she searched her mind frantically for a way to divert the subject to something safer. "What do you think it means? Having these dreams about each other?"

He immediately reined the horse in. "What did you say? You've dreamed of me as well?"

"Ever since that day sixteen years ago."

He grabbed her chin, turning her to face him. The leather of his gloves was soft and warm against her skin. His eyes bore into hers with an intensity that made her want to shrink away.

"What does this mean?" When she only continued to stare back, he released her. "Tell me about the dreams."

"They were often different, but you were always there, trying to tell me something. Usually sad. But I could never hear you or touch you. Well, except for my last dream." She felt him stiffen and looked at him, but his face was unreadable.

"Go on."

"There was a . . . woman. She was getting her head chopped off. I think you wanted to stop it, but couldn't." She shrugged. "I don't know what it could mean."

He nudged the horse, and they were moving again. He said nothing; his eyes were trained on the horizon, a muscle flexing in his jaw.

"What about your dreams?" she asked.

"The same."

"Do you know who the woman is?"

"Aye."

"Well?"

When he looked at her, she could practically see the wheels turning in his head. He didn't trust her and wasn't about to tell her about his plotting. For some reason this annoyed her, as if they should already be past all this because of the dreams. He said, "We have much to discuss. But not now. This has happened for a reason."

"Why?"

"I know not."

"So you just kidnapped me, hoping it would come to you?"

"It wasn't kidnapping."

She gaped at him. "What would you call it?"

"You were looking for me."

"I was working." She turned her head to avoid his perceptive gaze.

"Aye, working, I forgot." His voice was heavy with sarcasm. "I asked about you, and no one has ever laid eyes on you before. And the lass I spoke with told me she found you wandering about, wearing a fine woolen kirtle with a lad's shirt. You're a mystery, no doubt. But you're here for me." He cupped her cheek and turned her face forcefully to him. "You'll not run off on me this time."

She jerked away, afraid to speak and not wanting him to see the fear in her eyes. They rode in silence, the cold ball of dread in her stomach growing.

Audrey sat in front of the fire, a plaid blanket wrapped snugly around her. She watched the young man who had accompanied Brenden as he brushed the horses down and spoke softly to them.

"Who are you?" she asked.

"Gavin Ross." He inclined his head and turned back to grooming the horses. Brenden was trying his luck with the fish at a nearby stream.

"I'm Audrey."

He pushed a black curl away from his brow. "Well met, Audrey."

"How are you related to Brenden?"

He walked to the fire and poked at it with a stick. "He's my brother."

She looked closer to see the resemblance, but it wasn't there. He was younger than Brenden. They were roughly the same height. Gavin was a bit narrower through the shoulders and not as heavily muscled, but he was still a big man. His skin was fair, his eyes an unusually dark shade of blue. "You don't look like brothers."

He shrugged and sat across from her. "Same father, different mother." He pulled out a knife and carved the end of the stick. His head was bent, and his lashes were thick and sooty. He was very handsome. She wondered what his mother looked like.

"What happened to Brenden's mother?"

"Nothing." He smiled at her confusion. "My mother wasn't married to our father."

"Oh."

"Aye, I'm a bastard." He resumed his carving, laughing to himself. He apparently found the idea of his being illegitimate, or perhaps her shock, to be of great amusement.

"Are you a criminal, too?"

Still smiling, he leaned on his bent knee and regarded her. His slow appraisal made her uncomfortable. She pulled the plaid closer.

"And what makes you think we're criminals?"

"Kidnapping, for one. And I'm sure the reason we had to sneak off in the middle of the night isn't legal, either."

"Kidnapping, you say? Hmm. Bren didn't seem to think so. As for why we left Drochaid, that's not for me to be telling you." The shadows from the fire danced across his fair skin, making him look mysterious.

She scooted closer and pointed a finger at him. "That's exactly what he did! Kidnap me. And you helped."

He inclined his head into the black night. "Go on. You're free to leave. I'll not stop you."

Audrey looked around. She wasn't even sure which direction they had come from. "I can't go alone. I don't even know where I am!"

"We're a few miles east of Drochaid, which is that way." He pointed over her shoulder. He was making fun of her, and she knew it. As much as she wanted to stalk off into the night, she wasn't a fool.

She gave a yip of surprise when two big fish landed in Gavin's lap. She hadn't heard him approach, but now Brenden stood beside her.

He had bathed at the stream. His hair was dark and wet. In the back, near the nape of his neck, it hung in small, wet ringlets. She watched, mesmerized, as he ran his fingers through it, pulling the curls out straight only to have them bounce back.

He looked at her, and she quickly averted her eyes. "Are you hungry?"

"No," she replied, but her stomach growled traitorously.

"Audrey, this is getting tiresome. I'm not taking you back, so you might as well eat and quit your sulking."

She looked at Gavin in triumph. "You see! He admitted to it!"

Brenden looked between them with his hands on his hips. "What's she blethering about?"

"She claims you're a kidnapper," Gavin answered solemnly, then blinked owlishly at her. "I have to admit, he's sounding guilty."

Brenden shook his head. "She's like an old dog worrying a shoe with this kidnapping."

She was tired of being the butt of their joke. She stood up and picked her way gingerly in the direction Brenden had come from.

"Where do you think you're going?" Brenden asked.

"To wash up at the stream, if it's any of your business."

Brenden grinned. "You'll not find it that way."

Gavin was behind him, pointing into the darkness to her right. Her cheeks burned, but she turned in the direction Gavin pointed and marched off with as much dignity as she could muster with bare feet.

The water was freezing, and Audrey's teeth chattered. Finding that merely splashing her face with cold water wasn't going to cut it, she stripped and waded in. She washed her body the best she could, but her hands were shaking violently, and she had no soap.

Dawn was approaching, giving her a better view of the landscape. There were few trees, but one popped up on occasion to speckle the landscape. She dried herself with the blanket and dressed hastily, lest one of them come creeping up on her. She decided to stay by the stream and watch the sun come up. She needed some time away from Brenden to decide what to do.

She spread the blanket on the ground and sat down to rebraid her wet hair. She didn't like the way things were going. Brenden wasn't what she had expected, and she wasn't so sure she wanted to stay and see this through. She had no doubt now that the woman in the dream was the Queen of Scots. But was she going to let herself become involved in a plot to rescue her? One she knew was doomed to failure? What was the point?

Maybe she was there to persuade him to stop trying. To give it up before he became outlawed. After meeting him, she could liken that to beating her head against a brick wall. In her mind, she had given him a personality. She hadn't known his name or who he was, but because he'd haunted her dreams, she thought she knew him. And he wasn't the cold, hard, sarcastic man she just spent the night riding with. She felt sad for that loss.

She tied off her braid with a hollow sigh, realizing how lonely she had become. She was a fool. Part of her had always wanted to go to him, this sad man who seemed to need her as no one else had. Even before she had met her husband, Alex, she would muse about the mysterious man, comparing other men to him and finding them lacking. When Alex would turn away from her, she'd think, *The green-eyed man wouldn't do that.* But now it had all dissipated.

Still, she had no choice. He was the reason she was here. That didn't mean she liked his tactics. True, he was a sixteenth-century man, accustomed to a certain kind of woman. Maybe she should try being more docile, but she immediately dismissed the thought. She finally decided that she would just quit fighting with him. They would get nowhere if she kept badgering him, so she might as well be more agreeable.

She lay down, watching the rising sun with its oranges and pinks playing over the water. There were a few times since she'd met him in the hall that she thought the green-eyed man from her dreams was peeking through. She couldn't help but wonder, as she drifted to sleep, if he was in there somewhere.

Something roused Audrey from her sleep, though she wasn't sure what. She lay still, scanning the scenery in front of her. She didn't know where she was at first, but the hard ground and the figure sitting on a rock a few feet away brought it all back.

The sun had risen higher in the sky, and it was about midmorning. Brenden stared out over the water. The thick waves of his hair stirred in the breeze. He was a beautiful man. She felt a small stirring of long-dead desire. He scratched at the reddish-brown whiskers. She didn't usually like scruffy looking men, but his short beard was becoming. A ring on his finger glinted green in the sunlight—from its large emerald.

He glanced at her, his eyes a few shades paler than the emerald. He started to turn back, then jerked slightly in surprise. "You're awake! Do you feel better, then?"

Audrey stretched, hearing small popping noises in her back. "I think so."

"Why do you speak so strange?"

She stood and folded the blanket so she didn't have to look at him. "I told you before."

"And you were lying. Now I'll have the truth."

She pursed her lips, her usual rebuff to overcurious men rising to her tongue. But that was not the way to handle him. "We traveled a great deal when I was a child. So I suppose I never acquired an accent." It was the truth. She had lived all over the world since she was a child.

He nodded as if this made sense to him. "You don't have the look of a commoner. Have you lost your loved ones recently that you must resort to laboring in the kitchens?"

She sighed. "My mother and father are dead; so is my husband. I have no brothers and sisters. I have no one, okay? And I don't want anyone. I'm happy. I *like* being alone."

"You cannot be left to fend for yourself! You must marry again."

She waved this away. "I'll be fine."

He started walking back to their camp. He stopped to watch her pick her way around the sharp stones, scowling at her slow progress. Before she could protest, he lifted her into his arms. She held her body rigid, annoyed that he was pushing her around like some object.

"You're daft, woman. You don't even have a pair of shoes. You can't take care of yourself."

"I had a perfectly fine pair of shoes at Drochaid." He smiled at her in a condescending manner that made her angrier. "Besides, who dressed me? Didn't it occur to you I might need shoes to complete this ensemble?"

He half lifted, half shoved her into the saddle. He mounted behind her and wrapped a firm arm around her waist. "So now 'tis my fault, aye?"

Gavin was giving her another one of his infuriating raised-eyebrow looks.

"What are you looking at?" His eyebrows raised higher, and he rode ahead. "What's his problem?"

"'Tis not you. Doubtless, he's wondering what has possessed my addled brain to saddle myself with such a harridan."

"Well? What's the answer?" she asked, then added with a gentler tone, "I'm not usually so rude, but being dragged from a warm bed in the middle of the night to go riding with you and your strange brother doesn't put me in the best of moods."

"Aye, I suspect there's more to you. You always seemed so sad in my dreams. I can't help but wonder why?" He was silent, and she wondered if he expected an answer. Apparently he did, because he sighed. "Ah, mayhap you'll tell me later."

The sun warmed her, though the air was brisk. She relaxed against Brenden's chest. He was strong and solid behind her, and her anger dissolved. The rocky crags and heather-covered hills stretched out endlessly around them. She wondered how long they would be riding. It was almost November, and such mild weather was uncommon.

"Where did you travel as a child?" His deep voice resonated through his chest and into her shoulder.

"We traveled around Asia and Europe." He was silent, waiting for her to continue. "We lived in Turkey for several years."

"Your father brought you to live among infidels?" he asked incredulously.

"They're not infidels."

He grunted in disbelief. "So your father was a mercenary, aye?"

"What?" She frowned and started to protest, then realized there was no other reason for a sixteenth-century English soldier to be in the Turkish Ottoman Empire, unless he was a Christian renegade or a slave.

"Your father? Was he an officer of the sultan? Did he flay Christians alive and stuff them with straw?"

"Uh . . . no. He was very merciful. That's why we left." She decided against mentioning the three years she had spent there as an adult.

"Can you speak the heathen language?"

She shifted. She was sitting sideways on the edge of the saddle, and it was becoming extremely uncomfortable. "*Bu eyer kiçimi agritiyor,*" she said. *This saddle is bruising my ass.*

"Oh, aye?" He sounded a little surprised that she could actually speak Turkish.

"I said, I'm uncomfortable." She swung her left leg awkwardly over the horse's neck, so she was straddling it. He scooted back as much as he could and she found herself pressed closely against his stomach and chest. She tucked her skirts around her legs so they wouldn't be too chafed by the end of the day. He was silent though her ministrations, though his arm held her firmly around the waist.

She belatedly wondered how uncomfortable she was making him. "Am I making you uncomfortable?"

"I'll do." His voice was strained.

"You don't sound comfortable." She tried wiggling forward a little but only succeeded in wedging herself more firmly between his legs.

"Just . . . stop moving and I'll be fine."

The heat rose clear to her hairline when she realized the source of his discomfort. "I'm really sorry. I didn't realize . . . ," she stuttered.

"Don't apologize. I'll take no offense to having such a fine lassie rubbing against me."

Audrey's scathing retort was cut off by Gavin's riding toward them. "Redshanks," was all he said.

"Is it the kine?" Brenden asked.

"Aye. They must think we're fools, trying to thieve them in broad daylight."

Brenden and Gavin dismounted and led Audrey and the horses to an outcropping of rocks. Gavin pulled a knife from his boot, and Brenden grabbed a bow and arrows from the back of his saddle.

"You stay here." He pointed to the ground behind the rocks. Audrey crouched obediently, and they disappeared into the landscape. She had no idea what the "kine" were or what they were about to do, but if they needed weapons to do it, she wanted to stay out of it. She stole a glance over the edge of the rocks but saw nothing.

She turned, intending to sit down against the rock and wait, but what she found in front of her was a large, dirty man dressed in a plaid kilt. She started to scream, but he covered her mouth. He held her close, and she thought she might pass out from his stench. She struggled, but he pinned her arms to her sides.

He was babbling at her in another language. She couldn't understand him, but the suggestive tone of voice and the way he leered at her made his intentions obvious. She fought in earnest. He laughed as though he enjoyed it and kept yammering at her. The part of his face that wasn't covered with a scraggly beard was filthy. His long brown hair hung lank and greasy around his shoulders. He loosened his grip on her so his hand could grope her backside. She brought her knee up into his crotch, but he was quicker and blocked her with his thigh. She jerked her arm free and raked her nails across his cheek.

He yelled in pain. Red slash marks ran jagged down the side of his face. She tried to twist free of him, but he was angry now. He said something she took as the equivalent of a challenge to play rough and slapped her across the face. She felt wetness on the corner of her mouth and the sharp, metallic taste of blood on her tongue.

Her ears were still ringing when he grabbed a handful of hair and yanked her head back. He ground his lips against hers, trying to shove his fat tongue in her mouth. She pursed her lips tightly together. He pulled harder on her hair. She cried out, tears in her eyes, and he shoved his tongue in. One of his grubby hands found its way into the top of her shift and manhandled her breasts.

She was becoming sick with fear and revulsion. He stopped suddenly and threw her to the ground. Her blood stained his lips. He lifted his kilt.

She heard a whooshing sound. An arrow appeared in the man's thigh, the feathers on the end vibrating from the impact. She could see the whites of his eyes as he stared at the arrow in horror.

"Audrey!"

She turned, and Brenden was standing there like Robin Hood with bow and arrow, hair blowing in the wind and eyes blazing. She thought her heart would explode with gratitude. She scrambled up and ran behind him.

Brenden yelled something at the man. Now that the danger was past, she made the connection that they were speaking Gaelic. She peeked around Brenden's arm to watch the man limping off into the hills.

"Audrey, are you hurt?" He ran his hands over her arms, her shoulders, and even her head. She hadn't noticed before, but when he said her name, he rolled the *dr* sound. It gave her name an almost musical quality.

"I'm fine." She wiped the blood from her mouth. She self-consciously tried to smooth her hair, which she knew was coming out of the braid and standing out straight around her face.

He touched the front of her dress. The top buttons were missing, and it was gaping, exposing the snug shift. She held it closed with one hand.

"He ruined your gown."

"It doesn't matter."

He met her eyes. Her heart skipped a beat at the warmth in his gaze. He draped his mantle around her shoulders and helped her into the saddle.

Gavin was at the bottom of the hill with about twenty longhair cattle. She understood now. Cattle were "kine," and the man in plaid was one of the cattle rustlers. She had forgotten how close they were to the highlands.

"What are you going to do with those?" she asked Brenden.

"They belong to my father. We'll take them back to Creag Liath."

"Where's that?"

"Not far. Do you need to stop?" He looked up at her solicitously.

She shook her head. She was still a little shaken from the attack, but she could continue. Their exchange made Gavin look up and take in her disheveled appearance. He gave Brenden a questioning look.

"I got another one at the top of the hill. He thought to have some sport with Audrey."

Brenden mounted behind her and gathered her to

him. She had to stifle the sigh that almost escaped her lips when she leaned against him. *Idiot*, she screamed at herself. *Do not fall for this man!* He was trouble. But she couldn't stop the way her pulse sped up. She kept seeing him standing there with bow and arrow in hand.

She was really pathetic when she thought about it. As if saving her from her stinky rapist changed anything. She reminded herself what a fine judge of character she had been in the past. Her late husband, Alex, had seemed like a strong, able man. Instead, what she got was a man-child crawling with neurosis. She was not going to get into a relationship with this man. When they'd finished whatever they had to do, she would return to Drochaid and go home.

"Why are we going to Creag Liath?"

"Business," he answered shortly, then added, "I grew up there."

"Oh." Audrey felt pleased she was going to see where he grew up and became annoyed at herself again. "Your family is there?"

"Aye, but not at the moment. I hope to be finished before they return."

That was curious. Bad blood? Or maybe he just didn't want to explain her. "What will you tell them about me? If we see them I mean."

"What would you have me tell them?" His lips were near her ear, and she suppressed a shiver.

"Surely you're not going to tell them you're dragging me around because of the dreams."

"Nay, 'tis no concern of theirs. I shall tell them you're traveling with us and leave it at that."

He urged the horse to go faster, intercepting a wayward cow. Seeing its way blocked, the cow returned to the others.

"What is your business?"

"Right now, the same as yours."

"Perhaps you'd share what this business is with me."

He hesitated. "Will you drop the talk of kidnapping?"

"Yes."

"And you'll not try to run away if I'm not watching you every moment?"

"I promise!"

"The woman in our dreams is Mary Stuart, Queen of Scotland. And I plan to rescue her."

She'd known this from the start, but for some reason hearing him say the words shocked her to silence and filled her with dread.

"She's imprisoned at Fotheringhay in England. She was found guilty of treason and sentenced to death, but the warrant has yet to be signed. If the English queen stays true to character, it won't happen anytime soon. Just the same, I fear this will be my last chance to succeed."

She covered her mouth. This couldn't really be happening. She looked quickly at the emerald ring on his hand, then away. She fearfully looked back, knowing what she would find. The ring was still there. She stared at his hands, noting the long fingers and tended nails. They were large hands, and strong. But not strong enough.

4

It was twilight when they reached Creag Liath. A heavy mist was falling, but Brenden's mantle kept Audrey warm and dry.

The castle was built on a hill and was surrounded by a moat that was dry except at the back of the castle, where it extended out into a loch. It looked scummy even in the fading light. The enormous keep rose several stories above the thick, gray stone walls. Conical towers were placed every hundred yards or so in the curtain wall. It was much bigger than Drochaid. The drawbridge was down and the portcullis up when they approached the massive gatehouse.

Brenden reined his horse in before crossing the bridge and rummaged in the saddlebag behind him.

"Here, put these on," he said, presenting her with the leather shoes she thought she had left at Drochaid. "I fear I'll throw my back out if I try to carry you inside, wet as you are."

"You've had these all along?" She snatched them away and slipped them on. "You bastard! My feet are freezing!"

"That may be, but I didn't plan on chasing you about the hills if you had a mind to bolt."

The men at the gate called greetings to Brenden and Gavin. Brenden dismounted and held out his arms to help her down. She ignored him.

"I wouldn't want to cause you any undo pain on my account."

She saw a flash of white teeth as he laughed. "Your concern for my health is touching."

He led her into the castle, which opened directly into the great hall. She removed the dripping mantle, making sure to pull the front of her dress closed. Brenden handed it to a skinny middle-aged woman with a long face.

They exchanged a few pleasantries before Brenden introduced the woman as Glynnis.

"Mistress Williams." Glynnis nodded, taking in her appearance.

"As you can see, the lady needs something to wear. See what you can do. Put her in the apartments above mine and send a bath up. We will sup in my chambers."

Audrey followed her up two flights of stone steps and into a sitting room. It was similar to Brenden's room at Drochaid, with a fireplace and colorful tapestries hanging on the walls. A connecting door stood open, leading to the bedchamber.

Glynnis lit a candelabra on the mantle and another on a carved wooden table. She slipped quietly out of the room.

Nature was calling, so Audrey went in search of the bathroom. In the bedchamber, behind a colorful screen, she found a closestool with a padded seat. She returned to find Glynnis lighting the fire.

"This should do ye this evening." Glynnis pointed to

a chair with garments draped over it. "I'll have your gown mended."

"Thank you." Audrey removed her dress and handed it to her.

After Glynnis left, she removed Guendolen's shift, as well as her own bra and underwear. The new shift was made of linen and fit better, covering her cleavage. It felt cool and soft against her skin. The lace collar was large, but delicate, and rested flat against her shoulders. The gown was similar to the one she had just handed over to Glynnis. It was heavy green velvet with silver leaves and colorful flowers embroidered on the bodice. It tied loosely beneath her breasts, and the triangular sleeves hung loose. To her distaste it had a dark fur collar, but it was comfortable.

She was washing her face with the water and scented soap Glynnis had brought when she heard something behind her. She turned to find Brenden emerging from behind a tapestry.

Seeing her frown, he pulled the tapestry aside and revealed a door. "It leads to my chambers."

"How convenient." His familiarity made her nervous. "Ever heard of knocking?" she asked, drying her face. When she looked up, he was gone, and she found him behind her. He was inspecting her lace bra and panties closely. She ran to him and snatched them out of his hands.

"Do you wear them . . . underneath?"

"Yes!" She wadded them in her hands. She didn't like the expressions passing over his face, as though he was imagining her in them.

He offered her his arm, smiling broadly. "Come eat with me?"

She buried her undergarments under the discarded

shift and took his arm. He looked over his shoulder wistfully at the heap of clothes as he led her through the door behind the tapestry and down a short flight of stairs opening directly into his chambers.

Their meal consisted of overcooked eel, cheese, bread, and wine. It was already laid out on a trestle table when they arrived. Brenden pulled up two chairs and shooed the serving girl away.

They ate in silence. He had discarded the doublet and now wore a clean white shirt, open at the throat, which exposed a few auburn hairs. The shirt was large and blousy, with a large collar and ties that secured it down the front.

"This will all be yours someday?" she asked, impressed with the wealth she had seen so far. She had read that Scotland was a poor country in this century, so the apparent wealth of the Rosses was surprising.

"Nay, my brother Fillip will be the sixth Earl of Irvine upon my father's death."

Audrey choked. "You have an older brother?"

"Aye, he's two years older than myself."

But Ian had told her Brenden was the sixth earl! What had happened to Fillip? She felt ill and drained her cup of wine. The warmth filled her stomach, making her steady again. Maybe Ian was wrong. She didn't know when Fillip would die; maybe he would have a nice long life.

"Where is he now?"

"We just left him at Drochaid. He lives there with his wife most of the year."

She felt sick again, thinking about his wife. She poured more wine.

"Why aren't you married?" Her tongue was a little loose from the alcohol and curiosity got the best of her.

"You must be, what? Thirty-two? The nobility arrange all their marriages, don't they? Marrying cousins, stuff like that?"

He surveyed her with amusement. "I, uh, haven't met a lass I am interested in spending my life with. That was your first question, aye?" She nodded, and he smiled. "I am two-and-thirty. And aye, most marriages in my family are arranged, for profit." He looked at her speculatively. "Are you volunteering?"

"No! I was just asking!" She turned her attention back to the wine. Her cheeks burned with embarrassment.

"I didn't realize you found me so offensive."

"It's not you. I've been married."

"What's this? Stay you faithful to a memory? If the man is dead, would he not want you to move on? Only a selfish man would harbor such a wish that would cause you hardship."

A lump rose in her throat at his words, and she looked away. She shrugged, unable to think of a good answer. She felt him watching her and willed herself not to cry. Why was she ready to blubber anyway? She never cried about it anymore. She never even thought about it.

"Tell me of your husband. How did he die?"

Her stomach clenched in the familiar way at any reference to Alex's death. She couldn't see any way to avoid this conversation, so she blurted out, "He committed suicide."

She sat rigidly, watching the look of shock come over his face. It was the common reaction, followed by apologies, averted eyes, and quickly changed subjects. She always heard the unspoken question hanging in the air: *How could you let it happen?*

"He killed himself?" he asked in disbelief.

She nodded.

"Why?"

"Well . . . ," she started. She was at a loss for words. The only other person she'd talked about it with was a therapist. "Things just weren't going his way. At work, at home, with his family. I guess he thought he was better off dead."

She shook her head helplessly. She didn't have the answers.

"So he killed himself?" he asked again. "He was a coward."

She closed her eyes and took a deep, stabilizing breath until she felt the tears receding. When she opened her eyes, he looked angry.

"You won't allow yourself to weep for the man, because he wasn't worth it, I'd like to believe. But at the same time, you won't allow yourself to move forward."

"I really don't want to talk about this." She reached for the wine.

"Aye, I can't blame you. 'Tis much easier to tell everyone to go away; then you can curl up in your room with memories of your dead husband. That should keep you warm and fed."

She stared at him in disbelief. His green eyes regarded her knowingly, as if he knew all about her situation, had her pegged.

"You haven't got a clue. You just told me you've never cared for anyone, and yet you dare preach to me? You cannot possibly know what it's like." She stood and had to grip the table edge to steady herself. She was drunk.

He stood, too, and grabbed her arm. "Can you really love someone who would abandon you?"

She pulled away from him. Her head was too fuzzy to

have this conversation. The old thoughts were pressing their way in, the ones that said *she* must have abandoned him somehow, otherwise she could have stopped him. "I don't know." She started for the stairs and felt his hands on her again.

"I can do it!" She pushed him away and left him staring after her.

A small brass tub sat by the fire when she returned to her chamber, steam rising from it. She undressed and stepped into the water.

She used a ball of soap to scrub her body and wash her hair. The tub wasn't made for lounging, unless she hung her legs over the side, so she didn't linger. She kept glancing at the tapestry where she knew Brenden's door to be, expecting him to pop in at any moment.

She slipped her shift back on and combed the tangles from her hair. She washed her underwear in the tub and laid it on a chest in the bedchamber to dry.

After the bath was taken away, she sat by the fire wondering what Brenden was doing. The wine was starting to wear off, and she felt guilty about how she had acted during dinner. Maybe she should go to his room and apologize, but the thought of him taking a bath stopped her. Before she could stop herself, she had a mental picture of it and felt a blush creeping up her neck.

There was a knock from behind the tapestry, and Brenden stepped in. "I knocked," he said innocently.

She could only stare. She felt as though she had been caught doing something naughty, and her cheeks burned hotter. He had bathed and was clean shaven. He looked as he did in her dreams.

"You're supposed to wait until I say, 'Come in,'" she managed to say. His skin was smooth and his jaw, square and strong. He looked younger without the whiskers.

He grabbed a stool and pulled it beneath him. "I should have waited until morning, but I am troubled."

"Why?"

He leaned forward, taking her hand and giving her an appealing look. "I didn't mean to distress you earlier. I shouldn't have made you speak of it. It wasn't any of my concern. And I didn't mean to malign your husband. I know not why, but it grieves me to think you're suffering for what he did."

She was incredibly touched that he was disturbed enough to apologize. "It's all right. I just try not to think about it."

"That must prove difficult." He was looking down at her hand and caressing it gently between his. Her pulse raced. She considered pulling her hand away but seemed unable to get the signal from her brain to her hand.

"It's not so hard once you get used to it." Her voice had a breathless quality that made him look up.

"So you say." His caresses changed to more of a massage, and her hand became liquid under his touch, the sensation moving up her arm. His eyes moved over her face. She felt the need to break the spell, but no words formed in her head so she just gazed back.

"Has there been another? Since your husband died?" His voice was low, his hands kneading gently.

"No," she said, pulling her hand away.

He looked down at his empty hands. The top of his head was close. She wanted to touch the reddish-brown hair that looked so soft, a few wet strands interspersed in it.

He stood suddenly and smiled. "I will not broach it again." He started for the tapestry, and she followed. He turned back to her, his hand on the door to leave, regarding her silently. He placed his hands on either side of her head, smoothing them down her hair. It was all one length and hung to the middle of her back. He pulled some of it over her shoulders.

"When I dreamt of you, this is how you looked." He took a step back to observe her. "Even the expression on your face. So sad." He moved closer and touched her cheek with the back of his fingers. "I would wonder why you were so sorrowful."

"I'm not sad." Her skin was heating up from his touch. His fingers moved under her chin, lifting it, his gaze moving to her lips. She swayed toward him, longing for him to kiss her.

His hand moved under her hair, firmly circling her neck. His lips were soft and tentative, tasting hers. She slid her hands up his hard arms to grip his shoulders. He pulled her against him.

His mouth became more demanding, parting her lips to deepen the kiss. He smelled clean and warm and her hands found their way into the hair she had so desperately wanted to touch only a few moments before. She was surprised by her unrestrained response but seemed unable to do anything but press herself closer and meet the passion of his kiss.

Suddenly it was over. He set her away from him firmly, hands gripping her upper arms. His eyes were disturbed. She was trembling from the abrupt loss of his warmth, and her hand went to her lips.

"Something about this is wrong," he said. She felt a stab of pain in her chest. Was she the only one affected? She could hardly breathe from the rightness of it. She flushed in humiliation. "I feel as though I am taking advantage of a poor widow."

"You're not. My husband's been dead three years." Why did she say that? Did she want him to do it again? Going to bed with a man in an age of no birth control would be foolish.

She thought he was going to kiss her again, but he stepped away. "Nay." He shook his head uncertainly. "You're thinking of your husband right now. When I take you to my bed, I'll have you thinking of no one but me." He moved the tapestry aside and left.

When? She stared at the tapestry, her lips still tingling from his kiss. *When?* God, but he was arrogant. She was angry with herself for letting him kiss her like that. Now he expected it to happen. It was the wine. That had to be it. She rarely ever drank alcohol, and it had affected her.

This was not what she came here for. *It's not?* a little voice in her head asked. She stalked into the bedchamber and crawled under the sheets. She tried to blot him out of her mind, but every time she closed her eyes, she felt the heat of him again, his mouth. A small sigh escaped her as she fell asleep.

They rode out of the castle gates and into the countryside. The air was crisp, but Brenden had acquired a cloak for her. She was wearing the black dress he had brought her at Drochaid. It had been draped across a chair in her chambers when she woke, the neckline and buttons expertly mended.

Her head was clearer this morning, and she resolutely decided that if he tried to touch her again, she would firmly put a stop to it. He had said they needed to talk away from the ears of the castle, and she'd agreed there was much to discuss. She only hoped it had nothing to do with the night before. Against her new show of womanly indignation, she found herself watching him. His strong hands, his straight body, the muscular thighs that gripped the horse beneath him.

He was silent on the ride. She was thankful to have her own horse, a gentle brown mare, so she wouldn't have any physical contact with him. He glanced at her a few times, but his face was unreadable, making her wonder what was going on behind those eyes. The silence hung so heavy, she searched for something to say.

"So . . . is your family large? Lots of brothers and sisters?"

"Aye, I have three brothers and five sisters."

"Your mother had nine children?" She grimaced in sympathetic pain.

"Nay, she had four."

She'd forgotten about Gavin being illegitimate. "Are the rest by Gavin's mother?"

"Gavin is the only one from her. The others are from various mistresses." He grinned. "My father's tastes are fleeting . . . most of the time."

His father sounded like a wonderful person. "So, where are they all? I've only seen Gavin."

"Camden is back at the castle—you'll meet him soon, no doubt. No lass is within the vicinity long without him sniffing her out. Most of my sisters are married. The others are traveling with my father. You will like Camden."

What did that mean? Was he assuming she was some kind of whore who would throw herself at any anxious man? She cursed herself again for having let him kiss her.

"As long as he doesn't steal my shoes or make me go

riding in the middle of the night, I'm sure I'll like him fine," she replied acerbically.

He raised an eyebrow. "I see your tongue is as sharp as ever this morn. Did you dream after I left you?"

She felt a rush of surprise and excitement. "No, I didn't have the dream! Did you?"

"Nay, my dreams were far different." He was smiling, his eyes traveling over her face and body.

She ignored his innuendos. "Do you think it means anything?"

"I know not." He reined his horse in and dismounted. He tried to help her, but she was down before he could touch her.

"What is it you feel we need to talk about?" They left the horses to graze and walked, side by side.

"I want to know where you fit in."

She shrugged helplessly. "I don't understand any of this, either."

"How is it I have dreamed about you and the queen? It makes no sense."

She took a deep breath and decided to press on with her theory. "Maybe I'm here to stop you from making a big mistake."

"What makes you say that?" He sat and gestured for her to join him. They were on a hill, and she could see the castle in the distance, its thick walls shutting out the activities within.

"I know some things."

This sparked interest in his eyes. And suspicion. "What do you know?"

"What if I told you I know you will fail."

He leaned his elbow on his bent knee and regarded her with narrowed green eyes. "How do you know this?"

"I can't tell you how I know, only that I do. You will

fail, then be outlawed, and your wife will be bothered by soldiers coming to arrest you."

"My wife?"

"Yes, she is a beautiful woman and does a bunch of interesting things." God, she sounded stupid. She closed her eyes. They snapped open at the sound of his laughter.

"And you can't tell me how you gleaned this information? Is it part of your dreams you didn't tell me about?" His mouth was a line of barely suppressed mirth.

"No," she said in annoyance.

"Well then, your information means naught if you can't tell me the source."

"Why are you doing this? Power? Money? Do you want to put her back on the throne?"

Something changed in his eyes. They hardened, became cold. "If you can't give me your trust, why should I give you mine?"

"I didn't carry *you* off in the middle of the night. If you don't trust me, what is the purpose of my being here?" She was unreasonably hurt he didn't trust her. "I can't help at all if I don't know what you're doing."

"Tell me of my beautiful wife," he asked suddenly, the hardness gone from his eyes, although he still seemed distant. "What does she look like?"

"I don't know. Only that she was different from other women of her time." She almost bit her tongue off at the last part of her statement. He was looking at her strangely, making her uncomfortable. She hoped he wouldn't ask her to explain herself. "What?" she asked nervously.

"You're the only woman I know fitting that description."

She struggled to look unaffected and treat his remark lightly. But her mouth went completely dry, and she was having trouble swallowing. "Well, there must be another one out there."

He chewed his bottom lip thoughtfully. "I hadn't thought of marrying, but I think it pleases me. I'm not young anymore."

"Yes, well, I'm sure you still have a few more wild oats to sow. Thirty-two really isn't that old, and what's the rush? I mean, you have your plotting to keep you busy and whatever else you do. Why tie yourself down?" *Stop it! Stop it! Shut up!* She smiled tightly, afraid to open her mouth again for fear of what might come out.

He grinned at her sudden spewing of nonsense. "I think you flatter me, yet I understand little that you say to me at times."

She took a calming breath. "Are you going to tell me what your plan is to rescue the queen? Maybe I can help you figure out where I fit in."

"My plan is to not have a plan."

She looked at him incredulously. He didn't appear stupid, but it was absolutely moronic to go about rescuing the Queen of Scotland without a plan. She wondered if he had some form of land scurvy she'd read about once. It was blamed for some of the ludicrous plots formed by nobles.

"Don't look at me like that, I'm not daft. What I mean is, I'm not plotting with anyone this time."

"This time? How long have you been doing this?" She wondered what fruits and vegetables were in season this time of year. Maybe if she got some in him now, it might counteract some of this lunacy.

"Eight years." He stretched out on his side, impervious to the cold. She wrapped her arms around her legs, forming a ball huddled under her cloak.

"After eight years don't you think it's time to give up?"

"No."

She sighed. "So what is this 'no plan'?"

"The plotting I've been involved in up to now has either fallen through, or the correspondence has been intercepted by the English queen's spymaster, Walsingham. The last, a plot by Sir Anthony Babington, was reckless. I did offer my services but wasn't really involved. It was doomed from the beginning, with Babington claiming to have forces ready to invade England and men to kill the English queen."

"What happened?"

"The conspirators, the main ones at least, have all been executed. Queen Mary has been tried and waits for her death warrant to be signed."

"What are you going to do?"

"She's been moved to Fotheringhay in Northamptonshire. I've been gathering some men to rendezvous with us. We shall see when we arrive."

"Are you just going to walk up to her prison and break her out? Surely you must have a plan? With so many plots in the past involving her, she must be heavily guarded."

"Well, of course! And I 'ave no doubt they will be needing more." Gone was the Scottish burr, replaced with an English accent.

She had to laugh. "So you plan on pretending to be an Englishman? And you think they're going to buy it?"

"Why would they doubt me, when I 'ave all the necessary papers to prove my extensive military experience?"

She looked at him doubtfully. "You've been in the military?"

"They're not real. Forgeries, woman! I happen to know a certain muster commissioner in southern England who has strong Marian sympathies."

"It sounds dangerous."

"Did you not think it would be?" he asked seriously. "I want you to help me."

She looked at him for a long time, and he returned her gaze levelly. "You ask a lot, Brenden Ross. Why should I help you?"

"The dreams have left us little choice."

Audrey had dinner that evening with Brenden and his half brother. Camden was a stocky, handsome man, standing an inch taller than her five-foot–eight-inch frame. His hair was short and sandy blond, his eyes dark green. She guessed he was Brenden's age or a little younger. His smile was his most attractive feature, and she could tell he used it a lot.

The meal was served in Camden's chambers. Gavin and the steward, Leslie, were there. Immediately after the introductions, Camden seated Audrey next to himself and indicated for Brenden to sit on his other side.

"It pleases me to see you home, brother," Camden said to Brenden, then turned to Audrey. "And you've brought such a bonny lassie with you this time. Are you trying to rub my face in your continued good fortune?"

"Ah, Camden, you will find this one unmoved by your flowery words," Brenden said, smiling smugly.

"Oh? I can understand. One so fair must tire of hearing it so oft."

Audrey couldn't help it and burst out laughing. "I'm sorry, I'm sorry," she said, covering her mouth.

Brenden raised his eyebrows, grinning at Camden. "Do you see?"

Camden looked neither insulted by her outburst nor moved by his brother's one-upmanship. He shook his head. "Alas, all the lassies laugh at me. They think I'm but a wee blastie."

Brenden groaned and looked down at the table.

She didn't know what a "blastie" was, but he was obviously insulting himself. "I didn't mean to laugh at you. I've never had anybody say things like that to me. Thank you. It's very flattering."

"You play me false! I canna believe such a tale. Do you mean my brother hasn't been feeding you such speeches already?"

"No." She smiled sweetly. Brenden was watching them, the amusement gone from his face. "Tell me, Camden, what is it that you do here?"

Camden, another bastard son of the Earl of Irvine, ran his father's estates. He had a wonderful sense of humor and an infectious smile that had her laughing throughout the meal. Brenden, on the other hand, had little to contribute to the conversation and appeared to find his brother sorely lacking in the humor department.

Leslie excused himself, and this seemed to indicate the closure of the meal.

"Brenden, I must commend you on the find of such a woman," Camden said, leaning back in his chair and looking at her admiringly. A flush stole over her cheeks. "If I had such luck, I wouldn't find myself so sore alone."

"Please," she said, waving his compliments away in embarrassment. "I can't believe you're lonely."

Camden smiled and opened his mouth to speak when

Brenden cleared his throat loudly. His eyes were narrowed at her.

"I thank you, Camden, and assure you, I shall covet such a find." His biting tone suggested he would prefer strangling her. "Have you thought about the other matter we spoke of?"

Camden looked at Audrey in surprise, then frowned at Brenden.

"Don't worry, she can be trusted."

Camden raised his eyebrows in disbelief. "Did you learn nothing from the Babington fiasco?"

Brenden's mouth thinned. "Are you with me or not?"

Camden shook his head wearily. "I do not enjoy imagining my entrails being burned afore my eyes."

Audrey chose that moment to take a drink of wine, and her throat closed. Entrails? Being burned? She painfully forced the wine to complete its passage to her stomach.

"I hope that won't happen. I've ceased all correspondence since the affair."

"Brenden, support for Mary Stuart is dead. It died long before Bothwell."

Brenden's face hardened, then he stood. He walked around the table and grabbed Audrey's arm, pulling her to her feet. Gavin stood also, looking warily between his two brothers.

Camden gestured angrily at Gavin. "Is it not enough you put the lad in danger, now you've got the lass here, too?"

"Then you're not with me." Brenden turned to leave, dragging Audrey with him. Camden grabbed Brenden's hand, pushing back the loose sleeve of his shirt and exposing the scars surrounding his wrist. She saw the muscles flex in his forearm, but he made no move to pull away.

"I know every time you look at these you can't forget. But do you mean to lose everything for a dead man? A murderer?"

"That's enough," Brenden said sharply, glancing at Audrey.

Camden released him. "Ah . . . so you haven't told her everything, now have you?"

The tension between them was palpable. She could feel it building in her own chest as her gaze lingered on Brenden's wrist.

Camden turned to her with a defeated look. "I'd find out just what you're fighting for before you get pulled down with him."

Brenden was practically dragging her to the door when Camden's voice stopped him. "I'm with you, brother."

Brenden turned back, relaxing slightly.

"God help me, but I'm with you."

"What was Camden talking about when he said I should find out what I'm fighting for?" she asked Brenden on the way back to her chambers.

He was thoughtful. He led her into her room and shut the door. She turned to him expectantly. He still didn't answer, but walked to the fireplace to poke at the dying embers.

"You told Camden I could be trusted."

He gave her an obscure look. "Can you?"

"Yes." When his demeanor didn't change, she sighed in exasperation. "What choice do I have?"

"Do you trust me?"

Audrey hesitated. Could she? She was attracted to him, but that was nothing to base trust on. What did she know of him? He had taken her by force from Drochaid and seemed to have little regard for the feelings or safety of his own family members when it came to his plotting. Could she expect him to have any more concern for her, when he only had one objective?

He saw the indecision crossing her face. "Aye, that's what I thought."

He started to walk away, but she caught his arm. "What do you expect me to say? I hardly know you, and yet you're perfectly all right with asking me to do this! It's not like I have any choice, since you took me against my will, with no concern at all for my thoughts or feelings. I'm sorry, but that doesn't inspire trust in me."

He grabbed her arms roughly. "That's not how I feel at all. I feel like I've known you all my life." He released her. "It's absurd! I didn't even think you were real until a few days past." He laughed humorlessly. "What will make you trust me, Audrey? Shall I shower you with flattery? Perhaps I've been approaching this all wrong."

"Tell me what happened to your wrists," she asked, and immediately balked. It was obviously something terrible, and her lack of delicacy made her ashamed.

He pulled back the sleeve of his loose shirt. "This is what you want to know about?" When she didn't answer, he stepped closer. "I spent two years in a Danish prison, chained to a wall for murder. The scars are from trying to rip my hands from the fetters when we were left to starve. Do you trust me now?"

She swallowed, unable to tear her eyes from his. "I'm sorry."

"Aye, so am I. Had I never been there, my life would be a sight easier. But as it is, I can't change the past. I can only work on the present. I need my brother to do this, and I need you. Will you trust me?"

She backed away, needing to put some space between them so she could think. She walked to the cupboard and nervously fingered the comb and small mirror lying on it.

"I thought . . . I felt like I knew you, too . . . for a time. But you're so different. Not what I expected."

His hands were on her shoulders, and she stiffened.

"Would you rather me be like Camden? Someone who worships you for your sweet face?"

"Now you sound jealous," she said, trying to affect a light tone, but failing. His hands were at her hair, unbraiding it. He combed his fingers through it. Little ripples of pleasure ran from her scalp down to her neck and back.

"Mayhap I am," he said near her ear. "I'll not lie to you, Audrey. I don't mean to share you with my brother."

"You can lose the idea that I belong to you right now." She faced him and his hands moved to her shoulders. "I am not one of your . . . your women. I don't jump into bed with every man who happens to kiss good. Or every man who gives me a compliment."

His hands moved up her neck and into her hair. In spite of her bold words, another shiver ran down her spine.

"You only thought the kiss was good?"

"Well . . . better than good," she said, feeling confused suddenly. But she had no time to think; his mouth covered hers. There was none of the tentativeness of his first kiss. He pulled her against him, his hands moving over her shoulders.

She slid her arms around his waist and up the columns of muscle on his back. She could feel the warmth of him through his shirt, and her hands ached to touch his skin. The wall was against her back, his knee was pressing between her thighs.

Blood pounded in her ears—she couldn't think straight. She kept thinking that she shouldn't be doing this, but his hands seemed to be all over her body. Her ribs, her breast, one hand hitching her skirts up to stroke her thigh.

Her own hands were busying themselves while she returned the ardor of his kisses, pulling his shirt out of his breeches to feel the smooth skin of his back. She felt a sudden freeness at her chest and realized he was unbuttoning the front of her gown.

She turned her head away. "Stop," she said, her breathing labored. He stopped unbuttoning her dress, but kept kissing her. His mouth was hot on her neck, making the world recede again. Her eyes drifted shut, then she remembered why she had told him to stop. She wedged her hands between them, pushing at his chest. "I can't do this."

He stopped kissing her. "Why not?" Desire still burned in his eyes. He touched her face and pushed her hair from her cheek.

"I have no intention of getting pregnant."

He continued gazing at her incoherently for a few seconds before his face registered comprehension. He released her and moved a few paces away. The removal of his warmth worked wonders for clearing her head, and she rebuttoned her dress. He watched her with hooded eyes.

"There are ways around that," he said, reaching for her again.

She groaned and pushed his hands away. "Please, spare me the sordid details of your past."

"Fine." He sounded annoyed. "I'll not force myself on you."

Her eyes went to his shirt, which was half hanging out of his breeches, and she looked away quickly, her cheeks heating up. They stood uncomfortably, avoiding each other's gaze until he mumbled something that sounded like an apology and left.

She was still leaning against the wall and slid to the floor, covering her face. "What am I doing?" she moaned. Part of her reasoned that it had been over three years since she'd last had sex. What was the big deal? Hear him out on his sixteenth-century birth control and get it over with. It would probably be worth it.

But the rest of her knew her heart could never be so casual. What frightened her was how close she had come and how badly she wanted it to happen while it was in progress. *Still want it*, that little voice sang out, making her want to silence the owner.

Was she ready to give her heart away again? And would he be any better keeper of it than Alex had been? She shook herself. What was she thinking? She would have to stay here with him, and that was unthinkable. She was close to tears. She hadn't thought it was possible to be any more miserable than she was before she walked through the corridor, but Brenden Ross was proving her wrong.

Glynnis found another dress for Audrey to wear. It was burgundy wool, two-piece, with a bodice, skirt, and petticoats. She was also wearing stays, a type of corset stiffened with bones and laced up tight. It looked nice enough, making her waist deceptively tiny, but she found it uncomfortable.

It was early, and because she wanted to avoid any more intimate encounters with Brenden, she decided to go to the courtyard, an atrium in the center of the castle. It wasn't big, but was well kept and beautiful. It was dim inside the walls, the full light of dawn not reaching it yet. There were a few stone benches and some small trees lining the stone path.

She sat on a bench, burying herself in the thoughts and puzzles she had been trying to sort out since the night before. She saw movement out of the corner of her eye and turned. A man stood a few yards away by the wall, watching her.

Audrey stood up quickly, unnerved that she didn't know how long he'd been there. Since she hadn't heard anyone come into the courtyard, he must have been there all along. When he realized he'd been discovered, he approached her.

He was tall, standing over six feet. He appeared to be in his mid- to late fifties and was extremely handsome. His dark, reddish-brown hair was short, as was his well-groomed beard, heavily peppered with gray. He was dressed very finely in black velvet breeches with burgundy and silver ties below the knees to keep his hose up. His striped doublet was burgundy and black, quilted and embroidered with silver thread. He wore a black velvet mantle, lined with fur and secured across his broad chest with a gold chain.

"It's a beautiful morning, is it not?" He spoke with a faint burr, and as he got closer, she saw his eyes were a light green, fringed with thick russet lashes. Brenden's eyes.

"Yes, it is."

"Who are you? I believe if we had met before, I would remember."

"Audrey Williams," she answered uncertainly. He was looking her over in a bold way that made her flush.

"What brings you to Creag Liath, Mistress Williams?"

"I came with Brenden and Gavin Ross." She looked around furtively. "In fact, I was looking for them when I came to the garden."

He smiled charmingly. "Perhaps I could entertain you while you wait?"

"Who are you?"

"Alistair Ross, Brenden's father." He laughed at the look of surprise on her face.

She was at a complete loss as to what to do. After all, he was an earl. She should have known by his attire. He looked like royalty. Should she drop into a curtsy? Kiss his rings? How should she address him? Instead, she just stared at him. So this was the womanizer who had sired so many children. She could somewhat sympathize with the women who fell under his charms.

"Come." He held his arm out. "Humor an old man." He folded her hand over his elbow. "Where did Brenden find you?" he asked, as they walked the paths through the small garden.

She hesitated and decided to evade the question. "We've only known each other a short time."

"I see." From the way he said it, he didn't see at all. "I've never known him to take a lass on his travels. What is the nature of your relationship?"

Audrey smiled sweetly. "Is that really any of your business?"

He placed his free hand over his heart, in mock hurt. "My dear, I am distressed you find my question offensive. I am only asking out of concern for my son. He doesn't talk to me on such matters." He gave her a look of fatherly concern that made her laugh.

He appeared wounded by her laughter. "You doubt my sincerity?"

How could she describe the nature of their relationship when she didn't even know herself? He saw her hesitation.

"You seem to be a clever lass. I shouldn't have to tell you a man in Brenden's position will have to marry out of duty. But, as I am sure you are well aware, there is room for other . . . developments in such matters."

"We're friends," she said, with a hollow feeling in her gut.

"Friends?" he said with distaste. "Surely you jest?"

She placed her hand over her heart, imitating his earlier gesture. "You doubt my sincerity?"

He laughed, patting her hand. "Isobel will be pleased."

"Who is Isobel?"

"Gavin's sister, no relation to me. She's been staying with us since her mother died. She's quite fond of Brenden. I'd hate to see her scratch your bonny gray eyes out."

Her gut twisted sickeningly, but she managed to maintain a pleasant facade. "She won't have to fight me for him."

"Aye, she'll be pleased to hear you're 'just friends,'" he continued with a wicked gleam in his eye.

"Is she Brenden's . . . betrothed?"

"Nay, although she does need a husband, both of her parents were common, so she is unsuitable."

Brenden walked into the courtyard. He was frowning, and when his eyes lit on her with Alistair, his frown deepened. He strode over to them, looking from Alistair to her and back.

"I see you met my father."

She smiled tightly.

"I was just showing Mistress Williams my humble garden whilst she waited for you."

Brenden looked at his father in disgust. "And just

what did you plan on showing her next?" The inference in his question was obvious. Audrey's eyes widened in shock.

Alistair leaned toward her and shook his head sadly. "He always was a sullen child." He brightened immediately and removed her hand from his arm. "Perhaps you'll join me for dinner tonight in my chambers?"

Before she could open her mouth to answer, Brenden did for her. "We'll both be there."

Alistair looked at him in exasperation. "You act as though I'm luring her into some romantic tryst! Fillip and Gavin will also be there. Oh, and so will Isobel."

"Excuse me," Audrey said and walked into the castle. Brenden started to follow her, but Alistair stopped him, and they began bickering.

When she was in her chambers, she went straight to the tapestry with the door that led to Brenden's room behind it. She found what she was looking for: a lock. She slid the bolt and let the tapestry fall back in place.

She threw herself on the bed, berating herself for being so stupid. He was no different than his father: handsome, charming, and a rake. And he had almost pulled her in. She wondered how many bastards he already had running around.

She knew she was overreacting. The mere mention of another woman's name and she was locking him out, but it was better to stop it now, before he could hurt her. That made her smile a little. If the pain in her chest was any indication, it was a little late for that.

5

Audrey found the castle's book-lined drawing room and spent the day reading Sir Thomas More's history of King Richard III. It took her full attention to comprehend what the author was trying to say, as the spelling and wording were unfamiliar to her.

She was interrupted by Brenden knocking at the connecting door. She put the book down, uncertain what to do. He probably wanted to bring her to dinner with his father. When she didn't answer, he tried to open the door.

"Audrey, open the door." His voice was muffled through door and tapestry, but she could hear the annoyance in it. She was sick of him walking in on her any time he wanted. On top of that, he controlled every aspect of her life—what she wore, when she ate, what she did with her time—as if she were some sort of pet.

He went away, and it became quiet. Good, let him wonder what was going on. She hadn't come all this way to suddenly become a simpering female who melted every time he came near her. Never mind she had been doing just that. She was a captain in the air force, someone who commanded respect from people. She had always been capable of holding her own against superior officers as well as the muscle-bound security cops she was in charge of. Why was she letting Brenden push her around?

She went back to deciphering the book. The main door to her chamber burst open, and Brenden strode in.

"If you want to keep me out, you'll have to remember to lock both doors."

She was angry with herself for the stupid oversight. "What I want," she said, closing the book, "is for you to quit walking into my room any time you damn well please."

A confused frown pulled at his brows. "What's the matter with you?"

"To begin with, I don't like this dress." She stood, drawing herself up to her full five feet eight inches.

"What's wrong with it?"

"It's stiff and uncomfortable. No one asked me what I wanted to wear."

"If I let you wear what you wanted to, you'd be walking about in your shift."

"Don't be ridiculous. And I don't need you to dress me." She was warming to the battle now. He saw it.

He held up his hands in defeat. "I'll have dresses made for you. A stitch won't be sewn without your authority."

His droll remark brought up another point that was bothering her. She held up her finger, telling him to stay put. She ran to the bedchamber to retrieve her jewelry. When she returned, he was scratching his head in confusion.

"Here." She extended her closed fist. He opened his hand, and she dropped the jewelry into it. "You've been very generous with me. It's probably not enough, but I don't want to continue taking advantage of you."

He looked at the jewelry, then to her. His lips thinned. "What the hell is the matter with you?"

"I think we need to establish some boundaries in this relationship."

"What?"

She opened her mouth to explain further, but he shook his head. He grabbed her hand to give the jewelry back. She closed it into a tight fist and tried to pull away. He held her wrist and pried her fingers apart, shoving the jewelry into her palm.

"I don't want your baubles. And I don't know what all this talk is of boundaries. But if this is about last night, I swear I'll never touch you again." The way he said it made her think he no longer wanted to touch her.

"Fine." She lifted her chin slightly.

He walked to the door and waited for her to follow. "Lord Irvine waits."

She was rooted to the spot by the cold look on his face. When she made no move to follow, he sighed. "Will you join my father for dinner, if it pleases you?"

She swallowed the lump in her throat and followed him to Alistair's chambers. Her steps slowed when she entered. Servants hurried up the stairs and into his apartments, bearing platters of food. A long rectangular table was set up in one of the inner rooms. A young boy was placing a bowl of water next to Alistair's plate, which Alistair then dipped his fingers in to clean. The seat to Alistair's right was unoccupied, and he motioned for her to join him. Brenden pointedly sat across the table at the opposite end.

Gavin was seated on her other side, but she didn't know anyone else. Alistair introduced her to Fillip, sitting to his left. He had the look of both his father and Brenden, with dark-green eyes and brown hair. But his face was narrower and his eyes cold. Next to Fillip was a stunning woman with a mass of flame-red hair. Noticing the intimate way she spoke to Fillip, Audrey assumed the red-haired woman was his wife and addressed her as such.

She was appalled when Gavin leaned close to inform her that Fillip's wife was still at Drochaid and this was Jean, a good friend of his. Her mistake was met by a round of indulgent smiles, with the exception of the woman at the opposite end of the table, next to Brenden, who eyed Audrey coldly.

Gavin told her this was Brenden's mother, the countess. Audrey noted, with some discomfort, that the countess and Alistair did not address each other throughout the entire meal. On Gavin's other side, across from Brenden, sat Isobel. Audrey observed, with a pang of jealousy, that she was very pretty. Silky black tendrils escaped the silver net she wore to curl around a small, white face. Rosebud lips and enormous dark-blue eyes completed the picture.

When Gavin's head wasn't in the way, she was able to see Isobel smiling flirtatiously at Brenden. Audrey wasn't able to look much, though. Alistair kept her occupied, asking her opinion on everything from the wine to what she thought of King James's latest policy. Throughout the meal, Fillip made derisive noises in commentary on almost everything she said. It was becoming highly annoying. Alistair was ignoring him, which in turn appeared to irritate Fillip.

"You speak odd. From where do you hail?" Fillip finally asked, eyeing her suspiciously.

She was becoming weary of answering this question

and was ready to say she had a speech impediment when Alistair answered for her. "She was born in England but traveled extensively in her childhood. Her father was a soldier, or so I'm told."

Audrey smiled politely.

"Is that so? Where have you traveled?" Fillip asked.

"I lived in Asia for several years and have seen much of Europe."

Alistair nodded approvingly. "Brenden tells me she speaks the language of the Turks."

She grew a little warm at the thought of Brenden talking about her, but a giggle from Isobel quickly dampened the fire.

"Say something," Fillip ordered insolently, smirking at her as though he'd caught her in a lie.

"*May the fleas of a thousand camels infest your armpits,*" she said in Turkish, and smiled sweetly. They were distracted by the sound of choking from the opposite end of the table. Brenden's mother was slapping him on the back while he coughed violently.

"You're supposed to chew the food before you swallow it," Alistair said, grinning at Brenden. Brenden wiped his tearing eyes on his sleeve.

Fillip's green eyes were narrowed at Audrey. "What did you say? It didn't sound very polite."

"I said I found you to be a delightful dinner companion."

The coughing resumed, and Brenden finally excused himself. Fillip grunted in disbelief, and Alistair laughed.

"How charming," Fillip said, his mouth full of food. "She speaks like a heathen. Mayhap next she'll peel our skins off and make flesh dolls of us." Jean tittered next to him. He laughed, a piece of meat escaping his mouth to fall onto the stiff ruff circling his neck. Audrey noticed he was acquiring quite a collection of food items in the starched pleats.

It was a relief when the meal was over and she could close herself up in her chambers. She didn't know how she was going to bear the remainder of her time here when Brenden hated her. Part of her wanted to go to him and apologize for her earlier harshness, but she knew that it was better this way. If he kissed her again, she would be lost.

The next morning, the seamstress appeared. She listened grudgingly as Audrey held up her black gown and explained exactly what she did and didn't like about it. She felt like a nit-picking shrew, but if the seamstress was going to the trouble of making it, she might as well like it.

Gavin showed up at her door later and invited her to go hawking. She accepted, but to her chagrin found that not only was Brenden accompanying them but Fillip and Isobel as well. Audrey was apparently being ostracized, since Gavin was the only one even making eye contact with her. Rather than submit herself to more of Fillip's nastiness if he deigned to speak to her, she hung back, and Gavin rode with her.

She watched the smaller figures of the other three ahead while she and Gavin talked about hawking, a sport she knew nothing about. What she really wanted to do was ask him about Isobel. Audrey thought the dress Isobel wore was entirely improper for the occasion. It was very low cut and her breasts were close to bursting out of it. She was afraid that if Isobel's horse stumbled in a hole, they'd all get a good look at her nipples.

When she finally got up the nerve, she blurted out, "How old is Isobel?"

"Nineteen."

"When did your mother die?"

Gavin's face hardened. "Sixteen years ago."

"Isobel was only three? It was very good of Alistair to take her in."

Gavin's cobalt eyes cut to her and were full of hatred. "Aye, very good indeed." She was taken aback by the sarcasm that laced his words. Gavin had always seemed a jovial fellow. This was a side of him she was unprepared for.

"You don't agree?" she asked hesitantly.

"Seeing how he murdered my mother, I can't feel too grateful."

"But I thought . . . your mother and Alistair . . ."

"She was his doxy? That she was. But a tiresome one." He looked at her again with blazing eyes. She could almost see the tension running through him, and his mount felt it. The horse began prancing nervously and pulling at the reins. He spoke softly to it.

"He killed her because he no longer wanted her as a mistress?"

"Not exactly, but when the opportunity arose to rid himself of her, he took it."

"I don't understand."

"When I was two, he married her off to a stable hand, hoping her husband wouldn't tolerate her obsession with another man."

"Did he?"

"Well, my mother was thought of as a cunning woman, and her husband, I think, was afraid of her. When he died mysteriously, it was called witchcraft, and she was burned."

She gasped in horror.

"Aye. She was called *baobh dudh*, black witch. The

townsfolk said it was her familiar that did it, a large black dog she brought with her from the Isle of Skye. It was her only friend after my father discarded her."

"They thought the dog did it? Or her?"

"They thought she commanded the dog. But if you're enslaved by the devil, who's commanding who, aye?" There was a strange light in his eyes that gave her a chill. "Alistair was earl then and could have stopped it, had he the inclination. But he didn't. In fact, his sons were required to witness it. Be wary of the man. He's not what he seems."

"Why do you stay?"

"I don't have much choice. When I was fifteen, Bren began taking me with him when he went abroad."

"What about Isobel?" Audrey felt a new sympathy for the poor girl.

"She was but a bairn and doesn't remember it." He shrugged. "Alistair is kind to her and looking to wed her. I could do no better."

The others had dismounted near a large oak. It was a huge tree, its branches twisting and reaching upward. It leaned over an outcropping of sharp rocks, making the spot shady and inviting.

Isobel didn't join the men hawking. She found a sunny patch by the tree to sit and watch, and Audrey joined her. She noticed the girl couldn't take her eyes off Brenden. Audrey found her own eyes straying to him. He seemed happy, and she wondered how often he relaxed. He was so focused. Had his father and brother not shown up, he would probably still be doing whatever it was he did. She smiled wryly. She had no idea what he did. It seemed he spent all his time plotting. Alistair was probably tired of supporting a son who had nothing useful to contribute to the family. Was that why Brenden wanted to avoid him? Perhaps his father was trying to press him into a profitable marriage, and Brenden wanted to be free to continue his activities, not tied down to a wife. After the warnings Alistair had given her, it did seem logical. Guendolen, from Drochaid, had said Brenden's father had a match in mind for him. He probably feared Brenden would do something to mess it up, and he'd be saddled with his plotting son forever.

Isobel interrupted her thoughts. "Why are you traveling to England with Bren and my brother? You're an Englishwoman? Is he taking you to your home?"

"Um, yes. I'm just traveling with them." Inspiration hit. "He was a friend of my husband's."

Her face softened immediately. "So you're married?"

"Widowed."

She looked suspicious again, but the tension between them lessened.

"Mayhap you'll be there in time for the beheading," she said brightly.

Audrey grimaced. What a grisly thing for her to seem excited about. "Whose beheading?"

"Mary Stuart, the king's mother, of course!"

Audrey was curious about what a person of the times such as Isobel thought of the whole affair. Everything Audrey had read over the past months were judgments handed down by people hundreds of years removed from the actual events. She asked, "Why is Queen Mary imprisoned in England?"

"You have been abroad too long! You never heard of Kirk o' Field?" When Audrey shook her head, feigning ignorance, Isobel scooted closer, excited to share such a juicy tale. "Queen Mary was having an affair with James Hepburn, fourth Earl of Bothwell. He was a terrible warlock, just like his nephew after him, and he bewitched her."

Audrey tried not to smile. "His nephew?"

"Aye, the fifth Earl of Bothwell, Francis Stewart." She lowered her voice. "Better known as the Wizard Earl, just like his uncle."

Audrey raised her eyebrows, and Isobel continued her tale.

"She was so infatuated with him, they plotted together and killed her husband, King Henry, so they might live together as man and wife. They blew up the home where the king was lying sick, and his body was found strangled beneath a tree."

"Why did they blow up the house if they intended to strangle him?"

"I know not. I think mayhap he escaped, so Bothwell chased him down and strangled him with his bare hands. He was a terrible, fearsome man, but so fair to see, no lass could resist him." Isobel smiled as though she would like to be slave to such charm.

"Anyhow, they thought they were being quite clever and no one would think her love, Bothwell, had done it. But everyone knew it was Lord Bothwell who killed the king. The queen was distraught and did nothing toward finding the criminals. The people were becoming sore angry at the situation." She nodded knowingly. "Aye, they wanted blood for blood. Their king had been murdered, and the killer walked the streets of Edinburgh as though he owned them, flaunting his success. But things were getting worse, and the queen knew something must be done. A trial was held and her beloved acquitted."

"If he was so guilty, why was he acquitted?"

Isobel smiled wickedly. "The men who judged him were just as guilty as he and knew should they charge him with a crime, he would call them out for the part they played.

"Now the queen was free to marry and, of course, she wanted Lord Bothwell. But the people of Scotland were screaming for his head on a spike! What was she to do?" She shrugged her shoulders, as if pondering the question herself. "They devised a plan where Lord Bothwell would kidnap and ravish her.

"So they were wed. But their happiness was short-lived, for the Lords of the Congregation didn't want an evil warlock as king. They gathered their armies together to defeat them. But the queen gave herself up for Lord Bothwell's safety, and she's been imprisoned ever since. She escaped Scotland and asked for help from her cousin, the Queen of England. She didn't get it."

"What happened to Lord Bothwell? Surely a warlock as powerful as he could have saved the queen."

She frowned at Audrey, seriously considering the remark made in jest. "He tried, I think. But he's dead now." She waved the matter away as of no significance.

The relationship Isobel claimed the queen and Bothwell shared bore little resemblance to what Audrey had read. She was trying to separate the fact from the fantasy of the tale when something landed in the tree above them and began fighting to free itself. They stood as the men came running toward them. Fillip shaded his eyes and peered up at the top branches.

"What happened?" Audrey asked, but Fillip ignored her. He grasped the lowest branch and swung himself into the tree.

Gavin joined them. "The falcon got a heron that wasn't prepared to die so easy," he said, and laughed. "It put up a bit of a skirmish, and she dropped it in the tree."

"That looks a little dangerous," Audrey commented, noting some of the branches near the top where the bird struggled didn't look strong enough to hold a man of Fillip's size. Brenden joined them in their vigil. Fillip reached the top of the tree, but he still couldn't reach the bird. He shimmied onto a narrow branch and grasped the bird's neck.

"I got it!" he yelled triumphantly. He started back down. The sharp crack of splitting wood caused Audrey to cry out in alarm. The branch Fillip was on dropped suddenly beneath his weight. He grasped uselessly at the branches overhead.

"Fillip!" Brenden yelled. He grabbed the tree to climb up and aid his brother when the branch Fillip was on snapped. He landed with a sickening thud on the rocks below.

No one moved or spoke for several seconds that seemed to stretch out into hours. Audrey could do no more than stare at his body in horror. His head was lying at a strange angle, and he was motionless.

Gavin broke the spell and ran to the body. Isobel began making a soft sobbing sound. Audrey and Brenden slowly followed Gavin to where he was leaning over the body. Blood covered the rocks beneath Fillip's head and neck. The heron flapped uselessly on the ground next to his open hand.

"Is he—?" her voice faltered.

Gavin nodded grimly.

Brenden knelt beside Fillip, but his face was strangely blank. She placed her hand on his shoulder in comfort, mostly because she didn't know what else to do. She realized, with a wave of hopelessness, that Brenden was now the future Earl of Irvine.

* * *

Most of the castle was draped in black. Everyone was dressed in black, and the women wore dark veils over their hair. The burial was delayed a day, waiting for the arrival of Fillip's wife from Drochaid. Audrey's worst fears were confirmed when she learned that Fillip and Catherine had no son. Brenden was next in line for the earldom.

Audrey was becoming conscious of the passage of time. More than a week had passed. She only had a few days of leave left, and that wasn't long enough. Part of her wanted to leave. If time were passing at the same rate in her world, she could find herself AWOL when she returned. But she couldn't leave now; she hadn't accomplished anything that would ward the dreams off.

The funeral service was held in the castle's small chapel. She attended with Gavin and Isobel. The rest of the time Audrey spent in her chambers. Brenden was always with either his mother or father, and she saw very little of him. He neither looked at her nor spoke to her at the burial. He wore all black and was solemn and quiet.

One evening, almost a week after Fillip's death, Audrey slid the bolt, candle in hand, and unlocked the door connecting their chambers. She hesitated, asking herself again if she really wanted to do this. She opened the door and entered the dark stairwell. She knocked on his door. When there was no answer, she let herself in.

His rooms were dark. She lit the candelabra in the sitting room and waited. She didn't know what she was going to say to him when he returned, she only knew she needed to see him.

She had a desire to comfort him, and it disturbed her. She was overly conscious of the way her eyes followed him when he was near—watching every motion or gesture he made, even staring at the broad shoulders when his back was to her. It wasn't a good sign. She hadn't changed her mind. She did not want to get involved with him. That wasn't the reason she had been transported back to the sixteenth century. She was here to stop him. Why else did she have the dreams? It made no sense otherwise. They couldn't stop the queen's execution, so she had to stop him from going through with his plan. Even if it meant she had to follow him to England, badgering him the entire way.

It grew later, and he still had not returned. Audrey curled up in the chair sideways and went to sleep. When she awoke, the candles were out and a fire crackled in the fireplace. Her back hurt from the chair arm. She sat up and a blanket slid off her to the floor. She looked around the room and found him sitting at the small trestle table. His elbows rested on the table, his head in his hands. She didn't know what to do, so she just gazed at him, her heart aching.

"Why are you here?" he asked without looking up.

"I wanted to see you."

"Why?"

She bit her lip to hold back the tears. When she couldn't any longer, she turned to the fire, so he wouldn't see them. His fingers were on her chin as he knelt beside her. He studied her face, then pulled her against his chest. He spoke soothingly, running his hands over her hair and back.

Her tears had dried, but she didn't want to leave his arms. She pushed away from him finally, wiping her eyes with the sleeve of her gown.

"Why are you crying, lass? You didn't know Fillip very well, and he wasn't nice to you at that."

"He was your brother; I know his loss must hurt you." She turned away from him. She wished she could tell him the real reason she was crying. Because she felt useless. She had known Fillip was going to die, but why hadn't it occurred to her when he was climbing the tree? Could she have saved him? When Brenden didn't respond, she turned back toward him.

"What happens now?" she asked.

He leaned against the hearth and shook his head.

"Are we still going to England? Surely your father doesn't want you to leave now."

He ran a weary hand through his hair. "I care not what he wants. But I must stay for a time, as I am now heir and I will not make such a show of disrespect. We'll be delayed in our travel. I'll send Gavin tomorrow to tell the other men."

She looked down at her hands, thinking for the millionth time since she had walked into the passageway at Drochaid, *This can't really be happening.*

"Audrey," he said softly, and she looked up. "Have you made your decision? Will you help me?"

"Do I really have a choice?"

He grinned, and she smiled back. He looked very tired, and she decided it was time to let him sleep.

"Good night," she said softly, and walked to the stairs.

His voice stopped her at the door. "What's on the other side of that wall, Audrey?"

She looked back, but his face was shadowed. "What do the scars on your wrists have to do with Mary Stuart?" She moved slowly back into the room. His hand moved to his wrist, touching the scars.

"So that's it, aye? All I must needs do is bare my soul to find out." He was pensive, still rubbing his wrist. "Nay, you may keep your secret for now."

❧ 6 ❧

Audrey walked the castle grounds searching for materials she might use to construct a toothbrush. They had toothpicks and special cloths for washing the teeth. Glynnis had even given her a bottle of spiced wine to use as a sort of mouthwash and mint leaves to chew. She was probably getting her teeth clean enough through these methods for the short time she would be here, but she was used to brushing, and she knew nothing else would make her feel quite as fresh.

She picked up a feather from one of the many chickens that wandered freely about the bailey. She ran her finger along it, testing the strength of the vanes. She was suddenly aware of being watched and turned around self-consciously.

Alistair was practically hanging over her shoulder. "What have you there?"

"It's just a feather." She let it flutter to the ground.

He smiled. "Are you planning to construct some arrows? Don't tell me you're trained in archery as well as the heathen languages."

"No." She felt uncomfortable and wanted to get

away from him. She remembered what Gavin had said about him burning his mistress and no longer found him so charming. "I better go in." She started back toward the keep.

He caught her arm. "Nay, Mistress Williams, walk with me. We have much to discuss."

"Such as?" she asked, but allowed herself to be pulled along.

"Such as, I have been unable to find out anything about you."

"My father was—"

"Hold." He held up his hand, cutting her short. Her mouth closed and she stared at him nervously. "I'm not speaking of your childhood, though I suspect you have not been completely honest about it. What I speak of is from whence you came before Creag Liath and what has brought you to us."

"I'm from the village of Croughton. I was on my way to the highlands to visit my mother when I met Brenden."

He looked at her incredulously. "You travel alone? To the highlands? An Englishwoman?" He shook his head. "And what could Brenden have offered that detoured you from your travels?"

"Am I required to explain myself to you? I think it's sufficient to say I am with Brenden and leave it at that."

He grinned down at her as he led her back inside the keep. "Ah, I can see why Brenden is so besotted. You are delightful. But, you see, it's not sufficient. My son is involved in some suspect activities, and I have made it my duty to keep myself abreast of them."

She wasn't sure what he was implying, but when she tried to pull her arm away, he held onto it tightly. He led her up the stairs.

"Where are we going?"

"I intend to get some answers, lassie."

She began to panic and tried to pull away again. "I can't right now."

He dragged her to his chambers and shoved her in the room, closing the door behind him. She straightened her dress and hair before turning to him. He was the lord of the castle, and no one was going to rescue her from him. She didn't think he planned to extract the information he sought by force, so she decided her best bet was to be professional. She would deal with him the same way she dealt with any overbearing superior officer.

He removed his gloves and mantle, throwing them across a settle that sat in front of the fireplace. "What do you know of my son?"

"He's heir to the earldom. He's thirty-two. He's unmarried . . . uh . . . that's all."

"And that's enough for you, aye? I keep asking myself, of what interest are you to my son?" He paced the room meditatively, stroking the short gray and auburn beard. "Aye, you are beautiful and your manner is bewitching, but he is a man with grand plans and would not waste his time on you unless you fit into them."

"I don't know what grand plans you're talking about," she lied. "As far as I know, Brenden is dependent on you for everything."

He stopped pacing and turned to her with a furrowed brow. "Has he said this to you?"

"How else does the son of an earl support himself? Particularly one who is heir."

A smile spread across his face. "Indeed? How does one?" He approached her, and she backed away. "I think you are part of his design to rescue the condemned

Queen Mary." Her eyes widened, and he laughed. "Ah! So, it's true! I knew it!"

"I don't know anything about a plot."

He ignored her and began pacing again, but this time he was smiling. She watched him nervously. She knew Brenden and his father didn't get along, and he probably wouldn't be happy if she told Alistair anything about his plans. But Alistair might be just the ally she needed to convince Brenden to abandon his plot. Then she could go home! She wouldn't be forced to travel to England with him!

"Aye," he mumbled. "I can see how you might be of use."

"Brenden does think I might be of use, but I'm inclined to believe his plan will fail. I think he should abandon it. He won't listen to me. Maybe you could speak with him."

Alistair immediately stopped pacing and turned to face her. "Indeed?" he asked again, his voice rife with amusement. "What makes you think he would listen to his doddering old father whom he hates?"

She walked closer. "In the past, it might not have worked, but Brenden is in a different situation than he was a few weeks ago. He stands to be the Earl of Irvine one day."

He was still looking at her strangely. "And, my dear, think you this pleases him?"

"Of course!" she said incredulously. "Why wouldn't it? All this will be his! He won't be dependent on anyone anymore!"

"How would you suggest I handle this situation?"

"Threaten him. Tell him if he doesn't do as you say he will not be earl, but penniless. I bet that'll get his attention."

Alistair's voice was filled with laughter. "Aye, it would!"

She was confused. Was he making fun of her? She stood uncertainly in the center of the room.

"You are very clever, my dear Audrey." He moved closer. "And how does this arrangement benefit you? Would it please you to be a countess?"

She stared at him uncomprehendingly. Was he implying she had designs on marrying Brenden? "What are you saying?"

"I am saying you are base, a commoner. I would never allow him to marry so low, so put it from your mind." Her mouth thinned in indignation, but he held up his hand to silence any angry retorts. "As I have said before, there is room for other developments. You would make an engrossing mistress." His fingers touched her chin, tracing the line of it up to her lips. "But think, lass. I am earl already. Why wait for my death to begin reaping the rewards of such an arrangement?"

She slapped his hand away angrily and stepped back. "You are sick! I have no interest in a relationship with either Brenden or you!"

"Then state your purpose for being here."

"I want to stop Brenden from making a terrible mistake."

He considered her. "I, too, would like to put an end to his foolishness. Perhaps we could aid each other in this endeavor? I shall try threatening Brenden, as you have suggested. But if it fails, will you assist me in my plan?"

"What's your plan?" she asked suspiciously.

"When the time comes," he said with a small smile.

She hesitated, then nodded. "All right, I'll help you. Can I leave now?"

"Oh, aye!" He placed his hand on her lower back and propelled her to the door. He opened the door, but when she tried to leave, he pulled her back. He leaned close and whispered in her ear, "We shall discuss this further at a later date. I will send for you."

She nodded and turned, only to find Brenden standing a few feet away. He was apparently on his way to see his father. She was conscious that Alistair's hand still rested on her back, so she moved further into the hall, breaking the contact.

"Brenden!" Alistair said jovially. "A visit from my son! What an unexpected pleasure!"

The gleam in Brenden's eyes was deadly when he looked at Alistair. He turned his stony expression on her, and she swallowed, wondering what he was thinking.

"What were you doing in my father's apartments?"

Alistair said, "We were just talking."

"In your room?"

"Brenden!" Audrey said angrily. "What is—"

"Go to your chambers and wait for me there!" he yelled, and pointed down the hall.

She was shocked speechless that he would speak to her in such a manner and only stared at him. His jaw clenched, and he raked a hand through his hair. His voice was tight and controlled when he spoke again. "Please, Audrey, will you wait for me in your chambers?"

Alistair's brows shot up as he watched the exchange. Audrey nodded shortly and walked stiffly to the stairs.

Brenden slammed the door to his father's room behind him. "What did I tell you, old man? Stay away from her!"

Alistair shook his head. "You cannot see it, can you? You are a fool! I never thought I'd live to see the day when you became pathetic, but here it is, before me!"

"What are you blethering about?"

"She cares naught for you! She knows nothing about you, son! All she cares about is that you will one day be earl. She looks to raise herself through marriage to you."

Brenden frowned. "What are you saying?"

"I am saying that she knows nothing about your ships. She is only concerned that you will ruin your chance of inheriting by engaging in this plotting." He laughed and shook his head. "I must say I agree with her there."

"I don't believe you." As if to mock his words, his stomach clenched up nervously. Could that be all she was about? Was she some sort of witch trying to entice him into forgetting all that was honorable to him? All so she could be the countess?

Alistair was looking at him incredulously, then shook his head. "You are smitten!" He waved his hand in dismissal. "It matters not. You cannot wed her. Take her as a mistress, I care not, but you will wed a lass of breeding."

"Nothing has changed, father. I'm not your lackey to be ordering about. I will marry whomever I choose."

"You are a poor excuse for a son," Alistair said, looking at Brenden in disgust. "Shall you be leaving soon to rescue the queen? Will I be invited to watch your execution when you are captured in this foolhardy venture? You dishonor your family!"

"I'm leaving on the morrow." He gave his father a threatening look. "I will not warn you again, father. Stay away from the woman. She's mine!"

He stormed out and up the stairs to Audrey's rooms.

He paused outside her door, trying to collect his thoughts. This protocol she insisted upon, knocking and waiting for her to grant him entrance, having to phrase every question with the word "please," was annoying. Yet he found her easier to deal with when he granted such small concessions.

He had to knock twice and was about to barge in when he heard her reluctant permission to enter. She sat at the table, a closed book before her, her hands clasped on top of it. God, she was beautiful. It was still hard to believe this specter from his dreams was here, with him, that when he held her in his arms, she was warm and alive and filled with passion. Thick walnut hair hung in a fat braid over her shoulder, the end tied with a blue ribbon. Her skin was white and flawless, her mouth, wide and full. She was looking at him, her face expressionless, her large gray eyes anxious.

Every time he saw her he had to ask himself what it was about her that drew him so strongly. He had been with beautiful women before and not felt so helpless to their wiles. That was the strange thing—she had no wiles. Never did she attempt to charm him or seduce him, yet every move, every touch, made him desire her more.

She still didn't speak, and he closed the door behind him. He needed to know the truth about her. He needed to know whether he could have her or not. He knew if he were persistent, he could have her body, but he had to know if it ended there.

"What business did you have with my father?"

The dark lashes that framed her eyes were long and thick. She blinked, as if surprised by his abrupt question. "We were just talking."

"My father doesn't bring women to his chambers simply to talk with them."

She stood angrily. "What are you implying?" He started to speak, but she began railing at him. "Who do you think you are? Ordering me to my room! Telling me who I can and can't keep company with! I am not a possession! I'm a person and I'm sick to death of being treated like something you found and are keeping in a cage for your pleasure only!"

"Well, that would be useless, aye? Since you won't let me play with my pet."

Her face turned red clear to her hairline, and he almost groaned. She was really mad now. Instead of the outburst he was expecting, she whirled around and stood ramrod straight with her back to him.

He sighed, not knowing how to handle this woman. He went to her and placed his hands gently on her shoulders. She was one of the longest lasses he had ever seen. The top of her head came almost to his nose.

"Forgive me, I spoke out of turn."

She stepped away from his hands and turned to him. She didn't speak, but she didn't look angry anymore.

He said, "We're leaving tomorrow."

"For England?"

"Aye."

She looked nervous and crossed her arms under her breasts, gripping her elbows. "Please don't go."

"Tell me why I should stay."

"Because what you're planning to do is dangerous. You could die."

"Why should that matter to you?"

She was looking into his eyes, and her lips parted, as though to speak, though no words came out. A blush was painting her cheeks an appealing pink shade. He touched her face. The thick lashes came down against her skin, but she didn't move away.

He brought his other hand up to cup her face. Her skin was satiny, and he caressed it for a moment before forcing her to look at him. She stubbornly kept her eyes downcast.

"Look at me," he ordered.

She opened her eyes, but they were guarded.

"If I stayed, would you stay with me?"

Her eyes widened at his question. "Are . . . Are you asking me to marry you?"

There it was. It was what she wanted. Overwhelming anger coursed through him. His father was right about her.

"Nay, I want you to stay and lie in my bed," he said with a nasty smile.

Her eyes grew even wider, and she tried to pull away from him. His grabbed her waist and pulled her against him. "Is that a no?" He was angry, but if anything his desire for her grew. He kissed her hard, and she pushed at his chest. He trailed kisses along her jaw and neck.

"Brenden, no . . . let me go!" Her voice sounded desperate, but her breathing was ragged like his, and he knew there was something between them. She felt it, too.

He pressed his cheek against hers and held her tightly. She didn't fight him, but she held herself rigid. "Damn you, you greedy bitch," he whispered in her ear. "Why are you doing this to me? You haunt me every night of my life. You ruin all other women for me and when I finally have you in my arms, it isn't me you want but my title. I can give you everything—"

"Everything but marriage?" Her voice was cold, and he pulled back to look at her. "You're wrong, Brenden Ross." The eyes that were usually so wide and expressive were narrowed at him. "I don't want you or your father's money, and I certainly don't want to marry you, earl or not!" She gave him a hard shove, and she was free. She backed away quickly. "You are a hopeless fool who fills his life plotting treason. You have so much to offer to a potential bride!" Her voice dripped with sarcasm. "Safety. Stability." She shook her head. "I know why you can't marry me—because daddy won't give you your inheritance. And you dare call me greedy!"

He had no idea where she got these notions and just stared at her. He removed the dirk from his waist and handed it to her. "We leave tomorrow. Be ready at daybreak."

She snatched the dirk from his hand. "I need a knife?"

"Aye, wear it in your garter. It isn't wise to travel unarmed. Remember the friendly redshank? This way you can save yourself next time you're attacked, since it's obvious you don't need me."

Her eyes widened in memory of the highlander who had attempted to rape her. Perhaps she recalled that he would have succeeded, had Brenden, the hopeless fool, not shown up in time to rescue her. She looked as if she might apologize, but he turned abruptly and left. He slammed the door as hard as he could on his way out. What the hell was she talking about? He hadn't missed the comment about his plotting, and it had hit its mark, like a knife in his chest. But what about all the other rubbish she was spewing?

He thought he was going crazy all those years, dreaming about her. He'd learned to keep them to himself, and for so long, she was his alone. Now that she was here, he couldn't help still feeling like she belonged to him. He hated seeing her with his father or Camden and knowing they probably had designs on her. These selfish, jealous feelings were new to him, and he didn't like them.

He went to Camden's room. One of the lasses that worked in the woolshed was perched on his lap. His arms were wrapped round her ample waist, and they were both laughing. She jumped up at Brenden's sudden entrance.

Camden scowled. "Will you never learn to knock?" The lass tried to leave, but Camden pursued and caught her at the door. After whispering something to her that elicited a burst of giggles, she left.

Camden sighed and grinned at his brother. "What is it that couldn't wait?"

"We're leaving in the morning."

"But I haven't obtained all the forgeries! We need more papers, and how do we explain Mistress Williams's presence?"

"You can get the rest of the papers on the way." Camden rolled his eyes in irritation, and Brenden went on, "And Audrey will pose as my wife."

"Your wife? Why does she get to be your wife? Why can't she be my wife?"

"If you're married, then you won't be able to maul the serving wenches on the journey."

Camden winked at him. "I don't mind with a lass such as she as my wife. Mayhap by the time we return, I'll wed her for real. After all, Stephen needs a mum."

Brenden quelled the anger that seized him at his brother's words. Camden was full of jests and meant not a word of it. "She will be my wife, and we'll speak of it no more. Just be prepared to leave in the morn."

Camden raised a speculative eyebrow at Brenden's reaction but wisely kept further comments to himself. The door burst open, and Camden's son, Stephen, came in. His short blond hair was in disarray, and his face was covered with dirt and blood. His tunic bulged and moved. His arms were wrapped around whatever was trapped beneath his clothing. When he saw his father, he backed out of the room.

"Get back here!" Camden called, and went after him. He grabbed the lad's shirt collar and pulled him back in the room. He surveyed the boy's squirming midsection and gave Brenden a sidelong look. "Looks like you have a wee bit of a bellyache. Is that why you're not at your lessons? Perhaps we should fetch the healer to cut you open and see what's inside."

"No, Da. 'Tis naught. I'll be fine." He grinned and tried to walk past his father to the bedchamber. Camden put his hand on Stephen's forehead, stopping him. He squatted down in front of the boy and reached his hand under the tunic.

"Ow!" he yelled, and jerked his hand back. "What the hell do you have there?"

Stephen produced an enormous rat from under his tunic. "I named him Francis."

"That's a fine rat, Stephen. I'm sure he'll make a bonny pet," Brenden said, as he walked to the door. Camden shot him a dirty look. Brenden grinned as he shut the door on Camden lecturing his son about adopting castle vermin as pets.

"Mistress Williams?"

Someone was shaking Audrey gently. She cracked her eyes open. Glynnis stood over her holding a candle.

"What is it?"

"'Tis Lord Irvine. He says it's urgent that he speak with ye."

Audrey stared blankly at her. "Me?" Then she remembered that she was leaving with Brenden in the morning to go to England. She had told Alistair she would assist him in stopping Brenden. She sighed. "Let me get dressed." She had washed her bra and underwear earlier, and they were lying out to dry, so she would have to go without them until morning. She felt strangely naked, even dressed in her heavy sixteenth-century clothes, and hoped she wouldn't be here long enough to get used to it.

When she was ready, Glynnis led her out of the room. Instead of going to Alistair's chambers, they went down to the great hall, through the kitchen, and out through a back door. Audrey wrapped her arms around herself as the freezing, wet wind whipped around them. Glynnis extinguished her candle and only the moonlight and stars lit their way across the deserted bailey.

Audrey could make out the dark shadowy forms of the buildings and saw they were headed for the stable. "Why am I meeting him in the stable?" she asked in a loud whisper.

When Glynnis didn't answer, Audrey began to have misgivings. The stable in the freezing cold seemed like a strange place for a meeting. Glynnis pulled the door open and ushered Audrey in. The interior was illuminated by some foul-smelling oil lanterns. She was relieved to see Alistair was present with several of his burly guards.

"Very good," Alistair said when he saw her. "Forbes, give the lady a cloak."

It was warmer inside. She walked to where Alistair was leaning against a stall, a large black horse draping its head over his shoulder. Alistair was dressed warmly in boots, a heavy fur-lined mantle, and a hat. A velvet cloak dropped onto her shoulders, and she smiled appreciatively at the enormous man named Forbes. He stood at least six and a half feet tall with arms and neck the size of a stout tree trunk. A bushy brown beard covered most of his face, but his eyes were a surprising soft brown.

"Thank you," she said hesitantly, wrapping the warm cloak around her. "What is this all about?"

Alistair pushed away from the stall. "I told Brenden I would disown him if he went on this fool mission, but he cares not. So it's time to take more drastic measures and you, lass, said you would help me."

"What do you have in mind?"

He smiled. "I think my son is in love with you." Alistair nodded at her gasp. "It disturbs me as well."

"That . . . that's ridiculous! He thinks I'm some kind of gold digger!" Her head was spinning. There was no denying the strong physical attraction they had for each other, but love? She felt a deep emotional attachment to him, but that was due to the dreams. They had lived with each other every night for sixteen years, and she was the only one who could possibly understand the pain he endured from them.

"Perhaps, but he's past caring. You will go with my guards, Forbes and Dearg. They will take you to a place called Caisteal na h-Uamha. It's deserted and in ruins—Brenden will never think of looking for you there. Do not be alarmed, I have no plans to harm you. Forbes and Dearg are fine hunters, and I will send supplies along later. They have strict orders that your safety and comfort are of the utmost importance."

Audrey was so stunned that she could only stare at him in disbelief. The horses were being removed from their stalls and readied for the journey when she found her voice.

"This is kidnapping! I never agreed to do this!"

Alistair turned to her with raised brows. "You agreed to help me."

"I didn't agree to be kidnapped! I refuse to be part of this!" She turned to leave, but Forbes grabbed her arm and pulled her back to where Alistair stood.

"I so hoped you would be reasonable. I didn't want to force you."

"I don't understand how this will stop Brenden!" Audrey said desperately, struggling against her captor.

"I will give him a choice. He can promise to stop his plotting and I will return you to his arms when Mary Stuart has been executed, or he will never see you again."

Audrey stopped struggling. "And what if he chooses to continue his plotting?"

"Then he shall never see you again."

A chill traveled through her. "Where will I be?"

He laughed. "Don't worry, I have no plans to kill you or aught so gruesome! You will go abroad."

Audrey was about to protest again that she wanted no part in this plot when she heard a voice behind them.

"You can't do this my lord." It was Camden. His large white shirt was hanging out of his breeches and his sandy hair completely disheveled, with hay protruding from it like little spikes.

Alistair shook his head. "What are you doing here?"

"I had an . . . engagement." He gave Audrey a small grin, and a woman emerged from the darkness behind him and coughed nervously.

"You rut in the stables like a servant? What is wrong with you?" Alistair asked angrily, then held up his hand for silence before Camden could offer an explanation. He rubbed his forehead tiredly. He pointed to the woman. "You are dismissed. Get out of the castle now." He motioned to one of his guards, who grabbed the woman and started dragging her out of the stable.

"God damn it, father!" Camden yelled. He grabbed the woman's hand. "I'll take care of this. You just go for now." She nodded and left with the guard. Camden approached his father, running a hand through his hair and dislodging some of the hay so it landed on his broad shoulders. "I won't allow you to take Audrey away."

"I assumed as much. You will accompany her and ensure her safety."

"Like hell I will."

Alistair waved, and two more guards grabbed each of Camden's arms. He looked at his father incredulously. "This won't stop him, you know that? He will just come looking for her and go on to Northampton. You accomplish naught by doing this except to widen the chasm between you. He will hate you for this."

When Alistair didn't comment, Camden shrugged the guards off. "I will go, but only to see to Audrey's safety. I'm not part of your nasty plan."

I don't think this was a very good idea," Audrey said to Camden, who was astride the horse next to her, his hands bound like hers. "You should have stayed in the hay with your girlfriend. At least one of us would be free."

"I'm no coward that hides in the hay when a lassie is in distress. There was little else I could do." He nodded in the direction of Forbes and Dearg, both hulking men. "They would beat me within an inch of my life and still you'd have been spirited away. At least this way you'll have someone with you to be sure you're treated with care." He winked at her. "And who knows what might happen along the way once they relax their guard a bit."

She sighed. "What about your lady friend?"

"She'll be fine. She'll go to her family, no doubt. I'll support her if she can't find employment."

He didn't seem terribly concerned, and Audrey deduced the woman must have meant very little to him. No matter what century it was, it seemed men still treated sex in the same casual manner. She wondered how the woman felt about Camden and whether she would be hurt by his indifference.

"Why were you in the stable? Wouldn't it have been nicer for your friend to have been someplace warm and soft?"

He raised a blond brow and gave her a lascivious smile. "Beds are fine, but sometimes the location adds to the pleasure." When she looked away quickly, he laughed. "Don't judge so quickly. If I hadn't been rolling in the hay, you would be sore alone on this journey."

She did feel safer with Camden along, even though both Forbes and Dearg were extremely polite to both of them, almost apologetic for the situation they were forced into. They rode most of the day and into the night, only stopping to eat and rest for a few hours.

"Father's destination for us might not occur to Brenden," Camden said, when they finally had a moment away from the guards. He was thoughtful, scratching the blond stubble on his chin. "He knows of the castle ruins; we played there as bairns, but he hasn't visited them in years. We will likely be staying in the dungeons, since there's no shelter from the elements above ground."

"Sounds dangerous! Children shouldn't be playing around ruins!"

He looked at her oddly, then shrugged. "It was fun. It's by the sea and there are tunnels and caves leading to a cove. It's a good place for hiding. It was Brenden's place."

"Brenden's place?"

His mouth turned down slightly in the corners. "Aye, Brenden . . . well, he was always different. Has he told you about the dreams?"

She nodded.

"They tortured him something awful when he was

just a lad. He used to wake up yelling some nights, carrying on about killing someone or other and some lass in the hallway." He shrugged. "His mother thought he was possessed by demons." He looked skyward in scorn. "She had a minister come to exorcise him." At her gasp, he nodded. "Aye, it wasna a pretty sight. Poor Brenden, sitting there while the minister screeched prayers at him and made him recite verse. Of course, it didn't work. So the minister told our father only two options remained." He held up one finger to illustrate. "He could have it burned out," he said, as he held up another finger, "or he could have it beat out."

He let it sink in.

"He didn't . . ." She was aghast.

"Nay, no one wanted to see Brenden burn. So Da took it upon himself to administer beatings to Brenden before he went to sleep, thinking this would keep the demons from entering his body. Brenden swore after a week or so the dreams left him, but I slept with him and knew he still woke in the wee hours sweating and cursing. But he never spoke a word of it to anyone and took to roaming at night when the dreams woke him." He smiled wryly. "And Da was all puffed up, thinking he beat the devil out of Brenden."

They sat in silence a moment.

"Aye, he found the ruins on such a night. He let me come with him sometimes, but most of the time he wanted to be alone."

She was completely disgusted with this piece of information about Alistair and even angrier with him than before. A shudder went through her to think what a backward time this was that they thought Brenden was possessed by demons because of nightmares! Alistair wasn't a very good father, but she was in agreement with him about stopping Brenden from reaching Fotheringhay.

"Do you really think he'll come for us?" She felt silly asking such a question, but she wasn't convinced that Brenden would care enough to abandon his plans.

"Aye, I do."

"Do you think we'll still make it to Fotheringhay before the queen is beheaded?"

Camden's dark-green eyes were sad. "If he doesn't, he'll have a bigger demon to exorcise."

"Where is she?" Brenden demanded.

Alistair frowned at his son and threw back the covers of his enormous bed. The lass sharing it with him sank down as far as she could—only the top of her head and blue eyes peered at Brenden over the covers.

Alistair grabbed his breeches and pulled them on. "Could this not wait until morning?"

Brenden walked around the room, lighting all the candles. "No."

Alistair sat on the edge of the bed, rubbing his eyes wearily. "She is safe and will not be harmed. You have my word on that."

"Your word?" Brenden scoffed. "I could fetch a high price for the likes of your word these days, couldn't I?"

Alistair shook his head. "I cannot talk to you when you're like this. Have a drink; perhaps it will calm you." Alistair gestured to the bottle of whiskey on the table.

Brenden grabbed the bottle and sent it sailing into the wall. It shattered and the amber liquid ran down the paneling to puddle on the floor among the shattered glass and rushes.

Alistair looked at Brenden reproachfully. He turned to the woman in his bed. "Leave us for a moment, love."

She slipped her shift over her head and hurried to the door. "Have a care!" Alistair called to her. "Do not cut your feet." She skirted around the broken glass and out the door.

"Where is Audrey?" Brenden repeated.

"I will tell you. But first you must hear me out."

"I will not!" Brenden yelled. "You ask too much, man! You secret my woman away and now you want me to listen to fair words? You have gone too far this time!"

"She is hidden for now. She will be returned to you when Mary Stuart has been executed and not before." He met Brenden's hard gaze. "She will not be returned at all should you continue this foolishness."

"You don't make bargains with me," Brenden said in a low voice.

Alistair stood, frustration lining his face, making him look old. "I have lost one son. I will not lose another! And to disgrace. I will not allow you to get yourself killed for such a fool cause."

Brenden ran a calming hand through his hair, eyeing the broken bottle of whiskey on the floor. He could use a stout drink.

"This sudden show of concern turns my stomach. Who keeps your castles in repair, aye? Your fine clothing, from whence do the silks come? I have done well by you and asked for naught in return. This is how I'm repaid?"

Alistair's gaze was unwavering, and Brenden could see he was getting nothing from him.

"So be it," Brenden said, throwing his hands up. "I'll find her myself. My duty as your son ends now. Do you hear me?"

"Brenden, dammit!" Alistair called after him, but Brenden slammed the door behind him. He strode the halls to Gavin's rooms. He wasn't completely helpless.

Gavin had been in the tower gathering weapons for their journey and observed Audrey and Camden leaving with Alistair's most trusted guards. He knew the general direction they were traveling in, and if he was able, Camden would be leaving a trail. Gavin had already sent that elusive dog of his, Sebille, to track them. They wouldn't get far.

Since their traveling companions, the enormous Forbes and the large red-haired man named Dearg, were silent, Audrey and Camden talked a great deal.

Camden believed there was a possibility that Brenden and Gavin were tracking them. Audrey looked at the soft heather behind them, swallowing up any trace of their existence, and couldn't see how that was possible. On several occasions she spotted a large black dog that seemed to be following them. She attempted to point it out to Camden, but every time he looked, it would be mysteriously gone.

Camden was in good humor throughout their journey. At times he looked weary and as though he was trying to think of some means of escape, but for her, he generally wore a happy face. During their short periods of rest and nourishment, he assured her that he would figure something out and would not let her be kept prisoner indefinitely.

On one of these respites, she asked Camden for the hundredth time if he really thought Brenden could follow the nonexistent trail they were leaving.

"Maybe they sent that dog to track us or something," she offered.

Camden frowned and shook his head. "Nay, neither of them has a dog and none of my father's are black, so that can't be it. But they don't need a dog to track us. We are leaving a trail."

"Where?"

"The horses have been relieving themselves, as have we. And I've been gouging out every tree I sit by." He illustrated by ripping the bark off the tree next to them, which must have hurt his fingers. She looked around to see if the guards were watching. They were engaged in conversation a few yards away.

She sat on a fallen tree, turning her body to hide what she was doing, and pulled up her skirt and petticoat to reveal the dirk Brenden had given her poked into her garter. "Maybe this would work better."

Camden gaped at her leg. "You've had that all this time?"

She nodded. He grabbed her skirt suddenly, pulling it over her leg. He straightened, smiling at someone standing behind her. She turned to see Dearg looking at them curiously.

"The lady has hurt her ankle," Camden offered in explanation.

Dearg regarded her skirt–covered legs. "Let me see." He stepped over the log and knelt in front of her.

"Really," she said, standing and backing away. "I'll be fine. I was just telling Camden it's not that bad."

"Sit down," Dearg commanded. "Lord Irvine gave instructions ye were not to be damaged."

She looked at Camden for support.

Camden's face was bland, giving away nothing. "You're not a healer, Dearg. We'll have someone see to it in the next village."

"I can tell if it's swollen. I'll not stop in a village, announcing our presence by seeking a healer, unless 'tis troubling her."

Camden and Audrey answered at the same time, he saying it was swollen and she saying it wasn't. Camden shot her a warning look. Dearg looked between the two of them quizzically.

"Sit down," he said firmly.

She walked slowly back to the log and sat, offering him her foot. Camden stood close by, watching. She pulled her skirt up to her knees and held it firmly in place. She could feel the metal of the dagger beneath her hand and was terrified he would be able to see some of the scabbard from his vantage point. She looked to Camden, and he gave an imperceptible shake of his head, telling her it wasn't visible.

Dearg's hand gently probed her ankle. "Does this hurt?" he asked.

She shook her head.

"It doesna feel swollen, and she says it doesna hurt, but I canna tell with the hose on. Remove them and we'll have another look."

She looked at Camden in alarm.

"See here!" Camden exclaimed, sounding offended. "The familiarity you use with her disgusts me! I'm sure when Lord Irvine said he wanted her undamaged, he was referring to her honor as well!"

Dearg's face reddened, and he apologized profusely to her. She felt a little bad, knowing he was only trying to be gallant in his concern for her ankle. When he retreated, Camden exhaled, looking skyward. "From now on, keep your shanks covered!"

Audrey was filthy. Her hair was falling around her face, and her wrists were becoming raw from the coarse rope binding them. They finally stopped to sleep in a wooded area. She hadn't slept since Glynnis had woken her the night before, and she was looking forward to the rest, even if it was on the ground. They had a small fire, but it was still cold, since none of them were inclined to huddle around it together. Her clothes and thick wool blanket were warm, but she still shivered.

Camden moved closer. At first she thought it was because of her shivering and welcomed his warmth. It seemed like he was getting a little too close, but it wouldn't warm her much if he weren't touching her, so she said nothing. A moment later, she felt his hand on her arm and his warm breath near her ear. She readied her elbow to jab him in the ribs if he had anything other than asking her a question in mind.

"The dirk," he whispered.

She turned to give it to him, but she had wrapped herself tightly in the blanket. After a good deal of struggling and a grunt from Camden when she jabbed him by accident, she was free of the blanket, and it lay loosely over her.

He took the knife and quickly slipped it from the scabbard. She felt a small tug, and her wrists were free. He pressed it into her hand so she could cut his. Not being proficient with a knife, she fumbled around and stabbed him in the hand.

"The rope, dammit! Not my hands," he hissed through his teeth.

"Sorry."

She felt along his hands and the rope, grimacing when she touched blood on the heel of his hand, and sawed through the cord. When he was free, they both moved their heads to look at the guards. Dearg was sleeping, and Forbes, who had faced them when they lay down, was now partly turned away, looking idly around the trees.

"What's with him?" she asked. It seemed unusual, since he had been keeping a diligent watch on them so far. When she looked back at Camden, he had a wicked gleam in his eye.

"I believe he's giving us some privacy."

She didn't understand at first, but she quickly realized what their moving about and grunting must have sounded like. She looked at him in horror.

He chuckled softly and placed his finger to his lips. "Don't spoil it now. With him not looking, I might be able to take him by surprise."

She swallowed her objections to such a farce and nodded.

He pushed her backward, so that he was partly lying on her. His head was bent as if looking at her, but she could see his eyes, watching Forbes. She held her breath, waiting for him to make a move. She heard rustling in the trees above them and a scraping sound as Forbes shifted.

The next thing she knew, Camden had collapsed on top of her and was kissing her. She pushed against his chest and turned her face away, gasping for air. He was only an inch or so taller than she was, but he outweighed her by at least seventy pounds, all of which was lying on her.

"Camden," she said in a strained whisper. "Get off! I can't breathe!"

Her struggles stopped when she heard the crack of a branch breaking overhead and a muffled oath from the same direction. She looked up in time to see something big and dark fall from the tree on top of Forbes. A fight immediately ensued. Dearg sat up, and another figure dropped out of the tree on top of him.

Camden rolled off her and pulled her from the

ground a second before Forbes and his attacker rolled across their discarded blankets. She couldn't see much of the fighting in the darkness, but after a moment, one figure stood and turned to them.

"Brenden?" she asked hesitantly, taking a step forward.

"Aye, 'tis me."

He came forward from the shadows, and she sighed with relief. "Thank God! I didn't know what was hap—"

He grabbed her arms and shook her slightly. "What in the hell is going on here?" he growled in her face.

"Brenden?" Camden said, a note of apology in his voice.

Brenden released her and advanced on him. "You!" Brenden seethed. Camden backed up, anxiety crossing his face. "You goddamned lecherous bastard. I ought to kill you."

Gavin approached and watched the proceedings uneasily.

"Brenden, wait," Camden started, but Brenden grabbed the front of his doublet. Audrey's scattered wits were beginning to regroup, and she ran over, placing herself between them.

"Stop it, Brenden! What's the matter with you?" Brenden still held Camden's doublet over her shoulder. She tried to pry his fingers off. "Leave him alone."

"Audrey," Camden said behind her. "This isn't helping."

His words seemed to inflame Brenden even more, and he shoved her out of the way. Rather dexterously, Camden ducked Brenden's fist and ended up behind him, leaving Brenden swinging at empty air.

"You're but a great ox, brother! Surely you can do better than that!"

Brenden turned, a look of grim determination on his face. Gavin rolled his eyes and went to tend to Forbes and Dearg, who were moaning.

Brenden again lunged at Camden, who moved aside quickly and almost cleared him, but Brenden's fingers grasped the collar of his doublet, jerking him back. She decided to try again before anyone got hurt.

His fist was cocked to punch Camden, and she grabbed it. He tried to shake her off, but she held firm. "Why are you doing this?" she asked helplessly.

He released Camden and turned on her. "What were you doing rolling about on the ground with my brother?"

She looked at him in shock, then felt anger rising in her. Part of her brain acknowledged the fact that it probably did look pretty bad from up in a tree, but most of her was indignant that he would think such a thing.

"What exactly are you accusing me of?" she asked in a tight voice.

"Uh, Brenden? You should listen to her," Camden began again.

"Listen to what?" Brenden looked at them both. "That I have wasted my time searching for you, when Mary Stuart's execution draws nearer? I thought you were different. You're naught but a whore!"

She heard Camden groan a second before her hand shot out, smacking Brenden across the face hard enough to turn his head. The palm of her hand stung. His first look was one of astonishment, then she was afraid he might hit her back, not an uncommon thing in this century, her little voice reminded her.

"I am the one who is wasting my time!" she yelled at him. "Take me back to Drochaid now!"

He stared back at her, a muscle flexing in his jaw. His eyes left her to scan the campsite and fell on Camden, who was grinning at him, then to the blankets on the ground. He kicked them aside, revealing the cut rope beneath.

"I believe this belongs to you." Camden handed the dirk to Brenden. He took it, tapping it against his thigh. Still he was silent.

Seeing an apology was not forthcoming, Audrey became angry again. "Camden, will you please take me to Drochaid? I'm through with your brother and his plotting."

Brenden looked sharply at Camden. Camden said nothing for a moment, staring back at Brenden. Then he met Audrey's eyes. "Aye, but let's sleep now. I'll take ye in the morning."

"You leave with her, and you will regret it."

Camden looked skyward and walked away, shaking his head. Brenden stood absolutely still, watching his brother's retreat.

"How dare you call me a whore! Your brothers have been the only ones to treat me with kindness since I have come here! I don't care what you think you saw from that tree. Camden was trying to help me escape!"

He was still unresponsive.

She shook her head. "This was a mistake. Coming here was a mistake."

She turned and walked into the woods, wanting to escape from him and this place. Wanting nothing more than to be at Drochaid so she could go home. She was such a fool to think she could change anything. The nightmares were better than this. She heard him following her. She lifted her skirts and began to run. She didn't know where she was going, only that she hated him.

She hated him with such an intensity that it burned

in her chest and stomach. He was the reason for all this. If he wasn't involved in his stupid, precious plotting, she would never have had the dreams. He was the reason for sixteen years of misery. She ran faster, stumbling over stones and fallen branches but not stopping. She wore her twentieth-century leather flats, and they pinched her feet, but still she ran.

"Audrey!" he called behind her.

She didn't even look over her shoulder, she just kept running. Branches slapped her in the face and pulled at her hair. She reached up to push her hair away and realized her cheeks were wet. She was crying. If he touched her, she would go mad.

"Dammit, Audrey, stop!" He was closer, right behind her, and her heart leapt, the muscles in her chest tightening. She ran faster, grabbing the trees to speed her way. His hand clamped down on her arm, yanking her around to face him.

She fell against him and immediately jerked herself away, trying to run again. "Let me go!" she cried. "I hate you!"

He gripped her arms and shook her. "I hate you as well! What are you? Tell me!" When she didn't answer, he pulled her onto her toes so that her nose was inches from his and his light-green eyes bore into hers. "Do you know what it's like to want someone this way? All those years I thought you an angel, and when I have you here, you're the devil himself! You've bewitched me, woman, and left not a shred of sense in my head! But heed this, whatever you might be"—his grip on her arms tightened to amplify his threat—"you'll not disappear on me again. If I have to bind and gag you, I won't let you near Drochaid! Do you understand?"

She couldn't answer. She could only stare into the eyes that held hers. Eyes that she knew suddenly. The anguish, the sadness that was always there in her dreams was present again, and she was afraid. His eyes moved over her face with a desperate longing that made breathing impossible.

"Forgive me," he said in hoarse voice. Before she could answer, his mouth was on hers. The kiss was hard and demanding at first, and her fingers curled into the sleeves of his leather doublet. She had no will to resist him. Her anger and hate transmuted into an overwhelming need to be closer to him. She pressed against him, her body burning for his touch.

He swung her around so her back was against a tree and hiked up her skirt. His hand slid along her thigh, lifting it and wrapping it around him. She knew what was happening and tried to make herself stop. Instead she twined her fingers in his hair, turning her head to kiss him even deeper. His tongue slid over hers, his kiss ravaging her soul and leaving her mindless to anything but the taste and feel of him.

He stroked her other thigh, bringing it up to join the one at the small of his back. She hooked her ankles together, trembling with hunger for him to join with her, to be inside of her.

The bark of the tree bit into her back when he surged into her, but she hardly felt it. She gasped, thrusting her hips into his, yearning to meld with him. His mouth was on her neck, and she let her head fall back, swept away by the moment, letting him do what he would to her body. He made love to her forcefully against the tree until she thought she would die from the pleasure of it. But when it was over and her head rested weakly on his shoulder, damp with sweat, she wanted to die from horror.

His hands still gripped her thighs. He released them gently until she stood on her own feet. Her shoes had come off. She didn't remember that happening, but the twigs and stones hurt her feet.

"What have I done," she said under her breath, staring at the white collar of his shirt. How could she have let herself get so carried away? He touched her chin, lifting her face so he could look in her eyes. He was smiling slightly and his look was warm, causing a shiver to travel down her spine.

"This is only the beginning, Audrey—"

"The beginning of what? Of a relationship?"

He frowned, looking confused. "Aye, isn't that why—"

"That's all you want from me, isn't it? Sex." Why was she doing this to herself? Her chest was tight with humiliation. All he wanted her for was a mistress, a possession. She wasn't a person to him. When she had looked in his eyes, before he kissed her, she had been so sure there was more. That the two of them had somehow been thrown together. But it was over now, and all that hung between them were the words he had said in the past. That the only reason he wanted her to stay was to lie in his bed.

"What do you ask of me?" There was a hard edge to his voice.

She took a deep, calming breath. "That you release me so I can walk back to camp."

His expression became stony, and he stepped away from her. After retrieving her shoes, she tried to walk past him, but he grabbed her arm and led her back through the trees. She did her best on the walk back not to cry. She felt as though her whole world was crashing around her. It suddenly became clear to her that she had been moving toward this single moment her whole life. Joining this man. And she had just joined with him in a way she could never erase from her memory.

Brenden sat with his back against a tree while the others slept. Forbes and Dearg didn't put up a fight when they regained consciousness. Forbes had grown up with Brenden and Camden, his father being a guard to Brenden's grandsire. Forbes had no wish to fight with them, and he and Dearg agreed to accompany them to the English border. Brenden was glad. He needed all the help he could get keeping an eye on that damn woman.

When she had run from him earlier, he had been certain that she would disappear and he'd never see her again, or worse, that she'd haunt him for another sixteen years and when she returned he'd be too old to do anything with her.

He watched the humps of the sleeping bodies around the fire. She lay on her side, near Camden. She was bundled up tightly in the blanket. He wished he could lie with her and keep her warm. He pushed the thought out of his head. He still didn't understand what had happened in the woods earlier. He had been so angry at her for the misery she caused him by simply existing that he had wanted to shake her until her teeth rattled. Then she had looked at him with those huge gray eyes, and it was as if he were in one of his dreams with her, except he could touch her and feel her tremble beneath his hands.

Part of him wanted to tell her why he was doing this. Maybe if she understood, she would cooperate. But he didn't know if he could do it. He had never told anyone about his time in Denmark. Camden knew some, only because it was with his assistance that Brenden had been able to leave the prison.

He didn't know why he kept raging at her. He decided he would try being nicer. She appeared to be looking on Camden as an ally now, and Brenden thought that he could probably learn from Camden's example.

He heard something and turned his head sharply. Audrey was sitting up, rubbing her side.

He said, "Sleeping on the ground takes some getting used to."

"Yes, I'm going to have a terrible backache tomorrow." Her eyes dropped to his hands, and he realized he was rubbing the scars on his wrists. He stopped and gripped his thighs.

"When will you tell me what happened to your wrists?"

"Whenever you tell me what's behind that wall."

She sighed and looked at the ground. He thought she was going to lie back down, but instead, she wrapped the blanket around her shoulders and moved closer to him. She sat on her knees in front of him and looked at him with wide eyes. His pulse was already racing, and he knew she had no clue as to the effect she had on him or she wouldn't look at him like that.

"What *can* you tell me? Isobel told me Queen Mary and her lover Bothwell killed the king. Why would you want to rescue a murderess?"

He was silent, thinking, then said, "They didn't kill the king. They were lovers, so you can't excuse that betrayal. But King Henry Darnley was a nasty man. A drunkard, simple and cruel. He was plotting to kill the queen. The explosion at Kirk o' Field was meant for her. Bothwell merely tried to give the king what he deserved.

But Bothwell failed, and the murder was pinned on him anyway.

"They were married four weeks before they met with the Lords of the Congregation on Carberry Hill. The queen was always merciful and cared not for bloodshed. She gave herself to the lords on their fair words, and Bothwell rode free to regroup."

The firelight played across her white skin as she listened to him; there was a small frown between her brows. A gentle breeze lifted the loose hair that had escaped from her plait. "What happened to Bothwell?" she asked, moving closer.

"He tried to rally support for the queen over the next few months but was unsuccessful. He even came to Creag Liath to speak with my father, who was well known for his ever-shifting loyalties, but he sent Bothwell away. He had some success in the Orkneys gathering ships, but the lords sent a fleet after him and he was forced to retreat to Norway. King Frederick, seeing a useful political pawn, imprisoned him." He paused grimly. "And then forgot."

"He died in prison, didn't he? I remember read—uh, hearing about that. Was it in Norway?"

Brenden said nothing for a long time.

Her frown deepened at first, then became confused. "What? What's the matter?"

"Aye, he died in prison." He turned away, feeling as though his life, his past, were welling up inside him, wanting to burst, but he couldn't let it out. He couldn't tell her. Not yet. When he looked back at her, he could see her withdrawing from him.

She started to crawl back to the fire, then stopped and looked at him over her shoulder. "You know, my husband, Alex, used to keep everything inside. He was a proud man who couldn't admit to being hurt or scared; he thought it made him weak. He believed if I witnessed him showing an emotion other than anger or indifference, he would become less of a man in my eyes. But now he's not a man at all. He's nothing. Dead."

She lay down, pillowing her head on her arm. His throat was thick as he watched her. It had happened again. Another moment when he was certain she looked into his eyes and saw to the depths of his soul.

❧ 8 ❧

Morning came sooner than Audrey would have liked. Her body ached from sleeping on the ground, and her head was fuzzy with fatigue. They were mounted and headed south, leaving the trees behind for craggy rocks and rolling hills. The road they were on was more of a hoof-beaten path, rutted out from rain, and most of the time they rode beside it. She asked Brenden how long it would be before they reached Fotheringhay.

"A week, maybe more, depending on the weather. We haven't had much rain or snow, but I feel it coming." He looked upward and smiled as though he welcomed it.

She smelled the crisp edge to the air but didn't relish riding in rain or snow, clad only in the velvet dress and cloak she wore. As if reading her thoughts, he added, "We'll find you some warmer clothes in the next village. We'll get you something finer when we arrive in Northampton."

"I don't need anything finer. Just something warm."

"You'll need finery if you're to be one of the queen's ladies."

"Queen's ladies? What are you talking about?" She

had a bad feeling about that statement, and it didn't improve her mood.

"Aye. Since I am no longer engaging in correspondence of any sort, we have no means of telling the queen our plans. That's where you enter in." He grinned. "We'll get you in as one of her ladies, and you can relay my message."

"But I don't even know what a queen's lady does," she protested as Camden and Gavin rode up beside them.

"Do I hear correct?" Camden asked. "The lady doesn't know how to be a lady?"

She fixed him with a venomous stare.

"'Tis easy," he continued, choosing to ignore her dirty look. "All you have to do is follow the queen about and wipe her mouth after meals or wipe her arse after she shites."

Gavin punched him in the arm. "Don't be saying such things to Audrey, ye blastie. What's the matter with you?"

Camden rubbed his arm, an injured look on his face.

Gavin turned to her apologetically. "That's not true. Weel, the part about wiping her arse at least. You don't do much of anything. Help her dress, fix her hair, things such as that."

"But I don't know how to fix hair." Audrey pointed to her own hair, pulled into a simple braid. "See, I can barely fix my own."

"We'll remedy that," Camden said smugly.

"Oh?" she countered. "Don't tell me you know how to fix hair."

"I've fixed many a lady's hair." He smiled broadly and winked. "And dressed them as well."

"There must be more to it than that," she said skeptically.

"I think Audrey is right." Gavin nodded thoughtfully. "Who is she to be starting in such a high office with the queen? You have to be of noble birth to be allowed into the bedchamber. Camden is right, you'll be cleaning her closestool."

"Not the daughter of Lord Irvine! She'll clean no one's closestool!" Camden replied indignantly.

"I've heard it's an honor to clean the queen's closestool," Brenden interjected, making both Gavin and Camden look at him in disgust.

"Wait a minute!" She was becoming exasperated at this conversation. "Who is the daughter of Lord Irvine?"

"You are," all three of them replied at the same time.

When she gaped at them, Brenden explained, "You must be of noble birth to be a queen's lady, so you'll be my sister."

"But . . . but . . . the queen is a prisoner! A prisoner is given such consideration?"

They all exchanged looks, making her feel very ignorant.

"She's a sovereign," Gavin replied slowly. "Of course she has ladies. Not like the English queen, of course, but ladies just the same."

"She'll do fine," Brenden said, waving the discussion away. "We'll worry on making her one later."

Forbes and Dearg enjoyed a sideways look of mirth at that.

This was just great. She was going into the service of the queen with instructions from Camden! And no one had asked her how she felt about this. She was here to stop him from doing this, not to aid him. How had she gotten sucked into the discussion at all?

And Brenden was infuriatingly cheerful. She couldn't

imagine why, after the events of the day before. She rode closer to him. "You're in high spirits this morning."

He grinned. "Aye, and you're not, I see."

She scowled back. "Why should I be? I get to watch you rush headfirst into disaster, dragging me along whether I give my consent or not."

"Audrey," he said, shaking his head. "You're so full of doom and gloom."

"You know what you're full of?" He raised an eyebrow inquiringly. "Hubris."

He frowned. "Hubris? You liken this to a Greek tragedy?"

"That's exactly what it is. Your excessive pride will be your downfall. And I'm the audience, which already knows the outcome, watching in horror."

He threw his head back and laughed and continued laughing until tears ran down his face. He wiped them away with the sleeve of his doublet and tried to speak, but burst out laughing again.

"I'm glad you find this so amusing." She started to ride ahead, but he grabbed her reins.

"Don't be angry with me." He had himself under control, but laughter still danced in his eyes. "I just can't understand how you can know what will happen. Perhaps you are the witch you claim not to be. Is it within your powers to predict the future?"

She rolled her eyes. "I don't need magical powers to know you're going to fail! Is your father a warlock? Because he's predicting your doom as well."

He was still grinning and gave a small shake of his head. "Nay, my father's just an evil man."

She found it almost impossible to stay angry with him when he was looking at her so pleasantly. She looked straight ahead so he couldn't see her fighting not to smile back. "If I am to help you—and I'm not saying I will—I need to know why we're doing this. What stake do I hold in this?"

"Is this not where the dreams have taken us?" He rode his horse closer to hers so their legs were almost touching. "Have they not thrust us together and are now leading us to the queen?"

She couldn't dispute his logic, but it still didn't answer the question why. "I don't understand why Queen Elizabeth kept Mary imprisoned for so long. If she didn't want to help her, why didn't she just let her go? It seems so unfair."

"Mary is Catholic and the next in line for succession should something happen to Queen Elizabeth. It bode her well to detain Queen Mary in England."

"So it's all about religion," she murmured. It seemed deceptively simply.

"Aye. Alive, Mary is a danger to Elizabeth, the center of plots against her life and a symbol for English Catholics who would rise against Elizabeth and the Protestant faith. This, along with Mary's indisputable bloodlines, makes her a menace to the security of Elizabeth's throne. Even the pope has declared Elizabeth a bastard and Mary the rightful ruler of England. So Elizabeth has caged her, trying to contain the threat."

"In the twenty years Mary has been imprisoned, no one's been even remotely successful in any rescue attempts?"

"Several have lost their heads trying, but no, none have even gotten close to her person."

She watched him, sitting so straight on his horse. The breeze blew his reddish-brown hair back from his forehead.

"Did Queen Elizabeth have reason to believe Mary meant to depose her?" she asked.

"I don't think so. As far as I know, Mary asked only to be named successor and bore her cousin no ill. But there was enough of a Catholic faction to make Elizabeth uneasy. So when Mary came to her for help, she was locked away.

"After King Henry was murdered, some nineteen years ago, and Mary and Bothwell wed, well, no one was too pleased with such a development. Including Elizabeth, who bore no love for Bothwell and was aghast Mary would wed a man believed to have committed regicide. When Mary was captured by the lords, she was taken to Lochleven Castle in Kinross and held prisoner there."

Audrey had visited Lochleven when she was a child. The fortress sat on an island in the middle of a loch. It was practically impregnable. "Was Alistair one of these lords?"

His mouth thinned, and he looked down at his horse's mane. "Aye, but he backed out soon afterward. Despite how many felt about Bothwell, most weren't pleased with the treatment their queen was receiving. The nobles still loyal to her helped her escape and she fled to England, asking support from her cousin, Elizabeth. She was promptly imprisoned and told she would be released, even aided in regaining her kingdom, once her innocence in the complicity of King Henry's murder was determined. So they had a trial of sorts. She wasn't allowed to be present to give her own defense, and evidence was kept secret from those defending her."

"That's not fair!" Audrey gasped.

"They couldn't come to any decision on her innocence and decided to hold her. And"—his eyebrows raised incredulously—"she was expected to be the good prisoner and not attempt to escape. Even though she was being unjustly imprisoned without a proper trial." He shook his head. "I can't blame her for trying, but now she is to die for it."

"Are you Protestant or Catholic?" she asked suddenly.

"Protestant."

When he said nothing else, she asked, "Aren't you going to ask my religion?"

"It matters not. So long as you aren't overly pious . . . which I have determined you are not."

"I'm not sure how to take that. Isn't it desirable to be devout?"

"It would be a hypocrisy for me to expect you to be. I don't care for the lack of tolerance of the devout. Many of the Marians who lost their heads did so in the name of their faith."

"Doesn't it bother you to think other men have lost their lives for what you're attempting?"

"Of course it does," he said with no real emotion in his voice, gazing at the hills in the distance. "But I have to try. Nothing Bothwell did in life earned him the circumstances of his death. His last request will be honored. If I don't do it, it won't be done. A merciful God wouldn't let an innocent man suffer as he did."

His last words were edged with bitterness, and Audrey could only stare at him. Bothwell was the key to why he was doing this. She felt a surge of triumph at this discovery. He met her eyes and saw the look in them. His jaw tightened, and she knew it was a slip he hadn't meant to make. She decided not to press him—he would tell her when he was ready.

"I've never met a man like you, Brenden Ross. What

do you put your faith in, if not in God? You seem to know with such certainty you will succeed."

"It isn't faith. I have no choice. This is what I must do. The dreams won't go away, and I can't live with them." He paused. "I have a promise to keep and maybe I do have some faith that God will redress His wrongs." He looked at her with an apologetic smile. "But I won't know if I don't try."

They stopped in a small village and visited the local tavern for a meal. Camden disappeared, and when he returned, it was with heavy wool garments for Audrey to wear. She was pleased. Once she was able to get some privacy and put them on, she found them to be very warm. Which was a good thing, since the air was thick and cold. It had been raining on and off all day. The ground was soggy and the roads impassable in some areas.

They sought shelter in a stable for the night. It was still cold, but at least they were out of the elements and had the animals' warmth. Audrey headed across the stable to a comfortable-looking pile of hay to lay her cloak across. Camden sat beside her once she was settled. She had overheard him and Brenden discussing a son earlier that day and was curious.

"I didn't know you had a son."

He retrieved two clay bottles filled with ale and handed her one. "Stephen's a bonny lad. He'll be six in a week."

"You'll miss his birthday," she said sadly. She took a drink of the cool ale. She noticed no one drank water. Always wine and ale. She was getting used to it and even liked the taste. She also noticed her tolerance to the alcohol had increased. She could drink a good deal now without feeling the least bit tipsy.

"I promised him a pony before I left and to take him hawking when I return," he said regretfully. "He likes to watch the birds, but sometimes is a mite squeamish when they make a kill. He loves the wee beasties."

"I don't recall seeing him at Creag Liath."

"He has lessons in the morning and afternoons with James Sinclair, his tutor. He's a clever lad, too. Why, James tells me he can already translate several English writings to Latin."

"You're not married, are you?" she asked hesitantly.

"Nay, his mother wouldn't wed me, and she died during the birthing."

"Wouldn't wed you?" Audrey asked, shocked.

He looked embarrassed. "Well . . . there were some other lassies I was . . . familiar with at the time, and one of them happened to be her mother. She wouldn't speak to me when she learned of this." Audrey's mouth was hanging open, and Camden rushed on, "I didn't know or I wouldn't have been with *both* of them . . . at the same time."

"Tell me more about Stephen," Audrey said, returning to their original subject before she heard any more of the tawdry details.

He went on, bragging about Stephen until it was time to sleep. She was completely charmed by his love for his son and couldn't wait to meet him when they returned. He said good night finally and moved to the other end of the stable to sleep. She wrapped a wool blanket around herself and lay down. The stable was dark; the sound of snorting horses and the others rustling around in the hay nearby made her feel safe. The air was cold and filled with the scent of manure and peat smoke from the nearby cottage.

She heard movement, then saw a dark form walking

toward her. She could tell from the height and breadth of shoulders that it was Brenden. He spread a blanket and settled down in the hay nearby. Her stomach immediately bunched up in knots from his nearness.

"Camden was yammering your ear off," he whispered.

She thought she detected some jealousy and became annoyed at the spark of pleasure it ignited in her. "He was telling me about his son."

"Aye, Stephen. That's a braw lad if I ever saw one. Did he tell you how fine he was with a short bow?"

"No."

"I gave him one on his fifth year . . ." He talked for a good hour about his brilliant nephew, who was apparently the sweetheart of the entire family. She was moved by his affection for the boy. He didn't try to touch her, though his nearness was doing erratic things to her own body. She welcomed his closeness and let the deep burr of his voice lull her to sleep.

❧ 9 ❧

The next day they rode into another small village that was having some sort of celebration, or so Audrey thought. A procession of villagers traveled toward an open area with a raised platform. Instead of following her companions to the tavern, curiosity drew Audrey to the edge of the crowd. She couldn't see anything, but a man was yelling something about a witch. Gavin was with her, and they pushed their way to the front.

The man stood on the wooden platform. He was dressed mostly in black. His doublet was elaborately quilted and embroidered, with a small white ruff at the neck. He wore blousy breeches, and his striped hose fit tightly to muscular calves. His feathered cap was askew as though he'd been in a struggle. A girl stood with him. Her hair was long and blond and her clothes torn; her hands were tied behind her back. The man grabbed the girl's arm roughly, yanking her to a pillar protruding from the platform. Her head hung forward. Audrey couldn't see her face, only a glimpse of white skin.

"What are they doing to that girl?" she asked Gavin.

But it was Brenden who answered, surprising her,

since she hadn't realized he was beside her. "I don't know. Perhaps she's a thief or a witch."

The man was yelling and gesturing wildly. His Scots was so thick, Audrey could barely understand him, though he yelled "witch" and "Satan's whore" several times. He had a thin mustache that curled at the tips and trembled with the ferocity of his words.

Audrey realized, with growing horror, what she was witnessing. Either a witch trial or a lynching. It didn't appear to be much of trial, but in this century, it probably passed for one. The man grabbed a handful of blond hair and yanked the girl's head back, exposing the left side of her face and neck for the crowd to view. The lower half of her cheek, jawbone, and neck was covered with a cranberry-colored birthmark.

Gavin inhaled sharply. "'Tis the mark of Satan."

"Don't be ridiculous! It's a birthmark. Surely *you* don't believe she's a witch," Audrey said.

"Well . . . ," he began hesitantly.

Her comment drew scowling looks from the villagers around her, who apparently wanted very much to believe she was a witch.

The girl was young, maybe eighteen, and tiny. She raised her head. Enormous pale blue eyes scanned the crowd in despair, peeking out from behind the veil of blond hair that hung to her waist.

Gavin gasped. "Her eyes . . ."

The mustached man began yelling again. "She changed me into a horse every night for a sennight and flew me through the air to her Sabbat, where she bobbits and kisses the buttocks of Satan himself!" A hush fell over the crowd at his account. "Then she leaves me by day to languish from the sickness of it."

"This is ludicrous!" Audrey hissed at Brenden. He

wore a look of extreme skepticism, but merely shrugged at her comment. "What is he saying, anyway? What is a 'sennight'? What does 'bobbits' mean?"

Brenden regarded her strangely. "A 'sennight' is a week. Seven days," he added as though she were stupid, which was how she felt, "and 'bobbit' means dancing."

"She brought plague upon our village!" the man boomed on. "Is it not true that half the kine in the village have dried up, but her own are fair flowing?"

An answering murmur rippled through the crowd. The faces around Audrey nodded in agreement, eyes rapt upon the spectacle before them.

An old woman, her face enveloped in wrinkles, stepped forward and pointed a crooked finger at the girl. "I saw her! I saw the lass! At the graves of the dead bairns!" She turned to the crowd. "She cooks their remains to drink with her lover!"

The crowd seemed to be growing, pulsing, taking on a life of it own. Shouts of "Devil's whore!" and "The witch must pay!" rang through the square.

The blood chilled in Audrey's veins. They were working themselves up into a state of violence. Soon it would be too late to impose any calm on the proceedings. A stone sailed out of the crowd, hitting the girl's head. She fell to the ground, and Gavin grunted sympathetically. A crimson stain spread through her hair.

The man turned and pulled the girl to her feet. She stood unsteadily. She was conscious, but dazed.

"Una Sampson, will you confess yer sins?" he bellowed at her.

Una drew her head back and spit in his face. He retaliated immediately, smacking her. She fell to her knees. Blood trickled from the corner of her mouth. The man gestured to his right. A fire burned there, and another man withdrew a set of red-hot iron pincers from it. Audrey's mouth went dry.

Brenden and Gavin moved away from her. She didn't follow. The man approached the girl, holding the pincers out before him. Una Sampson stood again, long hair trailing down her back. Her eyes filled with terror when she saw the pincers. She tried to run, but the mustached man's accomplice caught her from behind.

"Will you be confessing your sins now?" the mustached man asked again.

Her bloodied lips trembled, but she raised her chin higher. "I'm not a witch." Her voice was steady and strong.

He grabbed her bodice and ripped it savagely downward, exposing her breasts. She screamed and struggled, her hair falling over her shoulders to partially cover her. The crowd screamed to burn the witch and "rip off the Devil's teat."

Audrey wasn't sure what Brenden's plan was, but Gavin apparently had one of his own. He lunged forward and tackled the man, wrestling him to the ground.

When a few others came forward to aid the man, Brenden withdrew his pistol. "What say we let the lads fight it out?" he asked in a good-natured voice. They backed away.

Audrey went to Una and untied the bindings from the girl's wrists. She looked at Audrey with wide eyes.

"I'm Audrey." She helped the girl stand. She was very small. Audrey guessed she weighed no more than ninety-five pounds. Una said nothing, looking around like a frightened rabbit.

Gavin, now in possession of the pincers, joined Brenden, shoving the bruised and bleeding man in front of him.

"These men are obstructing justice!" the man yelled to the crowd. "Arrest them!"

Several men started forward. Brenden put the gun barrel to the mustached man's temple and they stopped. "Now," Brenden said calmly, in a low voice, meant only for his prisoner's ears. "Let this woman go free, and we'll trouble you no more today." The man immediately started protesting. Brenden gave him a sharp rap on the head with the gun barrel. "I gave you no leave to speak." The man's face turned red, but he stopped talking. "As I was saying, if you give us any trouble, we'll be taking you along for the ride."

"She's mine." He stared defiantly at Brenden. His mouth was a thin white line beneath the bloodied mustache.

Brenden shrugged and nodded to Gavin. "Bind him."

Audrey handed Gavin the rope from Una's wrists, and he tied the man's hands behind his back. Brenden whistled. Dearg and Forbes rode forward, leading the horses.

"Sorry to disappoint you, but there'll be no witch burning today," Brenden called to the crowd.

They were mounted before the crowd could react. Brenden tossed Una onto the saddle behind Audrey. Una clung to her waist, burying her face in Audrey's back.

With some struggling, Brenden managed to get their prisoner mounted in front of Forbes, who smiled wickedly at him. The bushy brown beard made him look a bit evil. That Forbes stood at least a foot taller than him and that his arms were enormous didn't escape their prisoner's eyes. Despite the cold, his hair was becoming damp with sweat.

The crowd watched with only the barest murmuring, but once the shock had passed, a man stepped forward to protest, grabbing the bridle of Forbes's horse.

"Release Sir Synn Marshall!" he demanded.

Forbes withdrew his dirk and yanked Marshall's head back by his hair, holding the dirk to his throat. "Step back or I slit his gullet," Forbes said, still smiling.

They backed away.

"Where the hell is Camden?" Brenden asked. They didn't want to leave without Camden, but men were leaving the crowd to get horses and weapons to follow them.

The town boasted two alehouses, and as they rode past the second one, two of the windows burst, sending flames and smoke billowing into the street. Audrey's heart was thudding painfully in her chest, and the smoke choked her and burned her eyes. Una's hair whipped around wildly, slapping Audrey's face and blocking her vision.

The villagers' attention was diverted as they began screaming and trying to put out the fire. Thick black smoke rushed up from buildings, and flames licked skyward. After some hesitation, their pursuers turned back. Brenden reined his horse around to view the raging fire.

"Camden," he said.

Audrey looked around. "Where? I don't see him."

"Not here. I wouldn't be surprised to find this was his doing."

She was startled and a little fearful for him. "Then where is he? What if they know he started it?"

"Don't worry about Camden. They were too busy watching us to be noticing what he was up to. He'll join us as soon as he can take his leave." He turned his horse.

"Let's go, don't make his sacrifice for naught."

They rode hard the rest of the afternoon.

The blood was crusted thickly in Una's hair. She flinched as Audrey carefully cleaned the wound. It wasn't deep, but it had bled a lot. With the exception of the birthmark, her skin was as smooth and white as alabaster. She wore Audrey's other shift, one of Gavin's shirts, and a blanket wrapped around her.

It was late afternoon, and shadows fell across the clearing where they had stopped. It was littered with large stones and a few trees bereft of leaves. There was a stream about a quarter of a mile away, and Audrey could hear the faint sound of the rushing water.

Una had told them all the story of how she came to be accused of witchcraft. It seemed Marshall wanted nothing more than the land she lived on. When her father died, he pressed his marriage suit harder, and when she still refused, he raped her, thinking to force her through disgrace. When she escaped from him, he accused her of being a witch.

"He is the one who should be on trial! Did you hear that?" Audrey asked Brenden, who had watched her quietly throughout Una's telling of the story. "That man kidnapped her and raped her."

"What about the charges made by the villagers?" Gavin asked.

Una scowled at him. "If I could turn that ass into a horse, do ye not think I'd have left him so? Or turned myself into one, for that matter, and rode away as far as my legs would take me?"

"Why did the villagers say those things?" Audrey asked.

Gavin said, "Marshall paid them, I've no doubt."

"Aye," Brenden said, nodding. "Whether she's guilty or not, the villagers want a witch burning."

Una's eyes became huge and watery.

"What are we going to do?" Audrey looked over her shoulder at where Marshall sat, oblivious to their conversation and eyeing Forbes warily.

Brenden sighed, rubbing his hand across the auburn stubble sprouting around his lips. "Do you have anyone, lass, to stand in your defense?"

Una shook her head. "They burned my mother ten years past."

Audrey covered her mouth in horror and looked at Gavin. His arms were folded across his chest, his face a mask of obscurity. She wondered what he was feeling, hearing this story. Brenden glanced briefly at Gavin and back at Una.

"Mayhap if you talked to Marshall and told him you'd be a proper wife—one he wouldn't have to lock in his room, he might drop these charges. 'Tis better than burning, aye?"

Her cheeks flushed crimson. "I'll burn in hell before I share a bed with that beast again! Or any man, for that matter."

Brenden's eyebrows shot up at her venomous reply. Audrey shook her head at him, letting him know what a stupid remark that had been.

"Don't worry, no one's going to make you go back to him," she said soothingly.

Brenden grabbed her arm, pulling her next to one of the bare trees. "We can't take the lass with us."

"Do you suggest we give her back to Marshall? What else are we going to do? If we set her free, the villagers will try lynching her again."

"Then we leave her in the next village."

"Just leave her? What about him? What are we going to do with him?" She pointed at Marshall. "He'll come after her. And we're just going to leave her in a village with no money?" She was starting to get angry. After talking with Brenden last night, she had felt a new closeness with him. She couldn't understand how he could be so cruel.

He took a deep breath. "Now Audrey, you don't even know if the lass wants to come with us. What are we to do with her when we get to Fotheringhay?" She remained unmoved by his little speech, so he took a firmer stance. "Bringing you along is causing me more trouble than I care for! I don't plan to add another woman to my troubles! I did as you wished, and we saved the lass from burning. But we can't bring her with us. We leave her in the next village."

"I didn't ask to come along! Don't you dare complain about all the trouble I've been—you can thank yourself for that!"

"So you keep reminding me, and I don't plan to make yet another mistake!" He turned abruptly and joined Forbes where he guarded Marshall. She glared at his back and returned to Una, who was engaged in a reluctant conversation with Gavin. Gavin looked upset.

"What's the matter?" she asked.

Gavin drew Audrey a few feet away and said, "I can't say for sure, but the lass is talking like she means to take her own life."

Una had curled herself into a ball on a low rock and cast furtive glances over her shoulder at Marshall. Audrey's stomach tightened.

"What did she say?"

"She said she had naught to live for, now her da was

dead and she couldn't go back to her home. The bastard will kill her if she does." He threw a look of hatred over his shoulder at Marshall. "When I tried to tell her she could stay with us and we would help her, she said . . . well . . . some things I can't repeat."

"She did? Such as?"

He shook his head, red patches forming on his cheeks. "Nay, I can't. She can't be blamed for it. The lass must think all men are beasts after what she's been through."

Audrey touched his arm reassuringly. "We won't let her kill herself. Your brother," she said with distaste, "wants to leave her in the next village, but I don't think we will." He nodded, giving her a small smile. "For now, leave her to me. No doubt you're all frightening her."

She went back to the crouching form. Una's face was invisible, hidden by the golden hair that fell over her like a mantle. She touched the girl's shoulder. "We'll take care of you until we can think of something. What Marshall did was wrong, and he'll pay for it."

Marshall was on his feet, surrounded by Brenden, Gavin, and Forbes. They appeared to be interrogating him.

"I hope they kill him," Una said. Her blue eyes filled with tears that threatened to fall from her copper-tipped eyelashes. She blinked, and the tears spilled down her cheeks, unleashing a torrent she seemed unable to stop. Audrey pulled her close, trying to comfort her. Una resisted at first, but finally lay against her.

"I dinna want him to touch me, but I thought if I just lay there, it would soon be over. But he stank and hurt me. When I cried out, he hit me and called me names."

She shuddered, and Audrey held her tighter.

"I promise he will never touch you again." Audrey's voice was thick with emotion.

"I can't wash the feel of his nasty hands off me. What if . . . Oh, God! What if I carry his spawn in my belly? I can't live another day. I have naught left, and I won't bear his . . . his . . . beast!"

She was crying again. Audrey grabbed her shoulders and shook her. "You will not speak of such things! Nothing is that bad. Nothing is ever that bad."

Una pulled away. "You can't know what it was like."

Someone was approaching, but Audrey was too upset by Una's words to pay attention. "You're right. I don't know what it's like to be raped. But I do know what it's like to not have anyone or anything. To think your life is just a painful mess, not worth living." Una looked up. "My husband killed himself three years ago." She gasped, and Audrey nodded. "I lost my father two years before that. My mother's been gone close to fifteen now. I have no brothers or sisters. No family. I lived every day in the shadows of the nightmares that plagued me when I slept."

Una sniffed. "Why did yer husband kill himself?"

"Does it matter?" Audrey asked angrily. When Una only gave her a blank stare, Audrey answered for her. "No, it doesn't. No matter what he said his reasons were, or what you say yours are, it all comes back to one thing. Selfishness."

Una was confused. "Selfishness? But that's not how I feel. I'm just so . . . sick . . ." She closed into herself again.

Tears stung Audrey's eyes. "That's just what I mean. You think there's no one who can understand or care what you're feeling. So you carry it around inside, in a big ugly ball. Selfishly keeping it all to yourself. Not letting anyone else take some and help you carry it, so it's not such a heavy load." Audrey's vision was blurring. A firm hand was on her shoulder. "Everyone must sit around helplessly, watching you die slowly, while you hoard it all away inside for no one to see. Then you do away with the body. It's murder."

Through her tears, she could see Una staring at her in horrified silence. But something was cracking inside, and Audrey didn't know if she could stop it. The hand on her shoulder belonged to Brenden, and he forced her to stand. She let him lead her away from the others without protest. By the time they came to the bubbling stream, she had pulled herself together. She took a deep breath and wiped her eyes with her sleeve.

She laughed nervously. "What was that all about? I must have scared that poor girl to death! I can't believe I acted so foolish."

His arms were folded across his chest, and his gaze seemed to probe her, reading her deepest thoughts. "Your husband hurt you fair bad, aye? Why don't you accept it and go on? There are others out there. Men who wouldn't hurt you so."

She turned away from him. How could she tell him there were no other men? The only man who ever occupied her mind, her thoughts, her heart, was Brenden. And he was no different than Alex. He wouldn't share his hurt with her, either. He kept it to himself, believing that because he was a man he must bear his cross alone.

"I wouldn't hurt you." His voice was low near her ear. His hands rested on her shoulders. "I'm no coward, Audrey."

She turned to face him. "You're too arrogant to be a coward."

He pulled her gently toward him, his lips curving

slightly beneath the auburn whiskers. She moved forward, almost against her will, her head tipping back. She reached her hands up and grasped his wrists. She felt the smooth, puckered skin beneath her fingers. His lips were almost touching hers, but he stopped. His warm breath tickled her skin.

"Tell me, Brenden, and maybe I'll believe you," she whispered.

His hands moved to her neck, cradling her jaw. He ran his thumbs over her cheeks. The blood was racing through her veins and her breathing had become uneven, but she continued to hold his gaze. The light-green eyes were searching hers.

"You don't already know?" She shook her head slightly. "When you look at me like that, I feel as though you know things about me I'm not even aware of."

She was still holding his wrists and her grip tightened. Had she not thought the same thing about him only moments ago? He kissed her, and a sigh escaped from her throat. His tongue touched her lips, coaxing a deeper response from her, which she willingly gave. He crushed her to him, and she wrapped her arms around his neck, clinging to him.

She wanted him to make love to her again. Wanted it so badly it was a physical ache. That thought brought her to her senses. She turned her face away.

"We can't keep doing this," she said, trying to pull away, but he wouldn't release her. "This might mean nothing to you, but it means a great deal to me. I can't be so casual about it."

"How can you say that?" he ground out between clenched teeth. "I can't even breathe when you're near. I can think of naught but your eyes, so big and gray. They haunt me when I sleep still, even though the dreams have fled. You're as much a part of me as my very arm. As these scars on my wrists. How can you say it means nothing?"

"Then tell me why. Why must you do this? You will not succeed! If you care about me, listen to what I say!"

"Tell me how you know!"

"I can't!"

He shoved her away from him suddenly, and she almost fell. She shivered from the loss of his warmth. He was angry and seemed to have himself barely under control. He opened his mouth to speak, then shook his head and stalked back to their little camp.

Audrey sank to her knees, tears streaming down her cheeks. She couldn't deny the overwhelming physical attraction she felt for him, but it had become emotional, too. She realized that now, and the enormity of her task pressed on her chest. He would not be swayed from his mission. Then what would she do? Simply go along with it? Become some maid to the queen? Stand back and watch as everything he had worked so many years for fell apart around him? What would he do then?

When she returned to camp, Brenden was civil to her and she was relieved. She didn't think she could stand his coldness. He told her they would wait in the clearing for Camden to return. Marshall was sprawled on the ground, sleeping or unconscious, Audrey couldn't say, since the men had worked him over pretty well. She felt a tinge of compassion, seeing him lying there, all beaten up. She quelled it immediately. He deserved what he got, and worse.

Brenden said they weren't far from the Teviot River, and the English border was just beyond. Forbes and

Dearg would leave them in the morning and return to Creag Liath, taking Marshall.

"My father stands in good stead with the Earl of Bothwell. Mayhap he can encourage justice to be done." He gave the prone form of Marshall a look of disgust.

"The Wizard Earl?" she asked.

Brenden looked amused. "Aye. You've heard of him?"

"Isobel said he was like his uncle, the queen's lover."

He grunted.

"Does that mean he's not like his uncle?"

"He's a good enough man. But the talk of James being a warlock was just that—talk. Francis, on the other hand . . ."

"Come on!" She laughed incredulously. "Don't tell me you believe in that crap? There's no such thing as witches and warlocks. It's just superstition."

He glanced at Gavin, but said nothing. She frowned. She would have to get used to the nature of these people. They didn't have the technology her time possessed. When bad things happened here, it was reasonable to attribute it to witchcraft. She just thought Brenden was more intelligent than that.

"You really think your father will speak out against a rapist?"

"I've given Forbes orders to tell him what transpired in the village, and it's my wish he doesn't go unpunished for it. My father isn't completely unjust."

Audrey looked across the fire at Una. She was sitting as she had since they stopped: knees drawn under her chin, in a little ball. Gavin brought her another blanket. He sat a safe distance from her and tried to make small talk. His voice was soft, as it was when he spoke to the horses, and Audrey couldn't make out what he said to her. Una's face was almost completely hidden behind her knees. Only her huge blue eyes peered at him.

Brenden sat a few feet from Audrey, inspecting the wheel-lock mechanism on his pistol. The odd-shaped gun looked like a pain to use, and he told her that had he needed to use it back at the village, he wasn't sure it would have fired, since damp weather often rendered the gunpowder useless.

She said, "I think Gavin is taken with her."

Brenden didn't even look up. "Hmm, you may be right." He shrugged. "She's like one of his birds or dogs he's forever mending."

"He mends animals?"

"Aye, and he's fine at it, too."

"Well, I think it's sweet."

He scowled at her. "If this is some womanly ploy to convince me to bring the lass with us, it isn't working."

She swallowed hard and looked him straight in the eye. "If you leave her in the next village, you can leave me, too."

"Indeed? And what will you and the lass do? Mayhap you'll work in the kitchens? Like you were when I found you?" He smiled humorlessly. "Aye, you'll make a fine pair, her marked like a witch and you!" He gave a short laugh. "Your speech is queer as any I've heard and your manner, well, most men won't be so polite as I have been. Perchance on our way back to Scotland we'll find you've both been burned at the stake as witches?"

"I don't need you!" She stood up angrily. He was grinning, pleased with his own cleverness. "I think perhaps I'll take the advice you first gave me." She smiled back at him. "Yes, I think what Una and I should do is find husbands to protect and provide for us. You were absolutely right. Am I so queer no man will have me?"

He exhaled slowly through his nose, looking down at the pistol he held and turning it over in his hands. He was probably thinking about using it on her. When he finally looked up, she was surprised to see he didn't appear angry.

"Very well," he said with a wry grin. "She may come. But if you forget to feed her and she dies, don't come weeping to me."

"Thank you."

Before she could say more, their attention was diverted by the sound of hoofbeats. When the rider passed Dearg unimpeded, she knew it must be Camden. He dismounted and walked toward them. She wasn't so sure it was Camden anymore. The stocky, muscular frame was right, but the hair and face were dark. He stopped just outside the fire's light.

"What is everyone looking at?"

"'Tis good to see you, Camden." Brenden pounded him on the back. A puff of black rose from him, causing Brenden to choke.

Camden came near the fire. His hair and face were blackened. His eyes were smudged where he had tried to wipe the soot away. He smiled, his teeth a striking white against the black on his face, and waved his hand to disperse the cloud following him.

"What happened to you? Where have you been?" Audrey asked.

"The fire got a wee bit out of hand." He removed his doublet and slapped it against a boulder, causing a sooty cloud to billow around them. They all coughed and backed away. "Don't worry. 'Tis out now, and no one's hurt." His eyes lit on Una. She backed up fearfully, standing slightly behind Gavin. "This is the wee thing that caused us so much trouble?"

She moved completely behind Gavin, clutching at his sleeve.

"Come out, wee fairy. I'll not hurt you. I just want to look at what I got my eyebrows singed for."

"Leave her be," Gavin said, giving Camden a warning look.

Camden's eyebrows raised knowingly. "You're right, brother. I'll have to clean up proper before I present myself to the lady."

"There's a stream not far," Brenden said, gesturing for him to follow. Camden nodded, and they walked into the dark toward the bubbling sound.

Sensing the threat of danger gone, Una moved far away from Gavin.

"That was Camden." Audrey smiled reassuringly. "No one will harm you."

"Ye've been so kind. Forgive me. I willna hide when he comes back," she said, embarrassed.

"That's all right. It's perfectly understandable. Camden was looking rather frightening."

Una smiled, and deep dimples dented her cheeks, one on either side of her mouth. "I'm sorry about earlier." She touched Audrey's hand. "I was being foolish. I'll not try to hurt myself." She looked down. "I'm sorry about your husband. That's so awful. I don't know if I could be as brave as you."

Audrey covered Una's hand with hers. "I'm *not* brave."

"Aye, ye are. Ye travel alone with all these men, or is one yer husband?"

Audrey hesitated. They had been telling the people they met on their journey that she and Brenden were married, but since Una would now be traveling with them, it made no sense to keep the pretense up with her.

"No, they're just friends." Then she smiled and squeezed the girl's hand. "But I'm pleased to have another woman to keep me company."

Audrey grabbed one of the horsey-smelling blankets, wrapped herself up, and lay down next to Una. It wasn't long before Una was asleep. Brenden and Camden returned. Camden's hair was wet, but blond again, and with his face clean, she could see he hadn't really singed his eyebrows. She was glad he'd escaped the village unscathed. He winked at her when he caught her staring, and she smiled back.

Brenden stretched out beside her. Her entire body clenched up. She watched him warily as he covered himself and became still. He was facing her. His eyes were closed, and her breathing began to relax. It was difficult to be this close to him and not touch him. The fact that it was freezing didn't help, when she knew how warm she would be in his arms.

His wavy reddish-brown hair fluttered in the breeze. His beard was growing thicker, though it was still short. She remembered how it had scraped against her skin earlier when he had kissed her by the stream, and her stomach dipped down to her toes. She felt the heat creeping up her neck. She closed her eyes and forced herself to think of safe things.

They set out early the next morning, Una riding behind Audrey. Forbes and Dearg were returning to Creag Liath. Marshall would be on foot, wrists tethered to Forbes's horse. Brenden rode close to Forbes, extending his arm. Forbes clasped it at the elbow.

"God be with ye, milord," Forbes said, his voice full of emotion. "Camden, Gavin." He nodded to each in turn. "Mistress Williams, Mistress Sampson." He inclined his head to Audrey and Una.

They started off silently. Even Camden was unusually quiet. Audrey wondered if the reason for her companions' gloominess was the same as hers. They were entering England—and for her, the dreams were finally becoming a reality.

⇥ 10 ⇤

The terrain stretched out endlessly in front of them. Ridge after ridge of treeless moorland covered with a fine dusting of snow. It was desolate and empty and, according to Brenden, dangerous. Audrey found it difficult to imagine anyone would be out in such a bleak place, even to thieve.

Una rode on the back of Audrey's horse, with Camden riding beside them. Gavin and Brenden were riding ahead to scout out the terrain and make sure there were no border thieves lying in wait. It had been a few days since they had rescued Una from the stake, and Camden had finally gotten around to telling Audrey how he set fire to the alehouse to distract attention from them.

Audrey shook her head at his tale. "Well, I'm relieved you're unhurt."

"A wee bit of smoke never hurt anybody," he said dismissively.

He obviously hadn't heard of carbon monoxide poisoning. She looked him over surreptitiously. She decided he wouldn't be with them if inhaling the smoke had hurt him. And he looked well, his cheeks and the end of his nose pink from the cold. His dark-green eyes were clear. He ran a gloved hand over his hair.

"I don't know if I'll ever get the smell out of my hair."

"Tomato juice," Audrey said. Camden gave her a sidelong look. "You know, tomatoes?" He stared at her like she was speaking a foreign language. "It's a vegetable . . . or maybe not. I think it's actually a fruit . . . it doesn't matter."

"I don't know of a . . . tomato."

He looked at Una for support. She seconded his ignorance. Maybe it wasn't called a tomato yet. Brenden was riding toward them alone, and he reined his horse over to ride on Audrey's other side. He didn't speak, only listened to their conversation.

"It's reddish-orange and round. It grows on a plant. It's both firm and juicy inside."

Camden wrinkled his nose in disgust at her description. "I know of naught such as you describe. But tell me, what has this tomato to do with my hair?"

"If you wash your hair with the juice, it takes foul smells out."

"Brenden," Camden said, "in your travels have you come across this odious fruit? It's called a tomato."

Brenden shook his head. "I can't say for certain. I've seen many strange foods abroad, but I don't always feel the need to eat them . . . nor wash with them."

Camden still looked thoughtful. "Have you eaten this fruit yourself? Is it grown in Scotland?"

"Um, no, I don't think it's grown here," she said. It was only the sixteenth century; maybe tomatoes hadn't been brought back from the New World yet. She suddenly wanted to drop the subject.

Camden fingered his hair. He wore it shorter than Brenden and Gavin, but it curled at the nape of his neck and ears the same as theirs.

"So, you wash your hair with this runny fruit and it takes away the foul odors. Does your hair smell like a tomato, then?"

"If your hair still reeks when we return, I shall buy you as many tomatoes as you want," Brenden said brusquely.

Camden scowled at him and looked pointedly at Audrey. "Is a tomato fragrant?"

"No, not really. . . unless you're making tomato sauce; that smells very good."

Camden raised his eyebrows with interest and nodded. "I should like to find a tomato. Have you had a need to use one for this purpose?"

"Yes, I was sprayed by a skunk when I was a kid."

Una giggled behind her, and Camden was again staring at her as though she was from another planet.

"Your speech is so odd," Una said.

"What is a skunk, and why would it . . . spray you?" Camden asked.

Before she could answer, Brenden cut in, "Is it when you lived among the Turks that you ate tomatoes and were sprayed by skunks?"

Audrey hesitated. She was almost positive skunks were native to North America, as well as tomatoes. But to them, Turkey was probably as foreign as the New World. "Yes," she answered.

He gave her a smug grin.

"What's so funny?"

His eyes darted to Una, then back to her. He shook his head. "We'll talk later."

Her jaw tightened, and she looked away. She had

slipped somehow, and he'd caught it. Camden craned his head to look at Brenden again.

"What of Jasmine? Maybe ye could ask her—"

"Nay," Brenden said loudly.

Who was Jasmine? Camden was eyeing his brother strangely, and Brenden looked pointedly elsewhere. An old lover of Brenden's? The name was rather exotic, for this century at least. Maybe one of the women he frequented on his travels? She was perturbed to find jealousy gnawing at her, forcing her to probe into this mysterious Jasmine of whom Brenden was unwilling to speak.

"Who is Jasmine?" Audrey asked.

Camden grinned. "She's a verra skilled and knowl-edgeable—"

"Ship," Brenden interrupted.

"A skilled and knowledgeable ship?" Audrey asked in disbelief.

"Oh, aye," Brenden said, nodding with a bit too much enthusiasm. "She was a good ship, with a skilled crew. I sailed on her once, but won't again." When Audrey just stared at him, he explained further, "She leaned a bit to larboard."

"I see." Audrey forced herself not to pursue the issue. His past was none of her business. She needed to remember that she wasn't staying here.

It was late evening when they finally stopped in another hamlet for the night. The sky was dark and speckled with white, as snowflakes fluttered down on them. Brenden convinced the cooper to let them sleep in his stable. Una stood watching the men light a fire in the center of the small room. She had a blanket wrapped around her but was shivering almost uncontrollably. Marshall had ripped her dress to shreds. She had to be freezing in the shift and linen shirt.

Gavin was watching Una with a small frown. He unhooked the hip-length mantle he wore and swung it off, draping it around her shoulders.

"Don't want you to freeze to death, lass."

She smiled up at him. "Thank you," she said softly, and hooked it. It hung to her knees.

"I have an extra pair of stockings that'll keep your feet warm as well."

Una's cheeks were ruddy, and her eyes were shining. "That's not necessary. I don't want to take your garments. Then ye'll be wanting."

"Nay, they're getting no use rolled up in a blanket."

They smiled at each other for a long time. Gavin glanced at Audrey suddenly, and his cheeks began to redden. He cleared his throat and mumbled some excuse before walking away. Una followed after a minute, joining him where he was grooming the horses. Audrey had been assisting him with this duty in the past. Finding her services unneeded, she joined Brenden and Camden in the hay, where they had been earnestly discussing something, only to stop abruptly when she approached. It happened so often that she paid it no attention anymore.

"It seems I've been replaced." She gestured to Gavin and Una.

"Don't begrudge him. I think the lad's in love," Camden said and winked.

"You're taking this well," she teased. "I thought maybe you had designs on her."

"Nay, nay." He shook his head solemnly. "I fear my heart belongs to another."

"Is that so?" Brenden laughed. "And just who might that be?"

"I know not. But when I find her, she will come bearing many tomatoes." He arched a sandy brow at Audrey. "You don't have a sister you're not telling me about?"

"Sorry, I'm an only child."

Brenden slapped him on the back, a trifle too hard. "I guess you'll die a lone man, then."

"'Tis odd, I always thought it would be you." Camden's grin grew. "I keep seeing you as an old man sailing into the sunset on board that fine ship *Jasmine*."

They were staring at each other with an obvious challenge in their eyes. The tense moment made Audrey uncomfortable. She turned to Brenden and laid a hand on his forearm. "How long until we arrive at Fotheringhay?"

She caught the triumphant smile he gave Camden over her head before he looked at her with a much warmer one that made the heat rise in her cheeks.

"Another sennight or more. If the snow becomes a problem, we might have to hole up in an inn."

She nodded. She was glad to hear that if the weather got bad they wouldn't be braving it but staying someplace warm and safe. It was eating at her that they were still headed for Fotheringhay and, as far as she was concerned, doom. She had been searching for a way to convince Brenden not to go through with this, but she kept drawing a blank. The only thing she could think of was to tell him what he wanted to know: how she knew he would fail. But he'd think she was insane! Or worse, a witch! She took a deep breath and looked him straight in the eye.

"You said we would talk later. I think now is a good time."

He raised an eyebrow, but nodded. He stood and held out his hand, helping her to her feet. They moved to the corner, away from the others. Brenden spread a blanket and indicated for her to sit. She sat stiffly on her knees, her hands clenched tightly in her lap. He sat beside her, picking the dead grass off the woolen blanket.

"I've always known there was something unusual about you," he said in a soft voice, not looking at her, "but now I fear you're not like us." He reached down and dug into his boot, removing a velvet pouch. He turned it over in his hands. "Every time I think I've gone mad, this reminds me it can't be so."

He met her eyes and held the pouch out to her. She took it with trembling fingers and opened it. She gasped. It was her locket! She withdrew it and held it in the palm of her hand. She was speechless. When she looked up, he was smiling.

"I feared that you wouldn't know what it was and then I would be insane."

"You're not insane, Brenden." She closed her fist around the locket. "But we were brought together for a reason. We can't pretend the content of our dreams meant nothing."

"I'm not. 'Tis the very reason I wanted you with me."

She moved closer to him and placed her hand over his. "But I'm sure I'm not here to help you. I'm positive. I'm here to stop you from making a mistake. Please consider that possibility."

He shook his head and sighed. "We're back to this again. I have told you, lass, I can't pay heed to your words unless I know the source!"

"All right. I will tell you."

He sat up straighter. "Go on."

Her heart was thudding in her chest, and she squeezed the locket. She tried to withdraw her other hand from his, but he held onto it. She decided it might be better if she was touching him and laced her fingers with his.

"I'm not a witch or a fairy or anything supernatural like that. But I am different."

"Aye," he prompted her.

She swallowed. "I'm from another time. The future. The year I came from is 1996."

No reaction registered on his face. He continued to stare at her as though he expected her to say more.

"That's it?" he asked in confusion.

"Isn't that enough?"

He nodded slowly. "It explains a great deal. Your time is on the other side of the wall?"

"Yes, it looks like a corridor to me, but everyone else just sees a wall." She was amazed at his calm reaction. "You believe me?"

"I have no reason to doubt you. It explains why you seem daft at times and knowledgeable at others."

She frowned. "I can't believe you're taking this so calmly. I just told you I'm from the future! You're not ready to burn me as a witch?"

"Why would I want to do that?"

"Because that's what sixteenth-century people do! They burn outcasts for witchcraft!"

He scratched at his beard thoughtfully. "'Twill be a danger for you, I don't doubt, but I will protect you."

She could only stare at him in disbelief. "I'm not staying here. Whatever happens, whether you choose to listen to me or not, I'm going back home. I have a life there."

"You could have a life here."

She pulled her hand away. "As your mistress? I don't think so."

"As my wife."

She shook her head, though her throat became thick and her eyes misty. "Contrary to your belief, every woman does not want to be the Countess of Irvine. That is a job for another woman, a greater woman than I am. Besides," she said, looking away from him, "I've already been married to a closed-up man. I know better than to involve myself with another."

"Do you really feel naught for me?" he asked. "Because I can't believe it's so. I wasn't alone in those woods when we made love." Her cheeks burned. He grasped her chin and turned her face back. She let out a shuddering sigh as she met his light-green eyes, burning with anger and desire. "I can't let you go so easily. I'm not certain what you want from me, what would make you stay, but if you ask it, mayhap it's mine to give."

She couldn't answer him. She was fighting hard to keep tears at bay. She didn't want to love this man. He would hurt her; she knew it deep down. He would hurt her far worse than Alex had ever been able to.

He released her chin but took her hand again, pulling her close to him. "It's cold." He put his arm around her. She leaned against him. It felt so good, so right, to be in his arms that she allowed herself this pleasure, if only for the warmth it provided. "Perhaps I'm not the man you imagine me to be. You could give me a chance." When she didn't respond, he said, "Tell me why I will fail. I will listen and consider your words."

Her relief was so strong, tears almost squeezed out of her eyes. She forced them back. This was too important for her to become emotional. She needed to be able to impart this information rationally and thoroughly.

"I'm American. The country I was born and raised in is what you call the New World. The Dutch and the French both settled there, but mostly the British colonized it. After the War of Independence, immigrants from everywhere came to the country. That was in the late eighteenth century. Anyway, in the twentieth century, Britain is an American ally, and we have bases in your country."

"My country?"

She looked at him. "Uh, yeah. When Queen Elizabeth dies, your king will ascend to the throne of England, joining England and Scotland under one crown . . . Great Britain."

He let out a long slow breath, then nodded for her to continue.

"Anyway, I'm a captain in the air force . . . a component of the American military, and I'm stationed at Croughton Air Base."

"You . . . you're an officer? A woman?"

She nodded.

"You are of noble birth then."

"There is no titled aristocracy in America." This was a lot of information for him to digest, and she decided to get to the point; there would be time for questions later. "The information I have about you is simple. You attempt to rescue the queen, you fail, she is beheaded, and you are outlawed." She sat up so she could look at him. "We have been dreaming about each other and the queen. I'm sent here possessing this information about your future. Those are the facts. Doesn't it seem obvious that I'm here to stop you?"

He was pensive; staring at the others huddled around the small fire. She touched his thigh. The muscles beneath her fingers tensed immediately, and he looked down at her. "You have given me much to think on. Let's rest."

She nodded and started to rise, but he pulled her back down. "We'll keep each other warm," he whispered, and stretched out on his side, tugging at her hand. She was shivering and allowed him to pull her close. Why was she permitting this to happen? He arranged her cloak and his mantle over them. The thick wool blanket was beneath them. He wrapped his arms around her and she lay against him, her hands curled into his doublet. She could feel his hard thighs, thick with muscle, against hers. When he did nothing more than hold her, she allowed herself to relax.

He had proposed marriage to her, and she still didn't know how she felt about that. What did the proposal mean to him? He'd never mentioned love, although he used the word "care." She cared about him, immensely. But did she love him? She was pretty sure she did, and the knowledge made her sick. She could have all the foolish emotions she wanted, but she would not marry another man who closed everything up inside himself. She had told him what was behind the wall, yet she was still ignorant of what the scars on his wrists had to do with rescuing the queen.

Audrey woke the next morning feeling warm and comfortable. The smell of hay and the snorting of animals reminded her where she was. Thin streams of morning sun shone through the cracks in the stable wall. Brenden still held her close. She moved her head to look at him.

He was awake, and he met her eyes with a small smile. "I promise we will find more appropriate lodging tonight."

"Are we going back?" she asked hopefully.

He sighed. "Nay."

"Why?"

"I'm still thinking about all you told me last night. But we will continue south until I make my decision."

She breathed a little easier; at least he was thinking about it. "I told you how I know. When will you tell me why this is so important to you?"

"It isn't so easy to tell. I have difficulty thinking of it."

"That makes it even more important to share it with someone."

He looked deeply into her eyes. "I can't tell just anyone."

"I'm not just anyone. I thought I proved that last night."

"But you will leave me when this is over. That means you aren't the one I should tell."

She looked away from him. Why did he have to use logic on her? He had a valid point: Why bare his soul to a woman who told him she didn't intend to stay, regardless of the outcome? It still made her angry. If ever two people knew each other's souls, it was she and Brenden. They shared the dreams and the tormented childhood, they knew and understood each other long before meeting in the flesh.

"Fine," she said, and pushed away from him. She hurried over to the others before he could stop her. No one wanted to linger, so they were mounted and riding south in less than thirty minutes. Gavin had surprised everyone by swinging Una onto his horse in front of him and riding ahead of Audrey and his brothers. Una had seemed quite willing to be carried away.

Camden commented, as they watched them growing smaller, "Una is looking a bit too common, don't you think? She more resembles a vagrant than the yeoman's wife she pretends to be. I'll find her some decent clothing in the next village."

"How is it you're able to get your hands on women's clothes so easily?" she asked.

"Och, that. 'Tis nothing." He waved his hand to indicate its insignificance. "Everything's for sale in a brothel."

She gaped at him. "You mean to tell me I've been wearing . . ."

"Whore's clothes? Aye." He rolled his eyes at her look. "You don't look like a whore. The clothes were clean. The deed isn't done with them on." She was still speechless. "Does this offend you?"

She shook her head slowly. "No . . . I'm just . . . surprised. But it makes sense, I guess." She looked down at the gray wool dress she wore and frowned. "This dress doesn't look like something a prostitute would wear. It's not exactly . . . alluring."

"Ah, Audrey, never have I realized how lovely gray wool could be until I saw it on you." She scowled at the absurd compliment, and he laughed. "You don't think they dress like that all the time, do ye? They don't want to proclaim it when they go to market. Well, some of them do. They seem quite proud of being a harlot. But I've met some fine Christian women, as well."

She nodded at his little digression.

"What? Tell me what you're thinking."

Brenden, who rode silently beside her, said, "She thinks you're a whoremonger."

He gave Brenden a look of disdain and leaned toward her. "I'm not a whoremonger. I don't have intimate knowledge of the ladies in such establishments."

Brenden grunted rudely.

"I haven't failed you yet brother. I happen to know, from a very helpful lady I met while inquiring about another dress for Audrey, that the queen's death warrant has yet to be signed. In fact," he gave Brenden a pointed look, "Elizabeth has expressed the desire to have the matter removed from her hands."

Brenden looked at him in alarm.

"Worry not. Queen Mary's jailer appears to be an honorable man, by the name of Sir Amyas Paulet, who declared his disgust at the suggestion he assassinate her." He nodded knowingly. "Aye, though he won't kill her, I hear it said he bears no love for our most gracious majesty and finds her company tiresome."

"So she appears safe for now," Brenden said.

"Well, it seems the English queen's ministers are becoming quite anxious about this whole situation, and she made it clear she would not be adverse to being the subject of trickery."

Brenden frowned. "She is an odd woman. What manner of ruse has been put forth?"

"I know not of that."

"How does a prostitute know all this?" Audrey asked in confusion.

"'Tis a difficult thing to keep secret. It may not be known to the public at large, but there are travelers, messengers, statesmen who warm her bed and are loose of tongue." He smiled, his dark-green eyes crinkling at the corners. "It just so happens, she was entertaining a courier on his way with intrigues to our most illustrious king. For a few shillings she let me take a wee peek at his letters."

Audrey shook her head. "You never cease to impress me."

"I shall endeavor to continue impressing you, Audrey," Camden said, pleased with her compliment.

Brenden became silent and brooding until they reached York. They spent the night there and visited the marketplace in the morning. It was larger than any town they had yet been through. Tall, narrow townhouses made of wood and stone crowded onto the streets. On their bottom floor, a window opened to create a stall, with a table to display their wares and an awning. Brightly colored signs had pictures on them designating the services or wares being sold within.

The sound of hammers beating out barrel staves, candlesticks, and pots and pans rang out, intermingled with the cries of the merchants selling their wares or services. Some people rushed about in a great hurry, others browsed the stalls and talked with the merchants. Most were dressed like Audrey and her companions.

The charm quickly wore off when Brenden grabbed her arm a moment before she stepped in a pile of steaming innards from some unfortunate creature outside the butcher's. The butcher, an angry-looking fellow in a bloodstained smock, grabbed the neck of a honking goose that was tied in a pen just outside his shop.

The smells of fresh bread and smoked meat were overlaid with the stronger one of human waste. She saw why when a door to one of the townhouses opened and a woman dumped her chamber pot directly in the street, along with a bucketful of garbage.

A peddler stopped Camden. Audrey was surprised to hear him using an English accent to barter for dried meat. Just about everyone she saw wore a hat of some sort. Only some of the younger men and women were bareheaded. She saw a few people on the street who looked wealthy and wore more elaborate hats, which were made of velvet or silk and were oddly shaped, with feathers adorning them.

"Should we be wearing hats?" she asked Brenden. He just looked at her. "You know, to blend in? Like the cap I was wearing when I met you? Don't people wear hats in Scotland?" She was positive she saw people in Scotland wearing hats similar to these.

"Aye, mayhap you're right." He took some coins from his purse and turned to Una. Audrey spied Gavin crossing the busy street to the bakery and followed to look at some bread. A toothless vagrant sat on the ground nearby. Cloth was wrapped around his legs and was tied with rags to make pants. More rags were tied around his feet.

She had no money and eyed the fresh loaves of warm bread wistfully. She knew all she had to do was ask and Brenden would buy her whatever she wanted. It was the asking that was hard. She generally just took what he gave her and didn't complain.

Gavin said, "I'll take this and whatever the lady has been eyeing."

The baker, who had been watching her closely, laughed and selected the sticky pastries she had been staring at longingly.

"Gavin, no, that's not necessary . . ."

He waved away her protests and paid the baker from the purse at his waist. He took their purchases, and they started back across the street.

"Thank you," Audrey said, feeling a sudden shyness.

Gavin grinned, then frowned at something over her shoulder. She turned to see the vagrant staggering toward them, clutching at his chest. He fell. Gavin handed her the bread and ran to him.

"Is he all right?" she asked.

Gavin knelt beside him and shook his shoulders gently. "Open your eyes, man. Tell me what ails you."

The man's rank odor reached her even in her standing position. His hair was filthy and matted. He opened his eyes a crack and started clutching at Gavin.

"You're fine. Here, let me help you stand." He pulled the man up.

"Oh, thank you, sir," the vagrant croaked. He turned to walk away, but Gavin touched his arm.

"Here. Go get yourself a meal so you're not falling in the street from hunger."

Something passed across the vagrant's face as Gavin reached for his purse. A second later he took off running, leaving Gavin grabbing frantically at his waist.

"What's the matter?" she asked.

He looked alarmed at first, then his face reddened in anger. "The bastard cozened me! He was a filthy cut-purse!"

Then he was gone, too, running after the vagrant. Audrey followed. Luckily, Gavin was taller than most people, and she was able to keep track of him by the shiny black head darting through the crowd.

He disappeared between two buildings, and she followed, slowing her steps when she entered the alleyway. The buildings were so close together it was dark. It took her eyes a moment to adjust. She saw some movement at the far end and started toward it.

She was stopped short by a low, ominous growl behind her. She froze, terrified to turn around. The creature brushed against her leg, growling like an engine, then passed her by. It was an enormous black dog. It disappeared into the darkness.

She had started to back away on shaking legs when she remembered Gavin was at the other end. "Gavin! Watch out!" she called, uncertain of what else she could do.

He appeared out of the darkness and grabbed her arm, dragging her out of the alley.

"Did you see that dog? Are you all right?"

Before he could answer, a scream echoed from the dark alley behind them. She tried to turn, but Gavin continued pulling her until they were on the street again.

"What the hell just happened?"

He held his purse up. "I got my purse back."

She was about to ask how when Brenden appeared wearing a flat brimless hat, similar to the ones she saw other men wearing. He slapped one on Gavin's head. Gavin straightened it and grinned. Brenden was holding a third one, but it was full of dried dates.

"Where are Una and Camden?" she asked, taking the hat and eating some.

"We'll meet them at the inn."

She glanced back into the alley, wondering what in the hell had happened in there. At least Gavin had gotten his purse back. But some mad dog wandering around the streets made her nervous.

Camden and Una joined them an hour later. Camden was laden with nonperishable goods for the remainder of their journey, and Una carried a few items of clothing. She was wearing a linen kerchief and put one on Audrey, tying it at the nape of her neck. She also had gloves for them, made of a soft tan leather.

Outside of the village, Brenden and Camden removed their hats, both having obvious disdain for them, even though they still passed travelers entering the village on packhorses and in wagons.

"Why did you buy it if you don't like it?" she asked Brenden, as he crammed it inside his leather doublet.

"I don't think we should stand out."

"We're still far from Northampton, aren't we? What's with all the secrecy about who we are now?"

"I don't know who we might be doing business with. It wouldn't serve us well for them to be thinking a wealthy Scottish noble is traveling south in the wake of the Scottish queen's death sentence. Particularly since my sympathies have been no great secret."

"What about her son?" He immediately made a face of disgust. "King James? Doesn't he care that his mother is going to be executed? Why doesn't he send in troops or something to rescue her?"

"He cares not for her. Any protestations are merely for appearance's sake. He'll not damage his standing with Elizabeth. He stands to inherit the crown of England upon her death. If the cost is his mother's life, what cares he?" He raised an eyebrow. "And as you told me, that's exactly what happens. So I suppose he has made a wise choice."

"What do you plan to do with the queen when you free her?"

"I have arrangements being made for her passage to France."

She fell silent, not wanting to be a harpy, but at the same time, they were in England—they had just left York! She could turn around and see the guard pacing the rampart along the town walls. He planned on the four of them penetrating a prison? It was suicide!

"Brenden, please tell me you're still considering what I told you. I have come here to stop you. Please don't make this be in vain."

"Your appearance won't be in vain. Will you refuse to help me if I don't change my mind?"

"Yes!" she said emphatically. "I can't be a maid to the queen. Brenden, I am from another century! Do you really think I can pull something like that off?"

His jaw was tightly clenched, and he stared straight ahead. "You can't understand a man's honor."

Anger and despair rose in her chest. Camden rode up beside them in time to hear Audrey's response. "I can't understand because you won't tell me! It has something to do with those damn scars on your wrists doesn't it?" His jaw remained set, and he wouldn't look at her. "I hope your honor is a great comfort when you fail."

She spurred her horse ahead to ride with Gavin and Una. He was never going to tell her anything! She felt like crying and screaming in frustration. Her revelation had gained her nothing! When she chanced a look over her shoulder, she saw Camden talking to his brother earnestly. She wondered how Camden felt about this plot. She sensed he would rather not be involved but did it out of love for his brother. She wondered if he would be of any help in swaying Brenden's decision. She would have to talk to him.

⇥ 11 ↤

Five days later they stopped in Peterborough. They were very close to Fotheringhay, and Brenden said they would stay a few days to prepare. Camden needed to procure more forgeries. He got passports from someone he called "Jackman" while they were still in Scotland. He said they needed them to travel, but no one ever asked to see them. Audrey was finding that Camden left nothing to chance; he was very thorough. The forgeries he needed to get now pertained to the men's military service and to Audrey being Lady Tara Ross, Brenden's sister. Camden said he could usually find a likely forger in most alehouses, but he wanted something better, so he needed time. And there was also the matter of Audrey's wardrobe.

She hadn't had the opportunity to speak to Camden alone. Brenden guarded her jealously from Camden, as though she were a possession he might take away, and rarely allowed them a moment without his sulking presence. But today was different. Brenden and Gavin were both absent, having gone to rendezvous with their men. Una was at the market. Camden had brought a seamstress to the inn to measure Audrey. They were just finishing up, and he was arguing with the woman about which colors would best complement her complexion.

"Violet and brassel," he said, contemplating her for a moment. "Maybe even peach."

The seamstress stepped back and regarded Audrey. "Not peach. That'll sallow 'er out. Nay, she should wear dark colors."

"You're addled, woman," Camden said indignantly. "Her skin could not look sallow."

The seamstress shrugged and gathered her things to leave. He followed her to the door, repeating his instructions while she nodded impatiently. "I'll come down later to look at your cloth. Something in a borato or damask, I think."

He turned to look at Audrey critically again. The seamstress appeared dismayed that she would be subjected to more of his domineering attitude and slipped out the door before he noticed.

Audrey sighed and sat on the bed.

"What ails you, Audrey?" he asked, slipping back into his Scottish burr.

She shook her head.

"Let's see about making you a lady, then. Not to say you aren't a lady now. Just one fit to serve a queen." He grimaced, realizing he was shoving his foot deeper down his throat. "You know what I mean."

She nodded in compliance. She was losing enthusiasm for Camden's instruction. He was trying to teach her how to act like a noblewoman. Audrey was finding that the last thing in the world she ever wanted to be was a sixteenth-century noblewoman.

"I saw you running downstairs this morning." He

shook his head at her, his lips pursed together. "Ladies don't run."

"Sorry," she said sullenly.

He sat next to her on the bed and patted her hand. "What's the matter, Audrey?" But before she could answer, he blurted out, "Do you see my hand?"

She looked at his hand, laid over hers. "What about it?"

"You can't let a man be so familiar with you."

"But you don't mean anything by it. What's the big deal? It's not like I'm letting you grope me."

"But some men might get ideas in their heads just from touching you. And it's not a good reflection on you to be letting them get ideas."

She shoved him, and he almost fell off the bed. "Get away, then."

He regained his balance and looked down at her. "You're in a foul mood today. That's another thing. You shouldn't scold, it makes you sound low."

She glared at him. "I wasn't aware you thought so little of me. I guess I'm just some lowly promiscuous shrew!"

"Don't throw a tantrum. You remind me of my son, and he's just a wean."

She grabbed her shoe from the floor and hurled it at him. He dodged the missile, laughing at her. She grabbed the other shoe, but he caught her wrist, confiscating the shoe.

"Let's not be throwing things. 'Tis a certainty that isn't ladylike. Maybe I should take you over my knee like I do wee Stephen. Aye, that's a fine idea," he said wickedly, "but I fear I might find it too pleasurable to stop after you've been properly chastised." When she glowered at him, he sighed. "What's amiss with you?"

"Don't you realize how hopeless this is?"

He sat beside her again. "Have you no faith in Brenden? Or me, for that matter? How do you know it's hopeless?"

He was all seriousness now, dark-green eyes somber. This was the time, but how was she to go about it? She stood and went to the window nervously. It wasn't as though Camden had seen her walk through walls or dreamed about her for more than a decade. The idea of a time traveler might be impossible for him to accept. Snow fell slowly to the ground below, and intricate patterns of frost edged the window. "Why are you helping him, Camden?"

When he didn't answer, she looked over her shoulder. He sat dejectedly, elbows on knees, looking at his hands. She leaned her forehead against the cold pane of glass.

"Do you think I'm crazy?" she asked.

"No." His voice held a note of confusion. "You are most definitely an unusual woman, but not crazy."

She took a deep breath and turned to face him. He had an odd look on his face but quickly masked it. "I'm going to tell you something. But after I tell you, you may change your mind."

Brenden returned that evening to find Camden and Audrey sitting cross-legged on the bed and laughing. He didn't say anything but removed his mantle and walked over to them. Her hair was not bound in a thick plait as she usually wore it but was flowing shiny and dark around her shoulders. His brother had removed his doublet and boots, and they looked altogether too comfortable for Brenden's liking. He never should have left Camden alone with her.

"This is how you teach her to be a lady?" He arched a brow at Camden. "Or is she teaching you how to be a lassie, sitting around giggling all day?" His anger was barely held in check, but Camden was too excited to rise to his jibe. He jumped up and grabbed Brenden's arm, catching him completely off guard. "'Tis the most fantastic thing I've ever heard!"

Brenden frowned at his enthusiasm, giving Audrey a sidelong look. "What is?"

"Audrey! And the world she comes from. Did you know the Turks occupy no more than Asia Minor? Did she tell you of the motorcars? What think you of that? And the airplanes that fly like birds yet transport hundreds of people across the ocean!" Brenden's jaw dropped. Actually, she hadn't told him any of those things, and it annoyed him that he hadn't thought to ask. "And Audrey! Did she tell you what she does? A woman in charge of the security of an entire military base! I should very much like to go to this time and see these things." Camden walked away from him, rubbing his chin. "Do you think it works both ways? Could I go into the future if I tried?"

"I don't think so, Camden. Not if you haven't seen the corridor yourself."

"Maybe it's there for everyone to use, but you're the only one who can see it. When we go back you must point it out to me. I'll walk straight into the wall, if I must, to see if it works."

"You'll probably just end up with a bloody nose," she said, laughing and pushing her thick mane over her shoulder. "I told you about Ian MacKay. To me it looked like it was empty space, yet he leaned against it."

"Nobody is going through that hellhole!" Brenden said angrily. "I'll have the keep torn to the ground if I must!"

Camden sobered, and Audrey looked up at Brenden in surprise. "You know, brother," Camden said, walking over to stand in front of him, "you'd do well to listen to this woman on occasion. Why, she already knows the outcome of this folly, and you turn a deaf ear." He shook his head. "I never thought you were daft, but now you make me wonder."

Brenden turned to her. "Is this your latest tactic? You're recruiting my own brother against me?"

Her cheeks immediately flushed in anger.

"What else is she to do, you addlepate?" Camden grabbed Brenden's arm, turning him back. "You're like a stone wall when you get something in your head."

"Stay out of this," Brenden said, poking his finger in Camden's chest and turning back to Audrey.

Camden moved in front of him again. "I won't let you bully her, do you hear? We'll have it out right here if you lay into her."

Brenden's eyes narrowed in annoyance. "What is this? You style yourself her hero? You must be loving it."

He had just overstepped the lines of brotherly toler-ance with Camden, whose mouth was thin and eyes blazing. Brenden's chest tightened in horror. Camden really cared for Audrey. He didn't see her as another wench to bed but as someone to respect and care for.

"Camden." Audrey's voice sounded calmer than she looked. "Could you please excuse us for a moment? I would like to have a word alone with Brenden."

Brenden felt an apology was in order, but when he opened his mouth to speak, Camden turned on his heel and left, slamming the door so hard, Audrey jumped.

"How dare you treat him like that!" she yelled. "I'm tired of your jealousy! I do not belong to you!" She crawled off the bed and walked toward him. Her hair had fallen over her shoulders, and she shoved it back impatiently. Her enormous gray eyes were dark and stormy. She was going to be unreasonable, he could see that. He should have handled the situation better. She'd been angry with him for days; it wasn't likely she would listen to anything he had to say now.

"Why did you tell him?"

"Because I had to! You won't listen to me! He believes me. He sees the wisdom of stopping this insanity."

He grabbed her shoulders. "I believed you!"

"Then why are you still doing this?"

He shook his head, the words trapped in his chest, wanting to pour out but dammed up tight. "I . . . I made a promise." He turned abruptly and walked to the window. He scrubbed his hands across his face, trying to decide what to do.

He felt her hand on his back, then a touch on his arm. Her nearness was doing strange things to him, and he took a deep breath.

"You promised what? Not to tell anyone? It's about Bothwell, isn't it? I don't understand, Brenden. Help me to understand."

He turned to her, and her eyes were wide and questioning. He couldn't hold it in any longer, not when she looked at him like that. The words were halting at first, the memories rusty from being closed away for so long. "I was in Denmark . . . on business . . ."

⇥ 12 ⇤

He was forced down a ladder into a cellar. There were no windows; no doors, save the trapdoor they were sending him through. The stench of human excrement was so overpowering that Brenden gagged. At the bottom, he noticed another prisoner crouching and shading his eyes from the torchlight. His ankle was shackled to a thick wooden pillar in the middle of the cellar. The chain on his ankle was short, severely limiting his movement. *God, not that.* Brenden began struggling against his jailers.

They dragged him to the far wall and shoved him to his knees. An iron bar protruded from the wall three feet above the dirt floor. They chained the fetters he wore on his wrists to it.

"I trust you'll find your new companion more accommodating than Munk," Captain Lauridson said to the other prisoner, who rose, still shading his eyes. Smiling, the captain turned to Brenden and explained, "The earl's last roommate found his company unbearable and escaped. When brought back kicking and screaming, he promptly hung himself."

The prisoner dropped his hand, though he continued squinting. "If you'd be kind enough to leave a length of rope within my reach, I'd rid you of my presence as well." He answered in Danish, but Brenden could tell by his accent that he was not a native. His voice cracked from disuse. His hair and beard were long and his face filthy. He wore a rotting shirt that hung almost to his knees and no pants.

The captain smiled. He placed the torch in a wall sconce and turned back to Brenden. "We've caught him at a lucid moment! Pray, make the most of it."

Brenden watched them ascend the ladder, pulling it up after them. The door shut with an ominous thud. He tugged experimentally at the fetters and then at the bar, but they held firm. He peered up at the trapdoor. The other prisoner's leg iron rattled as he sat down.

"Someone has escaped from here?" Brenden asked.

The man started as if he'd seen a ghost. "You're Scots?"

"Aye. Brenden Ross."

"Tell me," he said, scooting as close as his leg iron would allow, which was only a few inches. "What news from Scotland?" His eyes were dark green and bore into Brenden with a fevered intensity.

"Morton is regent and keeps the young king like a prisoner. The English queen tried to give Queen Mary back for Morton to execute, but it never happened, I know not why. Mary is still imprisoned at Sheffield, I think."

The man sat heavily against the pillar. "So it was all for naught. The lords prevailed."

His voice was cultured. The captain had called him the earl. Something stirred in Brenden's memory.

"Who are you?"

"James Hepburn, Duke of Orkney, Earl of Bothwell, Lord High Admiral of Scotland, Keeper of the Hermitage and Edinburgh Castles, Sheriff of East Lothian, Lieutenant of the Southern Borders . . ." His voice held a note of irony, since they both knew he no longer held these titles. "Oh, and husband to the Queen of Scotland."

Brenden was startled to find out that this was Lord Bothwell. He had heard he was being held prisoner by King Frederick at Malmö, but the fact that he was now abandoned in the bowels of this godforsaken prison hadn't reached his ears. He had seen Bothwell once, nine years ago, after Carberry Hill, when he had come to Brenden's father to raise troops to rescue the queen from Lochleven. He couldn't reconcile the man slumped against the pole with the man he had seen then. The Bothwell of his memory had been a vigorous man who could hardly stand still. Though not of great height, he had been large, with broad shoulders and a heavily muscled body. That's when Brenden noticed the crescent worn deep in the dirt around Bothwell's pillar. Apparently he still had a penchant for pacing.

This Bothwell was thin and unrecognizable. The sheer presence he had once emanated seemed to have disappeared. Fear seized Brenden. Was this what was to become of him also?

Bothwell was regarding Brenden with suspicion. "Are you a Ross of Irvine?"

"Aye, my father is the earl." Brenden wasn't sure he wanted to admit this piece of information, since his father had been a sometime enemy of Bothwell's.

"Let us hope you have not inherited your father's character."

"Never," Brenden said under his breath.

Bothwell gave a short laugh. "Aye, I was never charmed by my father, either."

"How long have you been here? Last I'd heard, you were at Malmö."

Bothwell stared at the torch, no longer squinting. He answered in a flat voice. "I know not. What year is it?"

"Fifteen seventy-six," Brenden answered, his chest becoming tight from the implications of such a question.

Bothwell's eyes glazed over, fixed sightlessly on the torch. "Three years since I've seen the sunlight, even through the bars at Malmö. Nine since I've seen Scotland."

He started mumbling something to himself and shaking his head sporadically. Brenden was immobilized, dread filling him. Seeing the once vital earl in such condition was one thing, but to start wondering what he himself was going to be like in three years was quite another. Bothwell was in his forties. Brenden was two-and-twenty. How long would it take him to go mad? He pulled against his fetters until his wrists hurt. He yanked down, not caring if he ripped skin off his hands or broke bones. His hands were much too large to escape.

Brenden looked at the torch, which was starting to burn down. The mumbling became loud and angry, but completely unintelligible. Soon the darkness would be complete, and he would be alone, with whatever was left of James Hepburn, fourth Earl of Bothwell.

She was reaching for him, palms exposed, pale skin glowing in the darkness surrounding her. She mouthed something to him. Her full lips formed words he could not understand. Luminous gray eyes, framed by long, long lashes, pleaded with him . . . but for what? In spite of the woman's beauty, this was no fanciful dream. He could already feel the fingers of dread creeping up his spine. *Wake up!* he commanded himself, but it was useless. The woman turned away from him, dark walnut hair swinging around her shoulders, sparkling teardrops suspended from her lower lashes. His own eyes were turning, following the direction she now faced.

He braced himself for the sight he'd grown accustomed to. The ax glinted as it arced swiftly downward. He looked again to the woman, feeling somehow responsible for the horror she was witnessing, disgusted that he was powerless to stop it. She was screaming soundlessly, white hands covering her mouth. Then something smacked him in the head. He came awake with a start.

He didn't know where he was at first. He could see nothing in the darkness. The fetters on his wrists and the sharp pain in his neck from sleeping at an odd angle brought it all rushing back. His chest was still heaving from the intensity of the dream. His hair was wet with sweat, and he lowered his head to his hands, pushing it back. A knot was forming above his ear where something had struck him.

"Why did you hit me?" Brenden called out.

"You sounded as though you needed waking." The reply drifted to him through the darkness.

He rubbed his fingers across the bump gingerly. "You didn't have to strike me with a rock, did you?"

"That wasn't a rock—that was dinner."

Brenden hoped this was a joke, but the earl's voice held not a hint of amusement. The chain on Bothwell's ankle jangled as he moved.

"What dreams plague you?"

"A beautiful lass is trying to tell me something, but I can't hear nor understand her. Then something terrible

happens and I know it's because of me . . . something
I did."

"Ah . . . a lassie. That accounts for the heavy breathing."

Brenden's neck grew hot. "It wasn't like that. It was
frightening . . . I think I did something wrong and she
knew and blamed me."

"If you're doing it wrong, who else is she going to
blame?" There was humor in his voice.

"That's not what I mean! In the dream I think I killed
someone."

"I see. Well, 'tis just a dream, don't let it bother you
too much."

"I wager it might bother you if you had it every time
you closed your eyes for six years past! And I'm no
closer to understanding it now than when it began."

"I dream of a land I'll never see again and a wife I'll
never hold." Bothwell's voice was heavy and solemn.

"'Tis the price of treason. I guess you're lucky the
lords never did get their hands on you. Then your head
would be on a spike."

Brenden's caustic remark didn't have the intended
effect. Bothwell's laughter filled their dungeon. It took
on a slightly hysterical edge.

"Oh, aye! I am the lucky one! In death's stead, I languish in this privy hole, eating rancid meat and stale
bread. Never seeing the light of day!" He was laughing
so hard, he began coughing. After a violent coughing
spasm, he was silent for a moment. "And I get to share
my grave with the likes of you. Oh, aye, I am so goddamned lucky."

Brenden heard a scuttling nearby. For a paralyzing
moment he thought Bothwell was more mobile than he
looked. He exhaled, realizing it was only rats retrieving

the missile Bothwell had launched at him earlier. His stomach cramped from hunger, and his mouth was dry. How long had he been here? A day? A few hours? He wasn't sure. He felt panic rising again. He should think about escaping. He pulled on his fetters. He got to his feet, but he couldn't stand up straight because his fetters were chained so low on the iron bar protruding from the wall. He stretched his legs and sat down again. He felt along the wall and bar before him. It was solid.

"Dammit! How did this Munk escape?"

"He was chained to a ring in the wall, which he worried until it pulled out."

Brenden grasped the bar he was chained to and pulled. No give. "You've been here for three years and haven't escaped, yourself? I thought there wasn't prison that could hold the Earl of Bothwell."

Brenden had the sensation of those fevered green eyes boring into his back, even though the darkness was complete.

"I escaped from Malmö," he answered finally. "But they caught me and brought me here."

To die. To forget about. Just what they were doing to Brenden. He would die chained to a wall, surrounded by his own filth.

"Have you tried to escape?"

"How might I go about doing this, pray tell?" His voice was heavy with sarcasm. "They will not come near me. They think I'm insane."

Brenden couldn't blame them for keeping their distance. He remembered the brief look he got at Bothwell before the torch burned out, and it had been unnerving. His long reddish-brown hair and beard were streaked with gray and tangled, his legs filthy and scrawny. He looked like a beast.

"I'm sure you've done nothing to encourage this notion."

Bothwell snorted. "You'll be no better in three years."

"They can't keep me here," Brenden said with no conviction. "I haven't even been tried."

"If it's a trial you're waiting for, you might as well make yourself at home. Nine years and I've still not had one. I don't think they know why they keep me anymore."

Brenden remembered hearing that Scotland had been trying to extradite Bothwell for a trial several years ago, to no avail. He had been under the impression at the time that King Frederick was protecting Bothwell. Obviously, he was wrong.

They sat in silence for a long time. Brenden was slowly becoming agitated. The silence was oppressive, almost like a roaring in his ears. As if sensing his discomfort, Bothwell cleared his throat.

"This dream . . . you say you have it every night, and you don't know who the woman is?"

"I met her when she was but a lass. She was dressed like a lad and I thought her bonny, but I haven't seen her since. There's another woman in it as well, though she doesn't seem to be for me. She's getting her head cut off. I don't know who that woman is."

"Is this the murder you are responsible for?"

"I think so." Brenden had thought long and hard on this before and couldn't imagine how he would be responsible for a woman being beheaded.

"It must be a vision of sorts, a look at things to come. Perhaps even a warning. Hmm . . . Aye, you would do well to heed it."

"Aye," Brenden nodded. "I've thought much the

same myself, but I still know not what to make of it."

"View it as such: You will leave this hole one day to see a woman beheaded."

Hysterical laughter bubbled in Brenden's throat. He was truly grasping at straws now, and it suddenly seemed hilarious. He laughed until his sides hurt and tears ran down his face.

"That's more like it," Bothwell said. "Now they'll not think I'm the only one gone mad."

Dehaan, the short scrawny man who brought them food, descended the ladder with a torch. Brenden squinted up at him, shading his eyes. The light felt like daggers stabbing his eyes, but he welcomed the pain. It brought precious light.

It had become a ritual, this "mealtime." Brenden and Bothwell rolled their clay water flasks to Dehaan, since he wouldn't come near them. After replacing the burnt-out torch, he scooted filled flasks over with a long stick. Then he threw their food at them. His aim was fair, but sometimes Brenden was forced to work for his nasty dinner. Other times, he was so far off, Brenden would have gone hungry if it hadn't been for Bothwell, who either found a way to retrieve it himself, since his mobility was better, or shared his own.

Brenden had been trying to get up the nerve to ask him about the queen. The subject seemed off-limits, but with lack of entertainment, Brenden found his mind drifting back to the mystery chained across the room.

"So . . . was it worth it?" he asked hesitantly.

"Was what worth it?"

"Killing the king. Raping the queen."

Bothwell was silent for a long time. Brenden thought

perhaps he'd pushed him too far and he was going to begin his strange mumbling again. Brenden took a bite of the greasy, hard meat and willed his throat to open and swallow it.

"King?" Bothwell scoffed. "Henry Darnley was no king. But your question is a difficult one. Mary is a rare woman, and I have no regrets about loving her." He paused. "But when you view the results, I have to say it wasn't worth it. If it was only me, it wouldn't be so difficult, for I am responsible for my own actions and must pay for them in kind. But she was an innocent. Her only wish was to be free of an evil man, and she turned to me for help."

Brenden turned to look at him and saw his face lined with sadness and regret.

"Mary is imprisoned unjustly as many years as I have been, and her son is being brought up to believe she is a whore who murdered his father. If she knows this, then her heart is broken. I cannot bear I brought her to this."

Brenden kept his mouth shut. He knew without a doubt that King James's lessons included the continued debasement of his mother. He felt a twinge of guilt, as if he were somehow responsible for it.

"So the answer is no, it wasn't worth it. If I had it to do over again, I'd stay on the borders or keep to the sea, where I belong."

Brenden closed his eyes, wishing for the same. He could almost feel the salty air on his face, the motion of a ship beneath his feet.

The question was on the tip of Brenden's tongue to ask Bothwell if he had killed King Henry. But he didn't want to know, if the answer was yes. He was strangely touched by Bothwell's concern for the queen's feelings when his own life was now so meaningless. A lesser man would only have pity for himself. But not Bothwell. Brenden didn't want to hear any ghastly revelations.

"I did not kill him."

It was spoken so softly, Brenden wasn't certain he had heard him correctly.

"Then who did?"

"I know not whose hands did the deed."

"So you say," Brenden countered. "But what of the evidence of letters written to you by the queen? Or the confessions of your accomplices?"

"Those letters prove nothing, save that she loved me. Most of them aren't even from Mary. As for confessions, what would you say to get off the rack? After having hot pokers bore into your flesh, mayhap you would tell them just what they wanted to hear." He laughed softly. "I'd confess to killing Henry right now if it meant an end to this life."

"If she was your lover, why did you kidnap her?"

"I didn't really kidnap her." Bothwell laughed. "We might have gotten away with it, had she put up a struggle." He shook his head. "But no, she came with me most docile. Trusting me, as though I were her hero."

"What were you thinking, man? If you really loved her, you should have just stayed away. Think of how different things might have been."

"Do you not think I've had those same thoughts a million times over?" Bothwell asked angrily. "It wasn't so easy, Brenden. Had I left her alone, what then? She could trust no one, save me. The lords killed her secretary, Ricco, when she was heavy with child. They planned to take her away somewhere to give birth to the prince and then murder her."

Brenden remembered hearing about that, the lord's first act of treachery. Bothwell had been there to deliver the queen from the hands of those who meant to harm her. Bothwell was pacing now. Back and forth he went, wearing the crescent deeper into the ground.

"I had to try. She looked to me to protect her. I couldn't let her down."

How many years had he spent examining every move he had made? Wondering if he had done something differently, whether anything would have changed. Wondering if he was the cause of his wife's imprisonment. What frustration he must have felt, after being the queen's protector for so long and now being powerless to act. Brenden regretted making him think on it again.

"You're right. You did all you could," Brenden said gently.

Bothwell stopped pacing and looked at him. His brow was furrowed and his dark-green eyes anguished. He seemed on the verge of saying something, but shook his head and resumed pacing.

Brenden sighed. It was going to be a long day. He continued watching the torch as it sputtered lower and lower and finally extinguished. He longed to see the thread of smoke he knew drifted up from the torch when it finally went out. A sight he was never allowed to see.

Bothwell's pacing continued unerringly through the night. When Brenden awoke, he was still at it, mumbling angrily to the phantoms that haunted him, pulling at his hair and wringing his hands. Brenden had seen him when there was light to view it. If he didn't stop soon, Brenden was afraid for his own sanity. He stretched to the best of his ability and moved along the length of the bar. His limited movement was frustrating, but at least they were both granted some mobility so they didn't actually have to sit upon their own filth.

Bothwell finally sat with a thud. His breathing evened in sleep.

"Rest well, friend," Brenden whispered. "None needs it more than you."

Brenden lost track of any conception of time. His clothes were beginning to rot, and he sported a bushy beard. They spent much of their time talking. Mostly, Bothwell regaled Brenden with stories from his days as lieutenant of the Southern Borders and Lord High Admiral of Scotland.

"Tell me another one," Brenden asked, after Bothwell had just finished giving him a lengthy account about an ambush that had thwarted the Lords of the Congregation. Brenden knew he sounded like a bairn, but he loved hearing the stories. Besides, their other entertainment options were limited to sleeping and staring into the darkness.

"Nay, let's try something different. You tell me a story."

Brenden thought hard. "I have no stories to be telling."

"Everyone has a story! Even a young lad like yourself must have something to tell."

"No, nothing."

"What about your father?" Bothwell asked in exasperation. "Did he not teach you aught or take you anywhere? Or even tell you stories of his life?"

"Nay. My father has never cared for anyone but himself. I could tell you much about him, had I the inclination. Perhaps you'd prefer the story where he burned his mistress and had their six-year-old bastard watch it? That one makes for a nice evening. Or even better, there's the one where he was disputing with some cottars over rents and killed a man."

Bothwell was quiet, and Brenden continued, "He left the widow with seven bairns, he did. Instead of helping the poor woman, he evicted her. Aye, I suppose I do have a story or two, but they'll only make for nightmares, and I have my share of those already."

"Why are you here, Brenden? You've never told me."

"Murder."

Bothwell cleared his throat. "You don't seem like a murderer to me."

"Well . . . I'm not one, I'd like to think. It was self-defense. But don't try to tell the guards that when it's a noble you've killed." Brenden grimaced at the memory of the beating he had received for opening his mouth about it.

"Why were you defending yourself against a nobleman?"

"He was raping a lass. I guess I should have let him."

"No!" The word exploded from Bothwell, making Brenden jump. "You did the right thing Brenden. Never regret that."

"But if I hadn't saved the lass, I wouldn't be here."

"That's your father talking. I would rather share this prison with the noble Brenden who saves defenseless wenches from rapine."

Brenden was speechless. His tutors had rained much praise upon him for learning and such, but his father had showed nothing but annoyance when Brenden became indignant at his doings. He remembered the day he had given the small amount of money he had to the widow with seven children. His father took the strap to him, telling him that was no way to win the respect of subjects.

"I . . . I didn't mean to kill him," Brenden stuttered suddenly. "He turned out to be a bonny fighter and, well . . . it was kill or be killed."

"Don't worry on it another moment." Bothwell's voice was soothing. "It's always hard to kill. God help you when it becomes easy."

They sat in silence until the torch once again burned out and left them in darkness.

Brenden was awakened by the door overhead creaking open. Something wasn't right, he thought groggily. They had received food only a short while ago. Why was someone coming down now?

He saw the flicker of a torch, and the ladder eased down. Dehaan descended slowly, talking softly to someone above him. Then another figure started down, this one very small. It looked like a young boy.

When the boy reached the bottom, he removed his hat, and a swath of long blond hair cascaded down his shoulders. It was a lass!

She made a choking sound. "God! It smells like a privy down here!" she whispered. "Where are they?"

Dehaan held the torch higher to illuminate the greater part of the room and pointed to Brenden and Bothwell. Her eyes widened when she saw them. Brenden looked quickly at Bothwell, who was glowering at Dehaan.

"This one," Dehaan said, indicating Brenden, "is a murderer. But he's not crazy . . . yet."

She looked Brenden over, eyes wide. "But he's so . . . big and filthy. Does it not scare you to come down here?"

Brenden's neck grew hot. So now he was an animal

on display, to be stared at in amazement and revulsion.

"That's why I bring my stick." He held his stick aloft, and she nodded approvingly. "I never need it for this one. But the earl over here," he pointed to Bothwell with the stick. "I often have to apply it to him."

Her mouth was open in an O shape as she looked at Bothwell. The earl's venomous gaze was fixed on Dehaan.

"The earl murdered the King of Scotland and raped the queen!" He paused so she could make an exclamation of horror. "He then forced the queen to marry him. So I guess, in a sense, he's the King of Scotland! The lunatic King of Scots!" This caused Dehaan to fall into gales of laughter.

Brenden felt his gorge rise. He wanted to pummel Dehaan with his fists, and yet all he could do was sit and listen. Bothwell turned his head and stared at the far wall. This inflamed Brenden even more.

"You bastard!" Brenden yelled, hands straining against the fetters. "If I ever get my hands on you, I'll kill you!"

Whap! Dehaan brought the stick down hard across Brenden's back. For a paralyzing moment he couldn't breathe. Then he was wheezing, trying to gulp in the air he'd lost.

"You want some more?" Dehaan asked, raising the stick to strike him again. The lass stayed his hand, a pained look on her face. He shrugged and turned back to Bothwell.

"Sometimes I can get the earl to howl at the moon, just like a wolf." He began prodding Bothwell in the chest with the stick.

"Stop it!" the lass cried. Dehaan ignored her. Bothwell remained motionless, eyes averted.

"Wake up, earl! Wake up and howl for the lady," he jeered, jabbing Bothwell harder in the chest. She was grabbing for the stick when Bothwell's hand shot out and ripped the stick from Dehaan's grasp. Bothwell was on his feet and snapped the stick in two across his pillar. He threw the two halves at Dehaan, who dodged out of the way.

"Get out," Bothwell said in a low voice that made Brenden's blood chill. Dehaan grabbed the sticks and indicated for the lass to go up the ladder. She looked at Brenden and then Bothwell for a long moment.

"I'm sorry," she whispered, and climbed the ladder. Dehaan went after her, taking the torch with him.

"You'll pay for this." Dehaan's voice drifted down to them before the door slammed shut.

Their lives consisted of a long succession of hard meat, stale bread, and grimy water. They passed the time talking and telling stories. Brenden came to look upon Bothwell with much affection and was grateful he wasn't alone.

He knew Bothwell had spent the first three years of his confinement at Dragsholm in almost complete isolation. His only other cellmate had been a man named Munk who killed himself. But Bothwell said he wasn't much company. He was disease ridden and completely insane.

"Who do you think killed King Henry?" Brenden asked one day. He hadn't broached the subject again, for fear of Bothwell having another one of his pacing fits.

"I told you, I know not who killed him."

"You must have an idea? They meant to implicate you. Your name was called out on the streets of Edinburgh, both before and after the explosion. And one of your gunpowder barrels was found at Kirk o' Field, or so I heard."

"Ah, it is two separate things you speak of, the explosion and Henry's death. He escaped to be strangled in the garden. And aye, I know who was behind the explosion."

"You do? Well, why didn't you say something at your trial?"

"Because Henry put the gunpowder there."

"What? That doesn't make any sense."

"He had been plotting against Mary ever since she was with child. I think, when he realized he had the French pox, he decided to kill her, and possibly himself, too, since once she had seen he was poxed, he knew he had lost her forever. But it didn't work. Mary wouldn't stay the night with him at Kirk o' Field, despite his pathetic begging. Later that evening, I received word of what he was planning but did not believe it. He was always a dolt. I assumed he was incapable of such treachery. But I was wrong. I was the sheriff of Edinburgh and went to have a look. When I arrived, I saw for myself that he had filled the vaults below the house with gunpowder."

"I still don't understand. Did he blow the house up himself?"

Bothwell was silent.

"Well?"

"No. I did."

"What?" Brenden burst out angrily. "So you've lied to me? You said you didn't kill him."

"I didn't kill him. He escaped, and someone else strangled him."

"What's the difference? You might as well have been

the murderer." Brenden was upset at this revelation. He had been seeing Bothwell as a misunderstood hero. To find out his heart was as black as the lords he was always defiling was dispiriting.

Bothwell, as if sensing Brenden's change of heart, became indignant. "Pray tell, what was I to do? Let him live another day to try again? Or arrest him and charge him with treason? Behead the father of the prince?"

Brenden shook his head. The man made sense, but still . . . "What of your talk of it being hard to kill?"

"You didn't see how the bastard treated Mary. Nay, it wasn't so hard to send him to hell." Bothwell sounded a bit dispirited himself. "I never said I haven't sinned."

Once again Brenden's heart went out to the man. It wasn't as if he had planned it himself. The gunpowder was there. The man who was trying to kill the queen, inside. He supposed he might have done the same.

Brenden wasn't sure how long they'd been without food, but his best guess was four days. Life had taken on an ethereal quality. At one point he had been able to keep track of days by mealtimes. But in the past few months, it seemed Dehaan became less and less diligent about feeding them. Which also meant no light.

Brenden looked forward to having the torch illumi-nate the cellar for a few hours a day. He and Bothwell could see each other when they talked, and he could somewhat see himself. His hair hung past his shoulders and beard to his chest. They were both crawling with lice, and he spent a good part of the time scratching and trying to pick them out. Bothwell laughed and said he'd get used to it, but he still hadn't.

Once he tried to count the minutes in a whole day.

Every time he made it to sixty, he made a scratch on the wall. He tried to do it in his head, but it made him sleepy, so he counted aloud. By the time he had hit two hours, Bothwell was throwing his waste at him and yelling obscenities. So he gave it up.

Brenden had very little water left, and the last time Bothwell had spoken, he'd said he was in much the same situation. But Bothwell hadn't spoken in a while, and Brenden was getting worried. The cramping hunger was gone, but his mouth seemed constantly dry and he felt sleepy and listless.

"Bothwell?" No answer. "James! Wake up!" he yelled. It was an exertion to raise his voice.

"What?" Bothwell groaned.

"You need to stay awake." Brenden feared that if Bothwell went to sleep, he would never wake up. Then Brenden would be alone with a corpse.

"Why?" His voice was thin and weak. Brenden knew he was sick, in more than one way. The last time they were brought food, Bothwell had had one of his "spells." Dehaan enjoyed tormenting him when he was in such a state. But this time he made the mistake of getting too close, and Bothwell had attacked him. But he was weak and put down easily. Dehaan proceeded to beat him with his new length of stick and took his food back.

Bothwell hadn't been completely lucid since. Brenden tried rolling some of his food over to Bothwell, but he didn't think he ate it.

"Because you may not wake up."

"Oh, God, if only I am so fortunate."

"Dammit, James! This can't be the way you want to die!" Brenden was desperate. He could almost feel Bothwell's despair, it hung so thickly about him.

"It doesn't matter anymore. Do you think we're ever leaving here?"

"You can't say what may happen. When they realize they keep forgetting about us, mayhap they'll move us upstairs."

He sounded pathetic, and he knew it. They talked of escape and formed plans, some of them ludicrous, but both knew it was impossible as long as they were in the dungeon.

Bothwell laughed softly. "You dream, Brenden. You try to keep hope alive. That's what I love about you."

Brenden's eyes burned. Death was suffocating him. His death as well as Bothwell's. He hated feeling like a coward, but he desperately didn't want to be alone. Bothwell was the last thing holding his sanity intact.

"You're younger and stronger," Bothwell continued. "When I'm gone, mayhap they will move you. I'm the one Dehaan wants dead. Once you're upstairs, you could do it."

The thought had occurred to Brenden before, but he always put it out of his head. Now he did the same. "You are still strong, too!" Brenden lied.

Bothwell was silent. Brenden shifted his arms. They were stiff, and his shoulders ached from always being held in the same position. The fetters wore sores on his wrists, but they didn't hurt right now. He knew Bothwell's ankle was in far worse shape. He tried not to look at it when they had torchlight, but his eyes were always drawn to it, hoping each time he saw it that the festering would not be as bad. Brenden knew he was dying of more than starvation.

"Listen to me, Brenden." Bothwell's voice held a sudden strength that made Brenden sit up straighter.

"Do not make my death worthless. If they move you, you must escape."

Brenden sat stoically, trying not to let the words penetrate his heart. He always thought that if he did escape, it wouldn't be alone. "You are not going to die!"

"And if you do escape," Bothwell continued, as if he hadn't heard him, "grant me one last wish."

"Anything."

"Do not let Mary die in prison as I have. Do not let her suffer for a crime she didn't commit."

Brenden was silent, digesting this request. His throat thickened.

"Promise me!" Bothwell's voice filled the cellar.

"I give you my word," Brenden promised, tears making tracks through the filth on his cheeks.

Bothwell sighed suddenly. A weary, gut-wrenching sigh. "I'm tired now."

His breathing evened, and Brenden knew he was sleeping. Brenden squeezed his eyes shut and pressed his mouth against his forearm so that his sobs wouldn't wake his friend.

He awoke with a start. It was the dream again, only this time the woman seemed to be urging him to rouse himself. He couldn't hear her, he just knew. He sensed immediately that something was different. It was still pitch-black, but Bothwell was gone. He strained to hear his breathing across the room but heard nothing.

"James!" he called out. "Wake up!"

Nothing. Not a groan. Not a breath. Not the familiar jangle of his leg iron.

"James!" he shouted, his voice becoming hoarse.

Anger exploded in his chest, white hot. "God damn

you!" he roared. "We're still down here! Hear me!" He yelled in the direction of the door. "God damn you! I'll kill you for this, I swear it!"

He struggled with his fetters, pulling and yanking until he felt the wetness of blood running down his arms, and still he struggled. He pushed against the wall with his feet and tried to pull his hands out. Finally, he slammed his head against the wall in frustration.

"Take me with you."

He seemed to be drifting somewhere between waking and sleeping. He could hardly move his arms anymore and didn't care. His head lay against his hands, and he felt the cold iron of the fetters and the stickiness of drying blood against his cheek. It seemed to be what kept him conscious. Something brushed against his thigh. He had a vision of Bothwell's hideously bloated corpse dragging itself across the room, smothering him with its putrid stench. He shuddered.

Another brush and some scuttling. It was the rats. He realized, with some detachment, that they had become very bold. He felt paws on his thigh and could envision the twitching nose and whiskers, sniffing to see if he was dead so they could scavenge him, too.

He thought of Bothwell again with a sudden lurching of his stomach. Lying dead, now at the mercy of the rats. He found enough strength to move his thigh, and the rat scurried away.

He tried to think of his family, wondering if they even knew he was rotting away in prison. He thought of Gavin, clutching at his arm, begging Brenden to bring him along when he left. He thought of Gavin's mother, screaming as the flames engulfed her, the boy's face buried against his shirt. Their father turning away calmly. He shook the memories off. Could he think of nothing pleasant?

He willed himself to sleep—maybe the woman in the dream was an angel, and when he died, he would be with her forever.

There was light beyond his eyelids and a grinding, sawing noise. But he was too weary to open them. His sleep was blissfully dreamless, and he wanted to crawl back into it. But aches and pains were making themselves known. He was lying prostrate with his arms straight at his side. He wrenched his eyes open.

He was still in the cellar. Torches filled all the sconces, and three men were standing nearby looking at something on the floor. He tried to lift himself, but he was too weak. He looked around and saw his place against the wall, fetters hanging empty from the bar. His filth and rotting clothes piled around it. The sawing began to sound ominous.

He turned his head the other way. Bothwell was also flat on his back. His eyes stared sightlessly at the ceiling. Dehaan was sawing the fetter off his swollen, ulcerated ankle. Brenden closed his eyes tightly to shut out the scene.

"He's coming around."

No, I'm not! There was a hand beneath his neck, lifting. Cool clay against his lips, water running into his mouth, down into his beard. He choked. His head was laid gently back on the floor.

"His wrists look bad." It was the same man.

"Take him upstairs and dress his wrists. Try to get some food into him." Captain Lauridson. It seemed like a million years since he had last heard his voice. "I told his brother he was alive. Do not make a liar of me."

The man hauled Brenden up and over his shoulder to ascend the ladder.

"He's a big lad," the captain continued. "I think he'll be all right."

As they were slowly going up into the light, Brenden heard a rending snap and opened his eyes, peering down into the cellar.

"Finally! He's free," Dehaan said, and removed the fetter from Bothwell's ankle.

The gray-eyed woman was beckoning him closer. There was a sad smile upon her lips. Something was very different. The man with the ax was there, but the auburn-haired woman wasn't crouched over the block. He walked closer.

The gray-eyed woman held her hand out to him, and he extended his toward her. A jolt went through him when she took his hand. She was very close, and he could see how fine and poreless her skin was. She gestured to the steps leading to the scaffold.

A man and the auburn-haired woman embraced at the foot of the steps. He was a few inches shorter than she. Brenden's heart rose in his throat. It was Bothwell.

Dark-blue velvet was stretched across his wide shoulders. His short reddish-brown hair was cut close to his head. The auburn-haired woman, he realized now, was the queen. She pulled away from Bothwell and smiled serenely. She turned to climb the steps. Bothwell continued to hold her hand until her fingertips slipped from his grasp.

She knelt in front of the block and gently placed her

head on it. Brenden's grip tightened on the gray-eyed woman's hand. She moved closer and whispered in his ear, her breath warm, "Do not despair."

The executioner raised the ax above his head. Bothwell turned away, toward Brenden. His face was clean-shaven and filled out. A mustache framed his mouth. His eyes were filled with an undefinable sadness. He held Brenden's gaze for a long moment, then walked away. Brenden longed to call out after him, to apologize for failing him. But he couldn't.

The woman's lips were still close to his ear. "He doesn't understand . . . yet."

It was very late. A single candle burned on the table. Una had come to their room in the Peterborough inn that evening to sleep, but Brenden had given her some coins and told her to get another room. And so Brenden and Audrey sat across the table from one another until the early morning hours, while Brenden told his story. Now it was over, and Audrey could think of nothing to say.

It had been gut-wrenching to listen to; she couldn't imagine living through it. She stared across the table at him. He was leaned back in the chair, looking across the room at the window. The glass was of poor quality, and the diamond-shaped panes had fine cracks running through them. They looked black at night, the white snow scalloping the edges. He had taken his doublet off sometime during the evening and now wore only a rough shirt, the collar open, exposing the hollow of his throat. He had left all his fine clothes in Scotland, since they were passing as yeomen with their wives and, later, as soldiers. There was no need for fine linen and silks.

"How did you escape?" she finally asked.

"Camden had been looking for me for some time. He located me at Dragsholm and began paying Lauridson extra for my sustenance, which was why I was moved upstairs to somewhat better accommodations. I could see the sun." Her heart ached for him, but she couldn't speak. He looked at her, his light-green eyes warm. His short reddish beard had been trimmed recently and looked very handsome on him. He smiled slightly. "Camden managed to bribe one of the guards to leave my cell unlocked, and here I am." He paused, holding her gaze. "You were right. I do feel better."

"I'm glad," she said softly.

"Now that I've told you why I am honor bound to do this, do you understand? Do you realize it just isn't possible that you were sent to stop me?"

"If you felt this way, why did you allow me to believe you were considering returning to Scotland?"

His mouth hardened. "I won't allow you to leave me again. If I have to keep you away from Scotland forever, so be it. I'll put you on a ship, and we'll live in the New World. But you're not going back."

She stared at him incredulously. "How dare you make such decisions about my life! I will—"

He was out of his chair and a second later was hauling her out of hers. She didn't have a chance to react before she was crushed against him.

"No, woman! I am not such a fool!" His face was close to hers, his eyes searching. She was so surprised and aroused, she could hardly breathe. He saw it in her face and gave a small shake of his head. "I'm not a fool, am I? You feel it, too." She swallowed hard, wanting to deny it but unable to force words through her tight throat.

He began winding his hand in her hair. When he had

a firm grip on it, he tugged gently until she finally submitted, letting her head fall back and her eyes flutter shut. His mouth was hot on her neck, kissing a trail to her ear. She felt his breath against her ear, warm and ragged, and her knees almost buckled beneath her.

When he spoke, his voice was different. "I'm asking you not to leave me." Before she could answer, his mouth covered hers. Her lips parted immediately, welcoming him, and his tongue claimed hers. He pressed her backward onto the bed. A small part of her mind that was still capable of semicoherent thought urged her to stop him, and she almost did. He broke the kiss off, and she opened her mouth to ask him to let her go. But he yanked the shirt over his head, exposing his muscular chest and arms. She forgot her protests in her desire to touch him. His skin was warm and smooth. Auburn hair dusted his chest and stomach. Then he was on her again, and she wrapped herself around him, stroking the hard lines of his back.

He pulled her woolen gown and coarse shift over her head and lay beside her, running his hands along her body. She was trembling with need for him. She wanted him to take her then and pressed against him, trying to get closer, to be as close as two people could.

"Not yet," he whispered, pulling back from her. His large hand traveled over her stomach and ribs, where he cupped her breast and ran his thumb across her nipple. "I have thought long on being with you in this manner, and I don't intend to rush through it."

He lowered his head to suckle her breasts and a shuddering sigh vibrated through her. He kissed her body with a slow deliberateness, until she was begging him to make love to her. He finally relented, his hard body stretching over her, covering her with his warmth. He pressed into her, filling the ache he had made and creating a new need to have him even deeper and closer, to join completely with her.

"My Audrey, my love," he whispered hoarsely as he moved within her.

She cried out, but his mouth swallowed the sound as he kissed her. She clung to him, heat coursing through her.

Then it was quiet. The sound of their shallow breathing seemed to echo in the little room. Audrey tried to force herself to be upset about what had just happened, but he was still on her, their bodies damp from their exertion. His cheek was pressed against hers and his muscular arms beneath her back and shoulders, one of his hands cupping her neck. She felt protected and whole. As if sensing her train of thought, his arms tightened, hugging her closer to him.

He wanted her to stay. Judging from the pain in her chest at the thought of leaving, she was already very much in love with him. She cursed herself for allowing this to happen. She didn't belong here!

But he had told her. He had opened himself to her as no one had before. How could she leave him now? He rolled off her, but still held her tightly in his arms.

He took her hand and twined her fingers with his. "Will you help me, Audrey? Help me keep this promise that means so much to me."

"Yes," she whispered. It suddenly seemed inevitable that her dream was to become a reality. She had failed.

Brenden woke in the morning to an insistent pounding on the door. Audrey was just waking up and stretched in his arms. Her face was covered with hair, and he pushed it away. She yawned and blinked at him with hazy gray eyes. He kissed her before she could speak, and her entire body seemed to sigh in his arms. She wrapped her arms around his neck and kissed him back. He rolled on top of her.

"Audrey! I'm coming in!" It was Camden.

She pushed him frantically away and pulled the covers over her head. Brenden would rather have told his brother in a kinder way, but there was no helping the circumstances, and he was going to have to get used to it. As far as Brenden was concerned, Audrey was sleeping with him from now on.

Camden tried to open the door, but Brenden had locked it after Una disturbed them earlier in the evening. Brenden grabbed his breeks and pulled them on. He took a deep breath before unlatching the door and facing his brother.

Camden came in with a smile, but it faded quickly when he saw Brenden standing half-naked in the doorway. His mouth became grim.

"My boots."

Brenden raised an eyebrow.

Camden sighed in irritation. "I left my boots in here." He pointed to his feet. He stood in his wool stockings.

Brenden held up his finger and went to the bed.

"What does he want?" Audrey whispered, peeking out from under the covers.

"His boots."

She pointed to the table. They were resting beneath it. He grabbed the boots and took them back to the door. Camden snatched them out of Brenden's hands.

"Do ye have need for me today, milord? Or would you like me to keep the lassies company?"

"I want you to accompany me today, aye."

"I am yours to command, milord!" Camden said sar-castically. "I'll be in my room, awaiting your pleasure."

He turned and stalked down the hall. Brenden sighed. He would talk to him about this later. At the moment he was more concerned with Audrey feeling regret. He returned to the bed and sat on the edge. She was still beneath the blanket, an unmoving lump.

"You can't hide under there forever."

She pulled the covers down. "I feel like I've done something wrong. This feels very wrong." Her brow was creased with worry.

"Did it feel so wrong last night?"

Her cheeks turned pink, and she averted her eyes. He pulled her close. She was stiff at first, then wrapped her arms around his waist and laid her head on his chest.

"It feels very right now."

"Then mayhap I shall hold you always." He felt her shiver and smiled. "I must leave this morning. Camden and I will ride out to Fotheringhay to have a look around."

She nodded against his chest. He lifted her chin so she could look at him. "You will not sit in this room regretting our time together." She didn't say anything, and he gripped her chin tighter. "I mean it, Audrey. Think of the days ahead, of what we must do, but don't think you have made a mistake by giving yourself to me. You haven't."

He kissed her, and when he drew back, she was smil-ing at him. He didn't want to leave the bed or her arms, but he had many things to get underway. He rose and began dressing. She was lying on her side, the blanket draped over her body, but he could still see the generous swell of her breasts before they disappeared under the wool, a harsh contrast to her silky skin. Her hair hung around her pale shoulders.

"How did it go with your men yesterday?" she asked.

He and Gavin had met his men in Northampton to give them their needed papers and make certain everyone knew what was to transpire. "All that needs to be done is for Camden to obtain a few more forgeries." He smiled. "Elizabeth Curle received a distressing message from home and must leave the queen's service immediately. So we have a vacancy."

"I don't suppose you had anything to do with her distress?"

He shrugged. "It seems the letter said that Lady Tara Ross would be on her way shortly to attend the queen in Mistress Curle's absence."

Her brow furrowed, and she looked a little ill. "Me?"

"Aye. Don't worry, Camden and I will be with you at Fotheringhay, and Gavin will be in town in the event something does happen."

"How do you know they need you and your men? What if they turn you away?"

"They've been increasing the guard ever since the queen has been at Fotheringhay. Our position is a wee bit more precarious, as they may verify our previous assignments." He wasn't worried about this happening. He was sure the queen's jailer was far too busy with other things than to be verifying each man's background. "I'll have someone checking the dispatches, and if such a thing should occur, he has orders to detain the courier."

When he was dressed, he sat on the bed. She looked so inviting and beautiful, her long body stretched out lazily. He rubbed the curve of her hip and leaned down to kiss the tops of her breasts.

"What's the matter?" she asked when he straightened. He was pleased to see she looked disappointed.

"I must go. I will no doubt have to coax Camden to speak with me. It won't be very pleasant."

She nodded, and he forced himself to leave her.

The inn where they were staying was no Hilton, and Audrey slowly began to realize there would be no maid service to tidy the room up. Una had come in after Brenden had left with dried fruit and bread, but it sat on the table untouched. She dragged herself out of bed and began to dress. She didn't know why she was so tired lately. She felt almost drugged at times. She poured frigid water from the chipped clay ewer into the matching basin and washed her face before going to the table to look at her breakfast.

Her stomach began churning as she viewed the dried fruit and hard bread. She decided to clean the room. She found Camden's doublet lying over a wooden chest and felt awful. What had he thought? She cared very much about Camden, but she had never cared for him the way she did about his brother. She sensed he had feelings for her, but because he was such a womanizer, she never took him seriously. Besides, deep inside she had believed everyone knew she belonged to Brenden.

She hung his doublet over a chair back. She hoped he would still be her friend. She came upon the chamber pot and knew that if she didn't empty it, no one else would. She sighed and threw on her cloak. That would be one advantage to being a countess; she wouldn't have to empty the chamber pots. She froze at the thought. She could not be the Countess of Irvine. The locket immediately came to mind. *From the Countess of Irvine*

Collection, belonging to the wife of Brenden Ross. It couldn't be her! She couldn't marry him.

The chill air wrapped its icy fingers around her as soon as she left the inn, but instead of clearing her head, it made it spin faster. It wasn't possible that she had already been here and stayed. What did this mean? She dumped the chamber pot at the side of the inn, and her stomach gripped sickeningly. She held onto the corner of the building and threw up. She sank to her knees, unable to stop the violent retching. She wiped her mouth and sat a moment, trying to regain her composure. She felt her cheeks and forehead. They were cool.

"What the hell was that all about?" she muttered. The snow was melting and soaking through her gown, making her shiver. She started to stand and heard a low, keening whine behind her. She froze, her hair practically standing on end. She stood unsteadily and turned, pressing her body against the wall.

It was a big black dog. If she didn't know better, she would swear it was the same one she had seen in the alley at York. It sat on its haunches in the snow, looking up at the inn, whining sadly. It shuffled to her, not quite standing on four legs. It nosed at her hand. She patted its head hesitantly, and it stopped whining.

She knelt beside it. Its eyes were a dark cobalt blue. She frowned. How unusual for a dog! She scratched its ears. It didn't look like a stray; its thick black coat was lustrous and clean.

"Go home, boy," she whispered.

It started whining again. She felt torn, it looked so sad, but it was freezing and she was feeling weak and light-headed. At the doorway, she turned back to look at it, but it was gone. She returned to her room and forced some of the bread and fruit down her throat. Her hands were shaking, but she refused to think of what her bout of sickness might mean. About what everything might really mean.

Had they both been wrong all along? Perhaps she wasn't here to help after all. Perhaps she had always been here, caught in this circle of time. She had no future anymore. Her future was the past that she had read in history books. The idea that she might die before her father was ever born was so staggering, she had to sit down. She sat, staring weakly into space for most of the morning.

Una, Gavin, and Audrey sat around the fire waiting for Brenden and Camden to return. It was very late, and they were all becoming worried. Una and Gavin were getting along very well; they held hands often, and Audrey had even witnessed them kissing. She thought it was very sweet and couldn't help but be happy for the two of them. They needed each other.

They heard loud voices and laughter outside the door that was immediately recognizable as Brenden and Camden. They all exchanged looks as the voices moved directly outside the door. There was some fumbling around and more laughter and finally the door swung open.

They were obviously inebriated and holding each other up as they stumbled into the room. They came to the table, and Camden set a bottle of whiskey in the center. They both looked around blankly for something to sit on. Gavin reached for the bottle, but Una frowned at him, causing him to immediately withdraw his hand.

Brenden, who had found a stool and pulled it pointedly next to Audrey, sat down and draped his arm around her. Her face felt as though it was on fire, and she tried to smile politely at Una, who was staring at them with a knowing grin.

She turned her head toward Brenden. "You are drunk!" she whispered.

"I'm not drunk," he said loudly.

"Hmm." The smell of whiskey clung to him rather thickly, which would have given evidence otherwise, had the silly grin and lack of volume control not given him away.

Camden was still standing, swaying slightly. "Why are you just sitting here? Were you waiting for us?"

"Yes," Audrey said. "We were getting worried. You were gone a long time."

Before Camden could say anything, Brenden stood, grabbing Audrey's arm and pulling her up with him. "I'm tired. Good evening." He nodded to everyone and dragged her out of the room.

She couldn't breathe, she was so mortified. She said nothing until they were in her room with the door closed. He locked it and turned to her with a predatory look in his eyes that had her pulse racing even though she was angry with him.

"What do you think you're doing?" she asked.

He was in front of her before she had a chance to move away. He wrapped his arms around her waist and lifted her. She had to grab his shoulders to steady herself as he buried his face in her neck and began kissing her. A second later she was flat on her back on the bed, and he was on top of her. Desire pooled in her belly, and her breath was coming short. But she couldn't allow him to treat her like this and tried shoving him away.

"Brenden! Stop—" she began. His mouth covered hers in an overwhelming kiss that pushed all thought from her mind but how urgently she needed him. She was sinking deeper into the bed and his kiss, when he pulled his lips away to look down at her.

"I knew you'd be properly submissive," he said. She stared back him dazedly until she realized what he was saying and began struggling again. He laughed and held her closer. "God, I love you, Audrey. I love the way you smell and the way you taste. I love the way you feel in my arms." She stopped moving and closed her eyes, her heart lodged somewhere in her throat. "Look at me." She obeyed. He was gazing at her adoringly, and she felt tears in her eyes. "I love your eyes. They've haunted me for so many years. I've thought of naught but you today. I couldn't wait to come back to you."

"Then why were you getting drunk with your brother?"

He laughed softly and his lips brushed hers with feathery kisses. "He and I needed to understand each other. I think we do."

It was all the explanation she needed at the moment, and she wrapped her arms around his neck, pulling his mouth down to hers.

One of the dresses was delivered the next day, and Camden insisted that Audrey model it for him. As Una helped her dress, Audrey found this garment to be far different from anything she'd worn previously. For starters, by the heft of it, she guessed it weighed a good five pounds, and that was just the dress part.

The shift was a sheer cream-colored linen called lawn and left little to the imagination. It had a low lace collar, not stiffened, at her insistence. Atop that, she wore stays that pushed her breasts to near overflowing. She was sure the men would appreciate it, but it made her incredibly uncomfortable. Una produced a piece of material called a partlet that, to Audrey's relief, was attached to the bodice and collar and covered her cleavage. Then came a kind of hoop skirt called a farthingale that tied at her waist. It had a circular wire hoop at hip level and fell straight down in a cylinder. This one was a deep rose silk.

The sleeveless bodice was heavy and stiff, with a brocaded pattern of rose-colored flowers with intertwining leaves on a black background. A triangular-shaped insert, called a stomacher, also extremely stiff, was placed in front of the bodice. It was made of the same brocaded fabric, but covered with lawn. It came down to a point almost to her crotch. The bodice and stomacher fit together with cleverly concealed ties. Several petticoats went under the farthingale. A kirtle went over this, made of the same fabric and slit in the front to show the farthingale.

Next, Una attached sleeves, brocaded also. They were thick and padded and fit closely at the wrist, with the frill from her shift peeking out. The collar lay along her neck and shoulders. Underneath, she wore silk stockings, tied with embroidered bands above her knee, and green silk slippers.

It was hideous. Audrey hated it.

When Camden came in to inspect her, she glared at him. "What about her hair? She can't wear it like that," he said to Una. "Did we get her a head rail or bonnet?"

Una pushed Audrey down on a stool. She thought she might suffocate in the prison of a dress she wore. She had to perch on the edge of the stool in order to get any air into her lungs. Una parted her hair in the middle and twisted it, making rolls at the sides and braiding it at the back. She wound the braid into a bun and placed a small hood of lawn, edged with lace, on her head. It had wire running through the front of it, so it dipped over her forehead.

Audrey gratefully stood again, swallowing mouthfuls of air. Camden examined her critically, rubbing the blond whiskers on his chin.

"Well?" she asked impatiently.

He just grinned and unwrapped a parcel he had brought in with him. It was a long, gilded, silver chain. He fastened it around her waist. Suspended from it was a small rectangular mirror, a large hollow silver ball with perforations in it, and a small watch with only an hour hand.

"What is that?" Audrey asked, touching the chain. She looked in the mirror. "Yikes!" she cried, upon seeing her hair.

"This," Camden said touching the chain. "Is a girdle. And this"—he touched the ball—"is a pomander."

She brought it to her face to get a closer look and was assaulted by an overpowering smell. She dropped it as though it were hot.

"God! What's in it!" She covered her nose.

Camden laughed. "'Tis cloves. You breathe it when you're around diseased folk, to keep away the illness."

"Uh-huh . . . and does it work?"

"'Tis doubtful." He winked, knowing after the things she had told him about the future that it didn't.

"Do people really dress like this?" she gasped.

"Aye, the seamstress assured me this was what all noblewomen in England wear in the presence of their queen." He stepped back again. "Now that's a lady fit for any court, wouldn't you say?" he inquired of Una.

"Oh, aye, she's bonny all right."

Audrey was pleased she passed the test but was anxious to remove the clothes. She walked to the bed.

"No, no, no, no, no!" Camden cried.

"What?" Audrey stopped, looking at him in dismay.

He shook his head vigorously. "You walk as though you've something up your arse. I know you've never worn this manner of clothing before, but let's not announce it to the world!"

Audrey looked at him helplessly. "But Camden," she whined. "I can't breathe! I don't think I could bend over if I tried!" A thought struck her. "How do I relieve myself with this on?"

"You're asking me?" He waved at Una, giving her the floor on this particular topic. But she was at a loss as well. "I'm sure when the time comes, you'll figure something out," Camden said, bubbling over with mirth.

He spent the next half hour making her walk around the room until he was satisfied with the way she carried herself. She was about to undress when Brenden and Gavin returned from the village.

Brenden dropped some leather garments on the table. "She looks like she's in pain," he observed, nudging Camden.

"I wager she'll live," Camden returned, and laughed as she struggled to remove one of her slippers to hurl at him. Finding the task too difficult, she fell onto the bed and lay there pouting.

Brenden dismissed the others and sat next to her. He regarded her with sympathy. "Shall I play maid to you?"

"Please," she said, desperate to be out of the clothing. He pulled her back up to standing and, after much cursing, removed everything but the shift and stockings.

"I like this." He slid his hands down the length of her body, looking at the shift. She pulled away from him, enjoying the ability to breathe deeply and move freely. She walked to the table to look at what he had brought back from the village. There was a short jacket made of thick tough leather with metal plates sewn into it.

"What's this?"

"A jack. I can't be a proper guard, dressed like this." He walked behind her and ran his hand over her backside. "God's bones, woman, I can see everything you've got through that thing."

"Like it, do you?" She pressed herself against him.

He kissed her in answer, his lips and tongue gently exploring hers. He took her face in his hands and looked down at her. His breath fanned warmly against her lips.

"'Tis our last night together . . . for a bit."

"But it isn't night yet."

"Then it seems we have an early start," he said, before his mouth descended on hers.

❧ 14 ❧

Fotheringhay was a fortress. Two moats surrounded the hulking pile of masonry. A bridge connected to a lowered drawbridge led to the only entrance. Gavin and Audrey rode nervously to the monstrous gatehouse and waited for the portcullis to be raised.

Gavin's part was simply to play himself, Lady Tara Ross's half brother, escorting her into the service of the queen prisoner. He was dressed in finery, a black velvet doublet, trimmed with silver cloth, and black breeches. Black leather boots with gleaming silver buckles and a black velvet bonnet, also trimmed with silver, completed the picture. The sword and scabbard that hung from his slim hips were of shining silver, engraved and enameled with gold. He had a dagger at his waist, the hilt inset with several large jewels.

He was a handsome sight to behold, and Una had been swooning before they left. The clothing was a loan from Nicholas Jennings, a wealthy merchant in Northampton who was a business associate of Brenden's and with whom they had been staying while the message was conveyed to Sir Amyas Paulet that Lady Ross had arrived. Gavin and Una would continue in residence with Nicholas until they received word that it was time for them to flee.

Audrey was also dressed in black, as they were still in mourning for Fillip. Her mourning gown was a great deal more comfortable than her other new dresses.

Her eyes searched the guards on duty for Brenden and Camden but didn't see them. She wondered if any of the other guards were Brenden's men. They dismounted in the courtyard. She took Gavin's arm and followed a guard into the keep.

Audrey held onto Gavin tightly, and he patted her hand awkwardly, giving her a reassuring smile. They entered a great, brooding hall and were led to a set of huge oak double doors, where one of the guards removed Gavin's weapons. As the doors opened, Gavin leaned down and whispered in her ear, "Just keep your mouth shut." She had been instructed to speak as little as possible, in the hope that the peculiarities of her speech would go unnoticed.

They were ushered into the large study.

"Gavin Ross of Creag Liath and his sister, Lady Tara Ross," a man dressed in brown announced, before backing up to blend into the woodwork. The study was finer than the portion of the prison she'd seen so far. Shelves holding leather-bound volumes lined the walls. A large oak desk stood before them, but the man sitting behind it didn't bother to rise.

Sir Amyas Paulet was a middle-aged man with a rapidly receding hairline. A bushy mustache covered his upper lip and framed a weak chin. He was dressed somberly in black, with a starched white collar ruff at his neck. His doublet looked as though it was stuffed with something, giving him an unnatural potbelly.

He motioned for them to come closer. His small black eyes surveyed them coldly. He leaned forward, scanning his desktop. He picked up a parchment.

"Ah, here it is. You are daughter of Alistair Ross, fifth Earl of Irvine." His eyes darted to Gavin. "And you must be one of his bastards."

The muscles in Gavin's arm flexed under her hand, but his face remained impassive. "None other," Gavin replied, his icy tone matching Paulet's.

Audrey bowed her head, murmuring a greeting as Camden taught her. Paulet nodded curtly.

Gavin reached inside his doublet, retrieved a letter sealed with wax, and dropped it on the desk. Paulet picked up the letter but made no move to open it. He continued to inspect them, tapping the letter against his jaw.

"So you have come to serve your queen."

"Aye, she has," Gavin answered for her.

"She is a most tedious prisoner. She shall bore you to tears with her endless speeches on the unfairness of her life. Tell me, you are Protestant, correct?" When Gavin nodded, he continued. "Your father stood against her at Carberry, if memory serves me. What business have you with the papist?" He was looking at Audrey and arched an eyebrow sardonically when Gavin answered.

"The women in our family have served the queens of Scotland for centuries, regardless of religion."

Paulet pursed his lips together thoughtfully. "Burnes," he called sharply. The man who had announced them stepped forward. "Summon Hildie." The man nodded and disappeared. Paulet's attention turned once more to them.

"I think she will not accept you." He smiled humorlessly. "But I will send you to her anyway." He opened the letter and began reading it. At one point he snorted at something and glanced up at them but made no comment.

Burnes returned with a large broad-faced woman who could only be Hildie.

"Sir?" Burnes queried, making his return known.

"Take them in there." He waved to a door. "Inspect them, every inch." He directed his attention back to them. "If I find this is part of one of her popish plots, it will be you who is under lock and key." He motioned for Burnes to continue.

They were shoved roughly into the adjoining room. A screen was set up; Hildie and Audrey took one side, Gavin and Burnes, the other. She was subjected to a thorough and rather humiliating bodily inspection. Hildie stank strongly of unwashed body, and her hands were clammy. Dirt was caked under her ragged fingernails.

At one point Audrey heard Gavin say in a low and dangerous voice. "Put your hand there again, bugger, and I'll break it." It seemed he wasn't faring any better.

Gavin's face was grim when they returned to Paulet's office. "English hospitality. I forget how much I enjoy it until I'm subjected to it again."

Paulet gave them another of his emotionless smiles. Burnes informed him they were clean, and Paulet reminded him to search her trunk when it arrived. He turned his attention to matters on his desk, an obvious dismissal.

Gavin cleared his throat. "I will be traveling back this way shortly. Will I be permitted to call on my sister?"

"No," Paulet answered, not even looking up.

A muscle twitched in Gavin's jaw, and his lips

thinned. Burnes ushered them back out, closing the doors behind them. Gavin's weapons were returned.

"This is where we part, sister," Gavin said sadly.

Audrey's throat tightened, and she hugged him. She was terrified. After Brenden had left her in Northampton, the doubts began again. This was foolish! Doomed to failure! What was she thinking? But here she was. Every time she thought about what he had gone through in Denmark, though, she found herself going through the motions, against her better judgment.

He wiped a tear from her cheek and planted a kiss on it. "Take care and God bless." She watched him walk away, so tall and straight, and felt hollow inside.

Burnes gestured for her to follow him. He led her through the courtyard to a gray stone tower at the corner of the keep. She was amazed at the number of guards garrisoned at the castle. The place was teeming with them, but she recognized none, until they arrived at the octagonal tower. Two sentries were posted outside the door. One stood about her height, with sandy blond hair, a short beard hugging his jaw, and dark-green eyes. His stocky frame was clothed in a buff overcoat and leather breeches. Camden gave no indication he recognized her, but her heart felt lighter just the same.

He nodded to Burnes, an uncommon stoic expression on his face, and opened the heavy door for them. They ascended the crude stone steps until they reached a landing with another thick wooden door. Two more sentries were posted there, and one of them unlocked the door.

Several people were situated around the room. They all stood and made their way over, clustering around them. There were two middle-aged women, and six men of various ages. Audrey looked at the two women curiously, wondering which one was the queen and to whom she should kneel.

"Pray, tell who our visitor is." The voice, speaking with a soft Scottish burr, was approaching from behind the men. One moved aside quickly, bowing his head a fraction.

A sense of unreality washed over Audrey, and she was close to doing her dream check, something she hadn't done in weeks. It was the woman from Audrey's dreams. She stood several inches taller than Audrey, towering over most of the men in the room, despite her stooped shoulders. She was in her forties and thickening around the middle. She wore a voluminous black velvet gown, a rosary hanging from her neck and another from the girdle about her waist. A starched ruff of modest size circled her throat, parting under the chin.

This was the face Audrey recognized, yet different. She looked old and haggard, with a double chin. She wasn't very attractive, though she was not a homely woman. But there was a regal air about her that Audrey already sensed. The queen shuffled forward as if walking were painful, and one of the women rushed to her side to lend a supporting hand.

"Lady Tara Ross," Burnes announced, and left, the door slamming shut behind him. Shaking herself from her stupor of shock and remembering what she had been taught, Audrey dropped to her knees, her head bent.

"Greetings, Your Grace." She quickly snatched the hood of the cloak off her head.

"You may rise."

Audrey stood and met the amber eyes that scrutinized her. The queen's hair was dark auburn, but Audrey was almost certain it was a wig. Her nose was long and thin, and she had a wide mouth. It was raised slightly at the corners in a smile.

Uncertain whether she should speak or ask for permission, Audrey began hesitantly. "I come to serve you, as we were informed you have recently lost a most loyal servant, Elizabeth Curle. I know I cannot take her place but can only hope to ease your burden in the days ahead." Did she say that right? It sounded so strange coming out of her mouth, but no one made any move or gesture to indicate she had committed some breach of etiquette.

The queen looked at her thoughtfully. "I thank you, my lady Ross. Now please, join me. I should like to find out more about you if you are to serve me."

Audrey smiled and followed. The queen lowered herself, with the aid of one of the women, into a beautiful carved oak chair with a lavishly embroidered seat pillow. Not much of a prison, Audrey reflected, looking around the chamber they occupied. It was small, but the furniture was fine and colorful tapestries hung on the walls. A low stool was brought and positioned near the queen's feet for Audrey to sit on.

She waved the others away. "You are Scots?"

"Yes."

"I knew your father. He sat on my Privy Council on occasion . . . when he deigned to answer my summons, that is."

Audrey lowered her eyes. "He's always been a busy man, your highness."

"Aye." There was humor in her voice. "He had many sons to sire, if I remember correctly. He brought three of them to see me in France. Bonny lads, they were. Tell me, what of your brothers now? For I have heard little of your family since my incarceration. Only that your father is well and thriving under my son's rule."

"My brother Fillip died several months ago. As for my other brothers, they are well."

"Please accept my condolences on your loss," she said gently.

"Thank you." Audrey bowed her head, feigning sadness.

"What of you? Have you no husband? He cannot care to have you so far away, serving the papist queen."

When Audrey met her eyes again, she was sure the queen saw through the whole ruse. Audrey had the urge to tell her everything right then. But Brenden had said no, she needed to be assured of Audrey's goodness or she would surely suspect a plot against her after all she'd been through. Audrey didn't feel that lying to the queen from the beginning was going to inspire a great deal of trust, but the men were all in agreement that this was the only way to do it.

"I'm widowed."

"I must offer you my condolences once again, dear Tara. It seems you've had many hardships of late."

"But none as woeful as the one I find my queen in." Camden had instructed Audrey on the stroking of a sovereign's ego and had stressed that it must be done at regular intervals during any conversation. Audrey was finding it easier than she had imagined.

"Not woeful, Tara. No, never that. For this life has a purpose, one I have not recognized until recently." She eyed Audrey shrewdly. "It seems so odd that you should be sent to replace my dear Elizabeth. And so convenient. Your father signed a bond to kill my second husband, Lord Darnley. Did you know that?" Audrey shook her head. "No, of course, he wouldn't tell you. I only learned of it myself from my third husband, Lord Bothwell. Did you know he also signed another bond, endorsing my marriage to Bothwell?" Audrey shook her head again. Did Brenden know all this? "Oh, aye, Lord

Irvine, as well as the other lords, were very fond of signing bonds. I heard he signed yet a third one, to take Bothwell's life a short time after we wed."

Audrey's mouth was dry, and she could barely manage to swallow. The queen didn't miss her small act of nervousness.

"So I must wonder," she said, cocking her head thoughtfully, "what his daughter is doing here in my service. True, your aunt was a maid to me some twenty years ago, but for you, Lord Irvine's daughter, to come all the way to England and with my execution drawing so near . . ." She pursed her lips together, her expression hardening.

"I don't know what your highness is getting at. I'm here in goodwill, I assure you." Audrey's palms were sweating, and she laid them flat on her gown.

"This is part of the secret death Queen Elizabeth has planned for me, so her hands are not stained with my blood. I will not allow it!"

The women hovered close, keeping a watchful eye on the proceedings.

"No, no! That isn't why I'm here! I swear it!"

She eyed Audrey with disbelief. "What is your role? To place a poison in my drink? To admit the assassin in the dead of night? Or perhaps you shall do the deed yourself."

"Your Highness." Audrey dropped to her knees and lowered her head. "I wouldn't dream of committing such vile acts against your person. I am your humble servant." Her heart hammered against her ribs and sweat trickled between her breasts. How could this have gone so horribly wrong so quickly? Why wasn't this something Brenden had anticipated?

The queen said nothing for a long moment. Audrey's

knees were beginning to ache, and she was about to get up on her own.

"Please rise," she said. Audrey sat back on the stool, giving her a pleading look. "I know not why, but I trust you. I believe what you say." The tension drained from Audrey's body, until she heard the queen's next words. "But my judgment has always been flawed in the past, and I now find myself in a dilemma."

"You are not wrong to put your trust in me," Audrey said, causing the queen to smile.

"Then you shall stay."

It wasn't long before Audrey was settled. The queen had four rooms at her disposal, two downstairs and two upstairs. The ones on the lower floor appeared to be the "day" rooms; the ones on the upper floor, sleeping rooms. The queen had a large canopied bed, and several pallets and blankets—the subjects' sleeping accommodations—were stacked against the wall. The men slept elsewhere in the castle, and Audrey could see why, since the adjoining room was more of a closet.

She hung her cloak on a peg and was given a chest for her garments when they arrived. She descended the stairs in time to see their dinner being laid out. A trestle table was brought from against the wall, and stools were pulled up around it. The queen's chair was placed at the head.

Two sentries entered with serving girls, and the table was set with a modest meal. The smell of food made Audrey's stomach churn. It was doing a lot of that lately. It appeared the bout of nausea she had suffered wasn't an aberration, as she had hoped. Her period was well over a month late, and her nausea was becoming an increasing discomfort.

She did her best to hide it the week after Brenden left. It wasn't hard. Gavin and Una both knew Audrey's true feelings about the plot and attributed it to nerves. She was glad they hadn't suspected, because she desperately didn't want Brenden to know. She had no idea what his reaction might be. He had said he loved her, although he'd been drunk and had wanted to have sex at the time, so she didn't put too much weight on the declaration. Regardless of his true feelings, and her own, for she knew without a doubt she was in love with him, she couldn't stay. Especially if she were pregnant! She thought her child deserved a chance to live, and the odds for that dropped sharply by simply giving birth in this century.

Besides, she knew that once Brenden found out, whether he loved her or not, he would drag her to the altar. And she didn't know if she wanted to be married to him. He was unstable. What would happen when his father died and he became the earl? She couldn't remember what Ian MacKay had said, but Brenden had been doing nothing but plotting for the past eight years—what did he know about being an earl? No, the best thing for her to do was to go back to Drochaid when this was over, walk through that wall, and never look back.

The queen was walking slowly and painfully to the table. One of the women and a man approached Audrey while the others were seating themselves.

"I'm Barbra Curle, and this is Andrew Melville." The woman gestured to the man standing next to her. He was middle-aged and shorter than Audrey. He had a compact, athletic build and dark-brown eyes and hair. He smiled charmingly at Audrey.

Audrey nodded her head politely. Barbra took a

wooden trencher and began filling it with the various foods from the table. Everyone else chatted quietly, making no move to do the same. Andrew simply stood there, grinning at Audrey whenever she looked at him.

When Barbra was finished, she held the trencher out to Audrey. Audrey looked between her and Andrew in confusion.

"For me?" she asked in a low voice, frowning at them.

Barbra nodded and continued proffering it. Audrey's confusion was mounting. She was doing something wrong and had no idea what. Damn Camden!

Andrew leaned close. "Taste it." He made a little jerking motion with his head. She hesitantly took a piece of the hen and popped it in her mouth. It was good. She nodded and smiled. They still looked at her, so Audrey tasted a little bit of everything on the trencher.

"It's good," Audrey said, shrugging helplessly. "The vegetables are overcooked and a bit tasteless, but edible."

Barbra nodded, a small smile on her face. She withdrew the trencher but continued to stare at Audrey. Andrew bowed his head, but Audrey saw dimples deeply indenting his cheeks and knew he was laughing at her. She was doing something very wrong and was completely oblivious of what it was. Finally, Barbra nodded to Andrew, but instead of tasting it himself, he began presenting the different platters to the queen with great ceremony, holding a rod before him. He murmured some fawning words, and the queen smiled at him.

The others filled their trenchers, and Andrew returned to Audrey's side, urging her to follow suit. She picked up the plate she had tasted from, but she had very little appetite. The little scene had increased her nausea tenfold. She sat on an empty stool at the end of the table, and Andrew sat beside her.

"You haven't the slightest idea what is happening, have you?" he asked, his voice rife with amusement.

She shook her head and began eating, hoping he would elaborate.

"You were tasting for poison."

She choked, spewing the food in her mouth across the table. Everyone turned to look at her except Andrew, who was studiously inspecting the fowl before him.

"Does the meal meet with your approval?" the queen asked.

"Oh, yes, very good. Thank you." Audrey was trying to clean up the chewed food and spittle from the table. The man sitting across from her smiled weakly and seemed to have lost his appetite. "Good chicken." Everyone looked at her oddly, and she willed herself not to start babbling. Her cheeks felt like a furnace, and she riveted her eyes to her plate.

She tried to take her mind off her humiliation by imagining both Brenden and Camden lying on the ground, writhing in pain while she stoned them to death.

"You really did not know," Andrew said, chuckling softly.

She met his eyes. "What would you have done had I fallen to the ground convulsing?"

"I wouldn't have fed the food to the queen." He shrugged. "Anyway, we needed to be certain you were not an assassin. Had you poisoned the food, you wouldn't have tasted it."

Audrey added a third party to her stoning fantasy, her new fellow subject, Andrew. "What about me? I would be dead!" she said through clenched teeth.

"And died in service to your queen." He looked serious now, which made her angrier.

"I'm sure that would console my grieving family greatly."

He tried to remain serious, but his face broke out in a smile, and he shrugged again.

So this was part of her duties? Putting her life on the line every time the queen ate something! That was three times a day! What if she liked to snack? Audrey's stomach lurched sickeningly, and she forced the bile back down her throat, lest they think it was some form of poisoning and go into a panic. For the queen.

After a moment, she decided to humble herself. Andrew seemed an all-right kind of guy. Maybe he could help her. "I haven't done this before, so I'm not sure exactly what I'm supposed to be doing," she confessed.

"No!" His eyes widened in mock surprise. "I'm sorry. I'm sorry," he said when she glared menacingly at him. "It's easy. Your duties will be preparing the queen's bed and bath . . . and other associated activities." Audrey could see "cleaning the closestool" in large blinking lights. "There really isn't so much to do. Read to her or sing to her if she asks. She craves companionship as much as anything. We are very isolated."

"Tara," Audrey heard the queen say, not realizing for a moment that the queen was addressing her.

"Your Grace?" she answered hastily.

"I believe I've been frightfully rude by not making introductions. This is Father de Preau, my almoner." She motioned to the priest sitting across from Audrey, who inclined his head politely. "Jane Kennedy and Barbra Curle." The two women on either side of her. "Balthazzar, my tailor." She indicated a decrepit yet kind-looking old man with watery eyes. "Jacques Gervais, my apothecary, Dominique Bourgoing, my physician, and Pierre Gorion, my surgeon." They all exchanged polite greetings. "I believe you are acquainted with Andrew." Audrey smiled thinly at him.

The rest of the meal passed pleasantly enough, but the conversation was often in French, to her chagrin. When it was over, the serving girls appeared to remove the platters and trenchers. Audrey was just deciding to seek out the closestool, with the intention of depositing her lunch in it, when the door flew open, crashing against the wall.

Two sentries came in lugging Audrey's trunk. One, the dearest sight her eyes could behold, was Brenden. His beard had grown thicker, and his hair was ruffled from the wind. He looked enormous to her, clad in tough leather, amid these men of smaller stature. His green eyes passed over her, lingering for the barest second.

Her trunk was dropped on the floor with a thud. The lid lifted momentarily before slamming back down. They turned to leave, but annoyance ran through her at the state of her belongings. Her clothing was hanging out of the trunk, and some of it was torn.

"What is this?" she cried, running to the trunk and opening it. The lock had been pried open and was ruined. "Was it necessary to destroy my things in your search?"

Brenden's shoulders stiffened. Both he and the other sentry turned to her. "We had orders to search your belongings." His voice was flat and emotionless, but there was the barest warning in his eyes telling her to drop it. He was certainly playing his part with zeal. He was the one who had spent a small fortune having her clothes made quickly. Only for him to ruin them before she even wore them?

"Is there so fine a line between search and mutilate that you idiots don't know the difference?" Audrey held up a shift with the sleeve partially ripped off. She gasped in horror when she saw one of her bodices was ripped apart, separating the cloth from the boardlike material that stiffened it.

"The prisoner has been quite ingenious in the past in concealing her intrigues. We cannot be too careful," Brenden replied, stone-faced.

"In my bodice? You think something's hidden in my bodice?" But she was met with the slam of the door, and the key turning in the lock. She threw it down and turned to the others, hands on hips, still puffing with indignation.

The queen took one look at Audrey's face and started laughing. "Oh, Tara, you do me good! If you are expecting courtesy or courtly charms from those oafs, don't waste your time." She motioned for Audrey to join her and the other women seated about the fire.

"Balthazzar will repair your garments." She motioned for him to do so. The old man walked slowly to Audrey's trunk and began rifling through it.

"Thank you," Audrey said.

The queen and the other women were embroidering. Barbra rummaged in a basket by her feet, withdrew a square of velvet in a wooden frame, and handed it to her. Audrey looked at it with apprehension. She didn't know how to embroider! She did know how to sew. It couldn't be all that different. Barbra handed her a needle and some silken cord in purple. She smiled wanly and inspected the pattern.

It was a coat of arms. Luckily for her, it was already started, and she could see where she needed to continue the purple. She looked surreptitiously at the others' work. It was different than hers, but she could see how they were stitching.

"What did you think of Paulet?" the queen asked, glancing at Audrey momentarily.

"He was pompous and rude and subjected me to a humiliating bodily inspection."

The others gasped in horror, and even the queen appeared surprised. "He examined you himself?"

"Oh, no. It was a woman named Hildie, but it couldn't have been more disgusting had he done it himself."

They all laughed.

"Ah, Hildie. I think she finds water repellent, by the stink of her," the queen commented, smiling ruefully.

"Perhaps Paulet does not allow bathing," Jane Kennedy said wickedly. "He's afraid it will wash the purity from her heretic soul."

They all found this uproariously funny, so Audrey smiled.

"I'm sorry, Tara," the queen said, then turned to Jane. "Tara's family is Protestant." Jane's mouth formed a little O of embarrassment.

The queen smiled. "Andrew is Protestant as well, but not of the Puritan variety."

"Really, don't mind me. I'm not practicing," Audrey informed them. She didn't want them watching everything they said around her, afraid she would be offended.

The queen looked at Audrey with interest. "So you're not a follower of the late John Knox?"

"No. Who is he?" They gaped at her and she could have kicked herself. This was someone she should know about! Damn those Ross brothers!

"Well," the queen began, giving Audrey a strange look, "he was the instigator of my downfall." She shook her head. "Well, one of them. There were so many! He was leader of the reformed church in Scotland. His sermons incited rebellion more than once." Audrey vaguely remembered reading about him now, though too late to do her any good. The queen was nodding at her. "Ah, yes, I was the harlot queen. The jezebel cast out by God. Would he have lived to see this day! He wanted me burned for my religion then, and I will die for it now. But it will not be as he hoped, for they fear me. They fear me for all I stand for and others who see their path through my death."

Audrey was immobilized by her little speech. Not so much the words, but the look on her face. Audrey was by no means a religious woman, but the queen's countenance was the very definition of grace and serenity. And power. She saw power that she could not wield as a monarch coming through her death. Fear gripped Audrey. The queen wanted to die.

Audrey lay on a pallet staring into the fire. Everyone else was asleep, except the queen. The queen was at her embroidered kneeler praying silently to the crucifix on the wall. Audrey imagined that with her rheumatism, she must be very uncomfortable. But the queen didn't shift or move. She merely knelt quietly, hands clasped.

Audrey had made it through her first day as one of the queen's ladies. The rest of the day had been uneventful. Barbra and Audrey had aired and brushed the queen's already clean gowns, while Andrew bent studiously over ledgers, not appearing to do much.

The queen read some and embroidered. Barbra and

Audrey, accompanied by two sentries, took the chamber pots downstairs to be cleaned. When they were returning to the tower, Audrey made an offhand comment to one of the sentries, but he completely ignored her. Barbra informed her that they were not allowed to speak to them without Paulet or a superior present. The queen had a reputation for gaining the sympathy of her jailers, and Paulet wasn't taking any chances. They were harshly punished if they appeared solicitous in any way.

The evening meal passed without her being poisoned, after which they played cards. The day ended with Father de Preau saying prayers that accommodated both the Catholics and Protestants in their group.

Audrey was finding the concept of royalty confusing. She was not the only seemingly useless person in the queen's service. Audrey figured the queen could probably do away with all the women except one and combine the duties of the men. And Barbra commented on how the household had been reduced when they moved to Fotheringhay!

Audrey thought again how foolish all this was. She understood now why the plot would fail. The queen wanted to die! And Audrey was putting her child's life as well as her own in danger for nothing. Why was she here?

She turned over, but sleep was not forthcoming. She heard the queen rise and shuffle slowly to her bed. Audrey was right about the queen wearing a wig. She was clad in only her shift, and her hair was short and gray. She was only in her forties! She seemed so much older.

"What is it, Tara? You do not sleep." Her voice drifted softly to Audrey.

"It's been an unusual day, and I'm not tired," Audrey whispered back. She leaned on her elbow to see the queen better. She stood by the bed holding a candle. She motioned for Audrey to join her. She was having some difficulty getting into bed, so Audrey helped her.

"I'm glad you have come to me, Tara. You're like a spring breeze blowing through this hateful prison, with your youth and spirit. You make me feel young again."

Her eyes were wistful, and for just a moment, Audrey thought she could see her as a young woman. How regal she must have been! Standing almost six feet tall, with flowing auburn hair and lean aristocratic features. The woman who had captured the heart of Brenden's dear Lord Bothwell. Audrey wondered if she thought about him often.

"I'm happy I'm able to bring some happiness into your life," Audrey said, and meant it.

"It pains me greatly to think of how the others have suffered for me. Their imprisonment is voluntary, yet I have watched them let their lives slip by. I think God has made me suffer for my sins by making me witness the pain I cause those I love the most. I'm happy your own sentence with me will be short-lived." She looked truly sad, and Audrey's heart went out to her.

"It's not a sentence, Your Grace. I'm here of my own free will. I'll stay as long as you need me."

"My days are numbered. I feel it."

Audrey's secret pressed against her chest. She wanted to get it over with. Maybe if the queen knew there was a chance of rescue, she would change her mind.

"Maybe there's still hope," came out instead.

"Hope for what? My only escape is through death." This was said with that look of serenity once again coming over the queen's face. She welcomed it!

"I have heard Queen Elizabeth is merciful. Maybe she doesn't mean to execute you after all."

"Imprisoning me unjustly and subjecting a foreign sovereign to English law is merciful?" the queen whispered incredulously. "She is not merciful. She fears the shedding of royal blood, but only because it might lead to the spilling of her own. Nay, I must die. What I fear most is it will be a secret undertaking and I will not be given the public death I desire." Her face looked strange in the candlelight, and for a moment, Audrey was frightened of her, as though she were already dead.

"What about escape?"

"Impossible. Walsingham has gone to great lengths to stamp me out. For all of Paulet's pomposity, he runs a tight prison and runs it well. Nay, there is no hope for escape."

Audrey couldn't resist. "But what if it were possible?"

"I'm weary of plotting and intrigues." Her shoulders slumped tiredly. "It has always been a loathsome yet necessary task for me. I rejoice to wash my hands of it."

Audrey chewed her lip nervously; the words were poised on the edge of her tongue, waiting to spill out. The queen studied Audrey's face in the dark.

"Oh, dear Lord, no," she groaned. "Please spare me, I cannot hear it!"

"But your highness," Audrey grasped the queen's hand, and it lay limp in hers. "Lord Brenden Ross is here within these very walls with a garrison of soldiers. And Paulet thinks they're the English queen's men!"

The queen clapped her hands over her ears, shaking her head. "Silence!" she hissed.

Audrey obeyed and sat quietly. The queen's eyes were shut tightly as if she could completely block Audrey out. She slowly lowered her hands and regarded Audrey warily.

"You must cease this folly you have dreamed up," she said in a low voice. Audrey shook her head. "I command you." Her voice was harsh. "Who are you?"

"Audrey Williams. The man who wishes to free you is Brenden Ross."

"Why? Why is he doing this? Is he a fool?" Before Audrey could answer, she rushed on. "You would heap more suffering upon me? Have not enough brave men died in my name?"

"It's not for you that he does it."

Audrey was apprehensive about revealing this part. Brenden had told her of the necessity of it, and she had agreed with him. But if the queen truly loved Bothwell, it would be like reopening a wound and throwing salt in it.

"Then for whom, pray tell, does he undertake such an assignment doomed to failure?"

Audrey exhaled slowly. "Your late husband, Lord Bothwell."

She couldn't have looked more stricken had Audrey slapped her across the face. She stared at Audrey, speechless. When she finally found her voice, she was angry.

"What are these falsehoods you claim? Your words are fair, but such a thing is impossible! My husband died in prison over eight years ago."

"I know. Brenden shared a dungeon with him the last two years of his life." The queen was shaking, and Audrey became alarmed. "I'm not lying to you. He was imprisoned in Dragsholm in 1576. His only friend for two years was Bothwell. When Bothwell died, he made Brenden promise not to let you suffer the same fate."

"Stop! I beseech you! I cannot bear it!" Her hands were over her ears again and her voice was rising. Jane shifted and mumbled something in her sleep.

"Your Highness, I beg you, we must not wake the others!"

The queen wrapped her arms around her stomach and rocked back and forth. Tears streamed down her face, but she was being quieter.

"I'm sorry, I didn't mean to upset you." It sounded lame, but the queen didn't seem to hear. Audrey's own eyes were blurring from watching her. She awkwardly patted the queen's shoulder. The queen was lying on her side and turned her face into the pillow. Her body shook with silent sobs. When she was still, Audrey started to rise.

"Don't leave." Her voice was weak, and Audrey didn't move. "Lie with me." She patted the bed next to her. Audrey slid beside her, pulling the covers over them both. Their faces were a few inches apart.

"The few letters I received from him were all within the first few years of our imprisonment. Our communications were secret, of course, so there may have been more I never received. I never knew if he received mine." Her eyes became watery again. "In the last, he released me from our wedding vows. Without the burden of him, he thought I might regain my throne." She had to stop talking to compose herself. "I heard how he died. Was it . . . was it so awful?" Audrey nodded. The queen bit her bottom lip, squeezing her eyes shut, but tears escaped to stain her pillow.

"He wasn't alone. Brenden loved him dearly." She looked at Audrey, her trembling mouth trying to form a smile. "His last thoughts were for you. He loved you."

"You cannot know how much this means to me. Going so many years without a word . . . then hearing of his death." She swallowed hard. "Most of the time it seems more like a faraway dream. A tale of love and tragedy I read. There are days when I cannot conjure his face before me, no matter how hard I try. And I wonder, was it ever real?"

Audrey was crying, her hand covering her mouth to stifle it. The queen's eyes were distant, and Audrey knew she was with Bothwell again.

"He was always there to protect me, my brave knight. And when he was gone, I felt abandoned. But he hasn't abandoned me." She smiled at Audrey. The serenity had returned to her face, although her eyes were red-rimmed. "He's come back to me now when I need him most. His spirit will protect me."

"So you're with us, then?" Audrey asked, relief washing over her.

"No, there will be no escape. You must inform Lord Ross. I will not risk either of your lives."

"But . . . but this is what Bothwell wanted," Audrey stammered. "What about all I've just told you?"

"The gift you have given me is priceless. Since the moment I realized I loved him, he was the only person I could share it with. Not only have you given me a final message from him, but I've been able to bare my heart to you. I feel as though a weight has been lifted from it." She gripped Audrey's hand tightly beneath the covers.

"Do you really prefer death over freedom?" Audrey asked in disbelief.

"My dear, dear friend. For me, death is freedom."

🍃 15 🍃

Audrey loathed the thought of informing Brenden that his plan wouldn't work because the stubborn prisoner wanted to die. And in spite of the apparent comfort of her lodgings, it was still a prison. The queen wasn't even allowed to walk outside. Audrey was beginning to see that the queen had suffered greatly, was still suffering. And she wished she could help her. Could the past really be altered? But it wasn't the past any longer, was it? At the moment, it was very much Audrey's present.

She approached the queen the next morning after the Catholics had conducted a private mass in one of the adjoining chambers. The others were going about their morning duties, which would be finished soon enough, leaving much time for idleness. The queen seated herself at her desk, smoothing out a piece of paper to compose a letter.

"Your Highness? May I have a word with you?" The queen nodded, and Audrey pulled up a stool. "I beg you to reconsider. Lord Ross has many men garrisoned here, right under Paulet's nose. He has a ship waiting to sail you to France when we escape. I won't tell you it's foolproof, but I think there's a good chance for success."

She sighed. "Audrey, I know this is difficult for you to understand, but you must. In the past I was weak and did many things wrong. But while I did them, I never thought, 'I am sinning.' It was always later, upon reflection, that I realized how I had failed God in so many ways. I will not fail Him now."

"If you die, there will be no chance to redress those wrongs. And what about the injustice that has been done to you? You are wrongfully imprisoned! Surely you don't plan to let them win?"

"This is the only way I can win!" Her eyes took on an intense, feverish glaze. "You're mistaken to think there is a better way. I was a tolerant and merciful ruler when what Scotland needed was a tyrant. I was reviled by my Protestant subjects for being Catholic and disdained by my religion for being tolerant. I've never understood why we cannot coexist, but alas, we cannot. It's unthinkable Scotland would subject itself to my rule again. No, I can deliver no justice."

"But you would be free! You could live in France. You have family there, don't you?"

"You contradict yourself, dear Audrey! By virtue of my very blood, I am a queen. An anointed prince, who has to answer to no one but God for my actions. I cannot retire to the country, when, as you have pointed out, so much injustice has been heaped upon my person. I fear the reckoning has been a long time coming. I have this last offering for Him. The one thing that can make it all worthwhile."

"So you plan to die a martyr?" Audrey couldn't keep the scorn from her voice.

"I'm of little use to Him contained within this body."

"It sounds to me like you're giving up." Which was

what Audrey was getting ready to do. Whether she agreed with the queen or not, she couldn't refute her arguments. Hell, she couldn't understand her arguments! She had no deep religion, nor had she any concept of ruling a country.

The queen laughed. "Now you sound like Bothwell, trying to antagonize me into action."

"Well, that's fitting, since I do this for him," Audrey said, still annoyed that she was getting nowhere with her.

"I'm sure he would approve of your efforts." A tiny frown appeared between the queen's brows, and she stared blankly over Audrey's shoulder. Perhaps the mention of Bothwell and the fact that this was his wish was making her reconsider.

"What is it?" Audrey asked hopefully.

"I . . . I thought I felt him . . . his presence near me. But it was fleeting." She looked at Audrey again. "I woke late last night. The candle had burned out, and you were asleep." Her eyes became bright with tears. "I felt him. Unlike I had in years. It was so strong, I swear I could smell the warm scent of his hair on my pillow, as though he had just left." She looked down at the paper on the desk and ran her hand over it, caressing it. "I used to wake like that all the time, but it has been many years now and I hadn't realized how much little things like the smell of his hair meant to me." A single tear rolled off her nose to wet the paper.

"Maybe he is here. And is trying to tell you something!"

"Aye, he's telling me to come home." She stared at the paper a few more moments, her long white hand lying flat on it. Then she briskly wiped her eyes and looked at Audrey. "You must find a way to tell Lord

Ross I will not be a party to this. But he cannot take his men and leave, that would throw suspicion on him. He'll have to wait it out."

Audrey shook her head sorrowfully. "I can't tell him! He spent the last eight years of his life working toward this one goal. It means so much to him to honor his word."

"He sounds like a good man, but I cannot take the weight of his honor upon my already weary shoulders. Tell him I release him from the promise. But have a care, lest Paulet catch you. He would be most harsh with Lord Ross, even if he didn't know why you were speaking to him."

"I'll tell him." Audrey's heart was heavy with the weight of her task. She was immersed in her thoughts when the queen's voice pulled her out.

"Who is this man to you that you would risk so much for him?"

"I don't know," Audrey said, placing a hand on her belly, a move the queen's sharp eyes caught. Audrey tried to cover the unconscious slip by smoothing her hand over the dark velvet of her gown.

The queen dipped her pen in the inkwell and began to write. "You are here, are you not? Right in the thick of it. Your feelings cannot be trivial." Her voice was overly casual, and she continued writing without looking up.

"They aren't," Audrey said softly. The queen stopped writing and gave Audrey her full attention. "He's not the man for me." She shook her head. "It's difficult to explain."

"Go on, I'm no simpleton."

Audrey smiled slightly. She was trapped into this personal conversation whether she wanted to be or not. "He's arrogant and overconfident."

The queen laughed. "Would you rather he be sniveling and shiftless?"

"Well . . . no. But he's so driven . . . and honorable."

"I see, and those are all detestable qualities, really! I cannot blame you for fleeing from such a man!"

The queen was making fun of her, and Audrey smiled. "In theory those qualities are attractive, I agree. But when it's all directed at one goal"—she gestured at the queen—"plotting treason . . . well, it loses its luster."

"Bothwell was a man of honor such as Lord Ross, and I will share a secret with you." Audrey nodded and leaned closer. "Make him swear a solemn oath to you, and by God, he will not break it." The queen grinned. "But he knows this about himself, I am sure, and won't give his word easily. If he loves you, he will give it."

The queen patted Audrey's hand and went back to her writing, indicating that Audrey's audience was concluded. She excused herself and went in search of bread to calm her roiling stomach.

What was she going to do? Her sickness was as much from her new dilemma as from the baby in her womb. Brenden would never accept this answer. She could just imagine his reaction to her telling him, "Sorry, the queen wants to die a martyr. Let's go home." She cringed.

She took a piece of bread from the table. It was left over from breakfast and growing hard. How was she going to tell him? She couldn't seek him out, not when they were always accompanied by sentries. She had no wish to be the cause of any punishment. She chewed thoughtfully on the bread, feeling the contents of her stomach begin to calm. She would have to wait for him to make contact with her.

* * *

Several days passed without Audrey seeing either Brenden or Camden. Life in the tower was monotonous. Between prayers, embroidering, and eating, Audrey tried to persuade the queen again to see her point of view. The queen was steadfast in her decision, refusing to listen to any more of Audrey's cajoling. The queen only reiterated that Audrey must somehow communicate with Brenden to stop any rescue attempts immediately.

It seemed impossible! She found many excuses to leave the tower, hoping to pass one of them and somehow give them a sign. But there were so many soldiers, and two sentries always accompanied her.

Over the previous days, the queen had been composing a long letter to Queen Elizabeth. Audrey heard Andrew and Jane saying hopefully that perhaps Elizabeth didn't mean to kill Queen Mary after all. But on this morning their queen chose to dampen their spirits by announcing she had finished the letter to Queen Elizabeth and in it had begged the English queen to please end her miserable situation. If she intended to kill her, then get on with it.

Jane burst into tears and buried her face in Andrew's shoulder. The others all became watery-eyed, and her physician, Bourgoing, begged her not to send the hateful letter. The queen patted his shoulder kindly and handed the letter to Andrew, asking him to please deliver it to Paulet.

"He'll be wanting to read it, I'm sure. He so enjoys reading my correspondence, let's not keep him in suspense," she said sarcastically.

Audrey grabbed her cloak as Andrew was leaving, telling him she needed fresh air.

"I can't imagine why you'd want to be out in this weather!" He had to shout to be heard over the howling wind. The hood of her cloak blew back and the wet, icy wind pulled her hair from the loose braid that she had begun wearing again, since she had been unable to duplicate Una's efforts. The wind was so sharp that she could barely catch her breath and was thankful when they entered the keep.

Paulet was not in the drawing room. Burnes was there and went in search of his master. They waited outside the oak doors. She heard someone striding briskly toward them and turned, expecting Paulet. She tried to keep the surprise off her face when she saw Camden. He whispered something to one of their guards, who nodded and left, leaving Camden in his place.

She couldn't believe she finally had the chance she was waiting for and had no idea what to do. She couldn't talk to him with Andrew and the other guard present. She dared not even look at him.

"The wind is fair cold out there," Camden commented. Andrew started at his voice.

"Oh, yes," she nodded vigorously. "It's *bad* cold! Very bad." Andrew was frowning at her and shaking his head slightly. "It must be *terrible* to have to spend so much time out in it."

Camden opened his mouth to comment further just as Paulet arrived, looking extremely put out. Both of his arms were bandaged.

"What is it, Melville?" he snapped, his little black eyes sweeping over her, then moving to Camden and back to Andrew.

"Why, you are injured, sir! What tragedy has befallen you?" Andrew's tone was mocking, and Audrey tried to hide her smile.

"Mind yourself, Melville! What's this?" He snatched the letter Andrew held out to him. "Who is she blathering to now?"

"It's to Queen Elizabeth. My queen asks that you dispatch it at once."

Paulet smiled thinly, his eyes glinting with amusement. "Does she? I have no orders to bear her missives." He tucked it in his belt just the same.

"Is she no longer allowed to correspond with Queen Elizabeth? Surely you don't suspect her of plotting with the very woman who is putting her to death?" Andrew asked angrily.

"She is a condemned woman! I'll not send her knavish letter." His eyes were suddenly riveted to something over Audrey's shoulder. She turned to find Camden standing rather close, looking at her.

"You, soldier! What are you leering at?" Paulet asked suspiciously.

Camden looked at him in surprise and took a step back. "Nothing, sir."

"Indeed!" He walked to stand between Audrey and Camden. "Were you not conversing with the lady when I walked up?"

Her stomach dropped. She jumped in before Camden could answer. "No, sir. It's my fault. I was talking to him."

Paulet arched a bushy eyebrow at her, then turned back to Camden. Camden's face was expressionless. "Many a weak man is undone by lust. Do you think it's acceptable to go against my word, so far as the lass is pleasing to the eye?" He turned on her now. "And I thought she would send you away. I was wrong. Time has worn away your serpent queen's charms. So she brought in someone younger to beguile us."

"What?" she asked in confusion. "I was merely asking—"

"Enough of your trumpery!" His voice was loud and harsh, and she flinched. "Burnes!" he called. Burnes hurried to his side. "Assemble the men not on duty in the courtyard."

A sense of foreboding came over her. She looked at Camden, but nothing showed on his face. Andrew grabbed her arm and tried to pull her out of the keep. Paulet saw him.

"You're not going anywhere." He motioned to the guard, who blocked Andrew's path. "You'll watch his flogging. Mayhap your tongue will not be so loose in the future."

"Flogging? Flogging!" Audrey exclaimed in horror. It was impossible to tell by Camden's face what his feelings were on this, but she was aghast. They were only talking about the weather! "But it was me! I was talking to him! Why don't you flog me?"

Camden winced at her words.

Paulet tried to look down his nose at her, but couldn't since she was taller. "I've a mind to do it. But no, he has his orders, as he knows full well. His superiors and I are the only ones allowed to converse with the prisoner or her servants."

Andrew gave her a look warning her to drop it. He looked as miserable as she was to have to witness this. Camden wasn't even trying to argue or state his case; he just stood there. She would have to stop protesting, or Paulet might get suspicious.

They were led into the bailey, where a small group of soldiers formed up.

Brenden met them. "The men await you, sir." He was speaking loudly through the blustering wind. He looked at Andrew and Audrey curiously.

"Lieutenant, this is one of your men, correct?" Paulet asked, gesturing to Camden.

Lieutenant, was it?

Brenden looked at Camden and back to Paulet. "He is."

"I witnessed him chatting with this woman, one of the prisoner's servants."

Brenden's gaze hardened and turned on Camden, who returned his look impassively. Paulet held out one of his bandaged hands and the ever-lurking Burnes placed a whip of sorts in it. It was a thin pole, about a foot in length, with nine braided leather straps hanging from it, each knotted at the end.

"What say. . . twenty lashes? That should remind him of his duties." Paulet handed the whip to Brenden, who stared at it dumbly for a moment. He motioned for the sentries to take Audrey and Andrew back to the tower, but Paulet shook his head.

"I want her to watch what her wanton tongue has brought about."

Brenden hesitated only a second before ordering a guard to remove Camden's weapons. The guard reached for Camden's sword, but Camden pushed him away and removed it himself, along with his dagger and pistol. He slapped them forcefully into the waiting guard's hands. All the while, his eyes were locked with Brenden's.

Her stomach churned in earnest now. What in God's name were they communicating to each other? Camden removed the thick buff overcoat, metal helmet, jack, and coarse cream-colored shirt he wore. Goose bumps sprang up over his broad chest and shoulders as the freezing wind whipped around them.

He was led to a pole, more than six feet high. His wrists were tied to the pole, just above his head. Audrey's hands were shaking, and she was sweating, despite the cold. She wanted to cry out to stop this, but she knew there was nothing she could do.

Brenden swung the whip out and brought it down across his brother's back. Camden didn't flinch, but his hands tightened on the pole.

"That one doesn't count!" Paulet called, walking closer. "Come, Lieutenant, you wield that thing like a woman. Make him remember this day."

Brenden's lips thinned, but this time when he brought it down, the muscles grew taut along Camden's back and arms. White lines that quickly turned an angry red appeared. She covered her mouth to keep from throwing up. The next stroke broke the skin, and thin streams of blood ran from the wounds.

Andrew's hand gripped her elbow when her knees almost gave way. She squeezed her eyes shut to close out the rest. When the last hideous whack sounded, she opened her eyes and saw Brenden cutting the rope at Camden's wrists. His back was torn and bleeding, but he still stood straight and his face revealed no pain.

Camden's clothes and weapons were returned, and he was led into the keep. Her hand was still clamped over her mouth when Brenden walked back to Paulet. Brenden's face was devoid of expression, and he refrained from even looking in her general direction.

Paulet turned to her. "Let this be a lesson to you." His voice was harsh, and she saw by the white surrounding his thinly compressed his lips that he hadn't really enjoyed the sentence, either. Just doing his job. He motioned to the guards to return them to the tower.

Andrew held her elbow firmly all the way up the

tower steps, only releasing her when the door was shut behind them. The others looked up at their arrival. A look of distress passed over the queen's face when she saw Audrey.

"What has happened?" she asked.

Audrey raced up the stairs as Andrew began the tale. She reached the chamber pot just in time. Even after her stomach was empty, she continued to heave, finally dissolving into sobs on the floor.

Everyone was asleep upstairs. Audrey sat shivering in a chair, a quilt wrapped about her. Her shaking wasn't just from the damp cold. The afternoon's episode drove home what nothing else had since she had stepped through that godforsaken corridor. This was real. And it wasn't the relatively safe world she was accustomed to. The punishment Camden had received for his minor offense seemed hideously cruel in her eyes. But here, it was a fact.

It was her fault, and she was sick about it. She had been warned on more than one occasion not to talk to the damn guards. Yet her mind simply could not conceive flogging as a possible outcome. And now she couldn't go to him and apologize or make sure he wasn't suffering from the lashing.

She looked around the small room. A single candle burned on the desk beside her. This was a prison, with hundreds of soldiers guarding against escape. The prisoner they were guarding was a deposed monarch, unjustly imprisoned and waiting to have her head chopped off. Audrey covered her face as these realities slammed into her.

This wasn't a book or a fairy tale about kings and

queens and knights. There were no magicians or magic swords. They were real people, flesh and blood like her, who had lived and laughed and loved. And had suffered unimaginable fates. She knew the queen to be a kind and generous woman. And yet her own son was prepared to let her die to secure another kingdom. Her own people hated her for her religion! Her *religion*! America was, indeed, only a dream in this age.

She rubbed her temples. Her nausea, throwing up, and crying had only succeeded in giving her a thunderous headache that expanded when she closed her eyes. She wished she could lie down and go to sleep, forgetting, at least for a time, her predicament.

She froze. The door was slowly and quietly being opened. Was it the assassin the queen was so terrified of? Had they come to kill her quietly and deny her the public death she desired? A tall figure stepped into the room, quietly shutting the door behind him. She was fully exposed with the candle burning next to her and could see almost nothing of the intruder.

He stood at the door, looking into the room. "Audrey?" came the hoarse whisper. A choking sob rose in her throat, and she threw the quilt off. He met her halfway, squeezing her so tightly that she was lifted several inches off the ground. She buried her face into the cold leather of his overcoat, her tears dissolving the snow that dusted it.

He murmured soothing words to her, and at first, his deep mellow voice only made her cry harder. When her sobs finally died down to sniffles, he led her closer to the candle.

"You've not been sleeping, have you?" He pulled his gloves off and took her face between his hands to look at her closer.

"How's Camden?" she asked, choosing to ignore his question, since her haggard condition had more to do with pregnancy than lack of sleep.

"He's fine and wants you to trouble yourself not over it. 'Twas his own fault. I'd say we're lucky a flogging is all that came of it."

She shook her head. "I knew I shouldn't have been talking to him, but I had to let him know I needed to speak to you."

"It's not your fault." He held her face firmly, green eyes boring into hers. She felt her eyes filling with tears again. "He'll not be pleased to know you're up here making yourself sick over it. He's mending fine and will be back on duty tomorrow."

She grasped his wrists, feeling his scars. "What about you? That must have been awful to flog your own brother."

He sighed deeply and released her face. She thought he would talk to her of the pain the afternoon had caused him, but after a moment, he seemed to shake off whatever emotions he was feeling. "So what is this news you must be telling me?"

Dread filled her again, so she decided to stall. "How are you here? Are you sure this is safe?"

"Aye, it is. I put all my own men on duty and am here under the pretense of making rounds to be sure they aren't sleeping."

She looked at the door. "So your men are guarding us right now?"

"Aye. Now, has something gone wrong? Why did you need to see me?"

She swallowed hard and nodded. "She refuses to be party to the plot."

"Why?"

"She wants to die."

He stared blankly at her. This was apparently something that had never occurred to him, and he was having difficulty digesting it.

"Why?" he asked again.

"She wants to be a martyr for her religion."

"What?" It exploded from him in a loud whisper.

"Shhh!" She grabbed his arm. "You'll wake the others."

"Did you tell her about Bothwell? About the promise I made him? His dying wishes for her?" His voice was rising in anger.

"Yes! Yes! Calm down, please!" She led him to a chair and pushed him into it.

"I heard she cared not for him, that she tried to obtain a divorce to remarry. But after knowing Bothwell, I hoped there was good reason for it. To think he died loving her." His voice was bitter.

"That's not it at all," she protested, a bit annoyed at him for jumping to such a conclusion. "She was heartbroken when I told her. But things have changed in the twenty years since they were last together. I have a feeling she is much different now."

"So different she cannot honor the love she once held for him?"

She shook her head, struggling to explain something she didn't fully understand. "She didn't interpret the message from Bothwell the way you intended. She took it as a final message that he hadn't abandoned her, and it seems"—she made a face to let him know she had no part in these conclusions—"it only reinforced her belief that dying a martyr is the right thing to do."

He sat quietly, stroking his beard. "This isn't good."

"I'm at her every day about it. She won't budge an

inch. In fact, she releases you from the promise you made to Bothwell."

"She can't do that." He seemed to be under control again and very thoughtful. He wanted to hear everything Audrey had said to the queen. So she repeated all of their conversations over the past few days.

Brenden chewed his bottom lip. "She says she can't retire to the country, but neither can she regain the crown of Scotland. Remind her that is not so. Once she reaches her embassy in France, she can get word to Philip of Spain, who would surely help her, knowing she is at liberty."

Audrey sighed and shook her head. "Brenden, she's not stupid. I'm sure that has occurred to her. Don't you get it? She's happy to die. She *longs* for death!"

He stood. "I care not. She can kill herself when she gets to France."

She gave him a look of reproach. "The only person you're thinking of is yourself. What about her? She's been in prison for twenty years! Unjustly! The woman is practically a cripple. Why can't you let her have this?"

His eyes grew hard. "I do this for my friend, James Hepburn."

She felt a stab of guilt at her accusation. "I know, I'm sorry. But can't you see? She's not the same woman he knew so long ago. Perhaps if he saw her and talked to her now, he might understand, too."

"Since he's dead, I'm afraid that's impossible."

She dropped into the crimson velvet chair in defeat. "I feel like I'm standing between two brick walls, ramming my head into one, then the other."

He didn't respond. He just stared down at her with a veiled expression.

"Maybe you should talk to her," she suggested.

"Aye, mayhap you're right. I'll come back next week. We should be ready by then."

"Brenden," she said hesitantly. "I told you this would happen. Can't you accept that you tried? You did the best you could for Bothwell. It's not your fault."

He ignored her words. "I can't believe she really wants to die. This is the same woman who rode at the head of her army, wearing armor beneath her bodice. A woman who braved public outcry to marry the man she loved, even though he was suspected of murdering the king. Is that bold woman really gone?"

"I don't know."

"I have to leave," he said abruptly.

She nodded, desperately not wanting him to leave her alone in the cold tower that was as much her prison now as the queen's. "What if I need to see you again? I don't think Camden would appreciate a second flogging just to get you a message."

He was thoughtful. "I don't think it's safe. I'll come when I can, just try to wait." He leaned close to her with narrowed green eyes. "You don't look well, Audrey. Is something else ailing you?"

She shook her head. His attitude only reinforced her belief that telling him he was going to be a father would be a mistake. It was all a mistake, she thought suddenly, as her despair threatened to choke her. Coming to this time and loving him was a hideous mistake.

"Well then, I'll be back as soon as it's safe." His mouth descended on hers, his hand circling her neck. The kiss was hard and possessive, his beard scratching pleasantly against her skin. Then he was gone as quickly as he had appeared, and the room was cold and empty once more.

⊰ 16 ⊱

What passed next was a succession of long, idle days. The queen did a great deal of praying and talking with Father de Preau. Audrey was certain the queen was aware of her pregnancy. She was solicitous of her and made certain Audrey took proper care of herself. Audrey approached her many times on the subject of rescue, but the queen remained firm. Audrey told her of Brenden's visit and his feeling that Bothwell would have wanted her free. The queen just smiled sadly.

That night Brenden made an appearance. Audrey was expecting him. Paulet had come to the tower earlier and seized Andrew and the queen's priest, de Preau. They were taken away to be locked in the keep. The queen was distressed about what it all meant. She feared Paulet was planning a secret death for her and had removed the only two able-bodied men in her service to make it easier. Jane and Barbra were let in on Audrey's secret and were anxious for their mistress to cooperate. They sat around the fire waiting for Brenden while Jane read to them. The door opened, and the candles sputtered from the draft. As soon as Brenden entered, the room seemed to shrink.

He hesitated when he saw them waiting for him. He looked down as the queen's little long-haired terrier, Skye, came over to sniff the visitor. He whispered something and scratched her head. Skye wagged her tail vigorously, threatening to throw herself off-balance in her excitement. He removed his hat and walked over to them. He knelt before the queen. Skye perched herself against his thigh, pink tongue hanging out, waiting for more scratching.

"Your Grace, I am honored," he said with his head bowed.

Audrey felt a stab of pride. He was so handsome and gallant.

"Please." The queen smiled at him. "Be seated." Audrey relinquished her chair and pulled up a stool beside him. The queen motioned for Jane and Barbra to leave with the dog.

"Your Grace, I have come to state my case in person, since you turn a deaf ear to Mistress Williams. My plan can't fail. I have over fifty men stationed here, some under my command, some dispersed. I have people throughout Paulet's household. My own ships stand at the ready off the coast."

Audrey looked at him in surprise. His own ships?

"I hope for your sake you have been discreet. Naught passes by Walsingham unnoticed," the queen replied grimly.

"Not a word has been committed to paper. All transactions have been done in person, by my most trusted servants." He was calm, not begging, simply stating his case. The queen actually seemed to be considering it!

"Why were my steward and priest taken from me today?"

"Another plot against Queen Elizabeth's life was

uncovered. The French ambassador, Chateauneuf, is currently under house arrest. I suspect it was simply a concoction of Walsingham's to urge Elizabeth toward the signing of your death warrant."

The queen smiled. "Aye, it will not be long now. Walsingham will not be content until I am dead."

"I can have your grace on a ship sailing to France in less than a week, if you will permit me."

She looked at him for a long moment. "I want to thank you for your efforts on my late husband's behalf. He would appreciate all you've done. But alas, I must decline. There is a greater mission before me."

Audrey could see Brenden struggling to find the proper words to address the rejection. "You must understand my position. He didn't ask me to give you an option. Nor is he here to give me counsel on this matter. If you honor him, as he seemed to think you did, you will not let his request go unanswered."

"Lord Ross, I have answered his request. He made it at a time when he was still within the confines of this earth. I feel very strongly he understands what I'm doing." Her wide mouth was set, her amber eyes hard. "I am releasing you from any promises you have made. This is my greatest wish now, and I'm certain he would have you honor it."

A war was going on behind Brenden's calm facade. The thinning of his lips, the tightness of his jaw, his hand gripping his knee—it all spoke of barely held restraint. The queen saw it, too.

"You can do me a great service in another matter, if it pleases you."

"Aye?"

"I fear there will be a covert attempt on my life. See-ing how you have many men stationed here on my behalf, I would be gratified to know you're guarding against such a fate befalling me."

"Of course, Your Grace." He inclined his head.

She smiled. "It's time for me to retire. I'll leave you now. Mistress Williams has matters to discuss with you pertaining to her ill health."

Audrey shot her an angry look and helped her upstairs, where Jane was waiting. "Thanks a lot!" Audrey said under her breath.

"He needs to know," she reproved. "I think it might keep him from doing something foolish."

Audrey doubted the knowledge that she was pregnant would deter any of Brenden's plans, only complicate them. She went back downstairs. Brenden stood below, looking at her curiously. He wasn't nearly as upset as she had thought he would be.

"I told you," Audrey whispered. "This is what she wants. What are we going to do now?"

He glanced at the stairs, then pulled her across the room. "Next week, I'll take her by force."

"Brenden!" She was aghast. He *was* foolish! "Did you hear nothing she said to you?"

"Audrey, it can't fail—I know I can get her out of here, I know it! And you are to be helping me, dammit!" He looked angry and betrayed.

"Don't you see? It was never going to work!"

He grabbed her shoulders and shook her slightly. "No! This past you talk of is my future. It hasn't been written yet, and I'll be damned if you'll tell me I can't do it!"

She pushed away from him. She was shaking uncontrollably with anger. "Fine. Do whatever you want, Brenden Ross, and don't worry about who you trample in the doing of it! But when this is done, right or wrong, you will be alone. Do you hear me?"

A muscle twitched in his jaw, and he reached for her again, but she backed away. "Are you threatening me?"

"No! I'm telling you how it is! I'm leaving you when this is over and taking your child with me. I can't be with you. You care about no one but yourself!"

He stared at her for a long time, then ran a hand over his face. "You're with child?"

"Yes." She was dangerously close to tears, and his lack of emotion wasn't helping matters. A few tears spilled over her lashes. She fought to keep herself under control and not dissolve in a torrent of sobbing. He said nothing, nor did he try to comfort her. He began putting his gloves on.

"So you're just leaving? You have nothing to say?"

"What shall I say, Audrey?" His voice was curt. "Do you want me to beg you to stay? Did you hope I would abandon this folly in light of your condition?"

Yes! Yes! her heart was screaming, but her mind was indignant that he would dare throw these things in her face. "I didn't impregnate myself, you self-serving bastard! I wouldn't stay if you begged me! Get out!"

He stared at her. He had never seemed farther away from her than he did at that moment. A stranger. "How long have you known?" he asked.

"Since just before I came here."

He shook his head, pulling his other glove on. "What is that supposed to mean? You wouldn't have gone through with this had you known?"

"No, but I wouldn't have involved you. It's too late now." He turned to leave.

Her heart was breaking, but she didn't try to stop him. He stopped at the door with his back to her. He stood a long time with his palm pressed against the wood, obviously deep in thought. She knew he was angry, but she hoped his hesitation was because he didn't want to leave things this way between them. "I will think of something. I . . . ," he trailed off, and she knew he was struggling to get the words out. "I don't want you to leave me."

Brenden went down the tower steps as though in a dream. He walked across the bailey, thankful for the sharp cold, hoping it might clear his head.

The men at the gatehouse seemed lucid enough, despite the late hour. They were laughing and talking loudly until they caught sight of him. He raised his hand to acknowledge them. They waved back and resumed their conversation. He made a slow circuit of the grounds. Sentries were posted along the walls and at the towers where other prisoners were held. They didn't get the same consideration as the queen. The other prisoners lived on far less, sharing their few blankets and freezing cells with many people.

Brenden had enough guards so that they could slip away without being noticed for a time, at least long enough for a successful escape. Shortly before Brenden arrived at Fotheringhay, Paulet had requested reinforcements of well over one hundred men, both archers and foot soldiers. Inserting himself and his men into the equation was a simple matter of Camden's obtaining forged papers. Nicholas Jennings, an English Catholic and close friend, knew several muster commissioners who were Marian sympathizers and agreed to help. With the large number of men recently transferred to Fotheringhay, none of the papers were being verified. Everything was going according to plan.

Brenden came upon a sentry sitting against the wall

with his helmet pulled forward over his eyes. "Wake up," he said, kicking the inert foot.

The man came awake with a start. "I'm sorry, sir!" He scrambled to his feet.

Brenden knew he should upbraid the man, but he didn't feel like it. "Just keep your eyes open," he said, and walked on.

The cold gray walls rose high beside him, lit at intervals with torches. Everything had changed . . . or had it? What should an unborn child matter? He felt sick for even thinking such a thing, but there it was. He tried to push away the feeling that it was somehow her fault, but it burned like bile in his stomach. He knew the truth. Every time he had laid a hand on her, she asked him to stop. In fact, she probably conceived that night in the woods when she had been running from him because she hated him! This was *his* fault!

He entered the keep, nodding to the sentries he passed. He came to the room where Melville and de Preau were lodged. Camden was posted alone outside the door. He leaned against the wall, his arms crossed.

He raised an eyebrow when Brenden approached. "You're looking grim this evening. What ails you?"

He looked hard at Camden, trying to decide whether to tell him or not. He needed to discuss what they were going to do now, but he also knew how his brother was about Audrey. Camden straightened and became serious.

"What is it? Did something happen?"

"Aye, something has happened. She's with child."

Camden frowned. "The queen?"

"No! Audrey."

He fell back against the wall. He didn't say anything for a long time. "How did this happen?"

Brenden looked at him like he was a fool. "How do you think?"

Camden was shaking his head slowly. "But she knows already? So soon? It has only been, what, three weeks since you began sharing her bed?"

"No," Brenden said in a low voice, "that night in the wood . . . when I thought you two were . . . she and I . . ." He shrugged, not wanting to go into any details.

Camden's eyes widened. They were both silent. Camden rubbed both hands over his face suddenly and grinned. "This must be splendid news to you. So, what shall you do?"

"I don't know."

"What do you mean? You don't know how to be a father? You don't know how to treat a pregnant woman? Because I *know* I'm not hearing anything else."

Brenden knew what Camden was thinking. Audrey should be removed somehow from Fotheringhay. Taken out of harm's way. But that would take time. Brenden was afraid time was running out.

"Is she really so delicate? She's a strong lass, surely she can withstand it."

"I can't believe you're even thinking this! What if she loses the bairn? What then? I've known a good many women who lost their lives as well! Would you actually subject her to a beheading? Or if your futile plan were to succeed, a very brutal escape?"

"Keep your voice down, dammit!" Brenden looked around furtively. Camden was glaring at him, hands clenched into fists as though ready to lunge. "You're right, of course. I don't know what I'm thinking."

"You're thinking about your bloody honor. But you know what, brother? You're losing more honor than you can imagine in this venture. She's not like you and me . . . or any other woman. Such horror would be too much for her to bear. You know as well as I do that she doesn't belong here, but you're selfish enough to try and keep her as though she were a pet."

Camden's words were a knife twisting in his chest. Had he really dropped so low over this situation?

Camden regarded him for a moment, then a look of horrified amazement slowly spread over his face. "You think it's her fault, don't you?" When Brenden shook his head, Camden became even more surprised. "You're lying! I can tell! You know whose fault it is?" His voice dropped to a dangerously low level, his eyes narrowing. "You can blame yourself, you rutting bastard. Had you not been so eager to take her into your bed, none of this would have happened, now would it?"

"I think envy twists your words," Brenden said, matching his tone and demeanor. They stood silently for a moment, almost at a face-off.

"I'm out," Camden said suddenly.

"You can't leave."

Camden gave him a humorless smile. "Audrey needs someone to see to her safety. Since that man isn't you, I'll be sure of it."

"Are you hoping for special thanks?" Brenden sneered.

Camden leaned against the wall, his calm sardonic manner returning. "Why don't you finish your rounds, Lieutenant. I've grown weary of your company."

Brenden's fist itched to cave in the sarcastic smirk on his brother's face. But the truth of everything Camden said stopped him. He turned on his heel and left, going straight back to the gatehouse instead of finishing his rounds. He was glad he had a private room, unlike the other soldiers, who bunked together.

After stripping down to his shirt and breeks, he grabbed the untouched bottle of whiskey he'd found in the cupboard when he arrived three weeks ago. He took a long drink, the fiery liquid burning pleasantly as it went down. He sat on the narrow, ratty bed, replaying the events of the evening in his head.

He was wrong and he knew it. But failure ate at his soul so he could hardly think straight. Camden was right. He would never be able to keep her with him if he made her stay at Fotheringhay. He had probably lost her already.

"I'm truly sorry, Bothwell," he said, taking another long swallow of whiskey. "But you knew, didn't you? I remember the dream. You knew I would fail even then."

He decided to quit talking to himself before someone overheard. He crawled under the covers, but sleep did not come. He stared into the dark for a long time.

His door opened, and Camden entered, holding a candle. "I thought you might still be awake." He closed the door softly and pulled up a stool, setting the candle beside the bed.

Brenden regarded him warily. He sat up and offered him the bottle of whiskey.

Camden took a drink, and his lips curled in disgust. "This swill didn't put you to sleep?"

"I wasn't so much concerned with the taste as with the medicinal properties."

"Ah, is your heart ailing? I'm sorry, brother, I was a wee bit hard on you." He winked. "But I've been thinking, if we could get Audrey out somehow, without raising suspicion, we could move forward with your plan. She could stay with Nicholas."

"Aye, I think you're right. Elizabeth Curle was sent away easily enough."

"We'll think of something. I've never liked her being

here." Camden regarded Brenden for a moment. "What is it now? You should be in a fine mood, now we've solved the problem."

He was thankful for Camden's cool-headed logic. He tried to convince himself that this wasn't the end.

Audrey's life had turned into a big blur of nausea, heart-burn, and fatigue. The queen said it was normal and to eat lots of bread. The queen wasn't faring well, either. She limped into the room, heavily supported by Jane and Barbra. Her physician, Bourgoing, went to her after she was seated and began probing her leg joints.

He sat back on his heels and regarded her sadly. "I think I could relieve some of the swelling, but alas, I have depleted almost my entire supply of herbs. I have nothing that could help you now, Your Highness." He instructed Jane and Barbra to take her upstairs to lie down.

He took a deep breath, as though there were some distasteful task he must undertake and was resigning himself to it. Audrey felt sorry for him. He was as stooped as the queen was and a good deal older.

"I shall speak with Paulet. Perchance, he will let me venture to a nearby meadow. I believe I could find what I need there." He asked Audrey if she wanted to accompany him, since she generally accompanied everyone on their outings. She declined. She was starting to avoid the ones that involved seeing Paulet, since he always looked at her with contempt.

She followed the others upstairs and sat by the queen's bedside. Audrey admired her for the way she handled her pain. She complained of it very little, although it was obvious she was in misery. In the month they had spent together, Audrey had come to look upon the queen as a friend. She was a woman of great faith, and Audrey confided in her about the dreams that brought her to Brenden, leaving out the detail of time travel.

"My! They seem almost prophetic." The queen looked at Audrey oddly. "I fear you've been sent here for a much greater purpose than you imagine."

Audrey covered her face. "I am not a prophet or seer or any other perversion! I don't know why this is happening to me, but I wish . . ." What did she wish? That she had never come here?

"I've had similar dreams recently, and what they tell me is that this is God's will."

"I think maybe you're right," Audrey said, a strange feeling washing over her.

What *did* she believe? Someone had to be responsible for transporting her four hundred years into the past. But why her? Why not someone who was already here? The philosopher Boethius said that God not only exercised providence but that He lives in an eternal moment. If He lives in eternity, then past, present, and future are a single moment. It was daunting to think that this life was mapped out for her long ago. But God didn't exist in time. He was time. He was in the past and the future simultaneously—there was no difference to Him.

Things were turning sour fast. Brenden felt as though he had completely lost control of the situation. It was past midnight, and he found himself on sentry duty. He walked his little length of wall, stopping every so often. They had gotten word to Gavin, telling him to send a letter to his sister, Tara Ross, saying that her son was ill and they feared for his life. Brenden even knew the missive had arrived and was lying on Paulet's desk, opened but not acted upon.

Before he'd had a chance to worry about it, the garrison captain had called all the officers together. They were given orders to double the present manning and to triple it at the Scottish queen's tower, which was how Brenden found himself standing guard. The captain, being a brave man, even ventured a guess about the sudden increase in security. He was pretty sure the death warrant had been signed. After confiding this, the captain looked furtively around, as though he expected someone to jump out at him.

Brenden faced the wall and looked up. It was so dark, he could barely see where the wall ended and the sky began. Only the telltale twinkle of the stars let him know it was still up there. Any plan Brenden might have enacted was immobilized by these new developments. It was impossible now to have a majority of his men on duty, and there was no way he could get word to Audrey. Everything was slipping away.

He leaned against the wall, cold and bored and feeling like a prisoner. It had been days since he'd seen Audrey. Several men who looked to be gentry were arriving. No one was allowed to leave the tower, so he didn't even see her in passing.

When his shift was over, he returned to his room. He regarded the narrow bed he slept in with distaste. He sighed and lay down on it fully clothed. He could see her when he closed his eyes. Soft gray eyes looking back at him, fringed with the longest lashes he'd ever seen. When this was over, he would convince her to stay with him.

He'd send Camden off to do some of his sheriff business. Camden would have to go away. At least for a while, until they found a wife for him. He'd understand. Brenden was positive.

Brenden didn't get much sleep because he was needed early the next morning. The Earls of Shrewsbury and Kent had arrived. Shrewsbury looked particularly grim. He had been the queen's jailer for fifteen years before Paulet, and it was said she was removed because he bore her too much favor. They also brought more guards.

All Brenden could do was wait. They had a strange-looking man with them whom they called Bull. He carried a heavily wrapped parcel. It looked suspiciously like a wood ax.

Audrey had just sat down to dinner when there was a rap on the door. Paulet entered with four other men. They were all solemn, but one man looked especially pained. He was about fifty. His face was worn and lined as if he'd had many hardships in his life. His eyes reminded Audrey of a sad dog. They were red-rimmed as though he had been crying. The queen addressed him.

"Lord Shrewsbury, welcome." She didn't stand.

"Thank you," he murmured, averting his eyes.

Another man boldly stepped forward and identified himself as the Earl of Kent. In his hand he held a piece of parchment with a yellow seal hanging from it. Audrey knew what it was. Her heart seemed to stop beating for a moment, then started back up with a rapid hammering.

He read it aloud, looking around the room triumphantly. It was the warrant for the queen's execution. The one Brenden thought might never come. That explained the increase in security and the arrival of all the dignitaries.

The queen listened, calm and emotionless. Audrey was again awestruck by this woman. How could she sit and listen to the order for her death so peacefully? When the man finished, the room was quiet. Finally, the queen spoke.

"I welcome such longed-for news. I rejoice in the opportunity to shed my blood for my religion."

The men shifted uncomfortably at her words. Shrewsbury looked as though he might burst into tears.

"You are to die because you have attempted to murder my queen," Lord Kent spat at her. "We offer you the services of the dean of Peterborough to make ready for your end. You can now shed the folly of popery."

The queen crossed herself and gave him a look of reproach. "I decline your offer. This is the time for me to remain true to my faith. I request the services of my own chaplain, Father de Preau."

Shrewsbury shook his head sadly. "I'm sorry, madam. We cannot allow it."

The queen looked somewhat shaken. Audrey knew she had counted on Father de Preau hearing her final confession.

Lord Kent looked triumphant to have finally broken her calm facade. "Your life would be the death of our religion!" he exclaimed. "Your death will be its life."

Instead of having its intended effect, the queen's face radiated with joy. "He *has* chosen me." She turned her smiling face to Shrewsbury. "At what hour am I to die?"

"Tomorrow morning, at eight o'clock." His voice cracked as he bravely held back tears. At his answer, scalding tears started down Audrey's face. Jane and Barbra were clinging to each other, handkerchiefs pressed against their eyes. Bourgoing was sitting in a chair, his face buried in his hands.

"It's past dinner already," the queen remarked in surprise. "You haven't given me much time to prepare."

Jane broke away from Barbra and ran to Shrewsbury, clutching at his sleeve. "Please, my lord," she cried, tears streaming down her face. "You have always been a kind man. Can we not get a reprieve? The time is so short!"

He shook her off, his throat working to answer calmly. "There will be no delay," he said firmly, and motioned for the others to follow him out. After they left, the room was rife with sobbing. The queen looked at them all calmly and sympathetically.

"Come now! We all knew this would happen! We must be happy it has finally come to pass." She urged them to finish the meal and drink to her, which was an equally heart-wrenching experience. Audrey was beginning to feel sick from all her crying. She hated to be so selfish, thinking of herself, but she didn't know how she would be able to watch the queen die.

After dinner, the queen went to her wardrobe and began sorting her things. She separated them into packets—money, jewels, and special items—and wrote on the outside for whom each was destined. She gave the others instructions on whom to give each one to when they reached the continent after her death. To Bourgoing, she gave rings, silver boxes, and her beautiful velvet-bound music book.

To Barbra, she gave all of her miniatures. She gave Jane some more of her precious few personal possessions, along with things to take to Andrew. She called Audrey to her side.

"I have something special for you," she said.

Audrey could only nod, afraid that if she tried to speak, she would become a blubbering mass of tears. The queen slipped off her wedding ring and pressed it into Audrey's palm.

"The news you have brought me has been of great comfort to me in my final moments. I want you to have this, with the hopes that you will find as much joy in your life with Lord Ross as I found in my short time with Bothwell."

Audrey started to protest, but the queen shook her head. "The executioners are allowed to take all the items I wear upon my person for themselves. I would not have them getting this. No, it belongs with you."

She then set to writing her will and final letters to those who could not be with her. She wrote out her confession to Father de Preau, since she could not give it personally. While she wrote for hours on end, they went upstairs and readied the gown she would be wearing to her execution. It was a dark crimson, the color of martyrdom, with a black silk kirtle and bodice over it.

They dressed themselves in mourning colors. Audrey put on the black dress she had worn the day she arrived. So this was how it was to end. If she could go back and do it over—to not know the queen, to never come through the corridor—would she? She sat on the bed, turning the ring over in her hand. This was the beginning of it all. The queen's love for Bothwell. *En Ma Fin Est Ma Commencement,* 'In My End Is My Beginning.' It was the motto on the queen's cloth of state—before Paulet had ripped it from the wall and taken it away.

Audrey could finally see the truth of those words, in all the different meanings they must hold for the queen. *In my end is my beginning.*

❦ 17 ❦

No one slept on this night. The queen finished her final letter to her brother-in-law from her first marriage, King Henry of France, around two A.M. Afterward, she lay on her bed. Audrey and the queen's other servants gathered around her while Jane read aloud.

They could hear soldiers outside the queen's rooms and, at a distance, the sound of hammering on the scaffold being erected in the great hall. There was no chance of escape now. Audrey hadn't seen Brenden since their argument. He had said he would think of something. Instead of taking the queen by force, he had probably wasted precious time trying to find a way to remove Audrey from Fotheringhay and had failed. Now it was too late.

Audrey gazed upon the woman she had come to see as *her* queen and she lamented their failure to free her. And yet, Audrey was so confused. It was what the queen wanted. It was God's will. How could she begrudge her that? She knew it was the selfishness of grieving. She was already mourning the loss of a friend, and the queen's sad losses in life. Audrey wished it had been different for her, wished she had known more happiness than a blissful moment with Bothwell.

The queen opened her eyes at daybreak. They dressed her in silence. She embraced each one of them, bestowing a soft kiss upon their cheeks, and went to her oratory. She prayed for well over an hour and didn't stop when the relentless pounding began on the door. Audrey was sure it wasn't Paulet, since he always entered at will.

When Jane opened the door, the man identified himself as the sheriff of Northampton. Brenden and Camden were behind him, followed by a flood of soldiers. Brenden didn't look at her, but Camden met her eyes and looked away. The sheriff stood respectfully, waiting until the queen finished praying.

"Madam, the lords are waiting," the sheriff said when she stood.

She held her head high, without a trace of anxiety, as they left the tower. Audrey's heart was already beginning to pound in fear. It was unthinkable she was going to witness this. It couldn't really be happening. People weren't really beheaded. That was a thing from tales you were told as a child, not real.

Andrew was waiting at the entrance to the great hall, as was the sour-faced Earl of Kent, who blocked their way. "Only the condemned enters the hall."

The queen turned to Lord Kent and Paulet, who waited impatiently. "Please allow my servants to enter," she said, a note of pleading in her voice.

"No," Lord Kent replied. "They will raise such a ruckus with their incessant weeping that they will distract both you and the executioner." His eyes swept over them in contempt. "And I'll not have them dipping their kerchiefs in your blood for their popish relics."

Audrey's stomach heaved, and her knees buckled. A hand was at her elbow to steady her and was gone just as quickly. Brenden was beside her. Since soldiers surrounded them, his gesture went unnoticed.

"My Lord, I give you my word they will not do such things." The queen gave Lord Kent a hard look. "I refuse to believe your queen gave any such orders. Surely Elizabeth would not condemn me to die without my ladies to attend me."

Lord Kent looked uncertain and turned to Paulet. They whispered among themselves and the other lords standing nearby. Lord Kent turned back to her. "They may enter," he said reluctantly.

Only the occasional sniffle and choked sob broke the heavy silence in the great hall. A huge scaffold was before them, draped in black. Soldiers and hundreds of spectators, most of them common townsfolk, clustered around it. A fire blazed in the fireplace. The stage was set with two stools and a block, also covered in black. An enormous ax was propped against the block.

The queen ascended the scaffold, accompanied by the Lords Shrewsbury and Kent, and her ladies, Jane and Barbra. The commission for her execution was read aloud, and she listened with an air of detachment. A short, round dean of the church broke away from the crowd and rushed to the edge of the platform, enjoining the queen to embrace the true faith of the Reformed Church.

He began praying loudly, his voice ringing out through the crowd, filling the hall. Audrey wanted to cover her ears and scream. How could they force this final indignity on her? But the queen only opened her prayer book and began reading.

* * *

Brenden didn't know how much more he could take. He was sickened by the scene in front of him. He felt so powerless, impotent. He had failed. Failed miserably. Right now he was useless to Audrey, to Bothwell, and to the queen. He had achieved nothing. And now he had to set his mind to getting them out of Fotheringhay alive. Paulet had told them that morning that the queen's servants would be held as prisoners indefinitely after the execution. That was dangerous for Audrey. Queen Mary had been held indefinitely, and her detention had stretched into twenty years.

The dean stopped praying, blending back into the crowd. The queen stood, her own prayers finished. Two men in black stepped forward and asked her for forgiveness. She graciously granted it.

Jane and Barbra helped the queen undress. She seemed anxious to shed her clothing, getting her arm caught once and pulling at it impatiently. She was ready for this. Brenden realized then that she really did want to die and wondered if the outcome had been inevitable after all. She stood in her crimson petticoat and red satin bodice. It was cut low in the back, to accommodate the executioner's ax.

Jane and Barbra were weeping uncontrollably. The queen turned to them, an almost happy expression on her face. "Do not weep. Remember, I promised that you wouldn't cry. Rejoice! For we will soon see an end to all my troubles." She turned to the rest of them standing below. "Please, be comforted."

When she turned back to have the cloth wrapped over her eyes, Brenden was barely able to swallow the lump caught in his throat. Be comforted. For Christ's sake, how? Without the slightest indication of fear, she knelt onto the cushion set before the block. She was reciting in Latin as she felt for the block and laid her head gently upon it.

Brenden had seen people die before, but he wanted to flee the scene of this murder. Her whole imprisonment and farce of a trial were unjust. Now she was being executed for trying to regain her liberty. It was almost more than he could bear, but he braced himself for her death, his failure burning in his heart.

"Into Your hands, O Lord, I commend my spirit!" the queen cried, her voice strong.

One of the executioners placed his hand squarely in the middle of her back as the other raised the ax high over his head. Steel caught the light of the fire, glinting off the blade. The ax fell, and Audrey jerked beside him. The executioner missed his mark, hitting the back of the queen's head. Her lips moved.

"Sweet Jesus," she whispered.

The executioner swiftly brought the ax down again, severing the neck. Blood spilled down the sides of the block. Her head rolled off the block and onto the scaffold, her body tumbling backward. The executioner rushed to her severed head and pulled the blindfold off. He grabbed it by the hair, holding it aloft before the crowd.

"God save Queen Elizabeth!" he cried.

The lips were still moving, continuing her death chant. The head separated from the lustrous auburn wig and fell to the ground. The executioner was motionless, staring at the head in horror. Brenden looked at Audrey just in time to see her begin to sway gently as her eyes rolled back in her head.

Brenden caught her when she fell. Christ, just let it be a swoon, not the bairn, he prayed. The room was silent, all attention riveted on the grisly gray head and its moving lips. No one noticed Audrey's faint.

He slapped her gently on both cheeks, but she was unresponsive. He took a deep breath and smacked her. Her eyes fluttered open, and she looked at him blankly for a moment before her eyes filled with tears.

"Pull yourself together," he whispered harshly. "I need you here now. All of you."

She nodded and stood unsteadily.

The captain immediately began calling out orders. "Take the prisoners back to the tower and secure them," he called to Brenden, then turned to the other groups of soldiers. "Clear the grounds, get the townsfolk out."

Now was his moment to act. His men were widely dispersed. He nodded to Camden, who grasped Audrey's arm, holding her back while the other prisoners were led to the tower.

Audrey tried to push away the scene that kept replaying itself in her head, the queen's lips moving, chanting; still alive, yet dead. She started forward and felt a hand on her elbow, staying her. She turned and found Camden beside her. He gave her a brief, reassuring smile. Brenden had moved forward with the others but was lagging behind slightly. The townsfolk were streaming toward Audrey as they left the great hall. Someone screamed, and people began milling around.

The executioner had leaned over the body to remove the queen's personal effects when Skye appeared from beneath her skirts and bit his hand. He jumped back in surprise. The dog stationed herself underneath the body, her shaggy fur drenched in her mistress's blood, a deep sorrowful growl rumbling in her throat.

"Now," Camden commanded, pushing Audrey into the melee. He stayed at the edge of the crowd, moving out of the hall and toward the gates. She merged with the people who were continuing home instead of watching this new development. Her blood pounded in her ears. She snatched the white hood off her head to make herself less conspicuous.

An old brown cloak dropped onto her shoulders, and she jumped. A tall figure strolled beside her. She looked up, and a pair of cobalt eyes gazed down at her.

"Gavin!" she whispered. A brown cap was pulled low over his head, only a few black curls escaped at the neck. He gave her a warning look and grabbed her elbow, steering her toward the gate. He was dressed in a brown homespun tunic, like the rest of the commoners.

"I have horses outside the gate," he said in a low voice. "We need to move quickly, but don't draw attention."

Her heart beat faster with each step they took. She didn't dare look back. She could still hear Skye barking and people shouting. Her eyes focused on the enormous gate looming before them. Six guards were stationed there. One of them, a black-bearded man, made eye contact with Gavin and looked away casually.

There was more yelling behind them. "One of the prisoners! She's missing!" Gavin's grip tightened, and he began dragging her. The black-bearded guard pointed to a woman behind Audrey, and the guards rushed her.

They were through the gate and crossing the drawbridge. A man stood a few yards from the second moat, holding horses. A rending creak started behind them, and she turned in fear. The portcullis was lowering. Shouting came from inside the gates.

"Raise the gate! Raise the gate! One of the prisoners has escaped."

They ran.

The distraction of the dog was better than Brenden could have hoped for, but it wasn't enough. The captain joined them halfway to the tower and noticed immediately that Audrey was missing. Brenden took control of the situation. Pointing only to his men, he ordered them to find the woman.

Gavin and Audrey were through the gate, and the men he had stationed there were lowering it. Camden was waiting beside it. Brenden ran past a group of soldiers accosting a poor townswoman on her way home.

Someone shouted to raise the gate. Brenden's men pretended to struggle with it. The gate was halfway down, and Camden stepped to the other side.

Brenden ran to the men lowering the portcullis as though he were trying to help. "When it's down, jam it!" He ran to the gate and rolled under it. His sword hilt dug painfully into his side. The gate crashed down behind him.

Gavin pulled Audrey along, darting around the people trying to leave the castle.

"Stop them!" someone shouted not far behind.

She heard the gate close, so she knew some of Paulet's men were on this side with them. Her throat burned from fear and running and gulping so much air. The drawbridge ended and a longer bridge followed, spanning the two enormous moats. Then their feet hit dirt. Gavin grabbed her by the waist and tossed her in the saddle of one horse and swung himself into another.

The soldiers rushed them, brandishing swords and pikes. Her horse reared. Clutching with all her strength to the mane, she managed to hold on. Rough hands were on her, pulling her down.

She was halfway out of the saddle when the hands were suddenly gone and she tumbled to the ground. The horse reared again. She covered her head and tried to escape the flailing hooves.

She was grabbed again and turned to fight back, but it was Camden. She clutched his shoulders in relief. The guards who attacked her were on the ground moaning and bleeding. Camden pushed her back up into the saddle. He had just slid his foot into the stirrup to mount behind her when she saw a soldier disengage from the crowd to run at his back.

"Camden!" she screamed. He turned, pistol drawn, and fired. Smoke and sparks emitted from the barrel, and the man fell a few feet from them, clutching his stomach. Her ears rang from the gun blast, and the sulfurous taste of gunpowder filled the air around them. She tried not to look at the man, but he was so close she couldn't avoid it. The shot had taken out almost his whole midsection. She looked beyond him and saw Brenden, fighting with two other men, a third bearing down on him.

"Let's go!" Gavin yelled, grabbing the reins of her horse. Camden spotted Brenden's predicament and slapped her horse on the rump.

"Ride!" he yelled, and ran toward Brenden, drawing his sword.

Brenden pressed his foot against the lifeless torso and yanked his sword from the corpse's gut, releasing a flow of bright red blood. He turned to block his new opponent's assault. The man brought the sword down from over his head with both hands. As their blades clashed, the shock reverberated through to Brenden's hands and up his arms. Brenden planted his feet firmly and forced the soldier back.

The move threw the man off balance, and Brenden's foot met him squarely in the chest, knocking him down. He brought his sword down cleanly, separating arm from shoulder.

He turned his back on the throes of agony as Camden finished off the last guard. The other men had left with Audrey as he had ordered. There was only one horse, and Brenden ran for it, grabbing Camden's arm as he passed. A quick scan told him no more of Paulet's men were outside the gates.

They reached the horse, and Brenden mounted. Camden had grasped his hand to climb up behind him when a voice bellowed out from the rear.

"God save Queen Elizabeth!"

Brenden withdrew the pistol from his waist, but not before the crack of another sounded. The blast knocked Camden backward, and his hand was almost ripped from Brenden's grip. Brenden held on tight as Camden slumped against the horse, sliding to his knees. Brenden turned in the saddle, leveling his gun at a man with a bushy red beard, dressed in black and wearing a tall black hat. He was holding a smoking pistol.

"Perish all—" the man began triumphantly. Brenden heard the hissing of the charge being lit when he fired. The bullet slammed into the man's shoulder, cutting him off in midsentence. His hat tumbled from his head as he fell.

Camden regained his footing. "Can you make it,

brother?" Brenden asked, his heart thudding in fear.

"Aye, 'tis nothing." But his voice was weak and raspy, and it took all of Brenden's strength to pull him into the saddle behind him.

They rode hard for several miles before Gavin signaled them to stop. Audrey didn't dare look back. She was a fair rider but had never run a horse so fast. Her only concern had been staying mounted.

No one said a word, but she knew what they were doing. Waiting. Waiting to see if Brenden and Camden would make it. It was silent except for the sound of the horses moving about impatiently. A tightness was forming in the pit of her stomach. They shouldn't be that far behind! She stared hard at the empty landscape in front of them. It was flatter here than farther north, but there was still the occasional rise of a low hill. Which was what her eyes were trained on now.

It was turning out to be an unseasonably warm day, but the beauty was lost on her. She willed them to appear. All she saw was brown grass stirring in the breeze, a small tree devoid of leaves, and a bush, the thick leaves brown and curling. Her throat was thickening, and her vision blurred. It was not time to cry.

"Look! It's him!" one of the men cried. She dashed her tears and strained her eyes. Her heart leapt, seeing him galloping over the hill toward them, then dropped again, until she saw Camden was on the horse with him.

She smiled at Gavin, and he grinned back. "You shouldn't worry yourself on them—it'll take better men than English scrubs to bring them down."

Her happiness began to dim as they drew nearer. There was a strange expression on Brenden's face. Camden held on to Brenden's waist with one arm and swayed slightly. She urged her horse forward to meet them.

"He's been shot," Brenden said grimly. "I don't know how bad it is, but he can't ride much longer."

Camden groaned and looked around, barely noticing his surroundings. "You make it sound as though I'm going to die."

Brenden immediately began giving orders. The four men were to ride straight for Scotland for their own safety and to keep the English off their trail should they come looking for them. The rest of them were to head for one of Nicholas Jennings's manor houses outside town. Una was there, and Nicholas would hide them as well if necessary.

They continued riding hard, though now it had more to do with fear for Camden than fear of being followed. He didn't look good. His face was pale, and Audrey was afraid he might fall off the horse. But he held on, even making wisecracks to Brenden from time to time.

By the time they reached the manor around midafternoon, she was feeling the strain of being up all night and the fear and tension of the morning. Una ran out the door weeping and threw herself at Audrey.

"I thought I'd never see ye again!" Then forgetting Audrey, she launched herself at Gavin. The tall grayhaired figure of Nicholas Jennings appeared at the door, leaning on a shiny black cane.

"Thank the saints! You made it back alive!" When he saw Camden supported by his brothers, he frowned. "It's just like you to get yourself injured so we all have to wait on you."

Camden smiled weakly and pushed Gavin and Brenden's help away. "God's bones! I'm not an invalid." He walked slowly to the house, wincing every few steps. He held his injured side with his good arm to contain the jarring.

Audrey couldn't bear to watch him, so she ducked under his uninjured arm and grabbed his wrist, pulling it around her shoulders. She wrapped her other arm around his waist. He was startled and began to protest.

"I know you're brave, Camden, you don't have to prove it to me," she whispered, not letting him pull away.

"But it's such fun." He smiled and shifted his weight so she carried some. "What shall I prove to you next?"

"You can start by proving you can make it up those steps." She nodded to the stone steps leading to the huge double doors standing open.

"Had I known you'd be so easy to please, I wouldn't have gotten myself shot."

Once inside, they had another flight of stairs to contend with, but at last he fell exhausted on a huge bed. Una had gone ahead of them and stripped the covers off. She had a basin of water ready and several pieces of linen.

They struggled to remove his clothing and ended up cutting his shirt off. Her stomach clenched at the sight of his ravaged shoulder. The entry wound was large and jagged and dark red with oozing blood. By the condition of his shirt, he had already lost a lot of blood.

Una was in control of the situation. She poked at the wound for a moment, then asked Nicholas if he had anything she might use to remove the bullet. Nicholas barked an order, and moments later, Una was handed a needle-nosed probe. At Audrey's urging, she wiped it down with the whiskey Nicholas had provided to dull their patient's pain.

Una thrust the whiskey into Camden's good hand.

He looked at her uncertainly, then took a huge swallow. She started toward the wound with the probe, and he held up his hand to stop her. When she looked at him inquiringly, he took several more huge drinks. He wiped his mouth and nodded to her.

Before she could start, Nicholas stopped her. "Whoa, lassie!" He handed Camden a thick piece of leather, which Camden wedged between his teeth.

"Is everyone ready now?" Una looked around the room impatiently; when no one replied, she set to work. Audrey would have preferred not to watch, but since her services were needed to catch the spilling blood, she was left little choice but to press linen after linen underneath Camden's arm as Una worked. Brenden held Camden's hand. From the whites of Camden's knuckles and the sheen of sweat on his brow, it was clear the whiskey wasn't helping. Brenden looked to be in a great deal of pain, too, and Audrey wondered whether Camden could break his hand if the pain were great enough.

Finally, Una held up a large, misshapen lead ball, dripping with blood. Camden spit the piece of leather out and promptly threw up. He apologized repeatedly as Audrey cleaned the mess.

"Please, Camden!" she said in frustration. "I really don't mind!"

Una cleaned the wound and stitched his shoulder up. He had a profusion of curly blond hair on his chest, and it was thickly matted with blood. Audrey's hands were shaking as she washed him. She'd seen so much blood. So much killing. She didn't know how she was managing to stay calm.

When Una had finished, she wrapped a long strip of linen under his arm and around his shoulder, tying it to hold firm. Una thought a rib might be cracked, so they leaned Camden forward and wrapped his chest tightly with more strips of linen. His face was pale, and his jaw tight from the pain.

Una surveyed her work critically. "You were lucky," she said to him. "I knew a man who was run through with a lance in much the same place, and the blood was spurtin' out so fast, he was dead before we could do anything for him."

Camden gave her a look that said he could have done without this piece of information. "I thank you, Una. You did a fine job of it. Didn't hurt much at all."

Brenden laughed, opening and closing the hand Camden had squeezed, illustrating just how much it had hurt. Audrey felt somewhat better looking at him now. He was a big man, muscular and strong. She was sure he would be all right. Blood was already seeping through to stain the linen, but it wasn't excessive.

The men left, and Camden grinned at Una and Audrey. "It makes it worthwhile, having two bonny lassies washing and waiting on me." He rubbed at his beard thoughtfully. "I could use a shave." He arched an eyebrow at Audrey quizzically, a wicked little smile on his face.

"Now I know you're all right." She pulled the covers over him. "You be good and get some rest, and I might consider it."

A woman entered carrying a small vial with black liquid in it. "Drink this. It'll help with the pain." She handed it to him. He sniffed at it and made a face.

"Drink it," Audrey commanded, then wondered belatedly what she had ordered him to drink. Una followed the woman out, and Audrey turned to leave, too, so he could rest, but he caught her hand.

"Sit with me a bit, Audrey. At least until that swill puts me to sleep." He looked at her so appealingly, she couldn't refuse. She pulled a chair up by the bed.

They sat silently for a few moments before she spoke. "I want to thank you for rescuing me back there." Her voice faltered.

He looked at her strangely and opened his mouth to say something, then shrugged, wincing as the movement hurt his shoulder. "What else was I to do?"

"I don't know. I was just so scared . . . I've never seen anyone killed before." Tears were building in her eyes, but she forced them back. She had been the one to discover her late husband after he shot himself. For some reason, the day's events brought this vivid memory to her mind, and she couldn't push it away.

He took her hand and squeezed it. They sat that way until she noticed his eyelids becoming heavy. He seemed to be fighting sleep, but finally sighed deeply and gave in to it. She watched him—glad someone could sleep and forget for a time. She stood and gently tried to pull her hand away. His grip tightened, and his eyes opened.

They were glazed, and it took him a moment to focus on her. She smoothed the curling blond hair off his brow. It had grown longer in the past month and curled at the ends like Brenden's.

"Go to sleep," she whispered. "I'll bring you something to eat later."

"I love you, Audrey."

"And I love you," she said, her hand still resting on his brow.

His mouth turned down slightly at the corners, and he closed his eyes. "I know."

She stayed with him until she was sure he was sleeping soundly. His chest rose and fell gently. She tiptoed out, closing the door quietly. When she turned, Brenden was coming up the stairs.

"Is he all right?"

"Yes, he's sleeping."

Brenden put his arms around her, holding her close. She could hear the steady beating of his heart and was comforted. Feelings of warmth and safety rushed over her. But the constant question nagging at her was, what next? He had failed. What did failure as immense as this mean to a man like Brenden? And what was she going to do? If she loved him, how could she leave him to deal with this on his own?

He took her hand and led her to the room next to Camden's. She was relieved to see her gray wool dress and coarse shift were clean and lying across the bed. They were so much more comfortable than the dresses she had been wearing. She started undressing.

"A bath is being brought up, so you might want to wait."

He was wearing a cream-colored shirt and leather breeches. She was hesitant to resume the relationship they had begun before Fotheringhay. He had been rather callous about her pregnancy. He sat on the bed and stared into space. She knew he was hurting. She pushed aside her own doubts and joined him.

"He never wanted to be part of this, you know that?" He was talking about Camden, and she nodded. He became quiet again. She laid her head against his shoulder.

"I never did ask you, what is your religion?"

She frowned at the unusual question, but answered readily enough, "Protestant, I guess. I've only been to church a few times. Alex and I were married by a Justice of the Peace."

"Then you won't object to a Catholic ceremony?"

She stared straight ahead, unable to believe what he was saying. "Are you asking me to marry you?"

"Aye." When she was silent, he continued, "Nicholas keeps a priest. It will take place before dinner."

She stood and walked away from him. "I'm not ready to marry you. I haven't made the decision to stay here yet."

"You're carrying my child; the decision is made."

She looked at him incredulously. "That makes the decision even more difficult! Do you realize that in my time most women and their children live through childbirth? It's not something to fear!"

"Please don't leave." He sounded so desolate, she thought her heart would break.

She sighed helplessly. "Tell me what you're feeling, Brenden, please." She knelt before him and stroked his beard. He shook his head. "You did all you could. I know Bothwell doesn't blame you."

He gave a short, harsh laugh and grabbed her arms. "Is that all you can do, woman, talk?"

Before she could get any words out, he was kissing her. She wound her arms around his neck and let him pull her onto the bed. His hand was at her neck, moving down to her chest. He looked down. He lifted the silver chain around her neck. She had placed the queen's wedding ring on it with her locket.

"What is this?" he asked, turning it over in his hand.

"The wedding ring Bothwell gave Mary."

He released her and rolled onto his back, looking away from her. "You better wash."

She said nothing more and waited for the bath to be brought up.

* * *

I did this to you. Brenden stared down at Camden's sleeping face. The blood was drying on the linen bandages. Did Camden hate him? Probably not. It wasn't his way.

Audrey was bathing. When she was finished, Brenden would take her to the tiny room where mass was said and Nicholas prayed, and he would marry the only woman Camden had ever loved. *I did this to you.*

Brenden needed to think but was having a hard time doing so. What was his life now? That question was haunting him. He was about to marry a woman so extraordinary, he could hardly pass a moment without her face in his mind. She was carrying his child. His plotting was over. He could devote himself to his business again; he had left the reins of that in others' hands for too long. He should feel as though a great weight had been lifted from his shoulders. So why, then, did it feel like one was crushing him?

He sat there for what seemed like hours before Nicholas walked in. "The lass sits in your room staring at the wall like you. Mayhap this is not a good day for a wedding."

Brenden shook himself and stood. "Nay, fetch her. I'm ready."

Nicholas raised his eyebrows. He sighed and left. Brenden went to the tiny oratory. There was a picture of the virgin on a shelf, an elaborate ebony crucifix, and an embroidered kneeler. Candles were lit, and the priest, already in his robes, nodded at Brenden. She entered with Nicholas, and Gavin and Una followed. She was dressed simply in the wool dress that had been laid out on the bed. She didn't look happy.

She had lost weight. Her cheekbones stood out, and her eyes seemed larger than they ever had. Her face was pale. Brenden was afraid she might faint. *I am forcing her to do this.* The realization struck him hard, and he could only stare at her. The knowledge changed nothing. He would not let her go. But it increased the gnawing feeling in his gut.

He took her hand as they knelt before the priest. Before the man could begin, Brenden held up his hand. He turned to her. She was staring straight ahead, unblinking.

"Audrey, look at me."

She turned her soft gray gaze on him.

"Do you love me at all?"

Her eyes filled with tears, and his chest became tight, waiting for her answer.

"Yes." A tear spilled over her lashes, and she turned back to the priest. He squeezed her hand and felt some relief when hers tightened in answer.

After the solemn ceremony, they went downstairs to the hall in the center of the house. Brenden still held Audrey's hand tightly, and she was thankful. She seemed to be deriving strength and comfort from his touch. She still didn't know why she had gone through with the ceremony. Of course, it was because she loved him, but it was also the sadness in his eyes. How could she leave him?

She had seen that same sadness in Alex's eyes once. Audrey forced herself not to think about the similarities and instead admired Nicholas's beautiful house. It was bigger than the one Audrey had stayed at in town. The walls were covered with shining wood paneling. Beautiful tapestries, done in rich burgundies, greens, and golds, hung on the walls. In the dining room, they were all seated at a long table.

Nicholas was Catholic and was very disappointed to hear of the failed rescue. "As soon as I heard, I sent a man telling the *Marigold* to set sail, along with our other caravels resting in harbor. No doubt, as soon as word reaches London, all ports will be closed." Nicholas shook his head sadly. He was about fifty and in very good shape, despite the fact that his right leg was wood from the knee down.

Brenden leaned back in his chair. "I didn't have a chance to ask you how she fared on her last voyage." He had shaved his beard off and looked younger. His jaw was smooth and strong. She could see the thick muscles of his neck disappearing into his shirt collar.

Nicholas's brown eyes lit up at the mention of profit, and he smiled. "I think you'll be well pleased. She managed to intercept a Spanish ship off the Azores. It was laden down with gold and silver plate, and a little something extra we weren't aware of."

Brenden looked at him inquiringly.

"Pearls." He watched Brenden for a reaction, and when he got none, he frowned. "What's the matter, lad? Queen Elizabeth loves pearls and will probably buy the lot of them at whatever price we ask. You have grown richer yet! Should you not be happy?"

Brenden shrugged. "What was the return on the shares?"

Nicholas was grinning broadly. "Over five hundred percent! What think you of that?"

Audrey choked on the meat she was eating, making Nicholas laugh.

"You've not told the wife about your other activities?"

Brenden gave her a sideways look. "In time, I planned to."

"Are you pirates?" she asked in horror.

Nicholas shook his head vigorously. "No, no, my dear Audrey. Not pirates. Privateers. Commissioned by the Queen of England." He turned back to Brenden. "Ah, yes, Lord Burghley was so pleased with his five percent, he would like to front another voyage. He's most impatient."

"Who is Lord Burghley?" she asked.

Brenden looked mildly amused. "William Cecil, Queen Elizabeth's chief minister."

She was astounded. "The English fund your . . . privateering?"

"Well, not Brenden directly," Nicholas answered. "They don't like dealing with smelly Scotsmen." He grinned at Brenden and Gavin. "But they like me fine, and they certainly like the *Marigold*." He guffawed at that.

"What is the *Marigold*?" she asked, looking between them.

"A ship," Brenden said shortly, stuffing bread into his mouth.

"A ship! Do you hear this man?" Nicholas was warming to his subject now. "He owns a dozen or so of these fast ships!"

Audrey was stunned. She knew Brenden did a great deal of traveling and engaged in trading, but she'd thought his father supported him. Gavin was eating calmly, this obviously being old news, but Una stared at Brenden in awe. She turned to Gavin and punched him in the arm.

"You lout! Ye never told me this!"

"Oh, aye." Brenden grinned. "Don't think I sail alone! Gavin is a partner."

"Aye, my dear. Your future husband is no pauper," Nicholas added.

Brenden and Audrey gaped at them. "Future husband?" they asked simultaneously.

Una smiled sheepishly, her cheeks becoming rosy. "Well, with all that was going on, we didn't have a chance to tell you."

Audrey noticed how pretty she looked. She was wearing a pale-blue silk gown, the same color as her eyes. Her blond hair was braided and coiled around her head. Her birthmark even seemed less prominent.

"Er . . . uh . . . when?" Brenden asked.

"We'd like to get the matter with Synn Marshall settled first," Gavin answered, smiling proudly. "We don't want the charge of witchcraft hanging over our heads."

Audrey could see Nicholas was enjoying this interchange. She knew from the week she had spent with him before she went to Fotheringhay that he was not only a business associate of Brenden's but a good friend as well. He had been married for twenty-five years and widowed for three. He took to both Una and Audrey immediately, with a fatherly affection. He told them his only child, a daughter, had died when she was ten.

"Una asked me to give her away," he said, puffed up with pride. "So it looks as though I'll finally make it to that horrid country of yours."

"Congratulations!" Audrey said, becoming excited for them now that the shock was past. "So, what are you planning to wear?" And suddenly the air of gloom that had encompassed them since their arrival began to dissipate.

She was still fighting to sort out the misconception she had of Brenden when they went upstairs after dinner. He was self-sufficient! Rich! He hadn't simply been plotting for nearly a decade. He had a life outside it. She was beginning to feel relieved about her decision to go through with the marriage.

The tension and despair that had surrounded Brenden before had lifted, though he was still quiet. A fire blazed in their room, and Audrey was suddenly aware that this was their wedding night. Her stomach began to knot in anticipation, but she wanted to get some answers out of him first. Brenden looked exhausted and started undressing. She crossed her arms under her chest and looked at him expectantly.

"Well?"

"What?" He sat on the bed and removed his boots.

"Privateering? *Marigold*? You want to explain why I'm just now hearing about this?"

He pulled the ties on his shirt, exposing the red-brown curling hair scattered across his chest. "There's naught to tell."

"I was under the impression you lived off your father!"

"I don't know where you got that idea."

She frowned. It was true he had never offered the information and she had never asked. Still, she felt it was something he should have told her.

He saw her look and sighed. "If you stayed, I wanted it to be for me. Not for my coin or my titles." He grabbed her wrist and pulled her between his thighs. "Do you love me more now you know I have wealth? Mayhap you wouldn't have fought me in the beginning had I showed you my coffers."

"You're not funny."

"Aye, but you are. The oddest things bother you." He unhooked her bodice and pushed it off. "Just think, you'll never have to wear these rags again."

"I like this dress."

"Then you shall have dozens of them."

She smiled.

"The servants won't know the countess from the scullery maid." He pushed her skirt off.

She laughed and sat on the bed beside him, pulling her feet beneath her. "How did you meet Nicholas?"

He looked a little put out at her delay tactic, but stretched out on his side. "I met him when I was in Paris. He sailed his own ships then."

"Is that how he lost his leg? Sailing?"

"Nay," Brenden said, reaching his hand out to toy with the hem of her shift. "He took a fall from a horse and broke it. The bone went through his skin. The surgeon set it, but it became swollen and putrid, so they removed it."

She swallowed hard. That was right, there were no antibiotics. An infection in this century could cause the loss of an appendage.

"I see. So you met him in Paris and went into business together."

"Something like that." He grabbed her shift and pulled her to him. "Enough of this talking." He pushed her back on the bed. She felt weak with anticipation and wanting. He undid the ties that held the front of her shift closed and pushed it aside, pressing his lips between her breasts. "You are truly mine now," he murmured against her skin.

His words sent liquid fire through her. She longed to be possessed by him. There was nothing she wanted more. His hand moved over her breast, cupping it, stroking the nipple with his rough thumb. His breath was warm on her skin. His hand moved down her ribs to caress her stomach, his mouth covering her nipple, heating her sensitive flesh. Her hands were in his hair, holding him to her. She was trembling with need, the ache between her thighs becoming sharp.

He kissed her, his tongue delving deeply, his hand sliding up her thigh to rub her until she whimpered and pulled at his breeches. He shed his clothes, giving her access to the hard muscles that layered his body. His skin was fevered and damp, and he gripped her thighs, pulling her to him and surging into her with the same urgency that was filling her. He seemed almost wild with passion, and she abandoned herself to it, her nails digging into his skin, her mouth hungry for the taste of him.

Later, she lay against him, her cheek against the damp skin of his chest, feeling weak and wrung out from their lovemaking. He trailed his fingers gently up and down her spine, sending delicious shivers through her. She tightened her arms around him and let the feelings of foreboding and unease go. She loved him. She carried his child. The dreams were over. He was her life now, and she gave herself over to happiness.

Audrey woke to the thin light of dawn streaming through the window. She turned to Brenden. His face was soft in sleep, his hair rumpled. He looked so young, his thick, dark lashes lying against his cheeks. She eased out of bed, not wanting to wake him, and donned her shift.

After washing her face and teeth and tying her hair back, she tiptoed out of the room and went to see Camden. She was surprised to find him awake. He smiled weakly, and his face was flushed. She placed her hand on his forehead. He was hot.

"How do you feel?"

"My shoulder hurts like hell. I can hardly move it."

The blood on the dressing had dried to a rust color, and there was a new ominous dampness staining it. Trying to look unconcerned, she removed the dressing. The skin around the wound was an angry red, the area swollen from collarbone to neck. It had a discharge that smelled unpleasant. He was lying back on the pillows, not even attempting to look at it, for which she was glad. She was terrified. She had no idea what to do for an infection.

She pressed on the swollen skin around the wound. "Does this hurt?"

"Like fire," he mumbled.

"All right," she said, trying to gather her wits. "I'll be right back." She wrapped a piece of linen loosely around it and hurried from the room. Brenden was still sleeping when she burst in.

"Brenden, wake up," she said, shaking him.

"What is it?" He was immediately alert and threw the covers back to sit up.

"It's Camden." She willed her voice not to shake. "The wound . . . it's all swollen and infected. He's feverish."

He sat on the edge of the bed, staring at her. He bit his lip, as though he were thinking hard about this new development.

"I don't know what to do," she said helplessly. "In my time, he'd be given antibiotics. I don't know what you do for infection here."

He grabbed his breeches and pulled them on. "Get Una—she seems to know something about healing."

Audrey hurried to Una's bedchamber and knocked before entering. Una sat up groggily and rubbed her eyes, long gold hair falling over her shoulders.

"It's Camden. He's running a fever, and his shoulder is swollen."

Una shook her head to clear it. "Well, it's not strange his shoulder is swollen, I expected that. But he's feverish, ye say?" Audrey nodded. Una got out of bed, grabbed a blue velvet dressing gown and tied it beneath her breasts. "Go to him and clean it with water as hot as he can stand. I'll send some up. I'll see what I can find in the kitchen."

Brenden was sitting with Camden when Audrey

returned. Brenden wore his breeches, but his shirt was hanging out and half-tied. She looked at the tray of untouched food by the bed.

"You haven't eaten anything," she admonished Camden. He gave her a listless green gaze but said nothing. She tried to think of something to say, since they were all sitting there silently. "I'll give you that shave today."

He grimaced. "No, my skin hurts."

The water in the basin was cold, so she wet a towel and wiped his face with it. His skin was hot and dry, but she didn't think his fever was dangerous at this point. She sat on the bed next to him, trying to coax him into conversation. His answers were short and his smiles faked for her benefit, so she finally let the oppressive silence overtake them. Sun spilled through the window. She watched the particles of dust floating in the beam of light. Camden also seemed to be riveted by the dust show, but Brenden stared at the wall.

When the hot water was finally brought up, she set to cleaning his wound. The bullet had ravaged his shoulder, and she wondered if anything else inside him was damaged. She had never been badly hurt herself and had no idea how something this serious healed on its own. Maybe this was nothing, part of the healing process. But the story Brenden had told her about Nicholas's leg forced its way into her head, making her wonder where they would amputate if it came to that. The placement of the wound would make it impossible. What then?

Una entered as Audrey was finishing up. Gavin trailed in, sleepy-eyed, behind her. Camden looked around at everyone. Some life came into his eyes, and he grinned.

"I'm not dead yet, let's hold the funeral off a bit longer."

"Bah!" Gavin said, waving his hand at him. "You're

not going to die; that's just what you want us all to think."

"It's working, too. Why, Audrey is begging to shave me! I wonder what I can get her to do next." He winked at her.

Una was carrying a small wooden bowl, which she set aside so she could inspect his shoulder. After checking everything thoroughly, she began applying the mixture in the bowl to the wound. Camden did not look pleased and said as much. "Now I smell like a wee flower!"

Una ignored him.

When the wound was redressed, Audrey signaled Una to join her. They left Camden's room and went to Audrey's.

"What was that stuff?" Audrey asked after the door was shut.

"Mostly egg and oil of rose. Some other things I found in the kitchen."

Putting oil on a wound did not sound safe to Audrey. She knew putting butter on a burn was unwise, but maybe this was different. She certainly wasn't qualified to protest. "Will it work?"

Una shrugged. "I've seen it work before."

"I take it that also means you've seen it not work."

She looked dismayed. "Well . . . I'll be honest with ye, Audrey. I've seen men die from less than Camden's shoulder wound. Big, healthy, strong men. I've also seen them pull through worse. I canna say." Seeing the stricken look on Audrey's face, Una continued with a bit more confidence. "The only thing that really concerns me is his fever. His shoulder did seem a wee bit over-swollen, but the discharge is normal, I think."

"Maybe we should send someone into town for a doctor."

She sighed. "We're hiding, remember? We can't call attention to ourselves. Besides, do you know what a surgeon would do?" Audrey shook her head. "Scald it with oil or a red-hot poker to cauterize it, probably makin' it worse. So then he will die in more pain than he's already in."

Audrey couldn't stop herself; the situation seemed so awful, she burst into tears. "Please tell me he's not going to die."

"I don't know." Una put her arm around Audrey. "But I can say for certain it's too early for ye to be weepin' over it now. I told ye, I've seen men pull through it. My mother was a healer before she was charged with sorcery and burned. She taught me much of what she knew."

Audrey nodded, drying her tears. She took a few deep breaths before returning to Camden's room. Nicholas was there.

"Ah, the ladies are back. Good." He smiled at them. "I was just telling your men I'm expecting a visit from the constable any moment. He was spotted less than a mile down the road. I need you to stay up here, whilst I get rid of him." He started to leave, then turned back. "And if he feels the need to search my house . . ." He looked at Brenden. "Well, you know what to do."

"The constable? What's he doing here?" Audrey asked after Nicholas left.

"Nicholas is a Catholic, and we did escape in his general direction. I'm surprised they're just now coming to see him," Brenden said.

She looked at him in alarm. "And what is it that you're supposed to do if he decides to search the house?" She hoped it had nothing to do with killing anyone. She'd seen enough death. Brenden walked to a tapestry and pulled it aside. He hit the wall with the flat of his fist and a section of the paneling popped open. Audrey poked her head in. It was a small room with no windows. It took her eyes a few minutes to adjust to the dark, but when they did, she saw there were benches, a cupboard, and even a narrow cot.

"How convenient." She looked at Brenden nervously, wondering why someone would build a hidden room in their house.

He smiled at the look on her face. "This wee room has saved a few Jesuit priests from death." He looked around at the others. "Shall we?"

With Brenden's help, Camden managed to get off the bed. Brenden half carried him into the room, while Una and Audrey hurriedly tidied up to remove any clues to their presence and made the bed. A candle burned in the little room, and Camden was propped up on the bed, looking extremely uncomfortable. Audrey sat on a bench near him.

She hadn't thought of the men they had left behind at Fotheringhay, but the constable's showing up made her wonder what was to become of them.

"What about all your men?" she asked Brenden when he sat down next to her.

"What about them?"

"You left them behind!" She was surprised he could be so calm about it. "What's going to happen to them?"

"Naught, I imagine. They will continue on in their posts until security is dropped, then they'll go home."

"But won't they be associated with you?"

"Nay, Camden made certain of that." He nodded to Camden. "He made sure our forged papers, including those of the men that left with us, were different from the others. Also, they were sent under a separate muster."

"They cannot be traced back to us," Camden said from the corner.

Audrey felt some relief that no one else would suffer. Thank goodness for Camden. He was the oil that had greased the bearings through it all.

They talked quietly in the small room for close to an hour. The door popped open at last, and Nicholas's smiling face poked in. "All's clear!"

They filed out and settled Camden in bed once more. He looked as if he felt like hell, and Audrey desperately wished there was something she could do to ease his pain.

"What did the constable want?" Brenden asked.

Nicholas looked at Brenden wryly. "Well, they know it was you. But that seemed to be the only thing the constable actually knew. You did quite a job on the castle gate. It took them three hours to get it back up and then they only allowed one person to leave. He was destined for London to tell Queen Elizabeth the deed was done. The sheriff was finally allowed to go home this morning, and he sent the constable and a few men to check the surrounding area. They think you're halfway to Scotland by now."

Brenden nodded. "That's what I hoped." He gave Gavin a look of amusement. "They should be haranguing our father about my whereabouts before long."

Gavin grinned back. "He will appreciate that, I've no doubt."

"There was some talk you were tied into the French ambassador's alleged plot to kill Queen Elizabeth," Nicholas said with raised eyebrows. "But I don't think he's taking it seriously. There appears to be some doubt a plot even existed. The constable said he thinks putting the French ambassador under house arrest was merely one of Walsingham's safety measures."

"That's a different matter now," Camden said from the bed. "Liberating a prisoner and killing the reigning sovereign are not the same thing. Should they get their hands on you, I'll wager Walsingham will be finding a way to tie them together. You're forgetting the bond of association Queen Elizabeth's men have signed. They have sworn to execute anyone who threatens her royal person."

"Don't worry, they won't find me." Brenden sat in the chair by Camden's bed. "You better gain your feet again soon so we can head north."

Camden sighed. "You're wasting time. You should take the others and just go. I'll follow soon."

"Nay, I'm not leaving without you." Brenden leaned back in the chair, crossing his stocking feet in front of him.

"Don't be a fool. Every minute you stay, you put everyone in danger, including Nicholas," Camden said in frustration.

Nicholas put up his hands. "I'm not worried. You're welcome here as long as you care to stay."

Camden looked at Audrey for help. She sat next to him on the bed. "I'm not leaving without you, sorry."

He shook his head, but he gave them a small smile. "Dolts! The lot of you."

He lay back on the pillows, looking very tired. The others took the hint and left, but Brenden and Audrey stayed. She was reluctant to leave him again, fearing what she might find when she returned. Brenden seemed to share this feeling, and they sat quietly with him until he dozed off.

His fever rose steadily throughout the day. Audrey tried to get him to eat and drink some water, but he refused.

Around noon, she finally got some bread down him, but ten minutes later, he threw it up. After that, she pushed broth. He would take a few sips, then turn his head away in disgust.

She was becoming very worried. How could he fight off the infection without food? His whole body was like a furnace; face, chest, even his legs were hot. And he was dry, no sign of the fever breaking. He became more and more listless.

By evening, the discharge from his wound had changed from being almost clear and thin to thick and yellowish. When Una came to change the bandage and reapply the poultice to his shoulder, she shook her head grimly.

Sometime in the middle of the night, he opened his eyes and looked at Brenden and Audrey sitting wearily by his bedside. His eyes were bloodshot from the fever, and his lips were cracking. Audrey went to him and took his impossibly hot hand. His grip was surprisingly strong, and it gave her a spark of hope.

"What is it? Can I get you anything?" She began running down a list of things he might want, but he shook his head.

"It's Stephen," he said in a rasping voice. He cleared his throat. "I asked Brenden to care for him should anything happen to me." She started shaking her head, willing the tears not to fall. He squeezed her hand. "His mother didn't live through the birthing, and he's always been with me and his grandmother. I want you to raise him as if he were your own." He rushed on, as though he thought she might refuse. "He's a good lad, I know you'll love him. And I can't think of a better woman for the job."

She was unable to speak. Brenden stood abruptly and walked to the window.

"You're not going to die," she said firmly.

"Just promise me."

Hot tears ran down her cheeks. "I promise."

"The pony . . . I told him I'd get him a pony for his birthday. Please make sure he gets it." His eyes became watery. "Tell him his da thinks of him oft and to stick with his studies." His voice broke, and he couldn't go on.

Brenden mumbled some excuse and left the room. Audrey moved to the head of the bed and pulled Camden against her. He was quiet, but when she touched his face, his cheeks were wet and terribly hot.

"I never thought I wouldn't be able to say good-bye. God . . . I scolded him the day before we left. And it was so stupid. . . ."

She hushed him, unable to stand hearing the regrets he felt powerless to change. "He knows you love him," she whispered, touching his hair.

"God willing, he does."

They passed another day and night much the same way, his fever burning, his skin hopelessly dry. Audrey gave him every ounce of her attention and energy, but by the next morning, he had fallen into a state of delirium. It took Gavin and Brenden both to hold him down when Audrey and Una changed the dressings. She had never seen a person so consumed by fever, and she knew his body couldn't take much more of it. They continued bathing him in cold water and cleaning and dressing his wound. It was so swollen and putrid that Audrey knew it was hopeless. They were only waiting now.

Brenden sat beside him with dark circles under his eyes.

"Maybe you should get some sleep. I'll stay with him," she said, sitting on the bed.

He shook his head. "No, I couldn't sleep if I wanted to. I don't want to."

Dark whiskers covered his chin and jaw. He was still wearing the half-tied shirt and breeches he had donned when she first came to him about Camden's fever. She couldn't remember the last time he had eaten.

She went to him and tried to put her arms around him. He pulled away, leaning on the arm of the chair to get away from her. She was taken aback by his rejection, but she decided not to push it.

Audrey opened her eyes and saw morning's soft light filling the room. She sat up and rubbed her eyes. She hadn't meant to fall asleep. Brenden sat in a chair across the room with his face buried in his hands. Fear stole over her, and she stared hard at him, her chest becoming tight. In the edges of her vision, she could see the figure on the bed lying too still. She refused to look directly at it, instead focusing on Brenden. But part of her was watching, waiting for some sign of life: a moan, the smallest whisper of a breath, the motion of a chest rising and falling.

She stood and walked to the bed, looking down at last. His eyes were closed and the flush of fever had left his face somewhat. She touched him. He was still a little warm, but his chest was still. He didn't look dead. He looked as though any minute he might open his eyes and say something to make her laugh. *Please God, make him open his eyes.*

She didn't realize she was crying or saying these thoughts aloud until she felt hands on her shoulders.

When she turned, she was looking up into Gavin's red-rimmed eyes. She buried her face in his shirt.

Audrey took to bed, crying herself into an exhausted sleep. It was dark when she woke, and immediately images of Camden's bearded face lying peacefully against the pillow flooded her mind. Her head and body hurt from the sobs, but her heart didn't seem to care. She felt movement on the bed.

She turned and found herself staring at Brenden's broad back. She scooted close and slid her arm around his waist. His muscles tensed. She felt for his hand and took it in her own, wanting to comfort him. It lay limply in hers for a minute, then he pulled it away.

"Brenden, please don't do this."

She pressed her wet cheek against his back, feeling doubly hurt that he was rejecting her solace. He sat on the edge of the bed, moving away from her arms. Moonlight filtered though the window, outlining his back in silver.

"I killed him."

She got off the bed and onto her knees in front of him. She grabbed his wrists, pulling his hands away from his face. "You did not kill him."

"Aye, I killed him, as though I pulled the trigger myself." He yanked his hands away and stood.

"Stop it!"

"He never wanted to do this. I made him. I have brought naught put pain and death upon my family, and for what?" He grabbed her arms, lifting her to her feet as though she weighed nothing. "For what?"

She shrank away from him. "You didn't make him do anything, Brenden. He was capable of making his own decisions!"

"Was he? Could he choose whom he loved?" His grip on her arms was painful. "I would give you to him now if it would bring him back."

"Shut up!" she screamed, twisting away from him. "Just stop it! Now you're talking nonsense."

"Am I?" He advanced on her, his face dark with anger. "Why should I be the one to live? And have a wife and child and . . . God!" He covered his eyes. "And his son! I have taken everything!"

She backed away from him. "Brenden, he wouldn't want you to do this to yourself."

"How the hell would you know what he wanted?" He grabbed her again. "It was you he wanted and I hated it. Every time he looked at you, knowing he wanted you. I could have killed him a hundred times over for it."

"But you didn't, dammit! You didn't kill him."

"You don't really believe that, do you?" he said in a low voice. "I've been waiting patiently for you to remind me how you predicted this all along. What are you waiting for? You were right! How does it feel to have been right all along, saddled with a blustering ass of a man determined to have his own way?"

She hesitated a second too long, and he shoved her backward on the bed. He stood over her, glowering down at her as though he hated her.

"Is it not bad enough he died?" she asked, her voice shaking with anger and hurt. "Now you have to throw words in my face you know damn well I didn't mean that way."

He didn't respond, but continued giving her his hard green stare. She rose to her knees and moved closer.

"Please, don't do this. I don't want to fight with you now." She looked at him pleadingly.

"I forgot, you must talk everything out!"

She sat on her knees and looked down at her hands, unbearably hurt that he would treat her this way. At that moment she wanted to flee back to her time. Forget him and this place. She didn't even care if the dreams persisted after she left. It would be a comfort to be with the familiar.

He sighed deeply and rubbed his forehead. "Get some sleep. We're leaving in the morning." He headed for the door.

"Where are you going?"

"I need a drink. I'll be back."

"Wait," she said, crawling off the bed. "I'll go with you. I'm not tired."

"Audrey, please!" His voiced stopped her cold. He almost hissed it through clenched teeth. "Just," he took a breath to calm himself, "go to bed. I said I would be back."

Audrey stared blankly at the door after he left.

She was still rigidly awake when he came in a few hours later. Her eyes were accustomed to the dark, and she watched him struggle out of his clothes, catching himself on the chair once to keep from falling. He was drunk. He crawled beneath the covers next to her and leaned on his elbow to look down at her. His eyes apparently hadn't fully adjusted yet, because he started, realizing she was awake and staring back at him. Without a word, he turned his back on her and went to sleep.

Audrey sat on the bed sewing while Brenden stared down at her with annoyance. She tried to ignore him and not get angry, but she kept stabbing her finger with the needle. Her anger at him grew with each prick.

"Is there a problem?" she asked, her voice dripping with sarcasm. He had not been there when she awoke and showed up now only to ask why she wasn't ready to leave. She had been so angry with him that she had ripped her bodice in her violent dressing and was now trying to repair the damage.

"If you used a thimble, you wouldn't hurt yourself."

That was it. She threw the bodice in his face, catching him off guard. "You fix it."

He raised an eyebrow and sat in the chair to inspect it. He ripped out all the stitching she had done up to that point and started over. She watched him mend her bodice, not pricking himself once. His auburn head was bent, a small frown of concentration between his brows. His hands were large and callused, yet his fingers pulled the small needle deftly through the fabric. He tied it off, cutting the thread with his teeth. He tossed the bodice on her lap.

"Uh . . . thanks," she said, eyeing the repairs. He had done a good, sturdy job. "Where did you learn to do that?"

"There are no women at sea."

He seemed to be watching her as she put it on, but she could tell he was actually looking through her. His arms were crossed, a frown pulling at his brow. She knew he was hurting. She decided to swallow her pride and try to close the chasm between them. She reached out a tentative hand, touching his arm.

"Let's go," he said and left.

She looked around the room. The feeling that she had forgotten something, that she was leaving something behind, seized her. But she had nothing, so there was nothing to forget. She touched her locket and the queen's ring around her neck. She went to the door, glancing back uncertainly, that nagging feeling still tugging at her.

Una, Gavin, and Brenden waited in front of the house. Gavin looked up to the window of the room where Camden's body still lay. Una touched his arm, and they held each other until Brenden told them curtly it was time to leave. Nicholas was having Camden's body sent to Creag Liath for the funeral, and it would arrive shortly after they did. They were staying off the roads on the journey home, just in case the English were looking for them.

Home. It didn't feel like she was going home. What lay ahead of her? A world where people died in childbirth and from infections. A cold, drafty castle with no running water and an even colder husband. The feeling of depression that enveloped her had a niggling familiarity. Hadn't she been here before? Yes, except that the cold, remote man's name was Alex.

They were a party of grim, silent riders, once more sporting their crude wool and homespun. Una observantly pointed out that they had shoes, buttons on their clothing, and saddles and their horses were shod, all of which lent to the idea that they weren't completely destitute. It was something that Audrey hadn't realized but Una had picked up on when she first met them. It seemed they were a prime target for highwaymen. The reason they hadn't been accosted yet was probably due to the size of the men Audrey traveled with.

Gavin had a fine wardrobe made up for Una while they were staying with Nicholas. Nicholas was sending it along with the body. Una had gotten used to the luxury of living with Nicholas and told Audrey she wasn't looking forward to the harshness of travel. But it was better to look as though they had little.

Around midafternoon, they stopped to rest the horses and eat. It was a quiet meal, but Brenden was the only one brooding.

"What are we going to do when we get back?" Audrey asked him.

"I know not." He didn't even look at her.

"Maybe nothing will happen. Maybe you won't end up being outlawed," she said hopefully, offering him slices of dried apple.

He ignored her outstretched hand and gave her a look that told her the possibility of that happening was highly unlikely. A curious look passed between Una and Gavin, but they kept quiet.

"Well, then," she said, drawing out her words to show her growing irritation with him. "What are we going to do?"

"*You* will stay at Creag Liath with my father and Stephen. I don't know where I'm going. Away."

Una and Gavin left quickly, pretending to check on the horses.

"How long will you leave for?"

He sighed. "Do we have to talk of this now?"

"Yes, we do. If you're going to run off sailing on your boats—"

"Ships," he corrected her, taking a drink of ale.

"Your *ships*, don't expect me to sit around in this plague-ridden world waiting for you."

"Just what are you saying?" His green eyes were icy. "That child you carry is mine. I don't think you're going anywhere. You'll go to Creag Liath and care for Stephen as I've told you to, waiting for my return."

She didn't trust herself to speak. She stood with a great show of annoyance and glowered down at him. She wanted to kick him, he was making her so angry. He wasn't the only one who had lost Camden. Gavin had lost a brother, too, and she didn't see him biting Una's head off. She started for the horses, but he stood quickly and grabbed her arm.

"Don't even think of going back. I can arrange it so you'll never leave the castle without a guard shadowing you."

"So now you plan to keep me prisoner? Who do you think you are?" She tried to yank her arm out of his grip.

"I'm your husband, like it or not, and you'll do as I say."

He let her go and went to his horse. She followed him, refusing to let fall the hot, angry tears stinging her eyes.

* * *

An odd occurrence took place a few days into their journey. Early in the afternoon they came upon some ragged-looking men who begged them for money. Brenden told them he had none and gave them some bread. They eyed his clothing and horse with disbelief, but thanked him for the handout.

As the day wore on, Audrey noticed Gavin looking over his shoulder anxiously. When she turned to see what he was looking at, all she saw was empty landscape. That evening they entered a heavily wooded area, and Gavin calmed visibly. Audrey, on the other hand, became nervous. What had he been watching for? The woods were dark and cold and gave her the creeps.

Several times she thought she saw a large animal running beside them, but she could never see it clearly. Just a sleek black coat through the trees. When she asked Gavin about it, he shrugged.

"Likely just an old dog," he said.

She didn't mention it to Brenden, since he wasn't speaking to anyone, and when he was forced to, it irritated him.

That night they camped in the woods. She woke to find Brenden's hand covering her mouth. He held a pistol in his other hand, and his eyes searched the trees around them. Una lay sleeping close by, but Gavin was gone.

Brenden started to stand, then froze. They heard a low growl and a second later the sound of an attacking animal. He jumped up, peering into the trees. Screams of agony drifted to them as the animal snared its prey.

"Gavin," she whispered fearfully. Could it be him she heard being torn apart? But something told her it wasn't. The cries and the growling died away. Brenden lay back down.

"Aren't you going to see if your brother's all right?"

"Nothing's wrong with him. No doubt the highway-men are wishing they had chosen an easier quarry."

She looked at him hesitantly. Una was still sleeping! Audrey couldn't believe the ruckus hadn't wakened her. Brenden closed his eyes. She continued staring at him in disbelief. How could he lie down and go to sleep after what had happened?

"What is out in those woods, and why is Gavin safe from it?"

He didn't open his eyes to reply. "Some questions don't have answers. Leave it alone."

They headed north, skirting villages and roads and sticking to the rolling hills and forests. They came upon cottages built of dirty wood, with smoke rising from holes in the thatched roofs. Rags were stuffed in the cracks to keep the cold from entering, and piles of waste rested in front of the cottages, lending a distinctive odor to the air. Dirty-faced barefoot children clung to their mothers' skirts as the group rode by. The travelers were looked at with interest, but nothing more.

The wild dog incident wasn't mentioned by anyone, and Audrey was reluctant to hear the explanation, so she kept silent, too. She went days without speaking a word to Brenden. He didn't appear to notice, and Una and Gavin were ill at ease with him. He kept up some appearances, though. When they lay down to sleep, he pulled her close, his front against her back, his arm heavy around her waist. But when he remained silent and unmoving, she knew he was doing it because it was cold.

She woke one night, feeling alone and empty inside,

even though he was holding her. They had been travel-ing for a week, and nothing had changed. They were in Scotland and only a few days from Creag Liath.

She was at a stalemate with him. She didn't know what to do. He was hateful and uncommunicative. She was miserable. She kept telling herself that if she really loved him, she should simply be there for him. Maybe that's what she had done wrong with Alex. She had been so involved in her job. Being chief of security was stress-ful and time-consuming. She worked odd hours and was often called away from home unexpectedly. Guilt ate at her. She had been too wrapped up in her own life to notice how deeply he was hurting. Maybe if she devoted more time and energy into bringing Brenden out of this, she wouldn't lose another husband.

But the very thought of it was exhausting to her spirit. She couldn't live through it again. She couldn't sit and watch the man she loved hate himself until he had to end the misery that was his life. She couldn't stand to hear their words of condolence. See the real question in their eyes. *How could you let it happen? You were his wife.*

She turned to face him. Even in sleep there was a small frown between his brows. His whiskers were growing long again into a short beard. She did love him enough to try. On impulse, she pressed her lips against his.

His arms tightened around her, and his eyes fluttered open. He stared down at her. She felt embarrassed sud-denly, sure he was going to shove her away in revulsion. She steeled herself for it. Instead, his eyes closed, and his lips touched hers softly. His mouth moved over hers in a kiss that was all the more painful for its gentleness. After his coldness of the past week, this sudden warmth twisted her heart.

He pulled her closer, his knee pressing between her thighs as he deepened the kiss. His hand touched her face, and he drew away, frowning. He ran his thumb across her cheek. "Tears?"

It took her a moment to speak. "I thought you hated me."

"I don't hate you," he whispered, smoothing the hair away from her face.

"I want to go with you when you leave. I'm afraid."

"Afraid of what? That I won't return? Or that you can't wait for me?"

He was too astute by far. "Both," she said in a small voice.

He sighed deeply. "Whatever happens, I fear it will be what I deserve."

She bit her lip so hard, she tasted blood. She didn't want to hear him say these things.

"I can't bring you. Go to sleep now. I do love you. No matter what may happen, remember that."

Creag Liath was before them, looking somehow larger than last time Audrey had seen it. The gates stood open. Mule-drawn carts and people on foot passed through, making their way home in the coming twilight. She remembered the last time she'd ridden through the same gates. That was four months ago. Could so much really have changed since then?

Brenden acknowledged the greetings called to him with a nod. He tossed his reins to a young boy in soiled livery. Audrey started to dismount and felt his hands at her waist. She slid down, holding his arms. Something flitted across his face, and his mouth turned up slightly at the corners. Then it was gone, and he was striding toward the keep, the rest of them in his wake.

"Where is my father?" Brenden asked Glynnis before she could open her mouth.

"Supping in his chambers, my lord."

He climbed the steps and Audrey followed. Her tension mounted as they reached the landing and went down the hallway. What was he going to do? She hurried after him, taking two steps for each of his. He walked into Alistair's chambers without knocking.

Alistair sat at the head of the table, a silver goblet raised halfway to his lips. He slowly put it back on the table. Two of Brenden's sisters were at the table with him and Isobel, whose face lit up at the sight of him. Brenden's mother was at the other end of the table and didn't look pleased when she saw Audrey. She felt embarrassed at the state of her attire and the fact that she hadn't bathed in days. When she had, it had been a rush job in a freezing stream.

"You have returned," Alistair said.

Brenden faced his father defiantly. "I have."

"You failed as well and have been put to the horn. I received word a few days ago, in the form of a garrison of soldiers coming to take you to the Tolbooth." He shook his head. "I told you this would happen. I warned you."

"So I've been outlawed." It was a statement rather than a question, but Alistair chose to answer it.

"Aye, you have. This does not bode well. The heir to the earldom a hunted criminal. What shall we do?" Contrary to his words, Alistair didn't look worried. In fact, he seemed to be mocking Brenden.

"I'm leaving. Audrey and I have been wed." Isobel stared at them in horror, and the countess gasped. "She will stay with you until it's safe for me to return."

Alistair rubbed at his short beard, sharp green eyes taking in both of their appearances. "You leave your wife in my care?"

"Aye, she is with child." Another gasp. "And I shall kill you if a hair on her head is harmed."

Alistair raised an eyebrow. "Where are the rest of the weary travelers?"

"Gavin is downstairs. He has news for you." Brenden's jaw set. He knew what the next question was.

"And Camden, what of him?"

"He's dead."

Isobel's eyes became huge and watery. Brenden's sisters dissolved into tears and wailing. Alistair was speechless. He could only stare at Brenden in disbelief.

"He was shot and then died a few days later."

Audrey cringed at the harsh way Brenden was imparting the news to his family. Alistair opened his mouth to speak, then closed it. He swallowed and ran a hand over his face. A small blond head popped up from behind the table. Wide green eyes looked at Brenden. The boy held a wooden horse in one hand.

Brenden's face was stricken. "Stephen . . ."

"My da? Where is he?" Stephen looked from Brenden to Alistair.

Audrey's heart skipped a beat as she remembered her promise to Camden. She could never leave here. How could she turn away from a promise made to a dying man?

Alistair held out his hand to the boy. "Come to Grandda." The little boy went to Alistair. He was solid and sturdy, his blond hair cut short. He looked like a miniature Camden.

"Where is my da?"

"Steph—"

"Shut up!" Alistair roared at Brenden. "Have you not done enough already?"

Brenden's mouth snapped shut, his lips thin and grim.

Stephen crawled onto Alistair's lap.

"Your da has died. Like Uncle Fillip and your mother, long ago. He went to heaven to be with the angels."

The little boy's bottom lip trembled. "I don't want him to be with the angels. I want him to be here with me."

"I know, Stephen. I don't want him to be gone, either. But God decided it was time for your da to be with Him now." The little boy buried his face in Alistair's doublet, his shoulders shaking. Alistair shot Brenden an accusing look over his head.

Brenden stormed out and Audrey followed. She grabbed his arm to stop him, but he pulled away. Once they were in his chambers, she had to duck as the basin whizzed over her head and shattered against the wall. She moved aside quickly when the porcelain pitcher joined it. He was looking wildly for something else to destroy.

"Brenden!" She grabbed his arms. "Stop it! Please!"

His eyes were pained and slightly crazed. "I understand now."

"What? What do you understand?" She didn't let him pull away, holding his arms tightly.

"Those years in prison, I thought it was the solitude that drove Bothwell insane. But I was wrong. God, how I was wrong."

She forced his head down to her shoulder. He resisted for a moment, then wrapped his arms around her in a bone-crushing embrace. She felt tears on her neck. He hadn't cried when Camden died. He had been so angry, she didn't think he could.

She drew him to the bedchamber and onto the bed. They lay there for a long time, his face on her breast.

She woke to darkness. The shutters were open, letting in silvery light and a cool breeze. His hands were on her, unhooking her bodice. She helped him pull her arms out of it. She could only see the vague outline of him in the dark. His skin was warm and bare. He removed her skirt and shift, gathering her close.

She put her arms around him, feeling the smooth skin of his back. His hands fumbled with her hair until it was loose. He ran his fingers through it, combing out the tangles until it lay down her back. He ran a hand from the top of her head to her bottom.

"This is how I want to remember you," he whispered.

"But you can't see me."

"I don't have to. I see you every time I close my eyes." He pressed kisses against her eyelids, her nose, seeking her lips. His hands were warm and gentle on her skin; his touches slow and lingering, like his kisses.

He made prolonged love to her, whispering tender words and kissing her thoroughly. He laid his head on her stomach, caressing the small swell.

"What will you name it?" he asked.

Something about the way he was acting made it feel so final. Like he wasn't coming back. She fought back tears. "Why don't we wait until it's born; then you can choose a name."

He didn't say anything for a long time. "If it's a boy, name him Camden."

"And if it's a girl?" she asked, her voice shaking.

"Then she shall be Daryl."

"Isn't that a boy's name?"

"Nay, it means loved dearly."

She swallowed the enormous lump rising in her throat. "You're not coming back, are you?"

When he didn't answer, she began trembling with anger and grief. She was not going through this again. She refused to go through it again. She had lost one husband; she would not wait for another to succumb.

"I won't wait forever."

"I know."

"So that's it? No guards? No 'You'll wait here like the obedient wife until I return?'"

He had no answer for her, and a sob caught in her throat as her heart seemed to shred into a million pieces. She turned her back to him and buried her face in the pillow. He put his hand on her shoulder. "Don't touch me, you bastard. I hate you!" The pillow muffled her voice. He removed his hand. It was several minutes before she felt him roll away.

It was a long night. After the tears dried, she stared into the dark, watching the room slowly illuminate with dawn. The shape of the chair, a table with stools pushed neatly underneath, the lumpiness of the rush-covered floor, slowly became visible. All layered in various shades of gray. Colorless. Lifeless. He got out of bed. She suspected he hadn't slept either. He went to the chest at the end of the bed. The leather hinges made a soft cracking noise when he opened it.

Be there for him, Audrey. Don't make another mistake. Don't fail another husband. But the words of support were lodged in her chest, her own hurt too great to allow them release.

She listened to the rustlings of him dressing, the thump of his boots as he put them on, but still she didn't move. When he was done, the bed dipped under his weight, and she felt more than saw his presence next to her, as if the only warmth in the room generated from his body.

"I have a house. It's about twenty miles north of here. Should you decide to stay, I would feel better if you and Stephen were here among my family. But if my father gives you trouble, you can go there." She felt his hand hovering near her shoulder and her skin tingled, but he didn't touch her. "It's well equipped with servants that stay there year-round, so it's always ready for me. My factor lives there."

"Factor?"

"Aye, he handles my finances and such. Should you want for anything, you've only to send him word." He laid a piece of paper on the pillow next to her.

"What's this?" she asked, touching it with her fingers.

"Our marriage contract." She looked at him in confusion. "So no one will question the legitimacy of my heir."

"You've just thought of everything, haven't you?"

He looked away from the accusation in her eyes. He gathered some more things together and walked out the door.

She lay there, numbed by what had happened. What did it mean? He couldn't really be thinking of suicide. But then why worry about someone disputing his heir? He was making sure his affairs were in order. What kind of luck was it to have married two suicidal men? She tried to keep the old thoughts away, but they came creeping back, as ugly and evil as they were three years ago. This was somehow her fault. She didn't do enough. Other men experienced tragedy, and their families, their wives, helped them through it. She couldn't. She was useless, powerless to stop the men she loved from destroying themselves. She was lacking somehow, and it tore her up inside.

She wrapped the sheet around her and went to the window. His room was at the back of the keep, so she could see the stables, kennels, and wood yard from his window. There wasn't much activity at this hour, just a few men walking in and out of the wood yard. She was about to walk away when she saw Brenden's tall form striding to the stables. He was really leaving.

She watched him go inside with a sinking heart. A few moments later, Stephen ran in after him. What would she do? She had made a promise to Camden to take care of his son. But that was before Brenden had abandoned her. Could she leave? Go back to her time? Take up her life where she left off?

Her ears strained to hear any sounds from the stable. The bailey was deserted now, no one coming or going from the buildings, no sounds, as though time had stopped, waiting for her to make her decision. The spell was broken when a chicken sauntered by. How much time had passed in her world? Did it stand still while she was here? Or continue on? If it did, she would be AWOL.

She thought of Brenden's touch last night, so gentle and loving. She would wait for him if she only knew he would come back. She wished she could take Stephen back with her. But she was the only one who could see the corridor. She was as trapped by her own honor, her promise to Camden, as Brenden had been by his promise to Bothwell.

Brenden came out of the stable leading his horse. Stephen was in the saddle. She watched Brenden with a catch in her throat. Memorizing him. He walked the horse around the bailey, coming back to the stables after a few minutes. He lifted the boy down and knelt in front of him, speaking to him earnestly. She would have given anything to know what he was saying, but only snatches of his voice floated to her on the cool breeze. Stephen wrapped his arms around Brenden's neck and they hugged. Brenden took something out of his saddlebag and gave it to Stephen.

Brenden watched him run inside, then raised his eyes to her window. They were so brilliant, she could see the light green of them from where she stood. His hair curled at his nape, just a few auburn curls showing at the sides of his neck. He held her gaze for a long time. Finally, he turned and mounted. Her heart seemed to be leaving with him, tearing out of her chest to follow. She thought her knees might give way from the thought of never seeing him again. She longed to tell him she loved him and would wait. Maybe if he knew, it would keep him from doing something rash. But she still had enough pride left not to beg. They were more alike than she had ever realized.

His horse began to trot away, and she couldn't stop herself. She leaned out the window. *"Seni asla terket-meyecegim!"* she yelled, as though it were a curse. *I'll never leave you.* She knew he didn't understand Turkish, but she felt better having said it. He reined the horse and looked back at her. She laughed suddenly and hysterically. What must he be thinking? *Heathen wife!* He probably thought she had told him to rot in hell. At the moment, she wanted him to rot in hell, too.

"Cehennemde cürü!" she added. *Rot in hell.* Then laughed some more.

He rode away, shaking his head.

Una slipped in while Audrey was sitting on the bed staring into space.

"I heard he left," Una said. Audrey didn't answer. "It's a good thing; the guards have spotted soldiers approaching. They're wearing the royal arms."

Audrey looked at her in alarm. "Do you think he's far enough away?"

Una bit her lip. "I don't know. Maybe there's some way to detain them?"

Audrey used the staircase connecting Brenden's room to hers. She was relieved to see all her clothes were still safely tucked away in the chest as she had left them. When she was dressed, she hurried to Alistair's room and knocked. A few seconds later the door opened, and he stood in shirt and breeches scowling down at her.

"What is it . . . daughter?" He added the last mockingly.

"Soldiers are approaching. I don't know if Brenden is far enough away—he hasn't been gone long." He went back into the room, leaving the door open. She took it as an invitation to enter.

"I know," he said. There were several other men in the room wearing the burgundy livery with the Irvine crest. One of them held out Alistair's doublet and practically put it on him.

"Well? What do you plan on doing?" she asked impatiently.

When the doublet was buttoned, another man slid a belt around Alistair's waist with a sword on it. "What shall I do?" He looked like he had all the time in the world.

"I don't know! Stall them? Lie to them? Surely you don't want them to catch Brenden?"

"Hmm." He rubbed his beard thoughtfully. "Should I let Cain get what he has coming? That's a hard one. But no, I am becoming destitute of sons. The two I have left hate me, and Gavin is not a suitable heir." When he was finally fully dressed with all the adornments befitting an earl, he held his arm out to Audrey. "Shall we?"

"What are you going to tell them?" she asked as they went down the stairs.

"Doubtless, they've had some intelligence of him being here. They've been holed up at the stronghold of Clunie since their arrival. So the news would have traveled fast, as most of my servants would leap at the opportunity to exercise their disloyalty. I will, of course, lie. But you shall be the maltreated wife, left to yourself as he roamed the countryside committing unspeakable acts of treason and dishonoring you."

They waited in the hall. Despite Alistair's outward show of calm, she could tell he was nervous. He fingered the jeweled hilt of his sword and paced. At last, she heard the clambering of horses in the bailey and a few shouted orders. She and Alistair were flanked by guards. She recognized Forbes and Dearg and felt somewhat comforted by their familiar faces.

A group of soldiers entered with the metallic clinking of spurs and swords, all following one man with a commanding air about him. He removed his helmet as he approached, exposing reddish-blond hair cut close to his head and piercing black eyes.

"Lord Irvine." He bowed low before them, and his eyes immediately raked over her body in a way she found distasteful.

"Captain Ethan Moffat, this is my daughter-in-law, Lady Audrey Ross."

"Daughter-in-law?" he asked suspiciously.

"Aye," Alistair said, offering no further explanation. "To what do I owe this unexpected pleasure?"

"Perchance your daughter-in-law could answer that."

Alistair looked at Audrey expectantly, as did Captain Moffat. She feigned confusion. "I don't understand."

Alistair looked at the captain as if that should be answer enough.

"Are you the wife of Brenden Ross, who has committed treasonous acts against the crown of England?"

"How can he commit treason against the crown of England when he is not an English subject?" she asked coolly, meeting his black stare.

His thin lips curved into a smile. "Have you been married to him long? For if you had, you'd know he owns land in England and is therefore an English subject as well."

"Perhaps, but how can he be loyal to more than one sovereign?"

"Do you think attempting to assassinate the Queen of England is being loyal to King James? He was giving aid to the king's enemies, mainly the papists."

"I know nothing of him doing any such thing. I was only aware of his wish to save the king's mother from death."

"Against the king's royal authority? I think not, but he can defend himself at his trial. Where is he? I know he's been here." He stared accusingly at Alistair.

"I haven't seen my son in months. I know not of what you speak."

The captain considered this, obviously not buying it. He turned to her. "And how is it that the lovely Lady Ross is with you today? I don't recall seeing her when we were here before, and hers is a face I would surely not forget."

"She was unwell. She, too, heard of her husband's acts and was stricken he would dishonor her so," Alistair said blandly.

He looked at her with new interest. "So your husband makes you ill?"

"I don't approve of his activities."

Captain Moffat studied at her for a moment. He took a deep breath and glanced around the hall. With hands clasped behind his back, he walked to a tapestry and inspected it closely. She looked up at Alistair, and he rolled his eyes.

"This is quite a fortress ye have, Lord Irvine." The captain turned on his heel, giving them a charming smile. "I think it's more suited to our needs than is Clunie. We should like to garrison here, at the king's request, of course."

Alistair finally showed some emotion. His face flushed with anger, but his voice was controlled. "I know of no such request."

Moffat walked back to them, the smile still plastered on his face. "'Tis an easy matter to remedy. I shall tell him what an excellent location this affords us. The king will be displeased to hear you were most disagreeable. He is becoming sore weary of his unruly nobles." He moved closer to Audrey. He was young, in his early twenties, and big. His shoulders and arms were huge. Even though he only stood an inch or so taller than her, she felt dwarfed by him. "I know had I such a wife to warm my bed, I'd not stray far."

Alistair grabbed the captain's leather-clad arm. "You misspeak yourself, Captain. Remember your place!" Forbes's hand moved to rest comfortably on his sword hilt, an act the captain didn't miss.

"I apologize, *my* lady." He bowed to her. She didn't like the way he said "my lady," as though he meant something else entirely. "Let's not turn this situation ugly. Surely you have the room." He raised his arms to indicate the immensity of the castle.

"Very well," Alistair said. "Your men, in the gatehouse. Glynnis will show you to your room. The countess and Lady Ross will entertain you. I have business at court I must attend and will be leaving immediately."

"Why, I thank you for such hospitality, my lord," he said, smiling pleasantly.

Audrey hurried after Alistair as he walked away. He barked orders at the many attendants around him to make ready for his departure.

"What are you doing?" she asked him in the drawing room. "Leaving that . . . that man here for me to entertain. Did you see how he was leering at me?"

"Gavin's here. He won't let any harm come to you. I think you're capable of discouraging unwanted advances." He began rummaging through his desk.

"Why are you going to court?"

"To beg the king to pardon my son and heir, since it

was a noble mission he was on, not one of treachery. I will also be required to explain why I allowed my son to marry so low." He shook his head wearily. "I am forever making amends for his misdeeds."

Audrey had never looked at it that way and felt a pang of guilt for the part she played in Alistair's troubles. "I'm sorry about Camden. I know how much you loved him."

He folded several pieces of paper and stuck them in his doublet. "My dear, I love all my children." He looked troubled for a moment. "I will leave Forbes here for you, in case the lusty captain gets any ideas."

"Why wouldn't he? Thanks to you, he thinks my husband sickens me."

"Ah, well, had he thought otherwise, he might have decided to arrest you until Brenden came for you. He might still, but I think not. That's why I am letting them stay here. He thinks he's done something clever, but he is a fool. By the time Captain Moffat realizes his error, I hope to have secured a pardon."

He ushered her out, and she decided to go in search of her new nephew.

She asked Glynnis where she might find Stephen. She was directed to a room that served as a schoolroom for the Ross children. She peeked in the open door. It was empty except for a short, portly man. She noticed curious white smudges on the seat of his breeches. They were smeared as though he had valiantly tried to wipe something off. Strange. She was starting to back out when he saw her.

"Do not leave!" he called.

She walked hesitantly into the room. Small slates and books were stacked on a shelf. Several benches were pushed against the wall, and a battered desk was in the corner.

"Are you Lady Ross?" His graying hair stuck up wildly about his ears. He ran a smoothing hand over the unruly spikes, to little effect.

"Yes."

He rushed to her and grabbed her hand, pumping it up and down. "Oh, I am so pleased to meet you!"

When she regarded him strangely, he released her hand in embarrassment.

"I am James Sinclair. I heard about you and Master Brenden . . . I mean, Lord Ross. How extravagantly chivalrous and fantastic of him! To think, it was my lord that did it! I would have thought it more Master Camden's manner to go to such lengths for a lass." He surveyed her in amazement. "You don't look like a heathen."

"Uh . . . yes. Thanks?" she answered, not quite sure how to respond.

His face turned sad suddenly. "And poor Master Camden, I was so sorry to hear what befell him." He shook his head, pulling a handkerchief from his waistband and dabbing his eyes. "He was a clever one, that lad, just like his son."

"That's who I'm looking for." She looked around the room. "Where is he?"

"Who knows?" He shook his head again. "It was the same with him every time Master Camden went away and didn't take him along. He won't do anything. I'm fortunate he shows his face."

"Has he been here today?"

"Aye, he's been here," he said grimly, gesturing to the chair behind the desk.

She frowned and walked around the desk. The chair was covered with a white pasty substance that oozed onto the floor. Two half-moon-shaped indentations were in the center of the chair.

"You didn't . . . sit in it?" She covered her mouth, knowing that was what she had spotted on his breeches earlier.

He nodded, his face reddening.

"Does he do this often?"

"Like I said, only when his father goes away." His mouth turned down in the corners. "And now his father won't be coming back. No set of breeks is safe." He brightened suddenly. "But that's why I am so pleased you're here! I know Lord Ross is to be his guardian." He nodded sagely. "It's what the boy needs, a mother. Master Camden was a fine father, don't misunderstand me. But Master Stephen's tongue is sharp as a whip, and naught is done about it."

"Really?" she said, dread overcoming her. So he was a monster.

"Aye, Master Camden thought him amusing and nary laid a finger on the wee scut, when what he needed was the skin flogged off his arse. Of late, he is unmanageable. I wish you much luck."

"Where can I find him?"

He thought for a minute. "Try the woodshed. His father has dragged him out of there a few times."

"The woodshed?"

James shuddered in revulsion. "Spiders. He loves them." He wiggled his fingers in a feminine way that almost made her laugh. "Likes to leave them about as wee gifts."

"Uh, great." She turned to leave. She hated spiders. And snakes and anything else of the creeping, crawling variety.

"I hope you can induce him to resume his lessons," he called after her.

She left the keep and went to the woodshed. It was

dark inside, so she propped the door open and walked in, peering between the stacks of wood. Her skin crawled at the thought of spiders scurrying around within.

"Stephen?" she called several times. When there was no answer, she began searching the other buildings. She was surprised with the array of different buildings inside the castle walls. The buttery, woolshed, stables, kennels, bakehouse, smithy, brewhouse—there were more, but she decided to find him later.

She started to walk back to the keep and saw a little body scamper around the side of the brewhouse. The little bastard was following her! She tiptoed around the side of the building, but the rustling of her skirts gave her away. When she turned the corner, he was gone. She looked around just in time to see him dart inside the keep. He was fast.

She wondered what to do next. He obviously didn't want to talk to her, but then why was he following her? She was sure she'd never understand children. She went inside to Camden's rooms and pushed the door open. It was dark, but light shone from the connecting bedchamber.

Stephen sat cross-legged on the bed, a closed book in his lap and a candle burning beside the bed. They stared at each other for a long time.

"Didn't your father teach you not to play with fire?"

Dark-green eyes gazed unblinking back at her. "Uncle Bren says you are my auntie and I'm to mind you."

"Did he? What else did he tell you?" She sat beside him on the bed.

"That you have a wean in your belly and I'm to protect it when it's born."

"Uncle Bren was very thorough, wasn't he?"

He studied her for a moment. "He also said my da loved you and asked that you take care of me."

"Yes, he did." He did seem very smart. His eyes were bright and alert. She didn't know a lot of six-year-olds to compare him with, but she thought he was big for his age. He had the same stocky build as Camden. One difference, though—he didn't have the same ready smile, but she supposed he didn't have much to smile about.

"I know where weans come out of." He looked as though he had one up on her.

"That's nice . . ." She wanted to end this line of conversation before it moved into a realm she wasn't ready for. "James said you didn't want to study today."

"He is a corpulent pig, and he acts like a lass. Do you know what corpulent means?" The kid didn't crack a smile, and she tried not to.

"Uh . . . yes, I do. But that's not a very nice thing to say about someone."

"I know, I'm being obnoxious."

"Yes. Yes, you are." She finally smiled. He seemed to have quite a vocabulary at his disposal and enjoyed shocking people with it. She pointed to the book he held. "What are you reading?"

"It's my da's book. I can't read much of it. It's in Latin." He handed it to her. "Could you read me some?"

"I can't read Latin," she said, looking at the leather-bound book.

"It's easy. I'm still learning." He took the book back from her. "It's called *Secretum*—that means *My Secret*. Francis Petrarch wrote it. He's been dead a very long time. My da said it was a kind of diary." He considered the book, his sandy blond head bent over it. "What do you think his secret was? If it was really his diary, he wouldn't be wanting others reading it, so it must be a good one."

"You'll never know if you don't do your lessons. When you figure it out, you can tell me."

"If you can't read nor write, you're probably too ignorant to understand." He was so straight-faced when he said these things!

"I'll have you know, I can read, write, *and* speak another language. Just not Latin."

"Can you speak French?" She shook her head. "Greek?" She shook her head again, feeling increasingly stupid. "Spanish?"

"No, Turkish."

"You can speak like a heathen?" His eyes became owlish as he regarded her with admiration.

"Yes." She felt better that there was something redeeming about her in the little boy's eyes.

"Will you teach me? Then one day, I'll sail the seas like Uncle Bren and slay the evil pagans." He rose to his knees excitedly. "Just like the great Don John of Austria! I will carry the sultan's head on a spike!"

"They're neither heathens nor pagans nor even evil, and I will certainly not teach you anything you will use to slay someone." He looked at her as if she were no fun. "Their religion is Islam, and they have the same God as we do, they just call him Allah."

He thought on this. "Allah damn it!" he yelled, then shook his head. "It's not the same."

"You shouldn't swear."

"Why? My da swears all the time. So does Uncle Bren."

"Well, that's because they're grown-ups." Not a very good answer, she realized, but the best she could think up on such short notice. She changed the subject before this precocious child told her so. "If you learn your Latin, maybe I'll teach you some Turkish."

"A countess should know how to read and write Latin."

"Maybe you could teach me Latin, so I can be a proper countess."

He smiled finally, the idea exciting him. "Aye, let's start now."

They spent the next hour with him pointing out parts of his body and giving her the Latin names for them. She was impressed by his patience at her bumbling. They were interrupted when Gavin walked in.

He smiled at them sitting cross-legged on the bed together. "I thought I might find you here," he said, rumpling Stephen's hair.

"Uncle Gavin! Auntie Audrey is going to teach me to speak like a heathen!" He stood on the bed in his excitement.

"Is she now? She'll have to do it later—the countess is asking for her. Go find Glynnis, she's waiting your dinner."

He ran out of the room without a backward glance.

"He seems to have taken to you quick," he commented.

"It's the heathen thing. Works every time."

He laughed. "It appears we have guests for dinner, and the countess doesn't intend to entertain them alone."

She groaned, remembering Captain Moffat. Gavin told her she had enough time to bathe and change, so she hurried to her room. They were to be dining in the countess's chambers. Gavin said under normal circumstances, they would probably have a large meal in the great hall. But since they were back in mourning, the castle once again draped in black, they were keeping things simple. She was nervous about finally meeting the countess.

She wore her old black dress, which was her favorite. It was still in good condition. It wasn't as fine as the gowns she'd left at Fotheringhay, but she thought it was simple and elegant. It made her think about money. She possessed none, nor did she know where to get any. She needed new black dresses to accommodate the bulge in her belly, and she needed to buy a pony. She hesitated to ask anyone, and Brenden would have taken care of these things had he been there.

Well, she decided, she *was* his wife, so his money was hers. She would talk to Gavin about contacting his factor.

When Audrey arrived at dinner, everyone was already seated. There was an empty chair next to the countess, which she motioned for Audrey to take. The countess wasn't a very attractive woman, though regal in her own way. Graying brown hair was swept back from her face. She was fairly tall and had a long, thin nose. Her skin was very beautiful. It was honey-colored, as opposed to the porcelain white that Audrey had noticed the other women of this century were striving for. Fine lines gathered around her eyes and mouth, but otherwise it was flawless.

She looked down her nose at Audrey with greenish-blue, almost lashless eyes. "I had hoped you would be here a bit earlier so we might talk." Her voice was deep and husky, and it surprised Audrey when she heard it.

"I'm sorry," Audrey mumbled, already extremely uncomfortable. The captain was sitting across from her, staring at her cleavage. "Is something wrong, Captain?" she asked, hoping to embarrass him.

"Oh, nay, nay. In fact, everything is quite right." His

pupil-less black eyes looked at her warmly, before turning to the countess with a much more innocent expression. The countess gave him a tight smile.

It was a small dinner party; they were joined by a few of the more exalted servants, Gavin, Una, and another soldier who sat farther down the table. Poor Una looked as though she wished she could be anyplace else, and the countess didn't say a word to her.

"How long have you been married?" the captain asked Audrey.

She started to answer truthfully, but thought better of it, since it would place her with Brenden during his treasonous activities. "Six months," she lied, hoping he had been doing nothing wrong six months ago.

He frowned. "'Tis odd I hadn't heard of it. A great deal is usually made when a noble is wed."

"You must remember, Captain," the countess said pleasantly, "my son Fillip was still alive, so Brenden's marriage was of no consequence."

"I see. What was your name before you married? You're not Scottish. I don't think ye're English, either."

Audrey tried not to roll her eyes. Not this again! She thought she was through with the questions on her heritage.

"Her speech is odd because her birth is base," the countess said distastefully. Audrey was speechless that the countess would insult her in front of people, and even the captain shifted uncomfortably in his chair. "If you don't already know, my son is a man of his own means and therefore feels no obligation to honor his family. He did as he pleased when he married her, as he does in all matters. A very thoughtless man."

The entire table was silent, and Audrey stared at her food, her cheeks burning. The captain broke the silence.

"If I had to choose between great beauty and nobility, I believe I would opt for the former as well."

Audrey appreciated the attempt to give her back some dignity, though she doubted the sincerity of his statement; she just wished it hadn't come from him.

"If it was an ornament he wanted, I suppose he did well for himself." The countess's thin bloodless lips tightened slightly.

"'Tis a common thing to envy what one does not have," Gavin commented, as though he were addressing a different topic entirely. The countess glared at him, but he ignored her and leaned closer to the captain. "My brother didn't choose her for beauty alone, her head is far from empty."

The captain was watching Audrey closely. She felt ridiculously exposed by this conversation and wanted nothing more than to crawl underneath the table.

"So I've gathered," the captain said dryly. The conversation turned to other subjects, and Audrey excused herself shortly after.

This was a nightmare. Her mother-in-law hated her. The obnoxious captain was going to be a constant presence. She thought about Brenden's house and decided she would go there as soon as Alistair returned with news of Brenden's pardon. And she would not help her mother-in-law entertain again.

She moved her few possessions to Brenden's room. It made her feel better to have his books and things around her. She took one of his shirts from the chest to sleep in. It was more comfortable than her shift. She crawled into his bed. When she laid her head on his pillow, she smelled him and tears sprang to her eyes. She hugged the pillow to her, trying to ease the aching loneliness that filled her body. He had only left that morning, and it hurt. How she was going to survive this? After the evening she'd spent with the countess, if it weren't for Stephen, she would be on a horse riding for Drochaid. And what was Brenden doing while she was trying to make a place for herself in his family without his help? Was he feeling sorry for himself and thinking of ending it all? Where was he now?

Audrey sighed. She was tired, searching now in Camden's rooms for Stephen, but there was still no sign of him. She was beginning to realize why she had never seen him during her previous stay at Creag Liath. The child was amazingly elusive. Just when she was ready to give up looking for him, he'd pop out of nowhere. Or sometimes she would find him in Camden's rooms, looking at his father's things. Things that remained untouched as though Camden was still around somewhere and the room were waiting for him.

She wasn't sure what to do with Camden's things. Gavin had told her he had a will, but Brenden was the executor and Stephen's ward. Stephen wouldn't receive his inheritance until he was twenty-one. There was no hurry, but she didn't like the idea of the boy lurking about his dead father's room all the time. It couldn't be healthy.

Gavin was beginning to show her how things were done in a castle. She was able to send a letter to Brenden's factor, telling him of her new status and that she would like access to Brenden's money. She hoped there wouldn't be a problem. Her dresses were becoming strained across her belly, but not too noticeably, since she no longer wore stays. She was giving the dresses one at a time to the seamstress to take out.

She ran her hand over her stomach, wondering what Brenden would think if he came back while she was big with the child. She peeked under Camden's bed. No Stephen. She straightened and turned, jumping in surprise when she saw Captain Moffat in the doorway. She was beginning to detest the man. It had been two weeks since Brenden left, and he was still a fixture at Creag Liath. She knew he didn't buy the estranged wife story and was biding his time, waiting for Brenden to show his face. She could have assured him that was *not* going to happen, but he wouldn't believe her.

He leaned casually against the door frame, as though he had no other duties to perform but to follow her around all day. A slow smile spread over his face when he saw her immediate annoyance at his presence.

"Is there something I can help you with, Captain Moffat?" *Like your way out?*

"Can't find the wee monster, eh?" he asked, ignoring her question. The soldiers had taken an instant dislike to Stephen. He was managing to make their lives as miserable as a six-year-old boy could, but his favorite target was the captain. She'd heard that the captain must now be very careful to check his chairs before he sat and his food before he ate, and he certainly would not make the mistake of putting his boots on without shaking them out first, for fear of the many rodents that seemed to find their way into them when he was unaware. But Stephen was quick and had yet to be caught in the act.

"Oh, he's about." She gave the room another cursory search before going to the doorway and looking expectantly at the captain, waiting for him to move. He just stared at her with his black eyes. If it hadn't been for those dark, close-set eyes, he might have been somewhat attractive. She supposed some women found him so, although she was not one of them. He was causing quite a stir among the female servants, and she imagined he was having his way with them. His coloring was fair, darkened to a ruddy tan from spending time outdoors.

"Your brother-in-law tells me you lived amongst barbarians."

"Yes, and I generally flay the skin off men who stand in my way. May I please get by?" she asked, meeting his gaze coldly.

He raised an eyebrow and gave her a small smile. "I have to wonder, my lady, what is it that keeps your husband away so long? I expected him to at least try to sneak in to see his bride. I don't think I could have stayed away, heathen or no."

As always, she felt as if he were imagining her naked or in some other compromising position when he said these things, and it was extremely disconcerting.

"Perhaps it's the garrison of soldiers waiting to arrest him? Regardless of what you think, Captain, he's not a stupid man."

"Aye, I do think he is a stupid man, sweetings. To leave all this . . ." He straightened and took a step toward her. "Mayhap he waits for you to come to him."

She took a step back. "You're a fool if you think I'd endanger him in such a way."

"Ah, not so sickened by your husband as ye'd have me believe. I'm sure he'd be fair upset to know another man was forcing his attentions on you." He reached his hand out to touch her face. She slapped it away.

"The earl would be unhappy to hear you were accosting his daughter-in-law."

He laughed heartily. "You mean to tell me Lord Irvine hasn't been at you himself yet?" He saw the look that crossed her face and laughed again. He was no longer blocking the door, and she sidestepped him quickly. His hand bit into her shoulder, stopping her.

"Get your hands off me," she said through clenched teeth. He stood behind her with his hands on her shoulders. She stiffened; figuring a struggle would only drag it out. She was sure he wouldn't do anything to the future countess. But he quickly put a stop to that train of thought.

"You think you're something special now, but you must remember, when your husband was declared an outlaw he was stripped of all titles, present and future." She felt his mouth near her ear. "You're nothing more than an outlaw's wife."

"My lady?" Forbes poked his head into the outer chamber. The captain quickly stepped away from her. "Is anything amiss?"

She walked to the protection of Forbes's massive form.

"Nay, we were just looking for the wee blastie," the captain said casually.

Forbes gave her a questioning look, but she nodded her head that she was fine. He gave the captain a hard stare. Captain Moffat left immediately. She was thankful for Forbes; he had already shown up several times when the captain was acting inappropriately.

Captain Moffat was becoming a problem. She had planned to go to Brenden. It came to her while she was lying awake in bed, wearing his shirt, hugging his pillow, and generally feeling sorry for herself. She would go to him, and he wouldn't turn her away. She would force him out of his depression. She didn't want to make the same mistake she had with Alex by leaving him to himself. Once she was there, she would refuse to leave him. Gavin was the only one who knew where Brenden was. He hadn't told her yet, but Audrey was confident she could ferret the information out of him.

But now it was impossible. Not if that bastard Captain Moffat was going to be following her. She was stuck here until he figured out that she was useless to him. That's exactly how she was feeling: useless. She was of no good to anyone, except Stephen. If she didn't find the boy during the day, he came to her room in the evenings to give her a Latin lesson. She had been successful in coercing him to resume his lessons with James. Stephen's energy had been diverted by tormenting the soldiers, and James was enjoying the reprieve.

She knew she should speak to Stephen about his behavior, but she was enjoying it, so she kept silent. He didn't want to be mothered, so this left a great expanse of her day open. She thought about approaching the countess regarding the duties involved in such a title, but her biting comments the one time Audrey had joined her for dinner still stung. Audrey made a point of never being in the same area of the castle as the countess. It was an easy feat, since the woman rarely left her apartments.

That's when Audrey decided to approach Isobel. Surely she knew something, growing up among nobility. She and Una had taken to each other right away, both being the same age and about to become sisters-in-law. Audrey found them walking in the gardens with Gavin. She stopped to watch them, feeling like an intruder on their sweet moment. Una and Gavin were holding hands, and they were all laughing. Audrey backed up, feeling a pang of aloneness. All three of them belonged here together. Audrey didn't and stuck out like an extra toe.

Why should she stay? There was nothing here for her. She sighed and resigned herself to waiting until the pardon came through. But if he didn't want her . . . what was the point? Loneliness was more comfortable, for her at least, in the future. When she had her work to drown herself in. Now all she could do was sit and pine for her husband and chase a little boy around.

The letter came a few days later. Audrey peeked into the drawing room, wanting to get a book but not wanting to disturb Alistair's steward, Leslie, if he was busy. He was; his black head was bent over the desk in concentration. She started to back out.

"Gavin?" he asked, looking up. Seeing it was only Audrey, he waved her in.

"I just wanted a book, but I can wait until later."

He grinned. "Go, do as you please! Don't mind me."

She walked to the bookshelf. A few moments later Gavin walked in. Leslie looked at him in relief.

"Do ye know anything about this?" He handed Gavin a letter.

Gavin read it, his brow furrowing. "Aye, I know what this is. It's Camden's sheriff business."

Leslie rolled his eyes. "I know that. What do we do with it?"

"A new deputy must be appointed, but that will have to wait for Lord Irvine's return. Someone will have to go in his stead, since the quarter session is less than a fortnight away."

Leslie looked at Gavin pointedly. Gavin sighed. "Aye, I guess I'll do it."

"What do you have to do?" Audrey sidled up beside Gavin and peered at the letter over his arm.

"My father is the sheriff of Irvineshire. It's a hereditary office for some reason; it isn't like that in most places. It's most unfortunate, as it is a tedious duty. Camden has acted as his deputy since he was nineteen." He shrugged. "Truth be known, I haven't a clue what to do. Camden never had much to say on this business."

"How are you going to find out what to do?" She took the letter from him.

"I'll rummage through his papers."

"I'll do it," she said.

They looked confused.

"Ye'll do what?" Leslie asked.

"I'll figure out what needs to be done and be the deputy."

Leslie tried to suppress a smile, but it didn't work and finally he just laughed. Gavin didn't think it was quite so humorous and took the letter back.

"Don't worry yourself about this. Go on and help Una and Isobel. They're working on embroideries and such for the wedding."

She refrained from making a gagging motion at his male chauvinist attitude. She snatched the letter back. "I can do it."

Gavin's lips thinned, and he pulled the letter smoothly from her grasping fingers. "It's not necessary."

She reached for it again, but he held it over his head. Finally, she glared at him. "So what am I supposed to do? Sit around all day waiting for my husband to decide whether or not he wants to live? Or maybe I should start counting the days until the baby is born . . . let's see . . . it's well over one hundred now. Or, no!" She looked at them in mock excitement. "I'll join ranks with Stephen and put insects and rodents in everyone's boots." Leslie was laughing at her, but Gavin was not amused. "Gavin, please," she begged. "I'm so incredibly bored. I need something to occupy me."

Gavin and Leslie exchanged an odd look, and after a moment's hesitation, Gavin handed her the letter. "If it means so much to you, I'll not stop you. But I'm going with you."

"Fine, fine," she said, already lost in her strategy for trying to figure out her new job. "As long as you don't interfere."

As she was walking out the door, she heard Leslie say in a low voice, "And if you should, God help you then."

Audrey stood in Camden's room, a candle burning in her hand. It felt wrong to start digging through his things, but she didn't see what choice she had. She went to the cupboard and opened the right door. It contained the mundane things of daily life: a comb, a razor, a small mirror, all scrupulously clean and situated in its own place. She felt a catch in her throat, seeing these simple items that he had used every day. There was a wooden box on the top shelf, and she pulled it down.

Inside were letters tied with ribbons of different colors. She had a sneaking suspicion what they were and hesitated, wondering if she should check and make sure they weren't something she needed to read. But no, she was certain official correspondence to the deputy wasn't tied in bright ribbons. She put it back and opened the other side.

Ledgers, neat stacks of papers, and folded letters with the seals broken filled the shelves. She pulled out the ledgers. At first she didn't know what they contained because his bold handwriting made the contents seem almost poetic, but then she saw this one was simply a listing of expenses. The spelling was atrocious, but she was beginning to realize that there was no standardized spelling. People wrote things the way they sounded. She leafed through the rest of the ledgers. They were more of the same. Trying to decipher them was a strain on her eyes, so she didn't look too hard. She placed them back on the shelf.

She withdrew one of the stacks of papers. They were copies of letters he had written. She noticed they weren't in his handwriting, so he must have had a secretary do it for him. She was skimming through the first few, when something caught her eye: "Myne Abby Saynt Mary ys cruid yn stracture and yn neide of reparit, bot I desyris to maik yt yntoo a Unyvirsytie for skolars." She read the letter with renewed interest. She pulled up a chair and sat down with the entire stack.

Camden had an abbey. Since the Protestant reformation in Scotland, the old properties of the Catholic Church were no longer in use and had been distributed to the Scottish nobility. The abbey was a gift from Alistair. And he had wanted to make it into a university. She was impressed, but he hadn't reached any major point in his plan. According to the last letter, dated November 1586, he was having some repairs made to it.

Suddenly things started sliding into place. She remembered what Ian MacKay had said about the countess; she had founded a university, was sheriff of her shire, saved witches from the stake—she was the one who had finished Camden's work! Laughter bubbled through her. Had she really been here? With all the amazing things that had happened to her so far, she still found it difficult to believe she was the countess Ian had been speaking of. She put the papers neatly back on the shelf.

She didn't know how long she had been reading, but the candle was nearly gutted out, and the room was cast in shadows. A nervous feeling that she wasn't alone came over her, and she looked around. She was so involved in trying to understand what she was reading, anyone could have walked in unnoticed. She was about to turn back to the cabinet when she saw movement in a dark corner.

"You can come out now, Stephen. I see you."

He emerged from the shadows. His eyes were red, and tears ran down his face. She knelt in front of him.

"What's wrong? Why are you crying?"

He wiped his nose noisily on his sleeve. "Why are you going through my da's things?"

She pulled a handkerchief out of her bodice and wiped his eyes. "I need to know some things about what your father did. I thought I might find the answer in here."

"Why?" His face was so solemn, eyes so sad.

"Well, now that he's gone, someone needs to finish his work."

His bottom lip trembled. "Can't you wait until he comes back?"

"Stephen, your father isn't coming back. Remember what your grandda told you about him being with God now?" Camden's body had arrived a few days ago, and a hurried funeral was performed due to the circumstances of his death. Stephen had refused to attend, and afterward, she had been unable to find him until the next morning. So she knew he was having a difficult time dealing with his father's death, but she hadn't realized he wasn't accepting it.

His little throat was working, and he was fighting back tears. She pulled him against her. "It's all right, you can cry. We're all sad he's gone."

He cried for a bit, while she stroked his hair. "Is it true what I heard the soldiers say?" he asked.

"What did they say?"

"That my da and Uncle Bren were traitors. Captain Moffat called him Judas and said Uncle Bren probably shot him." He looked at her pleadingly, his green eyes begging her to tell him it wasn't so.

"No! Your father was a good man and so is your uncle. Brenden did not shoot your father. I promise. Your father was shot being very brave."

He gave her a small smile, then broke into tears again. She hugged him to her fiercely, and he flinched.

"Did I hurt you?" she asked, and loosened her grip on him.

"Nay," he shook his head against her shoulder. "My side hurts."

"Let me see." She started unbuttoning his doublet, but he pushed her hands away.

"It's nothing. I'm fine." He looked scared, and she became insistent.

"Stephen," she grabbed his arm, holding him tight, "why does your side hurt?"

He wouldn't answer her, so she finished unbuttoning his doublet and pushed his shirt aside. A huge purple bruise covered his ribs, turning yellowish at the edges.

"How did this happen?" she demanded. She tried to control her voice so he wouldn't think she was angry with him.

He burst into tears again. "Please don't tell anyone! I'm not a spy, Auntie. I promise."

"What are you talking about? Of course you're not a spy! Who said that to you?"

He sniffed a few times. "It was the day of the funeral. I was in the gatehouse, hiding under a bed. The captain came in and started jesting about my da and Uncle Bren. Calling them names and saying the English were going to cut Uncle Bren's head off." He looked at her apologetically.

"Then what happened?" she prompted him.

"I got very mad and came out from under the bed. He was sitting with his back to me, so I ran at him and started hitting him." He stopped again, so she nodded. "He . . . He threw me on the floor and k–kicked me. He said I was a traitor and a spy just like my da and if anyone found out, I'd get my h–head chopped off, too." He started to cry again.

Hate burned within her. How dare that man hurt and taunt a boy on the day of his father's funeral? How dare he do it at all? She grabbed his shoulders.

"Listen to me, Stephen. You did well by telling me. You are not a spy, and neither was your father or Brenden. I won't allow that man to treat you like that. If he lays a hand on you again or says one cross word to you, tell me."

He nodded, and she hugged him again. It was very late, way past his bedtime, but she had something she wanted to give him. She led him to Brenden's room.

"This is for you." She handed a book to him. He looked it over, inspecting the cover and opening it to flip through the pages.

"But nothing's written in it. What am I to do with it?"

"Remember how you told me about Petrarch's book, *My Secret*? This is kind of like that. It's your own book to write anything you want in. Your secrets or memories. Whatever."

He looked at it critically. "Why?"

"Well, maybe there are things you can't tell me or other people because you don't think they'll understand. There might be things you want to remember about your father. You write them down and you can come back and read them any time you want. Or maybe you're trying to figure something out about yourself. That's what Petrarch was trying to do."

He looked at her suspiciously. "I thought you couldn't read Latin."

"I can't. I learned about Petrarch in school. I read some of his writings translated into English."

He smiled shyly. "Thank you, Auntie."

She held his hand and walked him to his room. After she tucked him into bed, she walked across the castle, her anger growing with each step. When she reached the captain's room, she rapped sharply. She thought momentarily on the lateness of the hour but didn't care. She'd drag his ass out of bed.

She heard some muffled talking within, then a loud, irritable, "Who is it?"

"It's Audrey Ross. I'd like to have a word with you, Captain."

More muffled talking. After a moment, the door opened. He had dressed quickly. His reddish-blond hair was in disarray. His shirt was open at the throat and hanging out over the poufed breeches he always wore; they stopped at midthigh and showed off heavily muscled calves and thighs. He didn't open the door all the way, and his broad shoulders blocked her view into the room.

"My lady," he said, smiling. "What a most unexpected . . . and pleasant surprise."

"Whatever." She rolled her eyes. "I can see you're busy, but I need to have a word with you."

He thought it over for a moment, then opened the door wider for her to enter. One of the girls from the kitchen was hastily slipping her shapeless leather shoes on.

"Get out," he said coldly to her.

"My lady, I was just . . . just . . . ," the girl stammered, hurrying past her.

Audrey waved her away, and she scurried down the hall.

"I see you're enjoying your stay here," she said dryly when he had shut the door.

"Jealous?" he asked, regarding her intently.

"Please, don't make me ill. I have another matter to discuss with you."

He poured a cup of wine and handed it to her. She took it, then immediately set it on the table next to her, making him smirk in amusement.

"What is this matter that brings you to my room so late?" He walked closer, his voice dropping low. The man was incorrigible. He did not seem to understand that she found him revolting.

"It's about Stephen." That stopped him.

He frowned. "Stephen? Ye mean the little bastard that keeps putting mice and spiders in me boots?"

"Yes, the very same. If you ever touch him again, you son of a bitch, I'll kill you myself."

He was amazed at her outburst, then laughed. "Aye, I'd like to see you try. The wee bastard got what he had coming. I find him lurking about my chambers or the gatehouse again, he'll feel more of my boot on his arse."

"You think this is funny?" She was becoming angrier by the second. "I mean it, you hurt him . . . or . . . or threaten him with that ridiculous spy garbage again and I swear you will be sorry." She realized how empty her threats sounded and that she should have waited until tomorrow to speak to him. He was grinning at her mockingly.

She was getting nowhere, but at least she had made her point. She walked to the door. He was right behind her, his hand on her arm.

"Don't leave, love. You drove Bessie away. Stay and make it up to me."

She gave him a look to show her complete disgust at the idea. He laughed, but turned away. She hurried out the door before he changed his mind and decided to force himself on her.

She was glad she was taking on this sheriff business. It meant she would have to leave, and she was taking Stephen with her. She would gather all of Camden's papers together, and they would leave as soon as possible.

In the past, Camden had stayed in Brenden's house during the quarter sessions. The house was just outside the village where the quarter session was being held. Since the village had no inn, many of the officials attending would be housed with Audrey. It was a good thing she had decided to leave early. She had a great deal to do.

She was surprised to find how similar being sheriff was to her duties as chief of security, especially the administrative side of it. Unfortunately, quarter sessions were not one of the similar duties. She found copies of letters Camden had written before his past sessions. During the previous year, he had written those who needed to be present to inform them of their duty to attend and give them the date. The letters were fairly similar, so she wrote copies of her favorite ones.

She heard back from Brenden's factor. He sent her money and said he was coming to see her. She quickly wrote back, telling him she would go to him. She told Glynnis to have her things and Stephen's packed. They would be leaving the next morning. Once she had arrived, she would be very busy and was grateful for it. Maybe then she'd sleep more soundly.

She was dreaming again. Not the prophetic, strange dreams she was used to having. These were regular old run-of-the-mill dreams that could only mean one thing: She missed Brenden badly. She would wake, her belly so tight, it hurt, her breath short, still warm from the sensation of his hands and mouth on her. The tightness would move to her chest when she realized it was only a dream. A pillow wasn't much comfort; it didn't even smell like him anymore.

She shook thoughts of the dreams off and turned back to reading Camden's papers. There was so much to learn, and lucky for her, he needed to write a lot of letters to get things done. She also found a very impersonal journal he had kept while he was at the sessions, recording what went on. It was proving invaluable already.

There was a knock on her door, and Leslie entered.

"Lord Irvine has received a letter you need to see concerning the upcoming quarter session." He handed her the letter. It was fairly short and to the point, an unusual feature for sixteenth-century correspondence. It was from Francis Hepburn Stewart, fifth Earl of Bothwell. He wrote that since Alistair held Sir Synn Marshall in custody and his accusers were also there, as long as Sir Synn received fair representation, Alistair could try him. "In answer to your reqwest." Alistair asked to try him?

"Where is Marshall?" she asked. So much had happened, she had forgotten about the vile Sir Synn Marshall who had raped Una and tried to burn her for witchcraft.

"He's been downstairs locked up safely for near two months now. We had him over in the tower at Drochaid, but he escaped. The dungeon is stronger here."

"He's in the dungeon?" she asked in horror. She looked at the floor as if she could see him through it.

"Aye, he is. And a venomous fellow, no doubt." He nodded his head knowingly.

She thought for a moment about what needed to be done. "Make sure he's clean and has fresh clothes for tomorrow. Tell him he may write a letter to his lawyer if he wishes. Inform Forbes to increase the guard traveling with us since we will have a prisoner. Oh, and find Una—I need to speak with her and Gavin." She took her papers up again. He made no move to leave.

When she looked up, he was gazing at her with a bemused expression.

"Something the matter, Leslie?"

"If I didn't know better, I'd think ye were accustomed to giving orders." He grinned. "Right away, milady!"

It had been months since she'd been in charge of anything. She was enjoying the feelings of responsibility and importance.

"Did you know Marshall has been in the dungeon all this time?" she asked Gavin and Una when they arrived. They both looked surprised. "He's coming with us to be tried at the quarter session, so Una will have to come. Does Brenden have a lawyer?"

Gavin said, "Aye, his solicitor is in town."

"Good, when we arrive we'll have him draw up a bill of indictment for Marshall so we can have him tried." Audrey leafed through the papers, then looked at Una. "From what I've been reading, his offense could warrant death." Audrey watched her for a reaction.

"Good, let him hang," Una spat.

Gavin was watching Audrey with interest. "I owe you an apology, Audrey. I didn't believe you could do it. I thought you'd come running to me or Leslie, begging for help."

Audrey shrugged. "I like to keep busy."

As they were leaving, Audrey saw how Gavin's hand gently gripped the back of Una's neck to guide her. Since they didn't seem in a particular rush to get married, she assumed consummation hadn't taken place. But Audrey could see an intimacy between them, and it made her happy for them both. Gavin had seemed lonely when she met him.

Like Audrey was now. Maybe when she got out from under Captain Moffat's watchful eyes, she could send Brenden a letter. She shook her head; the captain was waiting for something like that. She desperately wanted to communicate with him, know how he was faring. Was he still beating himself up? Or was he coming to terms with it? She wished she could be there with him.

Brenden had been staying at Duncan Monro's stronghold for several weeks. Duncan was a distant cousin, but a close business partner, and had no qualms about hiding Brenden from King James's men. One of Brenden's ships was on the way, and he sent word to Gavin, asking after Audrey's welfare. He wouldn't leave until he heard back from him. He had to know if she was still there. He thought about her constantly, berating himself for not bringing her one minute, then glad that he hadn't the next. He desperately needed her comfort, her arms around him, but he couldn't let her see him this way. A shell of the man he had been. If he went to her now she would be disgusted that she had married another sniveling fool like her late husband. He couldn't show her the darkness within him. He must try to regain himself first. He feared he never would.

He sat at the table in the wee hours of the morning, as he had almost every night for the past week. A piece of parchment lay smooth and flat in front of him. Sometimes he poured his heart out like he had when he told her of Dragsholm. Other times he put on a brave face and said he was fine and would be back as soon as it was safe. But he always ended up watching the edges catch fire and burn in the fireplace, the words turning to ash as though he had never written them. But tonight, no words came.

He stared at the paper for a long time. Dipping the pen in the inkwell, he told her he loved her and not to leave. He leaned on his elbow and looked at it hard. She would think him weak and pathetic. He threw down the pen and crumpled the paper into a ball, launching it into the fireplace. He knew he should stop wasting Duncan's paper, but he seemed drawn to do it. The words would form perfectly in his head until he tried to write them. Then he couldn't even remember what it was he wanted to tell her. He stood abruptly, causing the inkwell to tip, then fall back, spilling a small puddle on the table.

He was crossing to the bed when the door began to open slowly. He panicked, since he was shirtless and unarmed, clad only in breeks. It was only Rois, one of the serving wenches. Several of the lasses took it upon themselves to try and cheer him—including, to his personal dismay, Duncan's fifteen-year-old daughter, whom he firmly rebuked. Rois was more persistent than the others.

She slipped inside and closed the door behind her, a wicked smile on her lips. "My lord is up late," she said, walking toward him. "What ails him that he canna rest?"

She was small, but her breasts were large, straining against the thin chemise she wore. Her hair was long and black, so black it was almost bluish. It hung down her back, swinging slightly as she walked.

She placed her hands against his stomach. His muscles tightened, and he grabbed her wrists. He stood still for a moment, part of him wanting to throw her on the bed and use her, the other part annoyed at the intrusion.

She looked up at him, making her mouth pouty. "Ye make me think you dinna like me." She looked down. Seeing he was aroused, her full lips curved into a smile. "He's not so dead after all, is he?"

"Get out," he said, pushing her away. Her face distorted with anger. He walked to the mantle and grabbed a bottle of whiskey, uncorking it with his teeth. When he looked up she was still standing there. "I have no need of your services. You may leave."

"Mayhap ye fancy the lads better, my lord," she said with a nasty smile. "There's a bonny one in the stables I've heard likes a good buggering."

He stared at her coldly. "If you feel better now, I want you to leave."

She looked as though she might cry. After calling him a few more choice names, scut and whoreson among them, she finally left. He sighed, leaning his forehead against the stone mantle and staring into the fire. The paper was no more than ashes now, gone as if it had never existed.

⊰ 22 ⊱

They were ready to leave around midmorning. Stephen was astride the pony Audrey had bought for him. It was the largest Leslie could find on short notice, and Stephen insisted on riding it. She was impressed with their little cavalcade, quite unlike their journey to England and back. There were several wagons with trunks of clothes and other necessities. When she commented on whether they really needed all this stuff, Gavin told her it would be much worse when the household moved to Drochaid, which they would be doing soon so Creag Liath could be cleaned. Brenden's house was fairly well equipped and their stay would be short, so not much was needed.

Captain Moffat approached her as she was mounting her horse. "I would like to offer my services in escorting yon prisoner." He nodded to Marshall's sullen form, already surrounded by Forbes and five others.

"No, thank you, Captain." She put her foot in the stirrup. He grasped her arm lightly to stop her.

"Let me speak plain. I harbor suspicions as to your reasons for leaving, but as you have a duty to perform, I won't stand in the way." He studied her thoughtfully. "But you won't rid yourself of me so easy, either. We shall escort you into town." He released her arm and motioned to his men.

"You'll have to find other accommodations in town, Captain. My house will be full." She looked down at him from astride her horse. The short metal brim of his helmet shadowed his eyes, but she could see he was tossing one of his lewd remarks around in his head. I could kick him in the face right now and feel no remorse, she thought in surprise. Propriety won for once, and he simply smiled at her before joining his men.

Since they were only able to travel a few miles an hour, due to the large number of wagons, it took all morning and the better part of the afternoon to reach Brenden's house. The whole way, Marshall eyed Gavin, Una, and Audrey hatefully, as though seeing their painful deaths in his head. When they stopped to rest the horses and eat, Marshall notified everyone in their company that the three of them were witches of the foulest kind. He was quickly silenced by Captain Moffat's fist and some disparaging words about the part of a horse he might be excreted from.

Brenden's "house" was more of a mansion, rivaling Nicholas Jennings's country manor in size and luxury. It was four stories of red stone and completely unfortified. No moats or gatehouse. There was a tall stone wall around it, enclosing the beautiful gardens in the back, and a wrought iron gate at the entrance.

Audrey told Forbes to contact the blacksmith to have the windows barred in one of the rooms on the top floor. Marshall had shown himself adept at escape and would be closely guarded.

By the end of the second day, Audrey was mentally

exhausted. She had brought James Sinclair, Stephen's tutor, with them, as well as the seamstress. She left Stephen in the care of James; not a situation the boy was pleased about, since James wanted him doing lessons all day. The seamstress was working on several new dresses for Audrey, one of which she was wearing—a simple black silk number, with an empire waist to accommodate her new addition. She was trying not to deviate too far from the current fashion so she didn't stand out. She was still wearing the multitude of layers—the shift, the petticoats. The gown hung loosely under her breasts, but she was looking forward to when it would fill out.

Being the deputy was a thankless job. The pay for the position was a fraction of what it cost to execute it in any competent way. She was lucky she had Brenden's money. She spent the day in town ordering an enormous amount of food for the officials who would be arriving soon.

She spoke with the chief justice who appointed the grand jury. He was surprised to have to deal with a woman, but became amiable once he had gotten used to the idea and saw she was capable. She hired a man to make a list of all the prisoners currently being held for trial and to deliver it to her that evening. Then she had to deal with the not-so-pleasant aspect of the job: executions.

There might be executions afterward, and it was her responsibility to see that they were carried out. She would have to hire men to do it after a decision had been made on the manner of the deaths. In the past, most were simple hangings, but she found some entries where Camden had ordered a large amount of "faggots," straw, and pitch for burnings. This was not something she relished, since the theft of a few shillings was punishable by death. She would have to resign herself to it since she had no control over the outcome of the cases. It was entirely in the hands of the attending justices.

When she was returning to the house, Captain Moffat appeared alone. Forbes and three other guards were with her, and she considered having them send him on his way. He reined his horse in to wait for her. Forbes glowered at him from beneath shaggy brown brows.

"I see you made a special trip to plague me today," she remarked with disdain.

"I have never seen a woman act as deputy before, although I've heard it has been done. I've always found women who styled themselves as men to be . . . repugnant." He looked her over suggestively. "But I must say, in you, it's a most enchanting quality."

"So I've done something to win your favor?"

"Oh, aye. I find myself hoping your husband has decided to flee permanently," he murmured, low enough so only she could hear.

"If he does, I assure you, that doesn't leave room for you to take his place."

He smiled. "You say that now, but a woman such as yourself must feel lonely. Wanting a man to warm your bed and lie between your thighs."

Forbes, who was carrying a lance, conveniently decided to switch hands, beating the captain on the back of the head and sending his helmet rolling in the dirt.

"I'm sorry, Captain. I can be so inept at times," he said in his deep growling voice, with a smile that more resembled a baring of his teeth.

Audrey stifled a laugh as the captain reined his horse over to retrieve it. With the opening made, Forbes rode next to her.

"I could squeeze the life out of that puss worm if ye'd like, my lady."

"Thank you, Forbes, but I think I can handle the captain."

He grunted his uncertainty. The captain kept his distance the remainder of the return, riding behind them.

Audrey had a houseful. Nine officials from the shire arrived, four of them accompanied by their wives. The meals were large and were served in the hall. She herself presided over them at the head. A few pointers from Gavin, and she felt she was handling it all quite well. Most of the men were disconcerted to have to deal with her but adjusted quickly. Two were polite enough, though they regarded her with suspicion.

She inquired of Brenden's solicitor, Peter Munro, where she could hire entertainment. He remembered seeing a traveling minstrel in town and arranged to have him play for her guests. The minstrel played the lute and sang bawdy songs. Her guests found him amusing and didn't seem to notice the stink that clung to him.

Peter and Una worked together and drew up an indictment to present when the session began. Marshall, in the meantime, spent his days systematically destroying Audrey's upstairs room. The guards were at a loss what to do with him. They bound him with ropes on several occasions, but he always managed to free himself to incur further damage on the furnishings. He even loosened several of the bolts on the bars across his window, which had to be repaired.

She considered talking to him but didn't think anything she said would make an impact on him. He knew what was happening and wasn't about to make it easy for them.

Adding to her problems, one of her guests turned out

to be related to Captain Moffat and requested he join them for dinner. She had no doubt the captain was behind the invitation, but she felt it would be an insult to refuse. Not that she minded insulting Captain Moffat; it was the guest she was concerned about.

The captain and his men set up a little tent city not far from town, so it was very convenient for him to show his face around dinnertime. The evening before the session was to begin, Audrey was retiring to her chambers when she found the captain wandering around upstairs. She clenched her teeth and balled her hands into fists. He would not go away!

"What are you doing up here?"

He looked at her innocently. "I was merely searching for the jakes."

"You know damn well they're downstairs. What's stopping you from pissing in the fireplace? That's what all my other guests do after they've had too much to drink."

From the look on his face, he didn't see a problem with using the fireplace as a urinal, and he shrugged. "I hadn't realized you were with child. It becomes you." He moved closer.

Her hand went involuntarily to her slightly protruding belly. She was a little over three months pregnant and showing, although the only outward indication was the cut of her dress. It hung almost straight down under her breasts.

"Yes, well . . ." She pushed past him to go to her room. "You know your way out."

He was so quiet, she didn't hear him following her, but sensed him there. She turned suddenly, and he almost ran into her. She did not want him to follow her to her room.

"What do you want?" she snapped. "I'm running out of patience with you. If I must, I'll have Forbes throw you out."

"I thought you might like some company. I noticed what a big bed you have and thought what a shame it was you're sleeping alone in it." His arm snaked around her waist, pulling her against him.

"You've been in my room? What the hell were you doing in my room?" She pushed against his chest, but he held her fast.

"You know what I was doing. But unfortunately, if your husband is corresponding with you, you're destroying his letters. I did find some bonny silk things I can imagine you wearing. Why don't ye put one on for me, sweetings?" He lowered his head to kiss her. She brought her knee up, driving it as hard as she could into his groin. He released her immediately and bent over, groaning and grasping his crotch. He wore a stiffened and decorated piece of cloth over his groin called a cod-piece, so she knew she hadn't done any serious damage.

"Get out of my house," she ordered in a voice loud enough to draw attention.

He straightened with some difficulty, bracing himself with the wall. He took the few steps it would take to reach her again. She was surprised he didn't seem angry, but there was something else unreadable in his eyes.

He grabbed her arm and placed his hand on her stomach. "You're a wildcat, love. I like that. But just remember"—he increased the pressure of his hand—"one well-placed blow and your husband will be without an heir. Perchance without a wife. I wager that will bring him back in a hurry."

She swallowed hard, meeting his black gaze. He moved away as Gavin came up the stairs.

"Good evening." He nodded to Gavin. Gavin looked after him, then turned back to her.

"Audrey!" He hurried to her side. "You look faint, do you need to sit down?" He led her into her chambers and pushed her into a chair. "What is it? What did he say to you?"

"He's a fool. He was searching my room, looking for letters from Brenden."

"Did he look elsewhere? Or just in your rooms?"

She shook her head. "I don't know. He thinks Brenden is so enamored with me, he can't possibly stay away or not write. The man knows nothing about Brenden."

Gavin looked as though he wanted to say something.

"Have you heard from Brenden?" she asked. His lips thinned, but he was silent. "You have! Why haven't you told me?" She glared at him and still he said nothing. A sick feeling came over her. "He told you not to, didn't he?"

"Audrey, he can't come back now, not with Captain Moffat here waiting for him. You know he must stay hidden until he's pardoned."

"Why doesn't he write me? I'd burn the letters after I received them. Just to know he's all right. That's all I want." He looked so pathetic, not knowing what to do or say to make her feel better. "What did he say?"

He sighed deeply. "He said very little. He asked after you and the babe." He shook his head sadly. "But I can tell he's still blaming himself. I think he and Camden were at odds about something when he died." From the veiled look Gavin gave her, she could see he knew their disagreement was over her, he just didn't know if *she* knew. "It must be very hard for him, thinking Camden hated him when he died."

She wrapped her arms around her stomach and went to the window.

"Please leave," she said quietly.

His slow footsteps echoed across the floor, and the door closed. What was she going to do? Tears burned at her eyes, blurring her moonlit view of the tree-speckled countryside, but she fought against them. What was it about her that seemed to drive men to depression? It seemed she was the cause of this whole horrible situation, and she could do nothing to rectify it. Even with him far away, he pushed her still further from him. The urge to ride to Drochaid and leave immediately was strong.

But she couldn't do it. There was Stephen and the child, her promise to Camden. She would stay until Brenden was pardoned. If Gavin wrote back to him and told him she still waited, maybe he wouldn't do anything stupid.

They didn't get to Marshall on the first day of the trials, but the other cases were settled without any death sentences, to Audrey's elation. She hadn't attended the other trials, so she didn't know what to expect at Marshall's.

Two justices presided over the "court," which was really just a room with a table and chairs for the judges. Brenden's lawyer, Peter Munro, was a young, blond man, all dandied up in a flowing velvet surcoat, complete with a stiff ruff around his neck and elaborate brocade shoes with pointed toes. He began the trial by reading the indictment. It said that Una had been taken by force in an effort to acquire her lands, raped in an attempt to force her into marriage, and when she still refused to comply, falsely accused of witchcraft. He finished by adding that had Gavin not intervened, she would be dead now.

The defense followed up with more ridiculous witchcraft charges and a plea that a higher court try the case. Peter then brought in two people who were present when Marshall tried to burn Una that day in the square. They testified that Marshall had paid them to accuse her. Marshall's attorney, in turn, had witnesses further stating Una's witchery.

The trial lasted less than an hour, and the justices took almost no time to deliberate. Marshall was pronounced guilty for making a false accusation of witchcraft and attempting to carry out the sentence himself. He was sentenced to the same penalty Una would have suffered had he succeeded: burning. Audrey swallowed the lump in her throat and feigned happiness. She was glad this whole mess was over for Una, but now she would have to prepare for Marshall's death, and her stomach was queasy.

The execution was set for the next day at noon. Marshall was dragged out, screaming curses at Una. He would be housed in the public jail overnight under a tight guard. "I'll see you burn before I do, foul whore!" he howled before the door closed, muffling the rest of his invectives.

Una shuddered. Gavin put his arm around her and pulled her close, but she pushed him away.

"You two go on ahead," Audrey told them. "I have some faggots to order."

"Nay, we'll wait," Una said, and they followed Audrey on her rounds as she prepared to execute her first criminal.

On the ride home, the air of depression surrounding them was palpable. Audrey understood why she was sickened, but she was confused by their long faces.

"What's the matter with you two? You should be happy! Now you can set a date for the wedding."

Una gave Gavin a sidelong look. "Aye, now that I'm safe to marry, I suppose we should."

His black brows creased in the perfect imitation of a basset hound. "What are you talking about? You've been acting strange for days now. What did I do?"

"I'll never know now, will I?" Una's mouth was set, and she looked straight ahead.

He looked to Audrey for support, but she shrugged. "What will you never know?" he asked helplessly.

Una gave him a pointed look. "What you would have done had Marshall been proven innocent."

"What the hell are you talking about?" Annoyance was starting to edge his voice.

"When I asked you if ye'd still marry me should Marshall go free, you said 'I don't know what will happen then.'"

Understanding dawned on his face, and he smiled gently at her. "I didn't mean I wouldn't marry you, love. What I meant was, if he wasn't proven guilty, I planned on killing him myself." He shrugged. "I couldn't say what would happen then."

"That would have been a fool thing to do, ye idiot!" she admonished him, but both Gavin and Audrey could tell she was pleased. After a moment, she reached her hand out to him. He brought it to his lips, pressing a kiss against her knuckles, his dark-blue eyes never leaving her face.

Audrey looked away and sighed.

Brenden walked swiftly to his chambers, the dampness from his palms staining the parchment of the letter he held. He didn't want to read it in front of Duncan and so endured sitting through the rest of the meal with him, trying to hide his eagerness to be gone. All the while his eyes continued straying to it.

Now within the confines of his room, he felt apprehensive. The wax seal held the mark of his brother's ring. He grabbed the flint and lit the wick of the tallow candle. He ran a nervous hand through his hair and sat, turning the unopened letter over in his hands.

What news did it contain? He examined the seal. It hadn't been tampered with. If they knew his whereabouts, they'd have been here by now. He broke the seal and slowly unfolded the paper.

Relief surged over him with a dizzying effect, making him squeeze his eyes tightly shut. *She hadn't left.* Gavin wrote that Audrey was fine, as was the child she carried. He opened his eyes and read on. His father had left to secure him a pardon; no word had been heard back from him. There was an unsavory fellow by the name of Captain Ethan Moffat haunting them about Brenden's whereabouts. Stephen returned the favor by making the captain's stay most inconvenient. Brenden smiled. He could guess what Gavin meant by that. He felt pity for the poor captain. As he read on, his brow began to furrow.

"She's gone and done what?" he asked under his breath. When he finished the letter, he leaned back in his chair, a smile tugging at the corners of his mouth. She was there, hanging on tenaciously, making the best of a bad situation. Deputy! He could hardly believe it. And spending all his money, as well. He didn't care—she could have it.

For the first time in nearly two months, he felt something stirring within him. He wanted to go to her. The uncertainty, the chance that she might leave him, had made him withdraw so it wouldn't hurt so badly when she did. That was why he had once again shut her out, refusing to talk to her. But now that all fell away, and he realized, with a wave of unease, that the very horror he had hoped to spare her, he was causing her by continuing his silence. He knew now, with powerful conviction, that she had been sent here for him. He could face anything as long as she stood beside him. He wished he had understood sooner so he could have reassured her before he left.

He had the urge to take one of Duncan's shaggy beasts and ride without stopping. But that would be foolish. He would have to wait, lest it all be taken away from him once he got there. He would send his ship waiting in Banff on its way. It had other business to attend and was costing him to sit idle.

What was she—close to four months along with the bairn now? He should be with her. His happiness dampened a little. She didn't need him. In fact, from the sound of it, she was getting along just fine without him. He could imagine the justices' reaction to a pregnant woman marching about town giving orders. No doubt she had charmed them all.

He read the letter again, laughing aloud in several places this time.

23

Audrey sat alone in the drawing room of Drochaid Castle poring over Leslie's account books. He was becoming used to her curiosity about the running of such a large estate and no longer gave her strange looks when she hung over his shoulder. Stephen sat near her feet with a deck of cards making a house. He was very good at it, and it was already four stories high.

They had been at Drochaid only a few days. It had been time to move on, since Creag Liath was in need of cleaning. Drochaid was smaller and not nearly as fortified, but comfortable. She walked by the corridor several times a day. It was still there. When no one was around, she sometimes stood looking into it. She saw Ian MacKay walk by twice. He would touch the wall and walk on. But she never stepped into it.

Captain Moffat was still with them, but now they were somewhat comforted by the presence of his men. When still at Brenden's house, she had been awakened on the morning of Marshall's execution and told he escaped. Two weeks had passed, and he still hadn't turned up. Una was sure he was plotting revenge.

Audrey hoped she was wrong and he had simply gone into exile.

There was still no word from Brenden. Gavin hadn't heard from him since his last letter. Sometimes, when she walked by, the corridor seemed to beckon to her, promising her an easier life. One of toilets and telephones, computers and standardized spelling. But she resisted and continued her waiting.

The door to the drawing room stood open, and servants rushed by, full of excited whispers. Something was going on. She toyed with the idea of checking it out, but changed her mind and went back to the ledgers.

Last year, the household had consumed thirty-five thousand loaves of bread and almost two hundred sheep! She was finding out how costly it was to maintain a household of this size and was feeling daunted. She looked up from her ledgers and frowned. The book-lined walls were shadowed, yet the servants were still scurrying about. She looked at the small clock on the table next to her. It was getting late. She sent Stephen to bed and decided to retire herself. She planned to ride to Camden's abbey in the morning and see what repairs were still needed.

She closed the ledger and bent to gather Stephen's cards when she heard heavy footsteps approaching. She looked up to see Alistair framed in the doorway. Her heart immediately began thumping in her ears. He was back, and he didn't look well. What did that mean?

He watched her silently, and she was unable to speak, only able to stare back into his light-green eyes. He looked older, as though he aged years in the two months since she had last seen him. More gray peppered his dark reddish-brown hair, and his beard was almost completely gray and white.

"You're back," was all she could manage, but it seemed to break the spell, because he walked in. He grabbed a chair and dragged it to the table where she sat.

"Aye, I'm back." He pointed to the ledger in front of her. "Are you my new steward as well as my deputy?"

"You heard."

He smiled, his eyes crinkling at the corners. "Aye, I heard. And your first condemned prisoner escaped." He clucked his tongue and shook his head.

She flushed. The guards had been knocked unconscious and later said they didn't know what happened, they hadn't heard or seen anything. They were mortified at having been foiled by the slight Synn Marshall, and she felt it was somehow her fault. He was her responsibility. She had never made such a blunder as chief of security and if she had, she would not have gotten off easy. She didn't offer Alistair an explanation.

He saw her embarrassment. "Don't be hard on yourself. Some things are beyond your control. I hear you did a bonny job of it."

She shrugged, then tapped the ledger in front of her. "I would like to speak with you about this when you have time. I think I could save you money by cutting back on much of the wastefulness I've observed."

He gave a short laugh. "I've heard. Gibson saw fit to meet me in the bailey, informing me that she is now forced to remove the skin from the chickens before she cooks them. She also said you won't allow her to use butter as she wishes. And what's this about steaming vegetables? She says you have some contraption set up in the hearth."

She hastened to justify herself. "Well, it's much healthier. The way she cooks, everything is full of fat and has lost all of the nutrients before it hits the table! And I have the baby to think of . . . and Stephen."

"Indeed?" He looked amused but indulgent. "Do as you will. I will tell her she must mind you." His face creased in pain suddenly, and he rubbed his arm.

"Are you all right?"

He waved his hand, as though to say it was nothing, and took a deep breath. When he exhaled, he seemed better. She waited for him to tell her what had happened at King James's court. After a moment, he rested his chin on his hand and looked at her intently. His scrutiny was making her nervous, and she was anxious to hear his news.

"A lass or a lad?" he asked.

She frowned. "What?"

He nodded his head in the direction of her stomach. "The bairn. What think you?"

"I don't know. A boy, I guess. Then he and Stephen will be like brothers."

His mouth curved into a smile. "Then a lad it shall be."

"Just because you say so?" She found herself smiling with him.

"I have a gift for these things." He straightened, apparently deciding it was time for more serious matters. He withdrew a folded piece of paper from his doublet. Her hands shook, and she dropped it once, trying to unfold it. It was a royal pardon, signed by James R. A teardrop splattered onto the ink. She dabbed at it frantically with one sleeve and mopped her eyes with the other.

She covered her face, sobs shuddering through her. He took it back to view the damage.

"Weep not. I can still read it." He folded it carefully and put it back in his doublet. "I will have a copy made. Do you know where Brenden is?"

She shook her head. "Gavin does."

"Tomorrow he will take it to him." He touched her hand. "We'll bring him home."

She looked at him closer, seeing the lines worry had worn on his brow. He wanted Brenden safe, too. They were silent for a few moments, contemplating their own thoughts.

"What of Captain Moffat?" he asked suddenly. "Has he been causing you much distress?"

She rolled her eyes. "Don't ask."

"Then I shall give you the pleasure of throwing his arse off my estate."

"An assignment I will relish."

He patted her hand before standing. "We'll talk more in the morning. Good night to you."

As soon as a copy of the pardon had been made—a long process, since Leslie copied it word for word—Audrey marched to the captain's chambers. He was still being lodged within the castle while his men slept in the gate-house. She'd noticed he was a late sleeper and had hoped to catch him in bed, or even better, in bed with one of their servants.

She planned to tell him exactly what she thought of him. Now that Brenden had been pardoned, the captain was harmless. She patted the blade tucked in her garter just the same. She had started wearing it after Marshall escaped. She knocked on his door and walked in. He was dressed and in the process of buckling his sword-belt. He looked startled at her barging into his room unannounced.

He didn't say anything, but looked at the paper she held in her hands. She could tell by his expression he already knew. News traveled fast in the little castle community.

"This is the pardon King James granted my husband. Would you like to read it?" She held it in front of his face.

He took it from her, black eyes skimming over it. "You're here to tell me to get out." He handed it back and walked to the door. This was too easy! But she was wrong. He closed the door and leaned against it. The expression on his face was unreadable.

"Yes, get out. Get lost. Adiós. I hope I never see your face again." She tried hard to think of more ways to say it but decided he had the general idea.

"Once again, I am smitten by your charm." He smiled. "But I don't think you came here just to tell me that. Surely ye have more words for me?"

She advanced on him. "I think you're a vile, disgusting bastard. You have managed to make a bad situation worse with your constant molestations. I hate you and hope you have nothing but unhappiness and misery in your life."

"'Tis a shame, for I am entranced by you." He grabbed her arm and pulled her against him. "Can't you give me one wee kiss before I leave?"

She pulled her head back from his searching lips. His breath was foul and made her stomach turn. "Let go of me."

He gripped the back of her neck. "You say you don't want it now, love. But once I'm in you, riding between those long legs, you'll wrap them around me and be screaming for more."

She turned her face in revulsion, and his mouth moved across her cheek. His fingers bit into her neck so she couldn't escape him. She reached down to retrieve the knife. He grabbed her wrist.

"What have ye there, sweetings?" he murmured,

transferring her wrist to his other hand and groping at her skirts. She kicked at his shins and punched him with her free hand. The movement was enough to make him cease his search and try to control her.

He grabbed her waist and lifted her. She had no idea what he was going to do, but she began struggling in earnest. He howled suddenly and dropped her. She scrambled away. He was bent over, holding his face. She looked frantically around the room and saw Stephen. He emerged from behind a chair, carrying a crude slingshot.

The captain saw him at the same time she did.

"Stephen! Get out!" she yelled, as she pulled the knife from her garter.

Stephen tried to dart past him, but the captain grabbed his arm, twisting it until he cried out in pain. "I finally got me hands on you, ye little piece of dung. I'll beat your arse so you can hardly sit down for that." He administered one resounding blow that landed across Stephen's back. Audrey was trembling with rage that he would dare hit Stephen again. The captain's attention was diverted from her, so he was extremely surprised to feel the blade of a knife against his throat.

"Put the boy down or I will kill you." Her voice was shaking, but she wasn't scared. He released Stephen and straightened. He made a grab for the knife, but she pulled it back, turning it in her hand so it would be easier to plunge into his chest if necessary. Stephen ran behind her, hiding his face in her skirts, but she didn't hear a whimper from him.

"Oh, you are an evil bitch." He looked at her contemptuously. "Will you set your husband on me when he returns? I should like to run him through in self-defense."

"I don't need to set my husband on you. You forget, I was raised with the Turks. I'll cut you up myself. Now get out. Move!" She was calming down. Her hand was steadier, her voice was stronger. He felt it, and shock registered on his face.

"Aye, I think you just might at that." He walked slowly to the table, never taking his eyes off her and gathered the rest of his things. He stopped at the door, a small smile on his face. "Adieu, little wildcat."

When she was sure he wasn't coming back, she dropped to her knees and pulled Stephen in front of her. "Are you all right, honey? Did he hurt you?" He shook his head, but he wrapped his arms around her neck, hugging her tightly.

She hugged him back, careful not to squeeze, since he was probably lying. Thank God for sneaky little Stephen!

"How long have you been in here?" she asked.

"I followed you. I came in while he was reading Uncle Bren's pardon."

She shook her head in amazement. She hadn't seen anything! Excitement shone in his eyes, making them a brilliant emerald.

"Is Uncle Bren coming home?"

"As soon as he can, he will be here."

"Do you want to go watch the soldiers leave with me, Auntie?"

"Sure, but let's watch from the tower." She'd had enough close encounters for one day.

They saw Gavin as they were passing by her time-travel corridor. He was outfitted for travel. "Are you going to tell him?"

"Aye, and I plan on bringing him back, so don't worry." He chucked her under the chin. "Do you have a message for him?"

She thought for a moment. Did she want to send a sappy message of her undying love and her vigilance in waiting for him? She looked beyond Gavin, seeing the same castle, but older and falling into ruins through a deceptively short hallway. "Tell him from where I stand, I can see into another world."

Stephen and Audrey watched Gavin leave from the tower.

Una was distraught that he had left with only a few men. She was certain Marshall would ambush and kill him. Audrey couldn't see Gavin being caught by anyone. The Ross men seemed to have a gift for lurking. Gavin took precautions for Una's safety in his absence, and she never left her rooms without a guard.

"Look!" Stephen cried, pointing a quarter of a mile to Gavin's left. "'Tis Sebille!"

Sebille? She strained her eyes. The men were already disappearing in the morning fog. She could barely make out the form of a huge black dog running with them.

"Sebille? Is that the dog's name? Whose dog is it?"

"She belonged to Uncle Gavin's mother." He turned to go down the tower steps. Her hair was prickling at the strange sight and Stephen's words. She grabbed his arm.

"What do you mean? Belonged? Is she a ghost?"

Stephen frowned, then shrugged. "I know not, Auntie, but she must a ghost or maybe a familiar. I only know what Isobel told me."

"What did Isobel say?"

"I think she was trying to scare me. She said Sebille was her mother's dog before she was burnt. Their mother was a black witch. Very bad. Isobel said she's Uncle Gavin's now."

She looked out the tower window, but they were out of sight.

Audrey could think of nothing else after Gavin left except the possibility of Brenden's return. If Gavin didn't bring him back to her, she didn't know what she was going to do. She had made a place for herself here. The work was not unpleasant, and she learned something new every day. Many of the documents she needed to read concerning Camden's abbey were written in Latin and French, so she sat in with Stephen on his morning lessons. James was delighted to have her as a pupil and rained constant praise on her progress.

As it turned out, Stephen *was* an incredibly smart boy—the praise had not been just the braggings of a father and uncle. He had a strong sturdy body and Camden's handsome features. When she thought about leaving him, it left a pain in her heart. She wanted to see the man he would become and be part of it.

She dined with Alistair in his chambers. It was a small party: Una, Stephen, Isobel, and Audrey, sometimes Leslie. Alistair seemed different somehow. Still the charmer he always was, but something was different. He liked Una, and Audrey was glad of it. Una gave him a hard time about everything, and he found it amusing. He called her "the wee witch," a term Una didn't find endearing, but he meant it affectionately.

One evening Audrey noticed Alistair looked unwell. He was pale and quiet, and he wasn't eating. He seemed distracted, focusing on something within.

"What is it? You seem unwell," she asked.

"It's nothing. I have trouble catching my breath at times."

His outward condition and what he said set bells off in her head. Being in the military, she was required to take CPR classes regularly, so she knew the warning signs of a heart attack.

"Do you have a tightness in your chest?" She tapped on her breastbone.

"Aye. And it hurts in my arm and face."

"You need to lie down." She helped him to his feet. "And stop eating all this meat." She gestured to the layout on the table, still consisting of far more meat than fruits and vegetables, regardless of the fact that Audrey harrassed Gibson on a regular basis. The plump cook resented Audrey's rise in status and defied her at every opportunity.

Alistair nodded absently.

Una looked at them in concern. "What's the matter?"

"It's his heart," Audrey stated, leading him to the bedchamber. Una trailed after them. They got to the doorway and Alistair braced himself on it, clutching his chest.

"Oh, God." Audrey moaned. She grabbed him around the waist and tried to hold him up. He made a strangled wheezing sound and fell. He was too heavy and almost pulled her down with him. The room went into an uproar. Stephen was screaming for his grandda. Una was trying to push Audrey out of the way.

Una knelt over him. When she looked up, she shook her head. "He's dead."

"Move." Audrey pushed Una aside. She tore at the buttons of his doublet and ripped off the ruff at the collar. Una's hands were on Audrey's shoulders. She was saying something about there being nothing Audrey could do. Audrey shoved Una across the room. After that, everyone kept their distance.

Audrey tried to remember everything she had

learned. She felt for a pulse. Nothing. She tilted his head and grasped his chin gently, setting it so his tongue wasn't in the way. Pinching his nose shut with one hand, she blew into his mouth and turned her head to see his chest rise. Everyone gasped in alarm. She settled herself in a position between his head and chest.

"All right," she mumbled. "Check breastbone. Palms flat, fingers up, elbows straight." She pumped fifteen times before going back to give him mouth-to-mouth. She was aware that she was being looked upon with horror but didn't care. She kept it up. She went through four cycles before she felt a weak pulse and saw his chest rise on its own.

She sat back on her knees, pushing hair out of her face with shaking hands. He didn't open his eyes or move, and she hoped he wasn't in a coma. It had all taken place over the course of a few minutes. She didn't think it was long enough for brain damage.

Una knelt beside him and inspected him. She looked at Audrey in amazement. "He lives!" she cried.

Guards appeared at the door. Audrey gestured to them. "Get him to the bed." They lifted him gently and carried him to his bed chamber, where they laid him upon the covers. She wet a towel and wiped his forehead. He opened his eyes slowly and looked at Audrey in confusion.

"It's all right," she said softly. "You had a heart attack. You need to rest now."

He closed his eyes in exhaustion and slept.

It was late when Brenden and Gavin arrived at Drochaid. Gavin had found him at Duncan's less than a week before and had brought him the pardon signed by

King James and a cryptic message from Audrey that filled him with dread. She was at Drochaid and could see into another world. Was it a threat? Or something to prompt him to hurry back to her? However she meant it, it induced Brenden to ride his horse to near collapse to return to her.

Brenden threw his reins to the stable lad and ran into the castle. As soon as he walked in, he knew something was wrong. Glynnis's long face looked at him fearfully as she hurried into the hall, Leslie not far behind.

"What is it?" he demanded, sparing no time for greetings.

Glynnis hesitated. "It's Lord Irvine. Lady Ross said it was his heart. He's fine now, but bedridden."

Relief washed through Brenden, followed by a stab of guilt. Alistair likely had to humble himself considerably to obtain the pardon. Brenden hadn't expected his father to go to such lengths for him. He would visit Alistair as soon as he saw Audrey. They still watched him fearfully. His chest became tight again.

Una descended the stairs. Her eyes were red-rimmed, and her lips began trembling as soon as she laid eyes on Brenden.

"What has happened?" he asked, his voice deadly quiet.

Una shook her head, unable to form the words at first. "She . . . she's gone."

"What do you mean, *gone*?" *Not dead. Please, not dead.* He grabbed Una's shoulders. "What has happened? The child . . . What do you mean?"

Gavin pried his fingers off Una's shoulders. "Una," Gavin asked gently. "What happened?"

"I don't know." Tears welled in her huge eyes. "Yesterday mornin' Stephen came to me saying he couldn't find Audrey anywhere. We haven't seen her since. She's just . . . gone."

Brenden ran up the stairs to his chambers. Glynnis entered behind him, setting a candle on the table before leaving. He looked around for signs of her. Had she left him a letter? Anything? A black silk gown lay across the back of a chair. He went to it, fingering the material. He lifted it to his face, the scent of her filling his senses. His eyes burned.

He was too late. She'd waited as long as she thought she could. Why? He crushed the material in his hands. He had been granted a pardon. Gavin was sent to deliver it to him. Could she not wait for word? Did she hate him so much now? He should have written her. Brenden's throat tightened. He had hurt her before he left and continued to do so by not sending word. Everything sounded so trite on paper. He wanted to be able to see her and touch her when he explained that it was she who had brought him home and nothing else. *He should have written!* The words danced through his quickly numbing brain, as they had countless times in the last three months. He should have begged her not to leave him.

He dropped the gown. A glint of silver caught his attention near the bed. He walked slowly to it.

It was the locket.

His hands shook as he picked it up. He stared at the delicate piece of workmanship lying in his rough palm. Was this the message? She was giving it back to him? He held it up by the chain, looking at it as though it somehow held the answer his heart was begging for. *Why?*

Where was the queen's ring? Was she not wearing it with the locket? He thought the necklace was unhooked and looked at the clasp. He frowned. It was still fastened, but the chain was broken. His heart stopped momentarily, and when it started again, it was with a wild thudding that he felt throughout his body. He looked around the bed. It was neatly made. He looked underneath. Her shoes were there. The glow of gold showed him the ring on the floor beside her shoes. He picked it up and walked back to the chair. Petticoats and stockings also lay on it. Why would she leave barefoot and in her shift? He looked at the broken chain again. Why would she leave it on the floor?

He ran to the door and roused the castle.

"Where were you night before last?" Brenden asked, drilling Una.

They were in the drawing room. A fire blazed, and Una sat at the desk with her hands folded in her lap. "I was with Isobel. We went to Tayside house for the week. We returned yesterday morning, and that's when Stephen told me," she said.

"What were you doing there?" Gavin asked.

"Lord Irvine is giving us a house as a wedding gift, and Isobel mentioned that I might like Tayside. So we went to have a look." She shrugged. "What do you think happened to Audrey?"

Brenden didn't know. None of the servants had heard or seen anything that night. Audrey was last seen leaving his father's room around ten o'clock and hadn't been seen again. Gavin told him about the odious Captain Moffat, and Brenden planned to pay him a visit as soon as he finished questioning the household.

"What about Marshall?" he asked, looking from Gavin to Una. "Has anyone heard or seen him?"

"Nay, not since he escaped," Gavin said.

"Have they been watching for him at the ports?"

"Aye, but he's not turned up."

Brenden paced, cracking his knuckles. Someone had to have seen something. Gavin was worried about Marshall taking revenge and had Una guarded at all times. But she hadn't been here, and he was certain Una wasn't the only focus of Marshall's hatred. It was Gavin, Audrey, and Brenden who had put Marshall in the position of being sentenced to burn at the stake. Someone *must* have seen something. Who could possibly sneak past the guards and make off with his wife without a sound? The thought flashed through his head that maybe she did return to her own time. It was the only plausible explanation.

No. She would not leave him. She had yelled it from the window in another language the day he'd left her, thinking he didn't understand. His chest hurt when he thought of how little time they'd had together. He never told her he spoke the Turk's language as well. He had meant to, after they had wed. He meant to ask her about all the places they'd both been, separated by four hundred years. Perhaps they could travel there together; he did much trading in the Mediterranean and with the Turks. She might be an asset. The idea that these things might never be, because of his own foolishness, burned.

He would question the guards again. With the exception of Forbes and Dearg, most could not be trusted. The Earl of Irvine was not known for his generosity, and many of his father's men-at-arms, unlike his own, shifted their loyalty quickly if the price was right. Luckily, the men guarding Una were employed by Gavin and Brenden. His hands curled into fists. This time when he interrogated them, he would be a bit more persuasive.

24

Audrey woke with the cold of a gritty dirt floor beneath her cheek. Her stomach hurt from lying on the baby. She pushed herself up to sit. The room careened crazily, and she closed her eyes, placing steadying hands against her forehead. Her head throbbed sickeningly, and there was dried blood in her hair.

She opened her eyes slowly, looking around the small cell. A torch on the wall was the only light, and the corners were draped in shadows. A chamber pot sat in a darkened corner. A windowless wooden door was the only other decoration. She felt a draft and looked around to see where it came from, but she couldn't tell. The smell of the ocean was strong, bringing the events of the past few days rushing back.

She had been in her bed at Drochaid sleeping when a hand covered her mouth. The hand tasted of filth and stank of fish and body odor. Her stomach immediately revolted. It was dark, and she couldn't see the form holding her but only felt strong arms clamping down on her and a body straddling hers. She panicked and struggled. Something crashed down on her head—then nothing.

But it wasn't over.

She was slapped awake and found herself staring into Sir Synn Marshall's belligerent eyes and flouncing mustache. She was fascinated that he still managed to curl the ends of his mustache so they danced as he spoke.

"Where is she?" he asked. His face was too close. His fevered brown eyes bore into her.

"Who?" Audrey asked dumbly, stalling for time. She was still in her room, now lit by a single candle. Marshall was not alone. There were five others, three of them Alistair's castle guards.

"The witch," he snarled.

"I don't know." She knew, but the guards who accompanied Una weren't on Marshall's payroll or he would have that information.

He backhanded her across the face, sending her sprawling. "You lie, bitch!" He grabbed her hair and yanked her to her feet. She heard a low growling noise and realized it was coming from her throat.

"Now tell me," he said menacingly, while he used his hold on her hair to shake her and she hissed in pain, "where is the witch?"

She gathered all the saliva in her dry mouth and spit in his face. His hand was on her throat, squeezing.

"I'll kill you if you don't tell me."

She gasped, her head clouding as she pulled at his hand. From far away she heard one of the other men hesitantly suggest it might not be such a good idea to kill her yet—and then nothing.

She was roused by the jarring trot of a horse. She was lying across a saddle in front of a smelly, leather-clad man on a horse. In the distance she could see the ruins of a tower, part of an old castle. It rose out of the angry sea like a black devil.

They followed the winding path leading up to it. Since the interior was so deteriorated as to be almost completely exposed to the elements, Marshall was using the dungeons as his camp.

She remembered being led down curving stone stairs, slick from the sea and wear, then tossed into the tomb she now occupied. She had been given hard bread and grimy water and left to herself. Due to the lack of natural light, she didn't have any idea how long she had been there. Maybe a few days, she wasn't sure. The pain in her head had been blinding at first, and she had been barely able to open her eyes. So she had lain there unmoving, eyes tightly shut, floating in and out of consciousness.

Now she held the wall and stood unsteadily. She touched her stomach. It was bruised and sore. She felt the faint fluttering movements and hoped they indicated the baby's safety. She wanted to curl into a ball and cry, yet her eyes were dry, her mind numb. Who would know where she was? Marshall must have left the three guards behind to vouch that they hadn't heard or seen anything.

If Brenden was coming back, he would be on his way. What would he think when he found her gone without a trace? She shivered. All she wore was her shift, with one of Brenden's shirts under it. One of the men must have had the decency to grab her shift and pull it over her head.

She heard the heavy bar being lifted from the door. She pressed herself against the wall. Marshall walked in again, smiling. "I have word the witch is back." When she only stared mutely at him, he continued, "Did ye see my lovely stronghold when you arrived? The locals call it Caisteal na h-Uamha—castle of the cave. There's a beautiful stretch of ground in the center, opening up into the heavens. Did you see that?"

It was the place Alistair had intended to send her and Camden to after he had kidnapped her. The place Camden said Brenden used to come after his dreams.

"I says to myself," he stroked his mustache, looking at her through half-lidded eyes, "I couldn't have picked a better place for a witch burning. I can just see it, flames licking up into the sky."

She tried not to let her horror at what he was implying show on her face.

"It shall be a festive occasion." He walked across the room, then turned back to look at her. "For I'll not be burning just one of Satan's whores. Nor even two." He watched her intently. "Nay, I shall have four."

What was he talking about? When she continued to look at him blankly, he smiled.

"Your husband and his kelpie brother have returned." His smile grew at her gasp. "I have dispatched a messenger to them. I informed them I hold you as my prisoner and welcomed them to pay a handsome ransom for your safe return." He pursed his lips and walked back to her. He wrapped his gloved hand around her throat and squeezed slightly. She caught her breath.

"I did not disclose our position, and their eyes will be covered for the journey. Should they think to have someone follow, I told them of my intention to kill you."

"You're insane. You can't really think any of us are witches." Her voice sounded hoarse and breathy because of the iron hold he had on her neck. When she breathed, she made a slight wheezing sound, trying to pull enough air into her lungs.

His eyes became dark and his lips thinned. "You and your family have taken everything from me." His fingers tightened. The edges of her vision were fragmenting. Her throat burned as she tried to suck in the wisps of air still being allowed entrance. She clawed at his wrist, his face floating before her. "I'm an outlaw, facing death should I stay in my own country. My home. And you did it, you foul bitch."

He released her throat, and she fell to the ground, gulping in the stale air. She continued to lie there, long after the door had closed and the bar had fallen, locking her in.

The messenger stared into the light-green eyes that were level with his. Under normal circumstances, Lord Brenden Ross would stand a head taller than him, but at the moment, Lord Ross held him against the wall by the front of his tunic. His toes barely scraped the floor.

"Now," Lord Ross said calmly. "I can make this easy for you, or it can be very painful, but I shall only ask one more time." He paused to let the meaning of his words sink in, and the messenger swallowed hard, tasting blood at the back of his throat. "What does Marshall mean to do?"

He shook his head. "I dinna know, milord." His voice was muffled, and there was a nasal quality to it, due to the blood running into his mouth and down the back of his throat from his broken nose.

Lord Ross's lips thinned, and his hand tightened on the messenger's tunic. He cocked his fist, ready to administer another blow. "Wait! Wait!" the messenger cried, squirming. "I'll tell ye." Lord Ross released him, and he sagged against the wall in relief.

"Tell me!" he roared. "And no more of this shite about a ransom!" He threw the letter at the messenger.

"All I know is he means to kill her, no matter what." When Lord Ross advanced on him again, he started stuttering. "He . . . he wants all of ye! Some men will arrive soon to take you to him. As soon as you and your brother leave to bring the ransom, he means to seize the witch . . . er . . . woman."

Lord Ross turned and looked at the only other person in the dark clammy room—a big lad with short curly black hair and the coldest blue eyes he'd ever seen. "What shall we do?" the blue-eyed man asked, never taking his eyes off the messenger.

"Give him the witch."

Blue Eyes looked at Lord Ross, raising a black eyebrow in question, then nodded. "What shall I do with this worthless dung heap?"

Lord Ross looked over his shoulder, as though he'd forgotten the messenger. "I care not." He started toward the stairs leading out of the bowels of Drochaid Castle. He stopped, turning back to Blue Eyes. "Before you . . . dispose of him, find out where Marshall's men are keeping themselves." And he was gone.

The messenger looked up fearfully as the tall muscular lad advanced on him. He sank to the ground. He knew just by looking in the lad's eyes that he would die today.

Blue Eyes squatted in front of him, arms resting on his thighs, hands dangling casually. "Suppose you tell me where Marshall and his men are hiding." He said it in a friendly manner, his lips curled into a slight smile.

"Why? Ye'll kill me anyway."

Blue Eyes's smile grew, a cool little thing that didn't quite reach the black-fringed eyes. "Do you know who I am?"

"Ye're one of Lord Irvine's bastards."

"Aye, that I am. But that's not all." He gave the messenger a wink that chilled him to the bone. "I'm son of Gavenia MacAskill of the Isle of Skye, *baobh dubh*."

The messenger inhaled sharply. The black witch who commanded devil dogs. "But . . . but . . . she wasna real. That . . . that's just a story mothers tell their bairns to scare them."

"She was real enough." The lad was grinning broadly, and the messenger felt terror's icy claws picking their way through his limbs, paralyzing him. Blue Eyes held up his finger, as though an idea just struck him, and slipped his hand into the small purse he wore at his waist. "She left something for me before she burned. Something I'd like to show you."

A growl emitted from somewhere in the depths of the dungeon. The messenger strained his eyes to see where the sound came from. A dark form was separating itself from the shadows.

The messenger turned back to look at Blue Eyes, and his eyes bulged, a scream caught in his throat. "I'll tell ye anything ye want to know!" he yelled, before his shrieks filled the dungeon.

Audrey huddled in a corner, squeezing her body as far back as she could into the small space. Her cheek was pressed against the wall, trying to get away from the torch Marshall held next to her face.

"Do ye know what it's like to burn, Audrey?" he asked, bringing the flames closer. She was too scared to shake or even talk. She could only watch the fire from the corner of her eye, feel the heat of it flushing her skin.

"It must feel like you're melting. The skin bubbling and running down your bones like wax." He was kneeling, and she could see his feverish eyes through the flames. "Or mayhap, it's dry. Your skin crackling and curling, your body screaming for water as you turn to ash."

She swallowed, breathing through clenched teeth. He was trying to drive her crazy. He came in several times a day, simply to torment and threaten her.

"'Tis a horrible way to die, methinks. And you. You almost brought me to it." He brought the torch a fraction of an inch closer. Her hair was down around her shoulders, knotted and tangled. She was terrified a few wayward strands would catch, setting her whole head alight. "If ye had your way, my ashes would be blowing in the breeze right now. Did ye plan on watching? Were you going to come and see which it was? A thick waxy death, or a dry crumbling?"

All she could do was pray to God to make him leave her for a while, even though she knew he'd be back. He was never gone long. She was afraid to sleep. She woke once to find him kneeling before her, touching her stomach. At the thought, she wrapped an arm protectively around the baby. He saw her action and pulled the torch back a little. She breathed easier once the heat wasn't baking her skin.

"I find myself wondering, what shall happen to the bairn? Will it burn within you? Or will it fall out once your belly catches, tumbling into the flames?" He was thoughtful, looking at a point on the wall beyond her. "I think I shall burn you first, with your husband watching."

The door opened, and Marshall stood, taking the torch far away. She didn't relax. Sometimes he found disturbances highly annoying, and when he came back to her the next time, he was worked up into a frenzy.

"Kerr and Roy have returned with the witches," he said, and started to leave.

Marshall turned back to her. "It seems we can get on with it now. Your husband has arrived, thinking himself your savior. The spotted witch will be here soon." He grinned and left.

That's when the shaking began. *Oh, please let them have a plan*, she prayed. They had an advantage, since Marshall apparently thought the castle was unfamiliar to them. She huddled in the corner she hardly ever left, somewhere past exhaustion and fright. She strained her ears for sounds beyond the heavy door, but heard none. In the last few days, she had somehow de-evolved into a creature ruled by fear. Scurrying over to the chamber pot to furtively relieve herself or snatch her food when it was brought, then hurrying back to her corner. Much of the time she felt like she was outside of her body, looking down on the pathetic figure crouched in a ball. But the times when she wanted most to leave her body behind, to absent herself from Marshall's tortures, she couldn't.

After a long time, she heard the bar lifting from the door. She eyed it warily, not sure what to expect. Two men were shoved in, and the door slammed shut behind them. She couldn't find her voice. They hadn't seen her. Their backs were to her, staring at the door. They were both tall and broad, although one was more heavily muscled than the other.

"Did you see more rooms where they might be holding her?" asked the bigger one.

"Aye, but none of them locked."

She forced a strangled sound through her dry tight throat, and they both whirled around. She tried to stand, but her muscles were stiff and sore. Hands were on her, lifting her, pulling her to the torchlight. She instinctively shrank from it.

"What has he done to you?" Brenden murmured, one arm holding her up, the other delicately touching her face.

She felt the first hot tears since she'd been there squeezing from her eyes. It hurt to cry, since her face and neck were bruised. "It's not as bad as it looks." Her voice was hoarse and rasping. Brenden's fingers lifted her jaw, and his gaze roamed over her neck. The green eyes hardened.

"Did he try to strangle you?" His voice sounded harsh and shook the tiniest bit.

She nodded and swallowed, wincing at the pain it caused. He held her against his chest. His arms were incredibly gentle, but she felt the muscles beneath his clothing quivering with barely held fury. She lay limply against him, letting his strength take over and hold her up.

"You came back," she mumbled against the wool of his doublet.

"Did you doubt it?"

When she didn't answer, he led her to the far wall, murmuring to her in a broken voice. He sat, pulling her onto his lap and cradling her against him.

"You can rest now. I won't let him touch you again," he breathed.

"What now?" she asked.

"We wait."

* * *

Brenden ripped a piece of her shift and cleaned the cut on her face, apologizing profusely every time she winced. When he was done, they sat in silence for a long time, their hands entwined, her head on his shoulder. Gavin roamed the interior of the cell, stopping every so often and asking no one in particular, "What's taking so long?"

He stopped suddenly and stood motionless in the center of the room. His eyes looked around, his face turning a fraction of an inch. He held up his hand. "There. Do you feel it?"

"Aye, I felt something," Brenden answered.

Gavin turned, as if being led by some force outside himself and walked slowly to the wall. He moved his hands in front of it, feeling for the origin of the draft.

"It's coming from this wall that faces the sea," Gavin said, inspecting every square inch of the wall in front of him.

"What's he doing?" Audrey asked.

"Do you feel the draft? I can almost taste the sea in this room. As a bairn I spent much time here and know the caves below well. There must be a passageway leading to the water," Brenden said, watching his brother. Gavin's hands roamed slowly across the stone wall. "I don't remember there being one here. It might have been closed off long ago when the castle was still in use and might mean nothing."

She watched Gavin with new interest. His hands touched each rock individually, feeling around the edges. It was a slow process, but finally he whispered, "There . . ." With both hands, he began moving a stone the tiniest bit, side to side, easing it out. Once it was out, he placed it on the ground and reached his hand into the opening. A section of the wall moved inward. The cool sea air wafted in through the crack.

"It leads down to the sea," Gavin said, not pushing it open any farther. "Do ye think we can get back up in time? What if they arrive while we're gone?"

Brenden helped Audrey to her feet. "We go. We're of more use to them free than locked in this room."

Gavin pushed the wall inward, and Brenden grabbed the torch from the sconce. He took her hand and led her into the blackness. They walked a few paces, seeing nothing but stone walls. Crude steps that had been carved out of rock lay in front of them. They were in the natural caves beneath the castle. The air was heavy with moisture, and the sound of dripping water echoed softly around them. They followed the stairs downward and were confronted with another wall. A lever was visible and Gavin pulled on it, opening another doorway.

They were in a stone corridor that branched off in two directions. She heard Brenden's almost inaudible "Ahh" of recognition as he took the lead. The walls were slick and wet; she could tell that when the tide was at its highest, there was water in the caves. The stone floor turned into coarse sand. She could see light ahead, and her heart beat faster.

Mist was falling thickly when they entered the small cove. Jagged black rocks jutted out of the sand. A many-oared boat was secured to a rock on the shore. Gavin untied it and pushed it out into the water, cutting off Marshall's means of escape. Brenden tossed the torch away, and they picked their way through the rocks, climbing back upward. The rocks were slick with mist and seawater, making her bare foot slip. She felt a stab of pain and gasped. The sole of her foot was bleeding.

Brenden surveyed the wound with concern. "Can you make it?"

She nodded. She had been through far more than a

cut foot in the past six months. She stepped more carefully, feeling guilty that she was slowing their ascent. The wind whipped her hair around, wet strands slapping her face like lashes. She could see the wall of the tower rising to their left some distance away. Brenden kept a firm hold on her hand, helping her over the larger rocks.

Once they were on flatter land, she saw a large party of riders approaching. They hid behind a huge boulder to watch. One of the riders was a woman, her light-blue cloak a splotch of color in the muted greens and grays of the overcast landscape. A thick gold braid hung down her back.

Audrey squeezed Brenden's hand. "It's Una! They have Una!"

Brenden kissed her forehead. "You stay here."

"Where are you going?" she asked fearfully, grabbing his hand to stop him.

He gave her a lopsided grin, their fingers still touching as he pulled away. "*Hiç korkma, geri gelecegim,*" he said. *Never fear, I'll be back.* And then they were gone, running swiftly and quietly toward the castle. She watched them, mouth agape. He had spoken to her in Turkish!

Her heart rose in her throat. They were fully exposed to the men who had captured Una. She saw more men coming out of the castle to meet the riders. She frowned. The men with Una made no indication that they saw the two figures now in the shadows of the crumbling castle walls, yet they had to have spotted them.

All her questions were answered in the next moment, when the riders started up the trail leading to the tower. Una reined her horse in, and fell behind. Swords and axes were raised and the men on horseback rode at the men approaching on foot from the castle. They were unprepared for the attack. Audrey watched in horror as they were quickly cut down. A few ran back to the safety of the tower. One of the men on horseback—it looked like Forbes—tossed a huge sword to Brenden, and they disappeared.

Una rode some distance away and turned her horse. It pranced nervously as she gazed at the castle. Audrey thought about calling out to her but was afraid to expose herself. She didn't know how many men were inside the castle, but she didn't think they outnumbered the men on horseback. Sounds of battle reached her hiding place behind the rocks. Bodies littered the ground outside the walls. She heard loose pebbles falling and turned, hoping it was Brenden. She was rudely disappointed with the vision of Marshall clambering up the rocks.

His eyes locked on her. "You can't escape me, bitch. If I'm to die, I'll take you with me!"

He lunged at her, murder in his eyes. She screamed and ran, her foot throbbing painfully as she stumbled across the sharp stones. Her ankle twisted, and she went down hard. He fell on her back. She tried to scramble out from under him, but her fingernails clawed uselessly at the sandy dirt and rocks.

He flipped her on her back and straddled her. He pulled a dagger from his boot. She bucked wildly, using her hands to push and scratch at him. All coherent thought ceased, her mind only focusing on survival. He put the blade between his teeth and grappled with her, trying to catch her flailing wrists.

Seeing a way to hinder him, at least momentarily, she struck his mouth with her palm. Her hand stung as it hit the blade. He made a strangled sound and fell off her. She rolled to her hands and knees. He recovered quickly, grabbing the hair streaming out behind her and jerking her backward.

"Audrey!" She heard the cry from both sides of her. One feminine, the other deep and masculine. Marshall yanked her hair savagely. One of his arms wrapped around her chest, the other pressed the knife against her throat. Brenden arrived from the direction of the cove, wielding an enormous bloodstained sword. Una stood by the boulder, her huge blue eyes filled with terror.

Brenden circled them slowly. Her hair was whipping wildly around them, and she felt Marshall shake his head a few times and spit. The cold wet metal of the knife burned her throat, and she knew he was cutting her. Brenden's eyes darted to her neck.

"Give me the witch, and I will let her go." Marshall shouted to be heard over the sound of the surf. Una's hand went to the neck of her cape, releasing the gold clasp. It fell to her feet in a billow of blue velvet.

"I'll come with ye, but you must release Audrey first."

"Una," Brenden started, a warning in his voice.

"No, my lord. 'Tis me he wants. This began between the two of us, and it will end there. Let her go."

Brenden took a step closer, and Marshall's arm tightened. His hand shook, making the knife cut Audrey deeper. She was afraid to swallow, since the motion might bring her skin in closer contact with the sharp blade. When Una was close enough, Marshall shoved Audrey at Brenden. He snatched Una's arm, pulling her against him and pressing the knife to her throat. Blood ran down from his mouth where Audrey had hit him. The curl had left his mustache. The ends hung limply, soaked in his own blood.

He backed away from Brenden, moving toward the

jagged rocks of the cove. Brenden pushed Audrey behind him and followed.

"Stay back!" Marshall made a threatening move with the knife. Una's arms were crossed at her stomach. She wore one of her more elaborate dresses, with slashed sleeves and the underblouse exposed. She fingered the edge of one of the slashes, and Audrey caught a glint of metal.

"Una!" Gavin's shout came from the cove. Marshall whirled, his foot catching on a rock. He moved the blade away from her throat momentarily. Una whipped a dirk from her sleeve and stabbed behind her. She gashed him in the side and tried to run. He yelled, falling backward but pulling her with him. They both tumbled down the rocky slope and out of sight.

Audrey heard Una scream and Gavin shouting something she couldn't understand. The wind had been blowing strongly before, but now the sky darkened and it began howling around them. Brenden and Audrey picked their way down the rocks. Marshall still held Una around the neck, but they were on the beach and moving toward the water. Gavin advanced on them with his sword drawn. Brenden was yelling at him, but the wind and sea stole the words.

Audrey stared in horror as a huge wave came toward the shore. She grabbed Brenden's arm and pointed to the solid wall of water moving closer. He looked down at Gavin, whose arms were stretched upward. Audrey started down the rocks again, but Brenden stopped her. They weren't safe from the wave, either, and Brenden tried to drag her to the top of the rocks.

She turned in time to see the wave rush over Una and Marshall. Then it hit Audrey and Brenden. She swallowed salt water and choked, unable to see where she was going, just grasping at anything in front of her. A strong arm caught her waist and pulled her down behind an outcropping of boulders. She could breathe again. Brenden sheltered her against him, her face pressed against his sopping shirt. When the water receded, they started back down to the cove.

Una was on the ground in the entrance of the cave, and Gavin faced Marshall on the beach, his sword still in hand. The clouds overhead were breaking up, the sea settling down. A strong wind still blew, but nothing threatening a tidal wave.

Marshall looked truly afraid. Gavin advanced on him and brought his sword down. Marshall ducked aside, stumbling and catching himself before he fell. Wet sand squished between Audrey's toes when she reached the beach. Marshall's words drifted to her on the breeze. "'Tis you. You're the spawn." His voice was high and shrill with fear.

Audrey thought she heard Gavin say, "Aye." Gavin's blade slashed down across head and shoulders. She squeezed her eyes shut to the sight of flowing blood and Marshall's head falling strangely to the side. When she opened them, his torso lay in the water, crimson waves rolling over it.

Her vision began to cloud, and she swayed. Brenden's arms were around her, behind her back and under her knees, lifting her. The sharp smell of blood clung to him, and her stomach heaved. She turned her head and saw Gavin running to Una. A huge dog stood over Una, sniffing at her inert form. A black dog.

Then everything went gray.

She roused when she was handed over to someone. *Must be Forbes*, she thought. She was lifted up and settled in front of Brenden on his horse.

His hand was on her stomach. "The bairn," he said softly. "Is he well?"

"I think so," she rasped, and swallowed, trying to get some moisture to her throat. He called for some ale, and a clay bottle was pressed against her lips.

"Let's go home," he said, nudging the horse.

⇌ 25 ⇌

At Drochaid, Audrey was bathed, fed, and put to bed. She found it difficult to sleep. Every time she drifted off, she woke with a start, looking around fearfully. Brenden finally crawled in bed behind her and wrapped his arm protectively around her stomach. After a while, she fell into a deep dreamless sleep.

She heard voices and thought she was dreaming, then she was floating upward, out of her warm cocoon, into the world of pain and sore muscles. Her eyes hurt, so she lay unmoving, eyes shut, trying to identify the voices.

"How long has she been like this?" It was Alistair, and he was beside her.

"Almost an entire day," Brenden answered in a low voice. He was still behind her, his palm flat on her stomach, the warmth of his body against her back.

"Do you think it was too much for her? What of the bairn?" Alistair asked.

"It's fine." He sounded like he was smiling. "I feel it moving from time to time. It isn't much. At first, I wasn't certain, but she's lying so still, I realized that's what it had to be."

"I'll have some food sent up. You should eat. I'll sit with her." There was something odd about this conversation between father and son. They were not only being civil to one another, but she was positive she detected warmth in Brenden's voice.

"Nay, she won't sleep much longer, and I will be here when she wakes." She could feel his deep voice through her back, and it gave her a little chill.

"Did you know she saved my life? Una said I was dead, and she somehow brought me back." Alistair was quiet for a moment. "I cannot understand why. I have done naught in this life to make it worth saving."

"She is very special," Brenden said softly.

"Aye," Alistair agreed, a note of humor entering his voice. "She dismissed my surgeon when he tried to let blood from my veins. She is giving Gibson apoplexy! Anyone who prepares food must now scrub their hands first." He paused. "Have you seen the cellar she has my servants digging in the bailey? She claims vegetables will keep longer down there."

Brenden laughed quietly. They were silent for a long time. Audrey had begun to drift to sleep again when Brenden said, "About Camden . . . I'm sorry."

"Don't apologize for something that was not your doing," Alistair said. "I know you would have stopped the shot with your own body if it were possible. Let us not dwell on such unpleasantness."

Brenden laid his head on the pillow next to hers, and his arm tightened around her. Sleep overtook her.

When she woke the next time, she was feeling somewhat better. Her body was heavy with sleep. She cracked her eyes open. A single candle burned on the table beside the bed. It was night. She closed her eyes again. The bed shifted and she knew Brenden was still with her.

"Are you going to open your eyes?" he asked.

She looked at her hand. Linen was wrapped around it. "What happened to my hand?"

"You cut it fighting with Marshall. It's not deep." He was shirtless and leaning over her. He seemed bigger and darker than she remembered.

"You came back."

"Aye."

"You speak Turkish."

"Aye."

"You lied to me."

"I don't recall saying I couldn't understand you." He grinned broadly, and she realized he was right. His smile faded. He was gazing at her with such a troubled expression.

"What is it?"

"I wouldn't have left you if I could have stayed. I wanted to bring you with me, but I feared for the bairn . . . and I didn't want you to see me as I was. I thought because of Alex, you would be disgusted." She frowned and started to speak, but he gently laid his fingers against her lips. "I should have told you these things, I know. I suppose I understand now a wee bit why your husband took his life. I never thought so before, but I can see why a person wouldn't want to live when every day is torment." She looked away from him, tears gathering in her eyes. She didn't want to hear this now. He touched her chin, turning her face back to him. "But you pulled me back. Knowing you were here, waiting for me. You and the bairn are my life now."

She held his face between her hands as tears spilled over her lashes. "I love you."

"And I you." He kissed her and held her close. The heartbreak of the past months began to lift, and she felt hopeful about their future. He deepened the kiss. She could feel him restraining himself, not wanting to hurt her. But she wanted him. It had been so long. He pressed his cheek against her hair. She could feel his heart pounding. She pressed kisses against his neck and chest, her hands traveling down the hard muscles of his stomach.

He inhaled sharply, grabbing her hand. "Will it hurt the child?"

"No," she whispered, freeing her wrist from his hold to touch him.

He rolled her onto her back, his hand sliding beneath her shift. He made love to her gently, being careful and solicitous of the baby. They clung to each other afterward, and Audrey thought of how close she had come to losing him and everything that had come to matter to her. This life was more real to her than anything she had ever had in her time. These people were more dear to her.

His arms tightened around her, and he said, "That corridor . . ."

"What about it?"

"Promise me you won't leave. Should you get angry with me, you won't run away?"

"I can't go back anyway," she said hesitantly. He drew back to look down at her, an eyebrow raised in question. "The corridor is gone." When he was still silent, she added hastily, "I had decided to stay with you anyway, and there was Stephen to think of. Anyway, it just disappeared. So I guess I'm stuck here."

Relief washed his features. "So it's over. Do you regret not leaving?"

"No." She traced the strong line of his jaw. "I told you I'd never leave you."

"Seni asla terketmeyecegim." *I'll never leave you.* The words formed surely on his tongue.

She smiled. "Where did you learn that?"

"I've been there many times. I have ships that sail to Algiers every year. 'Tis easy to be cheated when you don't speak the language." He took her hand and folded it in his larger one. "I shall take you there, and you can tell me how it will change."

"How is Una?"

"She's fine. A wee bit shaken, 'tis certain, but only a few bruises. She's been sore weeping for you, she's so worried." He smoothed the hair away from her face. "We all were."

"What happened? That was odd, the way that freak storm came and went." She watched him closely.

He averted his eyes and shrugged. "Aye, well. Odd things seem to happen when Gavin's about."

There was something not quite right about her brother-in-law that made her recall a legend Ian MacKay had recounted concerning warlocks and devil dogs. She decided not to pursue the topic. Whatever Gavin was, she loved him.

"How is everything with you?" She searched his face. He seemed calmer somehow, some of his intensity gone.

"Aye, I'll do." He kissed the back of her hand. "As long as I have my Audrey, I'll do."

Later they dressed and went down to show everyone that she still lived and the baby was well. Brenden held her hand and smiled down at her, looking the proud father. They passed the corridor. She felt a pang of guilt as she glanced down the long hall to the other end. It had been a small lie that she'd told Brenden, but for a worthy cause. A herd of twentieth-century tourists walked by, illuminated by harsh electric lights. Perhaps it wasn't a real lie at all, since the pull to return to that place was gone. She was finally home.